A Tree Called Fir

A TREE CALLED FIR

A Christmas Love Story

By
Bud Thomas

ISBN 978-1-7345471-0-8 (e-book)
ISBN 978-1-7345471-1-5 (paperback)
Printed in the United States of America

The Prayer of the Evergreen Tree

Thank you, Lord, for my creation.
The earth in which I live.
Sun, rain, and wind that nourish and cleanse me,
birds that nest in my branches,
small animals that I shelter from the cold.
For letting me be a part of your colorful landscape,
with the blue sky, evening sunsets,
and shining stars at night.
Most of all thank you, Lord,
for choosing me as the Christmas Tree,
to be part of your Son Jesus's Birthday Celebration,
which brings so much joy and happiness
into the lives and homes of so many people.
May my evergreen color be a symbol
of Christ's everlasting life.
Lord, I thank you!
Amen

PART ONE

CHAPTER 1

My Beginning

Imagine this! One morning you open your eyes for the first time ever, and you are standing on the side of a hill, looking down into a valley. You scan to the left, and as far as you can see, there are emerald-green trees, waving to you and welcoming you to Wildcat Mountain. You wave back. Then you scan to the right and see the mountains gently sloping into a valley, where the small town of Murphy, North Carolina, sleeps. A rising sun is peeking up from behind the purple haze, which floats like smoke over distant forests. You look behind you and see other young seedlings, all witnessing their first sunrise, greeting each other for the first time and all incredibly awestruck.

We are Fraser firs. They call me Fir, and this is my story.

I vividly remember that first day on my mountain. I was asleep inside a warm seedpod when I was suddenly awakened by something crawling all over my body. I had grown little tiny roots that I did not have when I last fell asleep, and the rootlets were searching for a way to escape from my cramped pod. I was laughing because the roots tickled, and I was scratching because they made me itch. During the night, I had grown a little trunk with branches with soft, delicate pine needles, and I had grown lots of wriggling, pesky roots. I was a baby tree, a teeny-weeny Fraser fir.

I yawned, stretched my limbs, and started pounding on the woody walls of the seedpod. It was like being in a very small, dark room with no door. I took a deep breath, just like the big, bad wolf, and blew hard against the wall as hard as I could blow, and *wham!*, the woody outer covering of my seed cracked. I stretched, pounded, and blew some more, and the pod burst open. I was free! My roots reached down into the moist, black soil and drank the cool, pure groundwater until they could drink no more. I was sated, so full that I thought I would pop, but I felt invigorated, alive, and reenergized. The nutrients in the soil were adding bulk to my body, and I seemed to be moving upward through the dense, loamy clay.

Still surrounded by a world of absolute darkness, I could feel the soil becoming warmer and, somehow, not as black. The color of the earth seemed to be more brownish as I got closer to the top, and I saw earthworms, beetles, grubs, and centipedes crawling in the soil all around me. I also felt warmed by a blanket of damp brown leaves on the top of my apical meristem (that's the top of my head). And just before I was officially born, I was startled by the antics of two cockroaches that were scurrying in the mulch above me. Ugly creatures that crawl all over everything, these two roaches were walking on my head and making me shudder.

Then it happened—I penetrated the last layer of soil, and I was suddenly blinded by what I had never seen before: light. I was surrounded by colors and sound and warmth. The sky was powder blue with white, wispy clouds floating everywhere. Birds of every color flew from tree to tree, singing their melodies and chatting loudly about everything from motherhood to food. Insects hopped from bush to bush and provided the buzzing *hmmm* that is so typical of a forest. Brown deer and white rabbits darted to and fro, nibbling on tender grasses and scratching their itches. A big bear lumbered by, almost stepping on me with his big foot. Berries were plentiful, and he stopped briefly to fill his belly before disappearing into the brush.

I was alive! I had been so apprehensive to leave the safety of my pod. I had no idea that there was so much beauty, so much life, so much happiness up here in the forest. I scanned the mountains from north to south, and I watched the sun rising slowly in the east. I was flabbergasted by the incredible beauty of the Blue Ridge Mountains. Then I heard many high-pitched voices, and they were all singing to me. Beetles, roaches, crickets, worms, and centipedes were marching single file around me and welcoming me to their forest. I was awed by the love that I received on this, the first day of my life.

All around me, new Fraser fir seedlings were witnessing their first sunrise, but none of these infant trees were as beautiful as Mary, the young conifer standing next to me. She breathed her first breath of mountain air just after I became a seedling. Mary was very pretty, and I think I fell in love with her on that first morning. But she talked too much, from her first breath as a baby Fraser fir. *Yackity yack, yackity yack*: that's all I heard from the moment she was born, but golly gee, she was so pretty.

Anyway, it was always nice to have a friend near me when the forest would get really dark and scary or when the weather would become especially harsh. Mary talked about the sky. She talked about the birds. She talked about the heat on hot days and the cold on chilly days. She never seemed to stop talking in the seven years that we were together.

On moonless nights her chatter would lull me to sleep, but on those terribly stormy days and especially frightening nights, I learned to pull my branches close to my body to muffle her incessant screaming. I loved Mary. She was a really good kid, and I thought maybe she would like to be my wife one day, when I grew older. But that's enough about my Mary.

CHAPTER 2

The Four Seasons

There are four magnificent seasons in western North Carolina, and I enjoyed seven years of each.

There were the brisk *winters*, when the light snows were sprinkled on the mountain like powdered sugar on a cookie.

I also watched seven *springs* usher in a multitude of delicate flowers, which decorated the hills and valleys in reds, blues, purples, yellows, and whites.

Summer was when animals played and none took life too seriously; when rains fell and storms raged; when the earth was cleansed and food was plentiful; when rivers and streams were swollen with water, and waterfalls cascaded to the rocks below; when the days were hot, steamy, stifling, and long; and when the nights were balmy and still. And the nights, oh the nights, the incredible, cool, awesome nights, where indescribable skies of black were decorated with star lights that twinkled and shone, where a moon walked across the heavens and disappeared in the morning, where the soft, cool breezes air-conditioned the valleys, and where the orchestra of insects blanketed the forests with its symphony of sound.

And then came the *autumn*, when the leaves changed colors, and the lush green of summer was replaced by the fiery reds and yellows of fall. The days got cooler, and the nights were cold, and we all shivered and sought the warmth and friendship of each other. The animals grew thick coats, and the hardwood trees dropped their leaves. The insects looked for places to hibernate for the upcoming winter, and the birds flew south. Food became scarce, and the nuts and seeds of summer were all safely stowed away in the ground and in the dens of squirrels and chipmunks.

Each season was special. Each made me happy. I loved this place. What's not to love? The air was clean and pure; the water was fresh and cool. The skies were blue by day and luminescent by night. The breezes cooled me in summer, and the sun warmed me in winter.

CHAPTER 3

November 16
A Very Bad Day

Everyone has felt the foreboding of bad things to come, a feeling you feel when you feel a feeling that you feel you never felt before.

And so it was on November 16, as I watched yellow leaves fall from the maples and felt the crisp wind chilling the mountain, that I felt that feeling. Something was very wrong; it's called *ominous* or *threatening* or *foreboding.* I could feel it in the wind. I could feel it in the soil. I could feel it in the darkened clouds that rumbled overhead.

I loved my mountain more than anything. But as another delightful fall day in November unfolded, my whole beautiful world as I knew it came to an abrupt and violent end. Huge, muscled men with chainsaws descended on my mountain, and the carnage began.

In the distance, I could hear the thunderous roar of gasoline engines whirring and sputtering. Trees were toppling to the forest floor as they succumbed to the sharp teeth of the power saws. I listened as my friends fell to the ground. I heard anguished screams as their trunks were severed from their roots, and I listened as my fellow Fraser firs cried.

Noxious blue smoke belched from cutting machines, and the forest reeked of exhaust fumes. I listened to the voices of men in trucks driving slowly and deliberately up Wildcat Mountain.

I heard the whispers of the wind and the warnings of the crows perched high above the forest, but there was nothing I could do but stand tall, wait, listen, and watch.

I had just turned seven years old, and although I had witnessed many a tragedy on Wildcat Mountain, I had trepidation for what I felt would happen today. Today would be a very bad day. I heard noises that frightened the squirrels and sent the birds into flight. I smelled an odor in the air that reminded me of the cars that raced down my mountain road en route to Murphy.

Whirring saw blades; sputtering machines; motors stalling, stopping, cranking, restarting; more whirring; chips flying through the air; trees crashing hard onto the grassy slopes; noxious gases of tired old chainsaws; and cigarette-smoking men speaking vile language and wearing perspiration-soaked clothes all replaced the sweet pine scents of Wildcat Mountain. A hell on Earth was taking place right before my eyes. Our ecosystem was being changed forever.

Suddenly, without warning, a tall, burly man was upon me. He carried a power saw, with which he sliced through my trunk like a sharp knife slicing through a ripe tomato. I screamed and crashed to the forest floor and watched helplessly as the man approached Mary. She fell next to me, pleading for me to help her, but there was nothing I could do. I'm just a tree.

Men were binding Mary with twine and bundling her so tightly in orange mesh that she could not even talk. A big, bald-headed man hoisted her up on his shoulder, carried her to a waiting truck, and threw her into the back. A burly dark-skinned man caught her and quickly threw my Mary onto the pile of Fraser firs stacked in the rear of the trailer. Trees were piled and stacked, one upon another, from the front of the truck to the very rear.

The forest was in tears, the mountain was crying, and the trees were all screaming in pain as they were sliced and diced and stacked in piles.

The bunnies had scurried off into the brush. Squirrels and chipmunks were watching from high in the maples, where they were safe. The birds had flown away, and all the larger mammals had fled to the other side of Wildcat Mountain.

Suddenly, the man who had thrown Mary into the truck was walking toward me, drops of perspiration dripping from his nose. He grabbed my trunk and dragged me toward a bundling machine. I was thrown, trunk first, into a big metal ring, like a basketball being tossed through a hoop. I came out the other side with orange plastic netting all over my body and my limbs crushed against my sides. I looked horrible, I was in a great deal of pain, I had lost a lot of sap, and my branches were bundled so tightly that I could not breathe. The bald-headed man carried me to the back of the truck, and I was stacked on top of my friends.

Broken limbs and torn branches littered the mountainside. A deafening, eerie quiet enveloped the eastern slope. Tree stumps and torn branches were everywhere. The large crows were silent for the first time in seven years. The whole mountainside was quiet.

Only hours before, this hillside had been glorified by the myriad colors of autumn and the incessant chatter of birds, but now Wildcat Mountain was without sound.

Ambling slowly away on a two-lane, winding asphalt road, there was a tractor-trailer laden with the stately Fraser firs of Wildcat Mountain. The rear doors had been closed and locked, entombing us young firs in a crypt of darkness. Bound with nylon cord and with sap oozing from our wounds, we were stacked ten high, ceiling to floor, in the cold, dark trailer of this refrigerated sixteen-wheeler. The trip from Murphy, North Carolina, to Lake Worth, Florida, would take fifteen hours.

CHAPTER 4

November 17
A New Home—Publix Supermarket

At 4:00 a.m. the truck stopped in front of the Publix Supermarket at the intersection of Jog and Lantana. Two very large, young, cigarette-smoking, white-skinned men popped the security seal and noisily opened the rear doors. They were both in their early twenties and wore heavy-duty calfskin leather gloves and long-sleeved shirts.

The shorter of the two was the boss. He had a small teardrop in the corner of his right eye: a tattoo. I thought that his teardrop meant that he shared my pain, my sadness. But this man was rotten to the core. He was like the men with chainsaws in Murphy.

Once the lift was fully extended, the taller of the two truckers engaged the handle and lowered the ramp. As the lift came within a foot of the ground, the one with the tattoo, "Bubba," jumped onto the platform, pumped twice on the handle, and rode up with the ramp. Bubba began pulling trees from their neatly stacked piles and tossing them onto the concrete roadway behind the trailer. The other big man, "Cree," was dragging the trees to the front of the store and displaying them in an upright position for the morning shoppers.

Suddenly, a gloved hand grabbed my trunk. I was jerked from my resting position and hurled through the air. I crashed to the ground with a thud. Hundreds, if not thousands, of my needles had been ripped from my branches. I gasped for air. I was dazed, terrified, and confused. Cree grabbed my trunk and dragged me thirty yards toward the front of the store. My limbs burned, and my head bounced along the brick pavers.

Grocery stores awaken at 5:00 a.m. Most people do not realize that deliveries have to be made, shelves have to be restocked, and floors have to be polished. The store manager is always the first to arrive, followed by the produce manager, the butcher, and the deli manager. The pharmacist, bag boys, and stock clerks all have tasks to perform long before the first customer arrives at 7:00 a.m.

Marshall Kemp, the produce manager, drove up and parked his car just as Cree was stacking the last Christmas trees in the Publix breezeway. Marshall carried a folded newspaper in his left hand and a hot, steamy cup of Dunkin' Donuts coffee in the other.

"Mornin', Mr. Kemp," said Cree as he removed his sap-stained leather gloves. Cree picked up his paperwork and asked for Marshall's signature.

"They're all there, Mr. Kemp. I counted them three times."

"Give me a sec, Cree."

Walking quickly and deliberately, Marshall disappeared inside the store and into the back, where his small office was located. He set the coffee on his desk, together with his newspaper, and retrieved a brown clipboard, which held the Christmas tree paperwork. The produce manager was responsible for tomatoes, apples, watermelon, grapes, and onions, and Christmas trees too, so before Cree could drive away, Mr. Kemp had to count every tree…

"Fifty-six, fifty-seven, fifty-eight, fifty-nine, and sixty. Right on, Cree; they're all there."

Marshall signed the receipt and gave a copy to Cree, and the two big men drove away.

It was Friday, approximately ten days before Thanksgiving, and I was one of sixty freshly cut North Carolina Fraser fir Christmas trees standing ready for the onslaught of holiday shoppers.

The temperature in South Florida had already climbed to seventy-one degrees. I was hot and thirsty, and my branches were still bound tightly to my sides with nylon mesh. I was continuing to drop needles, no matter how hard I tried to hold onto them.

Kenny was the young man in charge of selling the Christmas trees. He wore heavy gloves and a long-sleeved shirt and carried scissorlike shears to cut the orange webbing off our bodies. As my bindings fell to the ground and my branches opened, I could breathe again. Kenny started spreading my limbs and then reached in, grabbed my trunk, and pounded me on the floor. This helped spread my branches so that I would look more attractive to the Christmas shoppers.

Kenny was a big boy for sixteen, and he was very strong. I overheard him telling one of the other bag boys that he was six feet, six inches tall and played high school basketball.

CHAPTER 5

November 18
First Week at Publix

Publix is always busy, but this being Thanksgiving week, the store was particularly busy with early-morning shoppers. The crowds started arriving at first light and continued until closing at 11:00 p.m. Shoppers filled their carts with turkeys, bags of herb stuffing, yams, cranberries, and Christmas trees.

The first customer of the day was a rosy-cheeked, plump young woman with two small children. They asked the bag boy Kenny, who was assigned Christmas tree duty, "How much are the trees?"

Kenny told her, and she went inside to shop, but only after the older of the two boys broke one of my large lower limbs. The kid was hateful, and his little brother had yellow cream dripping from his nose. They hid behind me from their mother, trying to climb inside my branches to hide. That's when my damaged bough broke. It hurt so badly, and then I fell over, cracking the branch even more. The pain was excruciating.

As the fat mother waddled into the store with her two beastly children in tow, Kenny picked me up and rotated me so my broken branch was in the back. Forty trees were sold that day, but I was not one of them.

The Publix supermarket opens for business at 7:00 a.m. seven days a week, but the next morning, the parking lot was mostly empty, except for the usual vendors and a few early-morning shoppers. Nobody was looking at Christmas trees, so there I stood, in the same place where I had been left the night before.

Cree had dropped off another fifty freshly cut trees at five o'clock that morning, and Mr. Kemp had signed the paperwork and sent the truck on its way. I felt sorry for the new Fraser firs, because they were still bundled in mesh, and I knew how scared they were and how much their branches hurt.

I stood erect in the same spot for two hours and watched a few people trickle in and out of the store, mostly football fans buying beer and nachos for the afternoon games on TV.

A huge blackbird flew down from his roost and strutted through the breezeway. He was a scavenger bird looking for food. We had birds like him in Murphy, but I don't recall ever seeing one so large. He was so black that he shined, almost seeming to change colors as he walked slowly by. He looked up at me with one dark eye.

"Caw, caw, caw."

He was laughing at me.

"Caw, caw."

I did not like that bird. He laughed at me all day, and he seemed to get great pleasure out of annoying me. If only I could have moved, I would have fallen on that purple bird and crushed him like a bug.

I tried to move but to no avail. I was where I was, but I think that rascal crow knew that I was trying to get to him, because he suddenly looked up at me and flew noisily away.

This blackbird was the king of my breezeway. He gorged himself on anything he could get in his mouth, from donut crumbs dropped by customers to half-eaten sub sandwiches that had been left behind. I watched him swoop down and catch a curly-tailed lizard one day, and I couldn't believe my eyes when he swallowed him whole. I think he would have eaten one of the sparrows that had begun nesting in my branches if he could have caught one, but he never did. They were just too fast, and they were always watching out for each other.

Sparrows are small, fluffy-feathered, brown birds about the size of a golf ball. They flock together for protection. These cheerful little birds seemed to be ever present in and around the Publix supermarket. A number of them had made a permanent home inside the store.

I came to love the tiny sparrows, and I believe that they loved me too. They landed on my branches and sat for hours, nestling against my aching arms. They rubbed their beaks against my limbs and preened my needles. These wonderful little creatures delighted me. I loved my sparrows.

CHAPTER 6

The Homeless Man

The mornings were cool and pleasant that time of year in Lake Worth. The building provided shade for us trees until about 2:00 p.m. There was a heavy green metal courtesy bench bolted to the concrete floor near us. People came and went. They would sit on the bench and then walk away. I could see a scale inside the store near where the shopping baskets were parked. All day long I watched people weigh themselves. Most everyone frowned as they stepped off the scale. A trash can sat close to the entry doors next to a metal can filled with sand and cigarette butts. And all along the walls of the breezeway stood us Fraser firs, leaning against the wall.

Most of the Christmas trees had been tagged and were stacked neatly, side by side, up against the wall behind the bench, and Kenny had removed the orange plastic binding from about half of us. I was the closest tree to the bench.

Employees who smoked cigarettes regularly sat on the bench and expelled nicotine particulate from their lungs while taking a break from the toil and drudgery of their jobs.

Homeless people also sat on the bench. That's where I met Bobby Thornton, an Iraq and Afghanistan war veteran with a storied past. Bobby had no family in South Florida, so he had been spending the better part of this Thanksgiving holiday season on the cast-iron bench, talking with *me*.

Well, he wasn't really talking *with* me, because I hadn't talked to him yet, but that was about to change. Bobby sat next to me on the green bench, and he just talked and talked and talked, kind of like my Mary used to do. The way I saw it was that he must have been talking to me, because nobody else was usually around while he chattered away. Yes, I knew that he was talking to me, and that brought me comfort.

Bobby chewed a lot of gum—Double Bubble, I believe—and he was always creating these big, balloon-sized masterpieces that sometimes popped all over his face. Some days he'd forget to shave, and the gum would get in his hair and also in his scraggly beard. Somehow, he managed to get the Double Bubble off his face and back into his mouth, but it was really a sight to see when those massive bubbles popped all over his head.

CHAPTER 7

November 18
The Sad Little Girl

One day, not long after I was delivered to Publix, I met a sad little girl. Bobby was sitting on his bench when she approached, and he stopped talking and just stared at this beautiful but sad little human being. This smallish girl with a sad face walked up to me and just stood there, staring at me. She studied me from top to bottom. Her long brown hair was meticulously brushed, and she wore a red Christmas headband to keep the hair out of her eyes. She walked around me, to my back, and touched my damaged limb. "Oh, dear, you have a broken branch. That is so sad. Does it hurt, Mr. Christmas Tree?"

The little girl with the sad face held my broken bough in her small hand and gently closed her fingers. I could feel the energy flowing from her little body. It was warm and soothing, a magical tenderness that is unique to the innocence of a child.

"Missy? Missy, where are you?"

"Right here, Mommy, behind this beautiful Christmas tree."

Missy released the broken branch and stepped around to my right side. As she slowly reemerged into her mother's view, the sad little girl continued to delicately touch my supple needles, as if she was fascinated by the fingers of my soft hand.

"Please buy him for me, Mommy! I love him so much."

"Not now, honey. Come, we have shopping to do." The mom grasped her daughter by the hand and hustled her inside the store. I watched Missy disappear into the crowded Publix, her eyes following me until I was out of her view.

CHAPTER 8

Bobby Thornton, Bubble Blower
Fir Speaks to Bobby

B obby was seated on the bench and had witnessed Missy's repeated pleas for her mother, Natalie, to take me home. I had at last realized that God had given me a purpose in this world. I was sent here, to Lake Worth, to bring happiness and joy into that little girl's life. To bring a smile to her sad face.

Bobby already knew why I was here, at the front entrance of a grocery store, as opposed to my beautiful mountain. Bobby was introspective. He knew a lot of things about a lot of things. Bobby also knew that Missy's father had gone away and was not coming back.

"Life is very complicated, whether you are a Fraser fir with a broken branch or a human being with a broken life," he said.

Sitting in the middle of his bench, Bobby put two pieces of pink gum into his mouth and began to chew on the sweet juice. Bobby told me that you can't blow a good bubble until all the sweetness is gone from the gum. He spread his arms out and grasped the backrest with each hand. He continued speaking, and I'm sure he was talking to me, although passersby would assume he was daft and talking to himself.

"Yeah, there are more than enough raw deals to go around."

Bobby was popping bubbles that grew larger with every chew, but the chewing in no way interfered with his incessant talking. He was jibber-jabbering away, ranting and raving, waving his arms, one minute mad, the next minute happy.

"Raw deals; yep, too many raw deals."

Then Bobby changed the subject. "Why would you want to be a tree, man? Squirrels chewing on your nuts, having to stand in the same spot your whole life, and root rot. I heard the other day that you North Carolina fir trees were rotting to death. Yeah, must suck to be a tree.

"Bears must be your real nemesis, though. They walk up to you, turn around, and scratch their backs and their butts on your clean, pine-scented branches, and all you can do is grin and bear it. Ha, ha, ha...get it? Grin and *bear* it? I kill myself, hee, hee. You can barely stand it, get it? *Bear*-ly stand it? Ha, ha, ha."

Publix patrons passed by the bench, purposely keeping their distance from the unkempt man who was talking to himself and laughing uncontrollably.

"Seriously, you really must have lost your *bear*ings when you came to Lake Worth, ha, ha, ha."

That's when I could take no more of his jokes, and I whispered softly, so that only Bobby could hear me, "Yes, Booby, it can be difficult to be a tree, and bears can sometimes be especially troublesome."

"Who said that?" said Bobby as he turned around and looked at me.

"It's me, Booby! They call me Fir, and I don't think you understand how difficult it is for me to stand here all day and listen to your stupid jokes."

"My name is not Booby, Fir; it's Bobby, and I think my bear jokes are pretty funny, if I do say so myself."

"Well, Booby, I mean, Bobby, I *bear*-ly know you, and my mother told me never to talk to strangers that you *bear*-ly know! Ha, ha, ha, got ya!"

"Yes, you did. Wow, a talking tree. I must be going nuts. I must be having a nervous breakdown or something."

"No, Bobby, all trees can talk. It's just that most of us choose not to talk to humans. We do talk to each other and to the animals and even the creatures that are too small for the human eye to see.

We talk to the great spirit of the forest and his angels, and today, I am talking to you. I like you, Bobby, and I'm sorry about calling you Booby. I was just trying to be funny, like you.

"Anyway, since you are here and I am here, and since you brought up the *bear*, how would you like to hear my best bear story? It's about a huge bear that I knew in North Carolina. That's where I come from: Murphy, North Carolina."

"Sure, Fir, tell me about this bear."

CHAPTER 9

Spring and the Bear

"Every spring, the forest reawakens. Flowers decorate the mountain, the birds return, new tender leaves appear on trees, and the bears come out of hibernation.

"I don't like bears, but they are all over Wildcat Mountain. They are large, lumbering animals that have no respect for anyone or anything, kinda like you humans. No disrespect intended, Bobby. I had always regarded the bear as the animal that was on top of the food chain, but as I look back to the day when I was cut down, I see I was wrong. Man is the most fearsome. And man is definitely on top of the food chain, but I'm getting sidetracked. So let's agree that man is the *numero uno* predator and that we must be mindful that you humans can be very hurtful. But let's get back to my black bear. He was named Ted, and trust me, he was no 'teddy' bear.

"Ted was a newborn twin when I first made his acquaintance, playful and irresponsible. He had all the characteristics of a typical male bear cub, except he had a most cruel mean streak.

"Most of the young male bear cubs that I had come to know over the years were cheerful and happy, but not Ted. He never smiled, and he only laughed when he was causing harm to another animal or damaging a tree or bush. And as he grew up, Ted's ill temper worsened. He became a vile, destructive creature who was always scowling and snarling at everything and everyone, and he became the most feared and destructive beast on our mountain.

"Ted never went near water, except to drink, and because he never bathed, Ted reeked of a most disagreeable odor. You could always tell when Ted was around because of his rank black-bear smell, an aroma of spoiled meat and rotten fish, the foods that he wallowed in while he ate.

"Plus he had the scent glands that all bears use to mark their territory, and guess which tree on the mountain he regularly marked?

"That's right! Lucky little ol' me. At least once a week in the spring, Ted would wander by to pay me a visit. I could smell him a quarter mile away, and I knew what was about to happen.

"Ted would stand on his two hind feet and back up until my branches covered his backside. He would then bend over and spray me with his scent. I gagged and coughed. It was disgusting. Then he would wander off to share his stinking self with the rest of the forest.

"As Ted grew in age and in size, his meanness grew with him. He battered smaller animals and viciously attacked and bloodied other bears who had the misfortune to venture into his territory.

"Ted was very rough with me too, but Fraser firs are very tough trees, so I was able to endure his weekly assaults. Bears itch a lot, and dirty bears itch more because they are infested with ticks, chiggers, and other bloodsucking insects that make their life un-*bear*-able, no pun intended.

"And I was big, black Teddy's favorite scratching post, so when he waddled away from me each week, I was a stink-to-high-heaven mess. My limbs were bent, my cones had all fallen to the ground, and I was perilously close to falling over. But like I said, Fraser firs are tough, so I would shake myself for hours, until all my branches were again straight. And I would reach deep into the ground with my largest root, pull hard, and straighten myself.

"Not much I could do about the stink, so I secreted aromatic resins, kinda like pine-scented air freshener. They did a pretty good job of masking his scent, but I still stunk for a few days, and then I was my old self again.

CHAPTER 10

The Bear Trapper

"One day as I was preparing myself for the weekly assault by Mr. Black Bear, king of Wildcat Mountain, I saw a pickup truck pull off the road and park on the grass. I watched as a tall, skinny mountain man with a can of Budweiser beer got out of the truck and walked around to his tailgate. He finished the last of his beer and threw the empty can onto the grass by the road.

"He reached into the back and lifted some chains, a long metal stake, and a...*bear trap*. His brown-and-white dog sat in the front seat of the pickup, anxiously waiting for his master. The skinny hillbilly snapped a leather leash onto his dog's collar and opened the door of his Ford truck. Every human in North Carolina seems to drive an old, rusty Ford truck.

"Anyway, mountain man stumbled around among us trees with his hyperactive, sniffing dog pulling him in all directions. The bear hound walked in circles. He zigzagged through the trees, and he barked incessantly, until he got close to me. That's when he stopped dead in his tracks and started to bay, a sound like a screaming child makes in a supermarket. He pointed his nose right at me and howled like he was being beaten to death.

"Ol' Billy Bob Hillbilly pulled a hammer out of his overalls and pounded that iron stake deep into the ground near my trunk. I had to wiggle some of my roots so they didn't get crushed by the stake as it penetrated the ground.

"The mountain man put the hammer back in his pocket and then removed a red-and-white pouch from his other pocket. He opened the pouch, reached in, removed some brown stuff, and stuffed a hunk between his lower lip and teeth.

"Now, visualize this. I am almost seven years old. I'm about seven feet tall. This redneck in blue overalls is standing right in front of me. We are almost eye to eye. He has on no shirt, he is missing at least three front teeth, and he has sweat marks under his arms and stained onto his overalls. There is a big lump under his lower lip, he has a shaggy brown beard and no hair on his head, and he keeps spitting brown juice all over the ground. He also has brown drippings on his beard, and he stinks…worse than Ted. Awful body odor. He belches, spits again, and bends down to finish his work.

"I watched as the unkempt redneck and his bipolar dog drove off, and I began to feel anxious for Ted. The bear trap had been placed on the ground near my trunk and chained to the stake. Before leaving, Billy Bob had armed the device and covered it with leaves and dirt, but I knew exactly where it was. I had watched every move that this ugly human had made, especially the placement of the trap.

"Then I heard Ted coming out of the brush on the other side of the road. He had found a bush with wild blackberries and stopped to gorge himself.

"'Psst…psst!' I tried to get Ted's attention so that I could warn him about the trap.

"'Psst…psst…Ted!'

"Ted was so busy stuffing his face with blackberries that he didn't hear me calling to him; trees whisper, and that's why it's so quiet in a forest…kinda like a library. Anyway, purple juices were dripping from Ted's mouth, and thorny branches from the blackberry bushes were becoming tangled in his matted hair, and after a while, I couldn't tell who was the bush and who was the bear.

"'Psst…*psst!*' I whispered as loudly as I could, but to no avail. Ted was in his own little world, and nothing was going to disturb his feeding frenzy. But once the berries were all gone, Ted crossed the road and headed directly toward me. He was snorting and lumbering slowly in my direction, doing the cowboy walk on all fours.

"When he was within earshot, I again tried to get his attention, 'Psst…psst…TED!'

"He looked up at me and snarled.

"'Ted, watch out! There is a bear trap right here.'

"I pointed to the shiny metal stake that was pounded into the ground. 'It's covered up, Ted, with leaves and dirt. Be careful not to walk over here, or you will step in the trap and break your foot.'

"Ted walked around to my other side, looking down for any other traps.

"Just as I was telling Ted that there were no other traps, the rusty Ford pickup, with the dog in the front seat, pulled back up, off the road, and onto the grass. The skinny fellow in overalls got out of his truck and headed in my direction. He was carrying a beer, but there was no lump on his lower lip.

"I looked down and saw that he was coming back for his chewing tobacco. He had dropped the pouch when he was setting up the trap. He didn't see Ted, and Ted didn't see him. Things were about to get real interesting in a few minutes.

"With the help of a sudden mountain breeze, I moved my lowest branch toward the red-and-white tobacco pouch and skillfully dragged it onto the top of Billy Bob's bear trap. Ted was applying his scent to my back side and could not be seen from the road. He was also rubbing his back up and down my boughs to scratch those parts of his own back that he couldn't reach with his claws. He could not see the mountain man approaching, because I was in the way, and Ted couldn't smell the human because the wind was blowing toward the truck.

"The hillbilly couldn't see Ted because he was behind me, and he couldn't hear the bear because he was listening to country music through earbuds. Billy Bob couldn't smell Ted because he smelled even worse than my black bear, if that's possible.

"As Country Boy staggered closer, it was clear that he was very drunk. I watched him guzzle the last of his beer, crush the can, and toss it toward Mary, the Fraser fir next to me. I love Mary, but that's another story for another time. Suffice it to say that she too had been watching these goings-on with much anticipation and concern.

"The can made a muffled, tinny clink when it hit the ground, and it tumbled toward Mary's trunk. The noise distracted Ted, who was leaning against me and scratching up and down.

"'Huh?' he grunted as he watched the can roll to a stop.

"Meanwhile, the hillbilly had begun his search for his chewing tobacco, and he spotted the red-and-white foil pouch under my largest branch. He had forgotten about the trap and was focusing only on retrieving his chew. I think he was having a nicotine fit. Anyway, he tried to bend over to pick up the pouch but lost his balance and fell into my boughs. Billy Bob grabbed a limb and managed to stay on his feet.

"'Huh?' grunted Ted as I shook from the impact of the human falling into me.

"The mountain man looked down, saw the tobacco pouch, held on tight to my limb, and kicked the pouch with his boot. All these country boys wear steel-toed cowboy boots.

"*Sprang* went the trap.

"*Clank* was the loud noise that echoed toward Ted's side of the tree.

"'Huh?' grunted Ted again.

"'Eeyowww!' yelled the hillbilly.

"'HUH?' grunted Ted, and he turned his head around and craned his long neck to look at the other side of his marked tree.

"The redneck was screaming bloody murder and trying to pull his foot free from the trap when he found himself face to face, eye to eye with Ted.

"'EEYOWWW,' hollered the man at the top of his voice.

"'EEYOWWW,' bellowed Ted at the top of his voice.

"Both the bear and the man turned several shades of white. The man pulled his foot out of the mangled boot and high-tailed it toward his rusty truck, one foot dressed in a shiny cowboy boot, the other foot covered only by a dirty sock with the big toe poking through a hole. He jumped in his pickup and floored the accelerator, sending grass and small pieces of gravel flying into the air. When his spinning tire hit the paved road, it left a black rubber skid mark for a quarter mile.

"As for Ted, he ran in the opposite direction. They say a bear can run forty miles per hour, but I think Ted was doing sixty. Ol' tough guy turned out to be a scaredy-cat. He was running so fast that when he disappeared into the woods, the whole mountain shook.

"Mary and I laughed for days.

"We never saw Billy Bob or Ted again.

"It took about two weeks for the stink to go away, but then I had my piney scent back.

"And I still smell really good, don't I, Bobby?"

CHAPTER 11

Friday, November 20

B obby Thornton laughed about my bear story for what seemed like a whole week. Every day he would come to Publix, sit on the bench, and talk with me. I told Bobby some more stories, but he was particularly fond of the bear story, and he got to the point where he could tell it almost as good as me. Bobby would stand up and walk around and pretend to be setting bear traps. Then he would pretend that the trap clanked loudly as it closed on his boot, and he'd hobble off into the parking lot to a pretend pickup truck. The funniest part was always him running from a bear that was running from him.

Suddenly one day, as Bobby was gesticulating with his arms and laughing about the bear story, Missy and her mother appeared, approaching the Publix entrance. Missy broke loose from her mom and ran up to me. She wrapped her small arms around me and gave me a warm hug. Then she ran behind me and held my broken branch. It was so soothing. I felt her energy flowing through my damaged limb, just like before.

Bobby and Natalie McCord were not strangers. Natalie worked part time as a volunteer at the community center, but they had never spent time getting to know one another.

Bobby invited Natalie to sit next to him on the bench and enjoy the scent of the freshly cut trees. Natalie sat, and they talked for a while about the silly things people talk about when they are really only first developing a friendship.

Missy, however, was talking to me about how concerned she was about my broken branch. She told me about the time she fell off a trampoline and broke her arm. "It hurt really bad, Mr. Tree. I had to go to the doctor and get a cast. Maybe you should go to a doctor."

I decided to talk to this sad little child. "What is your name, little girl?"

Her ears perked up, and she leaned close to see if I would say anything else.

I told her my name and about the men in North Carolina who had cut me down and tossed me on the ground. "That's when my branch cracked a bit. Then, just last week, a mean little kid climbed onto my damaged branch and broke it even more. It must look terrible, and it hurts very much, but it feels so much better when you hold it in your hand, Missy. Next time when you visit me, I will tell you one of my best stories, the one about the white bunny, OK?"

Missy was so excited. She told me that she and her mother come to Publix every Wednesday at about four o'clock to do grocery shopping.

That's when her mother called, "Missy, come on. We have to go inside and get milk."

"Mommy, the Christmas tree talked to me! He's so beautiful, Mommy."

"Missy, Christmas trees can't talk."

"This one can, Mommy. His name is Mr. Fir. He told me his name, and he told me how his branch got broken. Can we take him home, Mommy?"

"Not now, Missy. We don't have the money. Let's go inside and do our shopping, and then we'll see the tree on the way out."

Bobby looked up from the bench and caught Natalie's eyes and said, "This is a magical tree, Ms. McCord. He can talk, and his name *is* Fir."

"Sure he can talk, Bobby. Everybody knows that trees can talk!" Natalie was being sarcastic to Bobby as she stared deeply into his eyes. Then she turned and said, "Gotta go, Bobby. I enjoyed talking with you...and your tree."

And Missy and her mom grabbed a shopping cart and walked inside the Publix Supermarket.

On the way out of the store, they saw Bobby still sitting on his bench. Missy ran around to the back of me and held my branch for a few minutes and whispered, "I love you, Mr. Fir."

Natalie sat on the bench and talked with Bobby the entire time that Missy was chatting with me. Bobby and Natalie seemed to be hitting it off, and I was the happiest I had been since I was on my mountain in North Carolina with my Mary. Missy held my branch the whole time, and it felt *so* good.

Then her mom called, and we all said our goodbyes.

Natalie held Missy by her small hand, and they walked off into the parking lot and disappeared into the sea of parked cars. Missy was looking back at me the whole time.

CHAPTER 12

November 25
Trey the White Bunny

Several days later, Natalie and Missy returned to the grocery store to pick up a few things for dinner and to do their weekly shopping. Bobby was sitting alone on the bench with his arms spread out on the backrest. When he saw Natalie McCord, he stood and motioned for her to sit, and she obliged while Missy came over to talk with me.

"Mr. Fir, do you remember when you told me that you would tell me about the white bunny?"

"Yes, Missy, that was last Friday, when we first met. You are going to love this story. It's one of my best." And with that said, I began to tell her the first of my many stories.

"Every year, in early December, the winter arrives with a vengeance on Wildcat Mountain, and with it comes a cold wind that howls through the trees and chills the forest with shivers and shakes. The nuts have all been buried, the grasses have all turned brown, and the leaves have long since fallen from the trees and bushes. Some of the winters are quite harsh. Food is difficult to find, snow is deep, and forest temperatures hover in the teens.

"It was just such a winter, three years ago, when I first met Trey. He tried to hop but kept falling down."

"Why, Mr. Fir?"

"Trey's left rear leg was badly injured, and his white fur was stained with frozen thick, red blood. I soon learned that my friend

41

Trey had been attacked by Len, a hungry coyote who lived down by the river.

"Food is scarce for the animals of North Carolina in the months of December through March. Birds fly south, squirrels and chipmunks sleep in the hollows of hardwood trees, and the lush, green vegetation of summer becomes a stark, barren landscape of brown sticks and leafless bushes, except for us hearty evergreens."

"Why don't you turn brown and lose your leaves, Mr. Fir?"

"We stay beautiful year-round, Missy. We have plenty of food because our roots grow deep. Thirst was never a problem, as I lived on a mountain with dense soil, and the loamy clay retained water like a sponge. Also, I have a waxy skin, which helps prevent excess evaporation in the summer and keeps me warm in the winter. I never get cold, and I never become too hot. I am the perfect tree, a hearty species that has lived on Wildcat Mountain for millions of years."

"Wow, Mr. Fir!" said Missy, with the wide-open eyes of a spellbound little girl.

"But rabbits are not Fraser firs. They don't have roots to feed them, so they expend huge amounts of energy foraging for plants and grasses. And bunnies are a very sought-after meal by meat-eating animals on the mountain.

"So here was Trey, the victim of an attack by a hungry predator, and I was the only one around to try to save his life."

"But what could you do, Mr. Fir? You are only a tree," questioned Missy as she continued to gently hold my broken branch.

"Well, he was lying face down in the snow, exhausted from his escape up the mountain. Even with a severely damaged leg, Trey was fleet of foot, and he easily outran the coyote. But upon his arrival at the top of the hill next to the road, only a few yards from me and Mary, Trey ran out of gas and collapsed."

Missy lowered her head and looked down at her feet and in a soft voice asked, "Was he dead?"

"Oh, no, no, no, no, Missy. Trey was just worn out.

"So I called to him. 'Psst...psst!' I whispered. 'Get up! Please, get yourself up!'

"The white rabbit heard my voice and raised one of his ears into the air.

"'Psst! Come on over here and hide under my branches.'

"Trey lifted his head and looked in my direction. His eyes were glassy from the loss of blood. I was holding up my largest lower bough for him to come and hide underneath.

"The white rabbit eased his bloodied body up and slowly crawled toward the safe place that I had created for him to hide in. It was a den-like hollow in the ground between two of my largest roots and just below the largest part of my trunk. Trey dropped himself into his new underground home, and his body went instantly limp as he curled into a ball and fell fast asleep. He slept for two days. His legs were twitching as he dreamed about his close encounter with Len, the hungry beast from the other side of our road. It was as if he were still running for his life from the brown coyote chomping at his hind leg.

"As the rain and snow continued to fall from the North Carolina sky, my needles accumulated a blanket of frozen water and large icicles under a layer of soft snow. An abundance of brown grass, Fraser fir needles, and juicy cones had fallen into the den where Trey slept, and when he finally awakened, he was famished. After gorging himself on fir seeds, Trey again lapsed into a deep sleep.

"When the bunny was not eating or sleeping, Trey and I passed our time chatting about our beautiful mountain. We laughed as we shared stories of loved ones and friends doing stupid things, and we cried as we remembered those who had passed away.

"Suddenly, as we were chuckling about the antics of two squirrels, we heard a snarling coyote. It was Len, the nasty varmint who had attacked Trey four days earlier. Len had tracked the rabbit's scent to this hiding place under my protective branches, and he was here to finish the job.

"It was very dark that night. Only the flickering starlight and the half moon provided illumination of what was about to happen. Len's eyes glowed an eerie shade of blood red, his teeth glistened, and drool dripped from his mouth as he inched closer to a shivering Trey. I never took my eyes off of the coyote."

"What happened next, Mr. Fir?" asked Missy with a furrowed brow and tears welling up in her eyes.

"Len lunged toward my bunny, his teeth prepared to crunch down on Trey's wounded leg, and that's when I shook all of my limbs as hard as I could. Snow and razor-sharp ice came crashing down on the brown coyote, with the largest icicle piercing Len's leg like a knife slicing through butter.

"Len yelped, howled in pain, and fell backward, rolling rapidly down the snowy mountain. He became a large brown snowball and rolled off the cliff. Len never came back to Wildcat Mountain. Trey's leg healed up better than new, and he's the fastest rabbit on Wildcat Mountain and one of my dearest friends."

"Wow, Mr. Fir. What a great story. Is that story true, Mr. Fir, or did you make it up?"

"Totally true, Missy. Cross my heart and hope to die."

Missy looked over at her mother, who was motioning for her to come and quietly calling her name. "Missy, we have to leave."

"I gotta go, Mr. Fir. Have a happy Thanksgiving."

"Bobby, I really have to say goodbye," said Natalie. "I need to get Missy to her Girl Scout meeting."

She called Missy again, "Missy, come!"

Missy came running around from the back of me, and she had a big smile on her face.

"What are you so happy about, honey?" asked her mom.

"Oh, Momma, Fir just told me the most wonderful story about a white rabbit and a coyote in North Carolina!"

Dismissively, Natalie ushered Missy into Publix, where they quickly completed their shopping. Mom and daughter couldn't have been inside the store for more than ten minutes, and when they exited the supermarket, Bobby was still sitting on the bench.

"Happy Thanksgiving, Bobby. I'll see you at the center this Friday, OK? We're serving a fantastic turkey dinner with all the trimmings, including pumpkin pie for dessert."

"You bet, Ms. McCord. I wouldn't miss it for anything."

As I mentioned earlier, Natalie was a volunteer at the community center, which was around the corner from Publix. The center doubled as a homeless shelter and a food bank, and Bobby would come in to enjoy a hot meal every Friday evening.

"And happy Thanksgiving to you and Missy, Ms. McCord. Isn't that a beautiful tree that your daughter is so fond of?"

"Yes, but I don't think we will be buying a real tree this year. Things have been kinda tough, with the recession and all. See you Friday, Bobby, and please, call me Natalie. Ms. McCord is my mother." As the two young ladies headed for their car, Missy kept looking back at me with her sad eyes as Natalie held tightly to her hand and they disappeared into the parking lot.

Natalie had no idea that Bobby was well aware of the fact that Glenn McCord had abandoned his family almost six months ago. There are no secrets in a small town. Everybody knows everything about everyone. Lake Worth is a small town, and a community center is like a small village, so the "secret" of Natalie's separation and subsequent financial problems was a secret to no one. Natalie was oblivious to the whispers, maybe because she was so busy tending to the misfortunes of others, or maybe because she was just naive. Whatever the reason, Natalie was having a hard time making ends meet, yet she never said a word to anybody. But everyone knew. Bobby knew.

CHAPTER 13

Night Life on the Breezeway, Cockroaches and Rats
November 25, Thanksgiving Eve

The days preceding Thanksgiving had been chaotic and in direct contrast to the serenity and peace that I had enjoyed when I lived in North Carolina. For seven years I was serenaded to sleep each evening by an orchestra of sounds found only at night on my mountain: the buzzing of insects, the rustling of leaves, the wind in the trees, and the thunder in our skies. And each morning I was awakened by the soft melodies of the blue birds, the rat-a-tat-tats of woodpeckers, the moist, gentle breezes of morning, and the warmth of a rising sun.

I often thought about my friends, the animals who were now so far away and whose faces were slowly fading from my memory. I supposed that I should be grateful for the blessings that I once had and prepare for the blessings that were yet to come. None of us know when tragedy will strike, when we will lose that which we love so deeply, but we also do not know what lies ahead. I knew that God had plans for me and that my destiny was in His hands, and His alone.

As I stood there with so many other Fraser firs and spruces and pines, drinking profusely from the water that had been sprayed on us earlier, I couldn't help but think of us as a new grove of trees, meeting for the first time and sharing stories of our time on distant mountains.

We were all different, some with long needles, some with short, some squatty and bushy, some tall and stately. But we were all

Christmas trees, and our destiny was to usher in love and happiness to loving families in Lake Worth.

Every day and every night brought with it a new story; speaking of which, the supermarket had been closed for almost two hours, and the night crawlers were awakening.

The cockroaches in Florida can grow to the size of a small mouse, and they would crawl all over everything at night, looking for food. They also have wings and sometimes would fly onto one of my limbs, making me shudder and giving me the heebie-jeebies. But they are not particularly fond of our Christmas tree smell, so they quickly flew away. But let there be no doubt about it: they, too, are creatures of the night.

The incessant buzzing of the Florida mosquitos can drive you nuts, but they were more of a nuisance to me than anything else. They, like the cockroaches, were repelled by my pine scent, and although they were of much bother to my sparrows, the little birds perched close to my trunk, where the pine aroma is most effective at warding off those pesky insects.

Cats are creatures of darkness too. So as I was whispering to my new friends about the joy of being a Christmas tree, I spotted a large pack of those dreaded feral cats. Actually, I think that they would be called a pride, not a pack.

Anyway, my understanding is that a group of cats in the wild usually consists of one dominant male and several, if not many, females. Splay—that was his name—was definitely the dominant male. He was as black as the darkness that he ruled, and he was probably twenty or so pounds of solid muscle.

The pride usually came out at night in search of food. They were voracious eaters, like the scavenger crow that also made my life so miserable, but these cats were something else. They took dread to a new level. There is nothing that smells worse than a cat litter box that has been sitting unclean for several days. The cat is proud of his scent, and the stronger his odor becomes, the prouder he becomes. It is the tomcat who does the spraying, and the biggest, meanest, dirtiest, most stinking tomcat in Lake Worth was Splay.

These cats came out at night with the male in the lead, their tails and heads held high, and the alpha cat, Splay, sprayed his scent on the sides of buildings, trees, and bushes, marking his territory and warning other feral cats to stay away or face the consequences.

According to my sparrows, he was named Splay because of what had happened one sultry June night near the field where Splay and his harem of girl cats lived. It was a moonless night, and the cats were hungry. Publix was closed, and it was after midnight.

Splay was the hunter and provider for the pride, and most nights he was able to find an ample supply of food to keep every stomach full. The favorite food of his tribe was the delicious field mouse. However, on this one particular dark evening, while on his nightly search for food, he encountered a rat the size of a small dog. Everyone knows that a rat tastes just like chicken, and since the feral cats just loved chicken, Splay's mouth began to water as he followed the scent trail left by the rat.

This rat was inside Splay's dumpster, feeding on garbage that had been discarded by the Publix employees earlier in the day. That garbage belonged to Splay. It was Splay's garbage.

Splay had heard about this giant rat but had never before encountered a rodent so large and intimidating. This intruder must have weighed in at twenty-five pounds, and the rat, Tack, as he was known, was outside of his territory. He had crossed the line, and not only was he in Splay's domain, he was inside Splay's dumpster.

There is no mistaking the smell of a rat, and although rats are usually light on their feet, this massive varmint was so large that he was no longer fleet of foot. But what he lacked in quickness, he more than made up for in size and strength. Tack was a fearless monster with a spindly two-foot tail and teeth that could chew through metal, and he wasn't concerned at all about the dangers of the darkness.

Splay crept up to the dumpster and leaped high into the air, softly landing on the green lid that acted as a top to half of the dumpster. The other half had been left open by the bag boy Kenny as he discarded the last plastic bag from the breezeway receptacle, and that's where the rat was, feasting on donuts and half-eaten sub sandwiches. Splay jumped down onto the gray rodent's back and sunk his teeth into the intruder's neck. Tack struggled, but Splay was too powerful, his bite too strong, and his razor claws too sharp. As suddenly as Splay had entered the bin, he jumped out, only this time his dinner was tightly clenched between his teeth.

If I were telling this story to Missy right now, she would interrupt me and say, "But Mr. Fir, I don't get it. I don't understand what the word *splay* means."

That's when I would explain that it means to cut something down the middle...like when your mother buys a chicken at Publix and takes it home for dinner. She gets her sharpest knife and slices it in half from top to bottom, so that the chicken is spread out and can be seasoned on both sides before roasting skin-side up in the oven.

The feral cats were proud of Splay. He splayed open that gigantic rat with his razor-sharp claws and passed huge pieces around to all his pride, and that is how he came to be known as Splay. He was indeed the king of their jungle.

But that night, as I watched the goings-on in my breezeway, I saw Splay challenge—or be challenged by, I know not which for certain—a quite large stray, feral tomcat, who was standing in a corner near Bobby's bench. The other cat was as large as Splay but much younger and therefore less experienced in the art of combat. This was a territorial cat fight, and to the victor would go the spoils of the territory and of the pride of girl cats.

Splay's claws were razor sharp, and his teeth could bite through a leather belt. As the fight began, the two cats circled each other, growling and snarling and hissing to intimidate one another. Their backs were arched up in the air, and the fur on their bodies was puffed up so that they looked to be twice their normal size. The noise coming from their mouths sounded like screaming, crying babies, only louder, because the sound was echoing in the breezeway.

Neither cat took his eyes off the other, and they continued to circle, each watching for that perfect opportunity to attack. Suddenly, Splay was on top of the younger cat, biting and scratching with his razor-sharp claws. Badly injured, the inexperienced tomcat ran toward the closest tree in the Publix parking lot and disappeared into the dense branches at the top of the tree.

Splay was unscathed, not even winded from his short skirmish with the other cat. He called to his girls, and they all followed him down the breezeway with their tails held high. He stopped near where I stood and left his scent (phew), then turned the distant corner and walked slowly toward the field behind Publix where the feral cats live.

But that night, as he fought yet another epic battle, Splay did no serious harm to the younger feline. He had made his point. He was the king of the forest, and we were *his* trees. That night there would be no fight to the finish, only the marking of territory, and that's precisely what he did as he walked away from me. He sprayed everything, walls, garbage cans, and yes, the other trees as well.

I thought maybe we should give him a new name. Not Splay... but Spray.

I smelled so bad for three days that nobody even came close in order to consider buying me. Kenny did his best to wash me three times a day, but it was not until the Saturday after Thanksgiving that that foul cat odor had finally dissipated.

CHAPTER 14

Thursday, November 26
Eddie the Sparrow

A most humorous thing happened on Thanksgiving Day. I was being hydrated by Kenny, along with the new arrivals that had been dropped off earlier in the morning by Cree. Kenny always seemed to take special interest in me. He appeared to really care for and have special affection for my well-being. I always seemed to get the most water, huge puddles of which were always left at the base of my trunk for drinking when my thirst became more intense. He knew that I had a broken limb and that I needed extra water to stay fluffy and to keep my needles from dropping.

My three little sparrows loved the soaking that I received every morning, and they would fly down to the concrete where the largest puddles accumulated and lie down in the cool water as if they were enjoying a tub bath. I watched them stir up the water with their wings, splash each other, and drink until they could drink no more.

So here we were, my three favorite little birds and me, enjoying our artificial rainfall, our morning ritual of being hosed down by Kenny, when a big, fat, green, juicy bug flew by. It landed on one of my higher branches, I guess to rest or maybe look for something to eat. I thought it was a grasshopper, but I couldn't imagine that it could be hungry. Its belly was distended from whatever this bug had been eating all morning. Maybe it was just too heavy to fly or tired from flying on such a full stomach.

Anyway, Eddie spotted the bug the moment that it flew by and landed on my branch. Eddie was the oldest of the three sparrows, since he was hatched first. His two brothers were one and two days younger—they were still kids, and all they wanted to do was play in the water. Neither had noticed the fat, juicy bug. Eddie vibrated and shook really hard to remove the excess water from his feathers, and he eyeballed the delicious-looking green insect, which was sitting very still so as not to be noticed by bug-eating predators. This juicy grasshopper creature was almost the same color as my needles, which made him especially difficult to see. I watched him cleaning his front appendages; I guess they were his arms, hands, and fingers. He looked as though he were licking his hands after eating a spare rib.

Eddie stood very still, watching every move the bug made. Suddenly, the winged grasshopper took flight, and Eddie left his brothers to pursue his morning meal.

Birds can do complex mathematical calculations very quickly in their heads, which allows them to predict exactly where a flying bug will be at any given time. That way, they can intercept it and catch an airborne insect in their mouth in midflight.

A quick calculation, and Eddie was on his way, flying at full speed to that exact point where he could nab the bug, but Eddie made one mistake. He did not see a car in the parking lot that also was also on a collision course with the bug. Just as Eddie grabbed the grasshopper with his beak, he hit the windshield of the red car and bounced to the ground. Like a golf ball, he rolled into the grass near one of the disabled parking spaces.

High above everything in the Publix parking lot is a fifty-foot royal palm tree with a new branch growing straight up into the air. On the very top of this branch sat the big black crow, and he had seen everything. He saw the large, juicy green bug flying in the parking lot. He watched the small brown bird snag the big green bug. He saw the sparrow bounce off the car windshield, and he saw the bug fall from Eddie's mouth. That's when he immediately flew to the ground, where the confused insect was trying to crawl away. Eddie was dazed but otherwise unharmed, and he heard the loud flapping of those big black wings as the crow landed near Eddie's bug. Just as the crow was opening his mouth to grab the grasshopper, the sparrow quickly flapped his wings and flew into the chest of the big blackbird, hitting him with a thump. Eddie grabbed the grasshopper and flew as fast as he could to the safety of my inner branches, where he swallowed the bug with one big gulp. The crow landed on the bench and squawked for almost an hour before he finally flew away.

"Caw, caw, caw! Caw, caw, caw!"

Eddie closed his eyes, nestled close to my trunk, and fell fast asleep. His brothers were still playing in the water.

CHAPTER 15

November 27
Black Friday

Black Friday was no different than any other day at Publix Supermarket. The managers began arriving at 4:00 a.m., followed by stock personnel, assistants, and baggers. The Pepperidge Farm bread man pulled up at five o'clock, followed by Lays, Pepsi, and Budweiser. Miscellaneous other trucks delivered everything from ice cream to fresh produce. Thanksgiving had left the shelves virtually empty and badly in need of restocking.

Food shopping would not be a priority today, but there were Christmas trees to be sold, and twenty fresh trees had been delivered by Cree. The shoppers did come to Publix on Black Friday, some to make returns, others to buy subs at the deli, and of course there were those who were buying their holiday trees. I was lifted and turned, dragged and dropped, and by the end of the day, I was still left leaning against the bench.

Forty-five trees were sold that day. Mr. Kemp was proud, Kenny was exhausted, and I was distraught because I had not been one of them. I was conflicted, confused, and so terribly lonely. As I was trying to rationalize my sadness, the lights went out. Publix was closing.

The cars drove away, and I was alone. Well, not totally alone; there were the unsold trees and the three wonderful sparrows that had chosen to roost in my branches. I guess they felt safe with me to protect them.

Suddenly I heard a noise. The little birds became especially quiet and tense. People don't realize how much noise birds make even when they seem to be silent. Birds talk about everything, non-stop chatter. They talk to each other about food, they chirp about the weather, they complain about the squirrels, and they laugh at everything. Even when they look sad, like when it rains, they're really quite happy. I could feel their vibrations as they reacted to and talked of the approaching noise.

"It's only Bobby," said one of the sparrows, and they relaxed, closed their eyes, and napped.

Bobby sat down on the bench and filled his lungs with the aroma of Christmas spruce, and then Bobby started talking out loud.

"Hey, Fir, you got any more of those Wildcat Mountain stories like you told me before? That bear story was really something. I had a dream the other night that I was a bear and I got my foot caught in a trap. I woke up in a cold sweat, and my foot was hurting me really bad. You are a real hero for saving Ted from that redneck, Fir. You are a real class act. I'm proud to be your friend, Fir. Now, about that story…"

"Well, let me think!" I said as I focused on one of those huge cockroaches walking toward Bobby's bench. Bobby spotted the roach at the same time as I did. Quietly, he took off his shoe and snuck up behind the massive bug. Bobby held the shoe in his right hand like a man with a hammer getting ready to pound a nail. The heel of his shoe squashed that cockroach to smithereens, sending splatter in every direction. Bobby nonchalantly put his shoe back on and said, "I hate those bugs, Fir. They crawl on me at night where I sleep in the woods. I had one crawl in my mouth the other night while I was snoring. I woke up coughing and spitting and couldn't fall back to sleep. Now, let's hear your story."

CHAPTER 16

Squirrels Autumn

"OK, Bobby, I'm gonna tell you about Tommy the white squirrel.

"Once upon a time, in the pristine mountains of western North Carolina, there lived a white squirrel and two chipmunks.

"The critters of Cherokee County are delightful to behold. Each is unique in beauty and personality. Although I was fond of most all of the creatures of Wildcat Mountain, my favorites, hands down (or should I say, limbs down), were Tommy the squirrel and the two rambunctious chipmunk sisters, Katie and Annie.

"Tommy was a long-legged white squirrel with a penchant for fir nuts, the ones that come from Fraser fir cones like mine and Mary's. The problem was that Katie and Annie also liked my seeds, and these three fuzzy critters were always stealing each other's food. Annie was the smart one. She would just sit and watch where Tommy would bury his nuts, and then she would watch her sister dig up the freshly buried morsels. But Tommy was a most vigilant squirrel, and he almost always caught Katie in the middle of her poaching, and then all hell would break loose. Tommy would bark, a loud kucking sound, and the chase would be on. He could never catch Katie. She was just too fast for the larger and clumsier squirrel, but there were a lot of close calls.

"Annie would just sit back and watch these two rodents irritate each other, and when the chase began, she would make a beeline to the buried treasure, dig it up, and eat the nut.

"Buzz the blackbird would get such a kick out of their antics that he would sit on my spire and just laugh and laugh, sometimes for hours.

"Annie was getting fat at Tommy's expense, but this all came to an end one day when Tommy caught Annie eating his stash. Annie was too fat to outrun Tommy, so when the speedy squirrel caught the plump chipmunk, Tommy viciously attacked Annie, fiercely biting and ripping at the smaller rodent's body.

"The only thing that saved Annie was Katie. She saw what was happening to her sister and blindsided the white squirrel. Tommy went rolling down the mountain and crashed into a big hardwood tree that grew perilously close to the edge of a bluff. Hundreds of feet below were boulders and river rock that had been sanded smooth by years of contact with the Nantahala white-water rapids. The Nantahala is a fast-moving river that snakes its way through the dense, lush valleys of Cherokee County.

"Tommy's collision with the tree rendered him unconscious and allowed the chipmunks to scurry to safety. When he finally awakened, Tommy was so disoriented and dazed that he was barely able to walk. Instinct told Tommy to seek safety from predators, so he tried to scamper up the tree by the ravine, but he lost his balance and fell onto the rocks below.

"Everyone ran to the edge of the bluff and looked down into the gorge for Tommy, but he was nowhere to be seen. Buzz flew over the white water for hours, but to no avail. Tommy had been washed away by the angry river and would never be seen again. We all cried that day. My dear friend was gone.

"Mary talked about this incident for three weeks nonstop. Everyone missed Tommy, but then one day Tommy, the white squirrel of Wildcat Mountain, reappeared before my very eyes. Mary was speechless. She thought she was seeing a ghost, but then she saw Tommy sit up on his haunches and wave to us. And then he gave us one of his toothy smiles, looked around, spotted the chipmunks eating his nuts, and the chase was on, just like old times.

"Mary was so happy that she cried, and I think I shed a tear of happiness too, come to think about it."

"That was a terrific story, Fir. I love your happy endings."

Bobby stood and stretched, raising his arms high over his head, fists clenched, and twisting his torso first left, then right, then left again. He lowered his arms and walked over to me.

"Our lives are going to have happy endings too, Fir. You just wait and see."

CHAPTER 17

Saturday, November 28

Natalie and Missy had not been to Publix since the Wednesday before Thanksgiving, and Missy wanted to come and talk with me in the breezeway. Missy spent all weekend telling her mother that we were out of this and out of that so that maybe, just maybe, Natalie would relent and take her to Publix. Missy could not wait to come see me again. She wanted to hear another one of my stories, and she begged and pleaded with her mother to *pleeeze* take her to Publix.

"Mommy, please take me to Publix. *Pleeeze*, Mommy. I'll clean up my room. I'll wash the car. I'll mow the grass. *Pleeeze*, can we go?"

Natalie explained that they had so many leftovers that there was no need to go shopping right then, but she promised that they would go grocery shopping on Wednesday, just as they always did.

"And besides, young lady, you are not old enough to wash the car or mow the lawn. As for your room, Missy, it better not need cleaning. We just cleaned it up yesterday."

Missy continued to pester her mother all weekend, but Natalie would not give in. She did tell Missy that maybe on Wednesday, when they did the weekly shopping, that they might see Bobby again, and if so, Natalie would like to sit and talk with Mr. Thornton while Missy chatted with Mr. Fir.

Missy thought to herself, *Well, Wednesday isn't that long to wait, I guess. Maybe Mom will need something on Monday. You never know.* Missy was so excited that she could hardly wait for Wednesday to arrive.

CHAPTER 18

Wednesday, December 2

Missy was a good student who made only As and Bs on her report card. She was attentive in class and was always timely in turning in her assigned homework, but on the Monday, Tuesday, and Wednesday preceding her next trip to Publix with her mom, Missy was not doing her classwork, and she had forgotten to turn in her homework. She could only think of me, the stately Fraser fir at Publix she had come to love.

Ms. Lee, her second-grade teacher, had noticed Missy daydreaming, and when she would ask Missy a question, the little girl who almost always got the questions right did not have a clue as to what was going on in the classroom. Missy just sat and stared out the window and imagined how beautiful I would look decorated with delicate bulbs, multicolored bubble lights, garlands, and Christmas presents with bows under me. Missy was in a trance.

"Missy, will you please pay attention!"

Ms. Lee had asked Missy to read before the class from their geography book, but Missy was in her own world, a world of dancing elves popping corn for garlands, a world where a real angel sat on top of her tree, a world where all her Christmas wishes would come true, and a world where her mother and father would celebrate Christmas together.

The bell rang, and Missy hurriedly loaded her books into her pink backpack with wheels and walked quickly toward the pickup area where her mother would be waiting. The minute Missy climbed into the car, she started begging and pleading that they could stop at Publix on the way home.

"No problem, Missy, I told you we would stop and do some shopping after school, and if Bobby is there, I would like to sit with him and talk for a while. We really enjoyed each other's company at the community center this past Friday, and I think he is a really good person."

"Can I talk with Mr. Fir, Mommy?"

"Sure you can, Missy," responded Natalie as they drove into the shopping center parking lot. At this time of day, there were few shoppers, and Natalie was able to pull into a spot quite close to the store. She spotted Bobby immediately, and she seemed to be even more excited than her daughter about stopping at Publix this Wednesday afternoon.

Natalie walked with Missy from her car to the supermarket entrance and sat down on the bench next to Bobby.

"Hi, Bobby, you look your usual handsome self. Did anyone ever tell you that you have a beautiful smile and gorgeous blue eyes?"

"Why, no, Ms. McCord...er...I mean, Natalie. You are the first. Most people just ignore me. They walk by as if I'm not really here, like I'm a nonperson," responded Bobby.

Meanwhile, Missy had disappeared behind the bench and was holding my broken branch in her small, warm hand.

"Do you remember when you told me the story about the white bunny, Mr. Fir?" Missy was looking up at me and talking softly so that her mother would not hear her. Natalie still did not believe that I was a magical tree.

Missy called to Bobby, "Mr. Thornton, can you come over and straighten up Mr. Fir and maybe get him some water to drink? He's thirsty!"

Bobby got up and walked around to the back of the bench. He reached his hand in among the branches, grabbed my trunk with his strong right hand, and lifted me off the ground. He carried yours truly over near the other trees that were standing straight against the Publix wall, well out of the afternoon sun. Kenny had left the hose connected to the spigot, so Bobby turned on the water and sprayed all the trees really well, especially me. The water puddled on the cement floor, and the trees drank a hearty supply of water and rehydrated themselves. They all puffed up and displayed their most vibrant green colors to attract prospective Christmas tree shoppers.

"That was nice, Bobby!" said Natalie. "For some reason, Missy loves that tree, but I've repeatedly told her that we cannot afford a real tree this year. We have an old artificial tree in the garage, and I thought we would decorate it on Christmas Eve, which has always been the tradition in our house. But this year, with Glenn gone… oh, that slipped out, Bobby. I'm sorry. I don't want to burden you with my problems."

Bobby looked into Natalie's sad eyes and reached for her hand. "Ms. McCord, I know about your husband leaving you. Mr. McCord did not appreciate what he had, a beautifully tender, caring, loving wife and a daughter who is second to none."

Missy yelled over toward her mother, "Mommy, Mr. Fir is going to tell me a story about a baby deer named Moe!"

Missy's voice was filled with excitement as she hollered to her mother from where she stood holding my broken branch.

Natalie looked at Bobby with a look of disbelief and shook her head back and forth. "This tree with the broken branch is Missy's imaginary friend, Bobby, and she claims to talk with the tree. Missy is enchanted with this tree. She is driving me nuts. Every day, it's, 'Mommy, can we go to Publix? Mommy, can we go see Mr. Fir? Mommy, we need milk. Mommy, we need cereal.' I think she has created this talking tree because she is having difficulty adjusting to her daddy leaving. I just hope this passes soon."

Bobby listened intently to Natalie's dismay over Missy's behavior.

"Ms. McCord, when I was a little boy growing up in Miami, I used to have plastic toy soldiers. My house was built up on blocks, and we had dirt underneath the house. I used to gather rocks and build little mountains; I made forests from small branches that I broke off of bushes; and I played war for hours with my toy soldiers. I had plastic cowboys and Indians and plastic horses. The dirt under my house was my fantasyland, and I got filthy dirty every day. I even got a ringworm once, and my mom said it was from cats making doo-doo in the dirt. I think that's when I quit playing under the house. But the point is that I talked to my soldiers and with my cowboys, and they...they talked to me, and they talked to each other. My cavalry chased and shot at the Indians, and the Indians chased and shot at the cavalry. Girls do the same thing with their dolls, so I wouldn't worry about her sudden fascination with this tree. But I will tell you, and you may think I'm a little goofy myself, but this is a very special tree, and that's all I'm going to say about that.

"I'll tell you what I'll do, Ms. McCord, I've got a couple of extra bucks. Why don't you let me buy this tree for you and Missy? I'll even help you load it on the car."

"No, no, Bobby. I appreciate your generosity, but this year Missy and I are going to have an artificial tree, and we are going to decorate it on Christmas Eve, just like we do every year. End of discussion."

CHAPTER 19

December 2
Moe the Young Deer

Meanwhile, while Bobby and Natalie had been discussing the special tree, I had started to tell Missy about the baby deer, Moe.

"Once upon a spring day, the sun was warm, the breezes were soft, and my view of Wildcat Mountain was breathtaking. Every morning I woke up in a cool forest, surrounded by my friends: the other Fraser firs, the birds, and the animals. I would watch the sun rise in the distance, melting the purple haze that defines the Blue Ridge Mountains.

"Mother deer with their spotted fawns would come out of the thicket and nibble on the moist grasses that grew at my roots. Does are very protective of their babies, and it only takes the slightest movement in the forest or the unsettling noise of a breaking twig to send them bolting into the underbrush from which they had come, with their babies right behind them."

"What would scare them, Mr. Fir?" asked Missy inquisitively.

"Golly, Missy, it could be almost anything. Thunder, a snake, mice, a falling branch, a bear, or a coyote. Remember Len, the coyote?"

Missy looked up at me with a mental picture of Len and his sharp teeth and said, "I would run so fast that Len would never catch me, Mr. Fir."

"Anyway, Missy, I became especially fond of Maddie and her freckled fawn, Moe. Moe was a jumper. He would run toward me as fast as he could, and at the last minute, Moe would jump over my lowest limb. Most of the time he would be successful, but not always. Sometimes I would see him coming, and I would lift my branch up, just a little, and Moe would trip. He would fall on the ground and start to roll down the hill like a brown pine cone with legs. His mother just looked at him and shook her head, wondering how she ever became the mother of such a silly little deer."

This part of my story really tickled Missy, and she started laughing. She laughed so loudly that her mother asked, "Missy, what is so funny?"

"Moe just tripped over Mr. Fir's branch and rolled down the hill!"

Natalie just stared at Bobby, again shaking her head, and Bobby just smiled at Natalie.

After Missy's laughter ceased, I continued my story.

"I loved Moe. He feasted on my tender little cones, the ones that he was able to reach. He would wrap his warm tongue around the cone and snap it off with his lips. I didn't mind. I could grow new cones in two days to replace the ones Moe had eaten.

"One summer morning Moe showed up alone and very sad. I could see tears in his eyes, and his head was down. He stood next to me, frightened, confused, and with his eyes darting in every direction. Usually, Moe would be feasting on my juicy cones, but today he just stood there, trembling and crying. I asked Moe what was the matter. I offered him some tender cones to eat, but he just stood there sobbing. I asked again, 'What's wrong, Moe? Where's your mother?'"

"Where was she, Mr. Fir?" asked Missy with a furrowed brow.

"Well, Missy, he did not know. Let me tell you what happened next. Moe's voice was shaky, but he snuggled real close to me and told me about his morning.

"'Mom and I were on the other side of the road.' He pointed to the asphalt two-lane road that ran through our forest.

"'There is a clearing on the far side of those trees'—he lifted his hoof and pointed to the dense thicket next to the road—'and the grass in the clearing is so high that you can't see me when I am next to my mother. Those green grasses are really sweet and tender over there, and Momma takes me to that same spot almost every day.

"'I heard a loud noise, and my mother suddenly ran into the forest, away from the sound that had scared her. I tried to follow, but the grass was too high, and she was much too fast for me, so I lay down, just like my mommy had taught me, and I stayed real still.

"'There were bad men with guns, and they were shooting at my mother. They went running after her, and I heard loud bangs, like the sound that limbs make when they crack off dead trees. They ran through the grass, right by me and into the forest. A giant of a man almost stepped on me as he ran by, but I didn't move a muscle. After they disappeared, the forest got very quiet. I heard nothing for a long time, no crickets, no birds, nothing—nothing but the sound that danger makes. I stayed where I was, next to a small log, for a long time before coming to see you. You are my only friend, Mr. Fraser Fir, and I don't know what to do.'"

"Oh dear," said Missy. "How scary to be without your mother."

"You bet it's scary, Missy, but I was with him, and I told Moe that I would stay with him until his mother returned. I told him some happy stories, funny things that happen all the time on Wildcat Mountain."

"Like what, Mr. Fir?"

"Like the time when old Mr. Crow ate too many berries and couldn't fly because he was too heavy."

"Will you tell me that story, Mr. Fir?"

"Yes, Missy, but first let me tell you about what happened next to Moe. I told Moe to sit behind me, between me and Mary and out of sight. 'If the men come back,' I said, 'they will not see you, Moe, and when your mother comes to look for you, I will tell her that you are safe.'"

"You are a good friend, Mr. Fir. I bet all the animals miss you very much, but I'm so happy that you are here with me. I just hope Momma lets me take you home."

71

"I hope so too, Missy. I think God sent me here to be part of your family, but let me tell you the rest of the story."

Natalie looked over at Missy, who had her head inside my branches, and said, "Hurry up, Missy, we have to go inside and do our shopping."

"OK, Momma. Mr. Fir is almost finished with his story."

CHAPTER 20

December 2
Everyone Has a Best Story

"Moe was a very good little deer. He remained hidden under my large branch all day, out of danger, and I was finally able to persuade him to eat some of my delicious Fraser cones. He was so hungry that he gobbled down all that he could reach and then started nibbling on the grass by my trunk, but he needed milk, his mother's milk. I stood watch all day, protecting little Moe and searching the forest for any sight of his mother. My sweet little friend was getting weak, and he could not stop trembling, even though I assured him that his mom would be there soon.

"As the full moon rose and the mountain began to glow in a soft white, I heard a rustling in the bushes. I immediately focused on the spot where I heard the noise, hopeful that it wasn't the men or a bear or one of the angry coyotes that lived on the other side of the road."

"Yeah, like that meanie, Len!" interjected Missy. Missy continued to hold my broken limb, and I continued my story.

"I whispered to Moe to be real quiet, and he stopped his crying. Suddenly, the most wonderful sight I had ever seen appeared out of the bushes—Moe's beautiful mother. Moe smelled his mom's scent and immediately ran to her side. They rubbed noses, Moe filled his empty belly with fresh milk, and they disappeared into the forest.

"The next day, Moe and his mother came to see me. Moe had told his mom all about how I protected him while she was gone.

I was so proud, and I puffed up my needles and became very tall and fluffy. Then I asked Maddie where she had been all day. She said that she was worried that the men would hurt Moe, so she had led them to the other side of Wildcat Mountain, away from her precious little baby boy."

"And then what happened, Mr. Fir?"

"Well, Missy, we all lived happily ever after."

"What a wonderful story, Mr. Fir. The next time I come back, will you tell me another, maybe about the bird that ate too many berries?"

"We'll see, Missy. Why don't you think of one of your good stories, and when you come back, you can tell me a story."

"C'mon Missy, we gotta go inside Publix." Natalie walked toward where Missy was standing next to me, holding my broken branch. She took her daughter by the hand, turned, and walked toward the open doors of the supermarket.

"See ya later, alligator!" I whispered to Missy.

Natalie turned around and looked at me as if she might have heard, but she just said, "Nah!" and then the two girls walked into Publix.

Natalie and Missy exited Publix about thirty minutes later with a shopping cart full of food. They were out of milk, cereal, chicken tenders, mac and cheese, and a whole slew of other tasty treats. Natalie was a bargain shopper, so she brought her coupons and also took advantage of the buy-one-get-one-free bargains. As they stepped into the breezeway, Missy broke loose from her mom and ran over to me. Bobby was still seated on the bench, so Natalie let Missy say her goodbyes while she said the same to Bobby.

"Mommy said we can come back on Wednesday, a week from today. Will you tell me another story, Mr. Fir?"

"I think we talked about this, Missy. It's your turn to tell me a story."

"But I don't know any stories, Mr. Fir."

"Missy," I said, "everyone has a best story. Everything that has ever happened to you in your whole lifetime is your story. Each day, as you go through your daily routine, you are living a story, but it's not just your story, it's all of our stories, Missy. We meet and greet; we agree, disagree, and sometimes agree to disagree. We love, and sadly, we learn to hate. We argue, we debate, we smile, and we frown. We fall down many times in our life, but the most important thing we can do when we fall down is to get right back up and get on with our lives. Because we are always finding new friends and, unfortunately, losing friends we've grown very close to, and all those people (and trees and animals—indeed, every living thing) become part of our stories. And you, Missy, become part of their unique stories too. Everybody who comes into your life, talks with you, plays with you, studies with you, and loves you, Missy, they are part of your story, 'The Missy Story.'

"The story of Moe, that was not my story, that was just one of Moe's stories, and he will have many more to tell as he grows up into a big, strong buck. I was just a small part of a Moe story with a happy ending. Look around. Watch. Listen. When you come back next Wednesday, tell me a story."

"OK, Mr. Fir. See ya Wednesday."

"Oh, one more thing, Missy."

"What, Mr. Fir?"

"Study, and pay attention in class!"

Natalie hugged Bobby goodbye and told him that she would see him at the community center on Friday and that they were having meat loaf, mashed potatoes, green peas, and corn on the cob.

"I love meat loaf, Natalie. I'll be there at five o'clock, *sharp*!"

CHAPTER 21

December 4
Meat Loaf and Brown Gravy

Bobby had this thing about being on time, and he was known to loiter around the exterior of a building before entering if and when he ever arrived too early, and he was always early. Tonight was no exception.

Bobby had taken the number-nineteen bus, which departed the Publix bus stop at 4:00 p.m., and since it was at most a ten-minute ride, Bobby would step off the bus at 4:10 p.m., almost an hour early. Although he could have walked the short distance to the mall, something told Bobby to take the bus. even though there was no sign of rain and an ocean breeze air conditioned the entire city of Lake Worth.

Bobby felt crisp; he was neatly dressed and groomed with a close-cut haircut and shave and smelling sweet from the aftershave the barber had smoothed onto his cheeks.

Maybe it was serendipitous that Bobby had decided to ride, for there had been an incident on the bus that required Bobby's attention. Two young, dark-skinned ruffians were tormenting an old lady, who, along with Bobby, had boarded the bus at the Publix bus stop. Bobby was not about to remain detached from the bad behavior of these two hooligans, so he approached them and, looking down into their dark eyes, demanded that they disembark at the next stop. Bobby pulled the cord to alert the driver, Manuel, that someone wanted to get off. The overgrown teens became confrontational with Bobby, so he grabbed them both by the shirt and escorted them to the rear exit. He whispered to them, "Don't make me hurt you!"

The boys, with clenched fists, begrudgingly complied, as Manuel, Bobby's close friend, accompanied Bobby and the two boys to the rear of the bus. Manuel returned to his driver's seat, reengaged the bus, and drove back onto the roadway. Bobby sat down next to the elderly lady, who thanked him profusely for coming to her assistance, and the ride continued uneventfully, except for the applause Bobby received from the other passengers and high-fives from several other homeless men riding on the bus.

The bus neared Bobby's stop, and Manuel instinctively pulled off the road to let his friend disembark. This particular bus stop was right in front of the community center, where an octagon of benches nestled in the shade of giant oak trees. The City of Lake Worth maintained the center, which was part of the municipal buildings and housed the police department, library, and sports complex for the citizens of Lake Worth. There was also a swimming pool and handball courts, and the entire facility enjoyed special attention from Public Works, which planted beds of multicolored flowers everywhere.

As Bobby sat on one of the black steel benches, he wished he could bring me to this beautiful place, if for no other reason than to share each other's company, but he knew that was impossible. Bobby looked up at the stately oak tree next to the bench, where Spanish moss was hanging just out of his reach, and said, "Mr. Oak! My friend Fir would love to meet you and enjoy sharing the wonderful stories of his life in North Carolina. I see you have two squirrels. Fir had a white squirrel and two chipmunks in Murphy, and he had rabbits and deer and bears. You ever see a bear, Mr. Oak?" Then he spread his arms on the backrest, closed his eyes, and thought of Natalie.

Bobby loved benches and sunshine and the billowy white clouds that decorated blue skies. He sat on a bench facing north, with the shade of the large oak tree partially shielding him from the direct sun. He opened his eyes, looked up at the sky, and admired the changing shapes of the clouds as they moved across the blue canvas above. He watched as white rabbits became floppy-eared elephants and wispy white pillows became fearsome dinosaurs.

Robins had already arrived from the north and were singing in the tree above. Mockingbirds were imitating their tweets, and pigeons congregated at Bobby's feet, begging for crumbs and crackers. They knew that he carried a bounty of goodies in his deep pockets. As the pigeons feasted on bread crumbs and bird-seed, Bobby stretched his arms out on the back of his bench and reflected on the beauty of the world. He began to hum a song that he loved:

> "I see trees of green, red roses too.
> I see them bloom, for me and you,
> and I think to myself,
> what a wonderful world."

Louis Armstrong, he thought, as the song sang on in his mind, *nobody ever sang it like you.*

As Bobby configured the clouds, he silently sang to himself and reflected on the pleasant memories of his youth. He thought of his mother, his wonderful mother, who had died before she ever really lived, the victim of a drunk driver who was too young to drink and too irresponsible to drive. Neither his dad nor Bobby ever really got over the loss of his mother, but the time they both shared with Mom had been the best of times. She had doted on her only child, spoiled him to a fault, cherished him, and adored him as only a mother can adore a child.

Bobby was looking at his watch when he realized that he had been daydreaming in the cool, blissful shade for forty-five minutes. It was time to go inside and sit with Natalie and eat meat loaf. He was more excited about seeing Natalie than eating meat loaf, and he absolutely loved meat loaf. How could life get any better than this?

So there he was, at exactly 5:00 p.m., anxiously ready to go inside the building, but a strange thing happened. Just as Bobby grasped the pewter handle of the front door, to his surprise, the door was pushed open from the inside by none other than Natalie. She looked like an angel with her arms spread out, ready to give Bobby a big hug. She had been watching the clock on her wall, and at exactly five o'clock, she knew Bobby would be walking through the front door. That's when she pushed, and that's when he pulled.

"Hi," she said as she embraced him with a friendly hug. "You're right on time, as usual, Bobby. I could set a watch based on your arrival at the center. When you say that you will be here at five o'clock, you are here at exactly five o'clock."

"I learned that in the military, Natalie. In boot camp, if you failed to arrive exactly on time, the whole platoon was punished, so we were almost always early, and *nobody* was *ever* late."

The aroma of meat loaf hovered in the air, subtly stimulating the senses of all who had come for this special dining experience. The room was already filled, almost to capacity, with homeless people—men, women, and children whose lives had fallen apart.

"Am I too late?" asked a concerned Bobby Thornton.

"No, Bobby, I've saved us two seats over in the far corner, near the kitchen, and I took the liberty of serving you an oversized portion, because I know how much you love meat loaf."

"Well, hot dang, let's eat." And with that, Natalie led Bobby to the reserved table for two in the distant corner.

Nothing ever tasted so good as meat loaf and brown gravy, at least as far as Bobby was concerned, and he was stuffing pieces in his mouth that were much too large to chew. Natalie had to slow him down.

"Easy, there, Bobby; there is plenty more where that came from, and I even have a doggy bag ready for you when you leave tonight, in case you get hungry later."

"I'm sorry, Natalie, but it tastes so darned good. It tastes just like the meat loaf my mother used to make."

Bobby's mother used to serve meat loaf every Friday for him and his dad. Bobby stuffed another forkful in his mouth and then wiped the gravy that was dripping down his chin. His cheeks were swollen, and he was again having difficulty chewing. He started to apologize to Natalie, but when he opened his mouth to talk, a large hunk of brown meat was expelled from his mouth and landed on Natalie's hand.

"Oh, I'm so sorry, Ms. McCord. I've misplaced my etiquette."

Natalie picked up a napkin, wiped the meat loaf off her hand, and handed a clean napkin to Bobby.

"No damage done, Bobby. You have some gravy on your chin." Then she reached over and delicately daubed the gravy off of Bobby's face. Bobby was a bit embarrassed and turned several shades of red.

Natalie was embarrassed too. "I'm sorry, Bobby; that was impulsive. I shouldn't have done that."

"Oh, it's all right. My mom used to do the same thing when I was eating meat loaf. I guess you are right; I need to slow down and tend to the p's and q's that I was taught."

Bobby smiled and thanked Natalie, his face still a light shade of red, as he looked down at his sumptuous plate of food. Bobby's plate was piled high with green peas, mashed potatoes, and corn on the cob, three of his favorite vegetables.

CHAPTER 22

December 4
Making Mother's Meat Loaf

The room was a-clatter with the sounds of forks colliding with plates, people talking too loudly, and dishes being refilled with second portions of the delicious food from the serving line. It was always an all-you-can-eat buffet for the homeless of Lake Worth, and it was unsettling to Natalie that there were so many single mothers with hungry children to feed. She was now a single parent, and any one of these women could just as easily be her. But her volunteer work at the center gladdened her heart, knowing that at least for one night her efforts and the efforts of others could make life better for these unfortunate women and their children, who could just as easily be Missy. When one sees the misfortunes of others, it makes one better appreciate what one has and be grateful for the heartache, pain, and suffering that has not yet visited one's personal life.

As Natalie was looking at all the single women and their children, she was silently thanking God for the blessing that she was not homeless.

Bobby, on the other hand, was immersed in thoughts of his childhood, which flooded his mind like a river overflowing its banks. He could visualize his beautiful mother, with her long, straight dark hair—hair just like Natalie's—slicing sweet onions and shucking corn. He closed his eyes, and he could see his mom in her kitchen, mixing the hamburger meat and humming the love songs of Johnny Mathis.

Bobby took another bite of his steamy mashed potatoes.

As he chewed, Bobby began to chuckle, recalling this one particular day when his mom was squeezing and squishing the ground beef mixture between both her hands, but she had forgotten to take off her diamond wedding ring.

His mind had drifted into the past, but the gentle touch of Natalie's soft fingers brought him back to the community center, where he was loudly chewing on his ear of sweet corn. Butter was dripping down his face, and juices from the bursting kernels were splattering on Natalie's cheeks. They both picked up napkins and proceeded to clean the raindrops of corn and butter from each other's face.

"Natalie, I've gone and done it again. I'm sorry. My mother did not raise me to eat like this. Look, I have a napkin in my lap, and I'm lifting my fork to my face, unlike all those other people, who look like dogs eating out of a bowl. And I usually eat slowly and chew my food well before swallowing, but this is meat loaf, and I seem to lose my senses when I eat meat loaf."

"Bobby, don't worry about it. My daughter eats the same way when we have meat loaf at home. Did you know that this is my recipe?"

"Are you kidding me, Natalie? The potatoes too?"

"Yep, the potatoes too. I leave the peels on because that's where the nutrients are, and I add sour cream for added flavor."

"The potatoes tonight are delightful. I think they are better than my mom's, Natalie."

Natalie had personally served him, and she took great care to give him extra-large portions of everything, especially the meat loaf and gravy. Bobby picked up his yellow ear of corn and began chewing off the kernels again, just like a typewriter would chew out the words of a letter.

"What are you laughing about, Bobby?"

Bobby was distant, detached from the present; his eyes were staring at his meat loaf, but he was far, far away, no longer in the building. He had mentally wandered out of the center and was a child again.

"Bobby? Bobby?" Natalie snapped her fingers in front of his fixated stare, and Bobby blinked.

"What were you thinking about, Bobby? You were laughing about something."

"Oh, I'm sorry, Natalie. I drifted off. That sometimes happens. I was recalling a funny story about my mom."

"Tell me the story, Bobby," requested Natalie as she watched him enjoy another bite of meat loaf. Bobby started to loudly laugh, and it attracted the attention of everybody in the dining hall. The noise inside the center had been almost deafening—everyone was talking, laughing, and truly enjoying this delightful Friday-night meal—but as Bobby's laughter increased in cadence, the hall became as quiet as a library. Disheveled men, women, and children stopped eating, and all eyes in the building focused on Bobby. Then a deep voice in the back of the room rang out, "It's story time. C'mon, Bobby, tell us one of your tall tales."

Bobby got so tickled that he had to put his fork down. His laughter was contagious, and before long everyone had a smile on their face, and many were laughing as loudly as Bobby and didn't even know why.

"What's so funny, Bobby?" asked Natalie.

The voice rang out again, "Story, story, story!" Almost immediately, the whole room was chanting, "Story, story, story!"

Bobby stood, lifted his hands in assent, and then sat back down and began from the beginning.

"My mother used to make meat loaf for me and my dad, and it was delicious, just like the meat loaf we are eating tonight, and I was just remembering the time my mother forgot to take off her wedding ring."

"Did she cook her ring in the meat loaf, Mr. Thornton?" questioned a little girl at the next table.

"No, that would have been terrible, but that's not what happened.

"My mama always prepared the meat mixture on Wednesday so that all the ingredients could marinate in the fridge, and then on

Friday, she just had to throw it into the oven about an hour before daddy got home from work.

"Well, when my mother made meat loaf, mixing the burger meat was always my job, but on this particular Wednesday, I was as dirty as a pig, so Mom had to start the mixing, and as I said, she had left her rings on.

"I had been playing in the dirt under our house with my plastic cowboys and Indians. Back then, in Miami, where I grew up, houses were built on big concrete blocks, which held the house about three feet off the ground. Grass can't grow in the shade under a house, and playing in the dirt was always a great way to spend a hot summer afternoon. My dog always kept me company, lying in the cool dirt on hot days and sleeping while I played. I also had plastic soldiers, tanks, and airplanes, and I would play war in the dirt when I tired of playing with my cowboys. Spotty (that was my dog's name) and I were as dirty as a dog and a little boy could get. So when I walked into the kitchen, I was told to go take a bath. Off to the tub I was sent to rub-a-dub-dub and scrub the dirt from my little boy body. I was only about eight years old. Momma wouldn't let me touch her cooking unless I was squeaky clean, and if I had been playing under the house, Mom would make me scrub under my fingernails with a toothbrush.

"By the time I walked back into the kitchen, clean as a whistle, my mom had the meat mixed with most of the tasty secret things that mothers use to make their homemade masterpieces. Her creation was almost completed when I entered the kitchen, sparkling like a new diamond ring. I was just in time to crack the eggs and add them to milk-soaked Italian bread crumbs, the part I always enjoyed the most. There was a certain fascination in breaking the shells and watching the yolks of the eggs drop onto the crumbs of bread, but then, the really best part was always grabbing that snotty-like egg and crushing it into slimy yellow goo, then squeezing all the ingredients together with my hands and forming different shapes with the ground beef. It was like playing with clay, or Play-Doh, and messy like finger paints.

"My mom always let me play with the mushy hamburger-meat mixture, building houses or forming balls, ropes of meat, and imaginary animal creatures, before she would make me hurry up and finish the mixing. I wore a white T-shirt, sat at the kitchen table, and was squishing and squeezing the meat tightly with my puppy-sized paws, just like my mother had taught me. When she thought that I had played enough, she would push me aside and form the actual meat loaf, cover it with Saran wrap, and put it into the ice box so that the flavors could all blend together.

CHAPTER 23

Mystery of the Stink

"Friday afternoon, about three hours before the meat loaf was scheduled to be placed in the oven, Mom pulled it out of the refrigerator so that it could sit for a couple of hours at room temperature. She said this was important so that the meat loaf would be thoroughly cooked all the way through to the center and that this further helped in marinating all the herbs and spices together.

"Mom also had a habit of smelling her food just before placing it in the oven or frying pan. She was always concerned that something might be spoiled, and she did not want us to get food poisoning. So at about four o'clock, she lifted the meat loaf dish up to her nose and took a deep breath, but then she started to gag, and she dropped the whole casserole dish on the floor. It shattered, and little shards of glass and large gobs of meat loaf flew everywhere. Mom was so upset that she started to cry. Spotty was racing across the room to eat the raw meat mixture, and Mom tearfully screamed at the top of her voice, '*Bobby, get that dog outta here!*'

"She was afraid he would get glass in his stomach. I grabbed Spotty by the collar and pushed him out the back door; then I ran back inside to my mother, who was on her knees, sobbing over her meat loaf disaster. I told Mom not to cry, and I got the broom, dustpan, and lots of paper towels.

"We cleaned up the mess, and then Mom sent me down to Winn Dixie on my bike to get some pork chops. Mom was a master at cooking up quick meals. By the time I got back from the store, which was only two blocks away, she was ready to start frying up the chops. She had the flour mixture ready and the egg mixture, and the grease was already hot in the pan, and best of all, the minute Dad walked through the door, the last pork chop was golden brown and bubbly.

"So in walked Dad to the wonderful smells of Mother's fried pork chops, and as usual, she met him at the door with her traditional big hug. Dad loved his hugs and kisses, so after he got about fifteen kisses from Mom and washed up, we all sat down and dug in."

"But I thought you were going to have meat loaf, Bobby, and now you're eating pork chops," commented a woman named Maria, who was sitting at the next table. "I thought this was a meat loaf story."

"You're right, Maria, this is a meat loaf story, but as I said, Mom threw the meat loaf away. She smelled it and said the meat was rotten. She said it smelled wretched, and then it slipped out of her hands, hit the floor, and shattered, so what was she to do? She took a bad thing that happened and turned it into a good thing; she made her outrageous fried pork chops instead. Anyway, I'll get back to that meat loaf debacle in a minute, Maria.

"My daddy also was confused about why we were having pork chops instead of meat loaf, but Mom said she would tell him all about it later.

"Now, my dad had a three-second rule, which I'll explain in a minute, but he was so hungry that no sooner had he sat down to eat, he grabbed one of the very hot, juicy chops off of Mom's serving platter. Rather than use tongs or a fork, like he should have done, he grabbed the pork chop with his fingers, but unbeknownst to him, these chops were boiling hot. They had just come out of the oil and still had bubbles of hot grease popping on the outside. That's when he burned the first two fingers and thumb of his right hand, and he tossed the steamy pork chop up into the air, while Mom, Spotty, and I watched, in what seemed like slow motion, as this pork chop rose higher and higher into the air and finally began to tumble downward until it hit the floor with a splat. Mom and I both stared at that perfectly cooked, steamy, golden-brown, breaded pork chop as it sat on our hardwood floor. Mom and I began to count, "One… two…" but we never made it to three. Daddy had grabbed that hot pork chop just before Spotty got to it, and then he started ripping huge bites off like he was starving to death. Spotty, Mom, and I just sat there with our mouths open, watching Dad devour his first pork chop. You see, Daddy had a rule, the three-second rule, which said that if our dropped food was on the floor for less than three seconds, then it was OK to eat. And he ate it."

"Is that true, Mr. Thornton?" asked a little boy not far from Bobby.

"Yes, Jimmy, it's OK to eat so long as you get to it before your dog gets it."

Everybody laughed, and then they got quiet again. They wanted to hear the rest of the story.

"The next day, Saturday, Mom made me take out the trash, even though the garbage man would not come for two more days. She was opening cabinet doors, cleaning out the pantry, and scrubbing floors on her hands and knees, and she had me working right alongside her. We cleaned the stove, took everything out of the refrigerator, washed every jar, spit-shined the insides of the icebox."

"What's an icebox?" asked Joey, a small child sitting next to a man named Larry.

"It's what we used to call the refrigerator when I was a kid, Joey."

"Oh, thanks, Mr. Thornton. Sorry to interrupt."

"That's quite all right, Joey."

"What was your mom's problem?" came that deep voice from the back of the room.

"Well," continued Bobby, "I did not have a clue. I thought my mother was losing her mind. I had never seen her act that way."

Except for an occasional cough, sniffle, or sneeze, the dining room was without sound. All were listening to this story and anxious to discover what it was that was wrong with Bobby's mom.

Bobby picked up his fork to take another bite of meat loaf. As he chewed and chuckled, he inserted his fork into the huge pile of steamy mashed potatoes and lifted a gravy-laden forkful into his mouth. He closed his eyes while he chewed, savoring every bite, and then continued his story.

"Mom threw out a perfectly good bag of potatoes, all the onions, and all the fresh fruit that we had just purchased from the Winn Dixie grocery store down by the new Burger King that had just opened. I had the honor of taking all this heavy stuff—that there was nothing wrong with—to the garbage can in our carport."

"Mr. Thornton, why did you throw out perfectly good onions and potatoes?" asked Santo, a young, dark-haired Mexican boy who sat next to his mother, Maria.

"Because my mother told me to toss them in the trash can, Santo, and I always obeyed my mother and father...well, almost always. Anyway, Santo, Mom said to throw them away, so I did what my mother told me to do. But you know what I was thinking, Santo? I was thinking that this madness had to come to an end. I just couldn't stand it anymore. I wanted to play in the dirt with the new Tonka trucks that my dad had bought me, but all Mom wanted me to do was to help her clean. So I asked her, 'Mom, what's with all the cleaning? And why are you throwing out all our food? Dad is going to have a hissy fit! We've been at this all day, and I want to go out and play!'

"Mom looked at me and said, 'Bobby, something stinks in this house, and I can't seem to find it. I've looked everywhere, and we've cleaned everything, and I have no clue whatsoever what stinks.'

"Dad walked through the door at about five thirty on Saturday, tired and sweaty from another hard day of driving trucks. Dad worked six days a week back then, and I don't remember him ever taking a day off, even when he was sick. Mom always rushed to the door to meet him, and she would give him a big, slurpy kiss and hug him real tight. She couldn't have weighed more than one hundred pounds soaking wet, and Dad lifted her off the ground, spun her around in a circle, and asked her, 'What's for dinner, Diane? Is that your *kapusta* that I smell?'

"'Yes, John,' she said, 'Are you hungry, honey?'

"'Starving, Diane,' he replied. 'I'm so hungry that I could eat a whole pig.'"

"Mr. Thornton, what is ka-poost-a?" asked Alberto, who sat with his uncle Jose; they were from Guatemala.

"Good question, Alberto. Kapusta, pronounced kah-poo-stah, is a Polish word for cabbage. My mother, however, added all sorts of ingredients to make a kind of pork-sauerkraut-cabbage stew, and boy was it delicious."

"Was your mother from Poland?" asked Jose.

"No, but my grandmother was from Warsaw, Poland, and Grandma Kaspersky taught my mother how to cook like a five-star Polish chef. She passed down all her Polish recipes to her daughter. If you've never had kapusta, you've never lived! It's delicious. Maybe we can get Ms. McCord to prepare kapusta for us one Friday night."

Natalie looked around the room and held her hands open like she was getting ready to clap and said, "Sure, why not?"

Bobby looked over at Natalie, held his right thumb up, and gave her a big smile, and then he said, "And I'll help you, Natalie, if you'll let me."

CHAPTER 24

Uh-Oh, a Pimple

Bobby continued, "OK, back to my story. While Dad was talking about how starved he was, my mom spotted a big, ugly yellow pimple that was festering on the side of my dad's nose, a blemish that had probably repulsed almost everyone who had seen Daddy that day.

"My father looked into my mother's eyes, eyes that were focused only on his nose. 'What's wrong, Diane?' he asked. Diane was the name of my mother, Diane Kaspersky Thornton. She was a real fox, and Daddy knew it. He loved my momma more than anything.

"Anyway, Mom said, 'John, you have a whitehead on your nose. Let me squeeze it for you. Sit down on the recliner, under the lamp, so that I have plenty of light.'

"Mom was always grooming Dad. She cut his hair, bought him nice clothes, and was always inspecting him for those ugly blackheads and pimples, and if she found one, she would grab a tissue and go to work like a surgeon working on a brain tumor.

"Well, this pimple was ready to explode. I think that if Momma had left it alone, it would have burst all over everything and we would be back to our cleaning."

"Yuck!" said little Lahoma, a dark-skinned girl sitting with her father. "That's disgusting."

Everyone laughed, and the room burst into a din of conversation about blackheads and pimples. Bobby took this opportunity to take several bites of meat loaf, peas, and potatoes. His corncob had been chewed clean. As the room grew silent and all eyes again focused on Bobby, he lifted his glass and washed down his food with a large swallow of cold milk.

"You're right, Lahoma, but it might be yuckier to walk around all day with zits on your face. We must always take pride in our grooming. That means combing our hair, keeping our bodies clean, using deodorant, brushing our teeth, and squeezing our pimples and blackheads. And my momma always made me brush my teeth and wash behind my ears. And she always inspected my dad for those ugly zits that pop up on everybody's face.

"Anyway, let's get back to my story. I turned on the light, and Daddy lay back in the lounge chair. He kinda had bad body odor from sweating so much, but Mom didn't care. She loved the man, and she loved his smell. As she got close to Daddy's nose with her two index fingers, Dad jumped out of the chair and yelled, 'Jeez, what stinks so bad?'

"Mother said, 'John, I don't know. Bobby and I spent the entire day today trying to figure it out. We cleaned the toilets, the icebox, the floors, the pantry. Bobby washed the dog twice, and we just can't find the stink.'

"Dad sniffed me and asked, 'When did you last take a bath, young man?'

"I looked down at the floor and quietly whispered, 'Right after I washed Spotty, Dad.'

"But just as suddenly as my dad was fussing at me, he was distracted by my mother, whose radiant smile and loving eyes captured his heart. Dad had always been a romantic, and as he looked up from his chair at his beautiful Diane, he seemed to forget all about me being the source of the mysterious stink. His eyes were all a-sparkle with love for his wife.

"She bent over and kissed my dad and whispered in his ear, 'You look hungry, John. Would you rather do this later?'

"'That kapusta sure smells good, Diane,' said Dad. 'Let's eat first and then worry about my nose after dinner, OK?'

"My mom agreed, and we all went to the table, including Spotty, who was hopeful that Dad would drop another pork chop.

"Mom seated us all in our usual places, with Dad at the head of our modest kitchen table.

"'I totally changed my mother's kapusta recipe, John,' she said. 'I hope you like it. I tasted it already, and I think that it is absolutely scrumptious. I simmered two racks of spareribs in a big pot of water with cabbage and sauerkraut, and I also added lots of red potatoes and some apples to sweeten the sauerkraut,' she told Dad. 'And I added some garlic cloves and onions, John. I think I have improved on Mother's recipe. I also made a skillet of hot cornbread with your choice of either butter or buttermilk. And to top it off, Bobby helped me bake a hot apple pie for dessert, just the way you like it, with a crisp, sugary crust, and we have vanilla ice cream to put on top of the apple pie.'

"We totally devoured Mom's kapusta and that marvelous cornbread, which Mom baked in her cast-iron skillet. Mom and Dad preferred to eat their cornbread in a bowl with buttermilk poured on top, but I ate mine with big gobs of butter spread generously on all sides. I still eat it that way, with oodles of butter.

"When the last piece of cornbread was swallowed, Dad sat back in his chair and said, 'Diane, that was outstanding! I'm as full as a tick. Can we eat the dessert a little later, like after I take a shower and read the paper?'

"'Certainly,' Mom answered, 'but first I have to deal with your pimple, so go sit in the recliner, and Bobby, would you turn on that lamp?'

"Dad went over to his La-Z-Boy recliner, and I turned on the light next to it.

"Mom was so proud of how much kapusta we had eaten. It was a testament to the goodness of her modified recipe. As she cleared the table of dinner dishes, she softly sang one of her favorite Johnny Mathis songs, 'Wonderful, Wonderful,' and I sang along with her, harmonizing as best I could. I always helped Mom clean up after dinner, and we took turns washing and drying the dishes.

"That night I washed while Mom dried and put the dishes away in the cupboard. Mama always took her rings off when she was cleaning; she said that the cleansers were abrasive and not good for her rings. Mom knew that she had cooked a first-class meal for three reasons. First, because there were almost no leftovers; second, because Daddy was sound asleep in his lounge chair, snoring along with Johnny Mathis; and third, because I had totally cleaned my plate, except for the bones. I almost never ate everything on my plate except when we had pizza or mac and cheese.

CHAPTER 25

Pop Goes the Pimple
The Stink Is Found

"My mom's new *kapusta à la Diane* recipe was a big hit, and we all just loved it. I ate a bellyful of pork and buttered potatoes that night, and Spotty must've had a dozen soft spare-rib bones to gnaw on. Spotty was in *hog heaven*, no pun intended, eating all those pork spare-rib bones."

"What's a pun?" asked Santo.

"Oh, it's a play on words, kinda like saying something serious but funny at the same time, like talking about something that has two meanings."

"I don't get it," said Santo.

"OK, Santo, spare-ribs come from pigs...or *hogs*, right?"

"Yep, I guess so."

"OK, and when you eat something really good, really tasty, if you close your eyes, you may feel like it is so good that you must be in *heaven*, right?"

"Yep, I guess so."

"Well, the dog was eating pork bones, *hog* bones...and they were so good that he thought he was in *hog heaven*."

"I get it, Mr. Thornton," said Santo with a big, proud grin on his face.

Most all the folks in the dining hall were grinning. Bobby didn't think that any of them really knew what a pun was.

"Now, back to my story," said Bobby. "Ma heard Dad snoring, so she put her rings back on and quietly snuck up to his nose. Momma brought her fingers close to the yellow volcano, silently preparing to puncture the ugly water balloon on Dad's nose. Just as her fingers neared Dad's nostrils, my father leaped from his chair and said, 'Diane, I think the stink is on your hands.'

"'That's impossible, John, you know how anal I am about washing my hands,' she said.

"Dad lifted her left hand to his nose and immediately threw back his head, withdrawing from the odor of what smelled like old roadkill. 'It's your hands, Diane!'

"Poor Momma ran from the room and into the kitchen, took off her rings, liberally poured Palmolive dish soap on both hands, and proceeded to scrub the tops and the bottoms of both hands with a Brillo pad. With her hands clean, Momma was so relieved that the mystery had been solved, although it really made no sense to her. Her hands had been in dishwater all day, and she had been scrubbing everything in sight with Mr. Clean and Pine-Sol.

"So, after thoroughly sanitizing her hands, Mom smelled her freshly washed hands and motioned for me to come smell them. They passed my smell test, so Momma returned to Dad's recliner, where my sated, tired ol' papa had once again fallen sound asleep. Mom softly kissed him on the lips, and Dad's eyes began to flutter. She whispered him awake, but I could not hear what she said, probably something about having dessert after she tended to the problem on his nose. I loved to watch my mother squeeze Daddy's zits, especially when they were on his nose."

Santo yelled out, "You were a *nose-y* kid, Mr. Thornton. A pun! I made a funny pun!"

The laughter was so loud that Bobby thought surely the plaster would crack and fall off the walls, but it didn't, and it was quickly eaten by the silence of anticipation of what would happen next. Everyone wanted to know about Bobby's dad's pimple.

"With the lamp shining brightly, I hovered over Dad's face as Mom brought her two index fingers closer to the zit. I leaned really close. I was fascinated with my mother's zit-popping exper-tise. Mom had long nails on her fingers, and they were quite sharp. She had barely touched the yellow bubble on Dad's nose when it exploded. I had zit juice all over my face, and Mom had it all over both hands.

"'Ugggggg, yuckkkkk!' I screamed, 'It's all over me, Mom.'"

"Uggggg, yuckkkk!" yelled all the kids in the dining hall.

"Disgusting!" yelled out one little girl, possibly Lahoma.

"Mom and I walked over to the sink and cleaned up. Momma saw her rings lying on the counter from when she washed her hands earlier, and she put them back on. She brought Dad a Kleenex to daub his nose, which was still oozing a yellowy fluid.

"Then Dad stood and asked for a dance with my mother. He nibbled on her neck and started gently chewing on her earlobes. He kissed her lips and smelled the fresh scent of shampoo in her hair."

The kids listening to Bobby's story began chanting in unison, "Oooooooh, oooooooh."

"Soft music was playing on the radio, so Dad reached for Mom's hand to give it a kiss and formally ask for this dance, and that's when he smelled the stink again.

"'Holy mokey…*jeeeeeze*, Diane!'

"Mom looked closely at her left hand, brought it slowly to her nose, and lurched back from the noxious smell.

"'*It's my ring!*'

"Mom took off the rings and went to the kitchen sink, and that's when she discovered that rotten hamburger meat had become embedded in the underside of her diamond wedding ring. The mystery was solved, and I spent the next day trying to salvage the food that Mom had thrown away. Unfortunately, the meat loaf mix-ture smelled as bad as her ring had smelled, because the meat had rotted even more in the hot carport. Mom never again mixed meat loaf while wearing her rings, but boy, did we have a clean house."

Suddenly, the bearded man in the rear of the room with the deep voice stood and said, "Bobby! Bobby Thornton!"

Everyone turned to look at the tall man, who had stood and was now addressing Bobby.

Bobby stood and asked, "What is it, Paul?"

Paul furrowed his brow and squinted his eyes as he looked toward Bobby. "You have a large pimple on your face, Bobby."

Bobby ran his fingers over his face but found no such blemish.

Then the man with the deep voice smiled and said, "Oh, that's not a pimple—it's just your nose."

Paul started laughing, Bobby started laughing, everybody started laughing, and then everyone applauded Bobby and the man who told the funny joke.

There was great joy and happiness in the dining hall as the throng of homeless people told their own funny stories and talked with each other. Natalie watched Bobby all evening. She never took her eyes off of him, and that night, as Bobby was leaving, she said, "You have a very beautiful smile, Bobby, and you tell a great story." Then she hugged him, closer this time.

CHAPTER 26

Wednesday, December 9
Bobby Spiffs for Natalie

Missy had studied really hard all week, because that was the last thing I had told her she needed to do. She had a feeling that I would not tell her a story if she did poorly in school, so she received all As and gold stars for turning in her homework each day. Missy was pestering her mother every single day of the week to go to Publix for something or another, but Natalie kept telling her that they could not afford to spend money on the nonessential items that Missy was asking for.

"Missy, money is tight right now. I expect to get a nice Christmas bonus and a raise early next year, but for now, we have to watch how we spend our pennies." Natalie kept telling her daughter that she got paid on Wednesday and that they would go to the supermarket to cash her check and buy groceries, and yes, she could talk to Mr. Fir.

Wednesday morning finally arrived. To Missy, it seemed like a month had passed since she last saw me, her new friend, the beautiful Fraser fir at Publix. Natalie, too, was excited, but she never let on to her daughter that she was hoping to see Bobby. Natalie was becoming quite fond of Mr. Thornton.

As Natalie was dressing for work and Missy was combing her hair, Natalie heard Missy talking to someone in the bathroom. She seemed to be reciting a poem, the poem they had finished writing the night before. Natalie crept closer to the bathroom and peeked in, where she saw her daughter standing on a stool, speaking into the mirror. Natalie stayed out of sight so as not to be seen by Missy. She listened with great pride as she eavesdropped on her daughter reciting the poem to her imaginary friend, Mr. Fir.

"…and I wrote it all by myself…but I did get a little help from my mommy, Mr. Fir," was all she heard.

The elementary school was nearby, and it was now 7:45 a.m. They had fifteen minutes before the first bell, so Natalie hollered into the bathroom, "Get your books, honey. We have to leave. We'll do the dishes when we get home, OK?"

Missy and Natalie had become quite a team since Glenn left, and every day they grew closer and more dependent on each other. They raced out of the house, into the car, and down Hypoluxo Road toward Missy's school.

"Don't be late this afternoon, Mommy; you know that we have to go to Publix after school!" Missy was kissing her mom on the cheek as the bell rang, and Missy took off and raced toward her classroom.

I knew it was Wednesday too. And Bobby knew it was Wednesday. He was busy all morning grooming himself. He stopped by the local YMCA and took a shower and shaved. He then walked to Big Al's barber shop for a haircut. They cut it just the way it used to look when Bobby was in the military: short on the sides but combable on the top. Next, Bobby went across the street to the Salvation Army and found a like-new polo shirt at a bargain price. He also tried on several pairs of size-ten shoes before finding the perfect pair that fit and looked good.

Lastly, some new slacks. There was a Dillard's outlet store at the Boynton Beach Mall, so Bobby sat on the bus bench and waited for the next city bus to arrive. He only waited about five relaxing minutes on a bench that was in a shady spot by a large oak tree. Bobby closed his eyes and pictured Natalie in a sheer yellow dress, dancing with him at a New Year's Eve ball. Every man there would envy Bobby because he was with the most beautiful girl in the world, with her ebony hair, skin like alabaster, and a smile that could melt any man's heart.

Suddenly he heard the squealing brakes of the bus stopping to pick up its only passenger. Bobby showed his pass and picked a seat in the front by the driver. Bobby knew all the drivers and all the bus routes. He was eligible for a discounted annual pass because of his veteran status and his disability. Bobby would transfer buses at Congress and take the number-twenty-three bus to the mall.

The number-five bus, which was driven by Pablo Suarez, was one of the newer buses and had excellent air conditioning, but Pablo's English was not so good, so Bobby just enjoyed the ten-minute ride.

It was approaching 11:00 a.m., and Bobby was beginning to feel hungry. There was a KFC buffet at Old Boynton and Congress, so he planned on making that his next stop; then, when his belly was full, he would walk across the street to the Dillard's outlet store to find a nice pair of slacks.

My fellow trees and I were watered down by Kenny, and as usual, Kenny gave the lion's share of water to me. I truly believe that Kenny knew, this being Wednesday, that Natalie and Missy would be here to shop and that Bobby would be here also. I also believe that Kenny had been listening to my Wildcat Mountain stories, even though he always pretended to be doing something else, like sweeping fallen needles or rearranging trees.

At three o'clock, Bobby disembarked bus nineteen at the intersection of Jog and Lantana. He was walking tall and strutting as he crossed the parking lot toward our bench. I could not believe my eyes. Bobby looked like a professional golfer, except that he was wearing no hat and had no golf clubs. He wore beautifully tailored and pleated beige slacks, a bright orange polo shirt that emphasized every ripple of muscle in his arms and chest, and a spiffy new pair of spit-shined brown loafers. I almost didn't recognize him, he was so…so…normal looking. He sure didn't look homeless.

Bobby sat down, turned his head to look at me, and said, "How ya doin', good buddy?"

I looked him up and down and answered, "Not quite as good as you, you handsome dude. Why are you dressed up like that? Are you expecting a lady? Who could that lady be? Natalie, maybe?"

Bobby was a little embarrassed that I had figured it out.

"Is it that obvious, Fir?" asked Bobby.

Just then, before I could answer, Natalie drove up and parked her car not far from the bench. She looked rather spiffy too—bewitching, in fact. She was dressed in a sexy yellow chiffon dress that hung just above the knees and flowed with the breezes as she walked toward Bobby. Bobby stood up, and all I could think was that Natalie looked like Cinderella, and Bobby was her prince. They told each other how nice they looked and then sat down on the bench to talk.

CHAPTER 27

Missy's Story for Fir

M eanwhile, Missy released her hand from her mother's grip and raced toward my broken branch. She gently held my damaged limb in her warm hand, and again I could feel her energy flowing into my body.

"Ooh, Missy, that feels so good. Did you think of a story to tell me, Missy?"

"Mr. Fir, I wrote you a poem! Is that all right? I worked on it all week, and my mommy helped me. She taught me a new word that I wrote in the poem: *nary*. That means none, or nothing. You want to hear my poem?"

"Sure, Missy! You said the new word is *nary*? And that it means *nothing*?"

"Right, Mr. Fir, *nary* means 'none at all.'" Missy reached into her pocket and pulled out a neatly folded piece of lined notebook paper, unfolded it, and began to read.

"I love to go to Publix to see
my dear friend, Mr. Fir, the Fraser tree.
He tells stories of flowers
and he talks for hours
of the birds that sing
and the beauty of spring
that only the beautiful flowers can bring.

And then he speaks of summer and fall,
when I shall grow old, and he shall grow tall,
and together we see the squirrels and the birds,
and I listen intently to his beautiful words.
The colored leaves will fall to the ground,
making nary a noise, nary a sound.

And winter will come to chill the nights.
The stars will twinkle, such an awesome sight.
But there will be warmth for Fir and warmth for me,
because we love each other, don't you see?"

"That's beautiful, Missy." A tear of pine sap dripped from my eye, and I thought Missy might have heard me sniff.

"That's a poem about you and me on Wildcat Mountain, Mr. Fir. Now will you tell me a story?"

"Sure, Missy. I'll tell you about the Wildcat Mountain kitty."

CHAPTER 28

The Wildcat Mountain Kitty

"Once upon a time, when I was about six years old, an old, beat-up car came driving down the two-lane road that winds through Wildcat Mountain. It slowed down near where Mary and I were growing tall, bushy, and beautiful. An old mountain woman, with her front teeth missing, tossed a small black-and-white kitten out of the window, and the poor little thing landed near us in a patch of grass."

"Oh my gosh, Mr. Fir, that's terrible. Was the little cat hurt?"

"Fortunately for the kitty, no."

"The tiny ball of fluffy fur landed in an area of tall, emerald-green grass, which broke her fall, and she didn't even have a scratch. Kitty did have the wind knocked out of her, though, and she was frightened.

"Maddie the deer and Moe, her fawn, were visiting us that afternoon, and we were talking about the men who were shooting at Maddie with rifles just one week earlier.

"When we heard the kitten hit the ground, we all looked in the direction of the baby cat noises that were coming from within the patch of three-foot-tall grass, 'Mew, mew, mew.'

"Moe was a most curious little deer, and he walked over to the grass to investigate. He had mother's milk all over his face, and the smell of fresh milk must have attracted the hungry kitty, who was trying to find its way out of the dense grass. The rustling noise led Moe to an opening where he could peek in and see who was there. At about the same time the baby deer stuck his head in, the kitty stuck her head out. They almost bumped heads, and the small kitten licked milk off of Moe's face with a big slurp from her little pink tongue. Moe jumped back, and the kitty jumped forward. Kitty wanted more milk. She was famished. Moe was startled and retreated to the safety of his mother. The kitten came right up to Moe and said, 'Mew, mew, mew.'"

Missy interrupted again, "She was still hungry, wasn't she, Mr. Fir?"

"Yes, Missy, and when Moe lowered his head to look closely at the kitty, our tiny black-and-white kitten started to lick Moe's face all over, cleaning off every drop of milk.

"'Mew, mew, mew,' cried the kitty, so Moe suckled his mother, again letting mother's milk cover his face, and he lowered his head again to share with the kitten. But the hungry kitten was not getting enough to drink, so I told Maddie that she should lie down and let the kitty and Moe suckle together, and that's what Maddie did. It was adorable to see a baby deer and a black-and-white kitten sharing milk from a mother deer."

"Aw, Mr. Fir, that is so cute!"

"Yes, Missy, it was a sight to behold, but it was a struggle for the small kitten."

"How so, Mr. Fir?"

"Well, if you can imagine trying to drink out of a glass that is too big or trying to suck fruit punch through a straw that is as big around as the lid of a mayonnaise jar, or a baby trying to wrap its lips around a nipple that is the size of a beach ball."

"So, Mr. Fir, how did baby kitty drink?" asked Missy, with her head turned and her brow wrinkled.

"Well," I said with a smile on my face, "it was quite humorous to watch. The kitty struggled at first, but it kept looking over at Moe, who was drinking milk like there was no tomorrow. Kitty noticed that Moe was pushing down on the bag of milk with his face, so kitty did the same thing, but she used her paws. Suddenly, and without warning, a stream of warm milk hit kitty right in the face. She licked her face the way you would use your tongue to moisten your lips, and then she pushed again at the bag of milk. A second stream of white liquid hit kitty right between the eyes and dribbled down toward her mouth. She licked, just as before, but then looked over at Moe and noted that he had his mouth over the stream. Kitty was a fast learner, and on the third push against the bag of milk, she held her mouth open and successfully captured the entire stream. From that moment on, it was push, squirt, and swallow, push, squirt, and swallow.

"No sooner had they finished drinking their bellies full, the two little ones began to burp, and they belched at the same time. It sounded rather funny to hear two babies burping simultaneously, and Mary started to laugh. She said that she thought she saw burp bubbles floating up into the air. I didn't see any bubbles, but Mary has a tendency to exaggerate.

"Maddie got up on all fours and towered over the kitten, who seemed to have thought that Moe's mom was her mother too. Kitty followed Maddie everywhere she went and kept licking Moe's face. Moe liked this kitten and asked his mom, 'Can we keep her, Mom? She can be my sister!'

"'No, Moe,' Maddie said. 'We have to run real fast through the forest and jump very high to avoid danger. The kitten is too young and too slow. She could never keep up.' Moe looked down at the ground with big, sad baby deer eyes and started to cry.

"'Don't cry, Moe,' I offered. 'Your mother is right. We need to find another one of our forest friends to adopt Kitty, and I have just the right mammal in mind.'

"'Who?' asked Moe.

"'Who?' asked Missy.

"'Cindy the Skunk,' I said and looked at Moe, who was holding his nose.

"Missy was holding her nose too.

"'Cindy just had a litter of two pups,' I said, 'one a boy, and the other one a little girl. They have plenty of room in their den, and she was expecting three pups, but only two survived, so she has plenty of milk, and I'm sure she would raise Kitty as her own. I'll talk to her this afternoon. She always comes around at about this time of day, and she's a very loving mother.'

"I asked Maddie if she could hang around for a bit, and after Maddie nodded, she walked over to the high grass to begin feasting on the tender shoots. Moe and Kitty followed, but the little ones were really not old enough to eat grass, and besides, it didn't taste as good as mother's milk.

"Almost on cue, Cindy the skunk came waddling by. She was black with a white stripe down her back, or was it white with a black stripe down her back? I'm not sure. Anyway, she held her tail up high as she walked through the Fraser firs on her way over to talk to me. We really liked each other, and I wanted to ask how her twins were doing."

"Twins? But you said one was a boy and one was a girl. How could they be twins, Mr. Fir?"

"They are called fraternal twins, Missy, when one is a boy and the other is a girl. Anyway, I always told stories to Cindy, stories about the mountain, Missy, just like I tell you my stories. And Cindy loved my stories just as much as you seem to love them."

"Oh, I do love your stories, Mr. Fir. What happened next?"

"Cindy had left the twins in the den. They were not yet old enough to go outside. Too many predators, too dangerous, and their scent glands were not yet developed.

"When Cindy saw me looking at her as she walked toward me, Cindy spoke first. 'Hiya, Fir. How have you been doing?'

"'Oh,' I said, 'you know how it is here in the mountains every spring. The dogwoods are in bloom, the azaleas are producing thousands of red flowers, and the creeping phlox are everywhere.'"

"What is creeping phlox, Mr. Fir?" interjected Missy. Missy had been listening so intently and asking so many questions that it was taking me forever to tell this story.

"Creeping phlox are the beautiful wildflowers of spring, and they grow everywhere."

"What color are they?"

"White, pink, and lavender, and they decorate the ground like stars decorate the night skies, only in color.

"Now, back to the story, Missy. I introduced Cindy to Maddie, but the doe was reluctant to go close to the skunk. Moe, however, went right up to Cindy, and they rubbed black noses. Kitty was watching Moe and followed him to Cindy and did the same thing as Moe: rubbed noses with the skunk. From that moment on, we were all friends. Maddie even came over and touched her nose to Cindy's too."

"What happened next, Mr. Fir?"

"Well, the black-and-white kitty took a special liking to Cindy and started purring and rubbing herself back and forth against the sides of Cindy's fluffy body. And Cindy, being a mother and all, couldn't help but fall in love with this tiny, black-and-white, homeless kitten. She licked the baby with her long, wet tongue, cleaning its tiny body from head to toe and from front to back.

CHAPTER 29

Homeless Kitty Needs a Mama

"A newborn kitten is extremely helpless and always hungry, not unlike a speckled fawn, and while Kitty was bonding with Cindy, Moe followed his mother, Maddie, to the bounty of lush green grass where the baby cat had landed when tossed from the car. Maddie was feasting on the tall, succulent blades of juicy grass, while Moe pushed his face against his mother's underside and began to nurse.

"Kitty smelled the milk dribbling from Moe's mouth and plodded a wobbly course toward the sucking sound. Her eyes had been open for several days, but the kitten's vision was still somewhat blurry; however, the keenness of her other senses led her straight toward Moe. Kitty repeatedly jumped into the air, trying to snag one of those delightful sources of mother's milk that Moe had a hold of but each time missing her mark. Being a tenacious little cat, Kitty continued to jump even though she continued to fall short. She was, quite simply, much too small to reach the warm milk that Moe was enjoying, so after each leap she would fall to the ground and bounce like a black-and-white tennis ball on a green tennis court.

"Moe was much taller than Kitty, even though they were both just babies. Moe was a fawn, and Kitty was a baby cat, but there was a huge difference in their height. Moe's mother was taller still, but the milk, which was always waiting for Moe when he got hungry, was easily accessible and readily available to him because fawns have long legs. But Kitty had short legs and was built low to the ground, and try as she might, she was repeatedly unsuccessful in reaching the milk that Moe was gorging himself on. Each time kitty would fall to the ground, Moe would bring his nose down to Kitty to help her get back on her unsteady feet. Kitty would lick Moe's face until it was spotlessly clean of milk, and then Moe would return to his nursing."

"Poor little kitty," whispered Missy. "We have a mango tree in our backyard, and I love mangos. They are sweet, juicy, and delicious, just like peaches, but they always seem to be just out of my reach. I jump and jump and jump, but I just can't seem to reach them. Sometimes I fall down, just like Kitty. Poor kitty."

"That's just what I said to Mary, Missy! 'Poor little kitty!'"

"So, after watching three failed attempts, I whispered to Maddie that she had another hungry baby to feed, and she turned her head and saw the forlorn kitten looking up into her eyes and mewing. Maddie lay down next to the high grass, and Kitty tried to latch on like Moe. But kitty's mouth was just too small, and as hard as she tried, Kitty was just not getting enough milk. She pushed like before, but there was very little milk squirting into Kitty's mouth. She was getting some nourishment but not very much.

"'Will you just look at that, Fir?' said Mary. 'I think I've seen everything now. Next thing you know, a baby kitten will be drinking skunk milk.' Cindy looked up at Mary, and then Cindy looked up at me, and she just shook her head in disbelief of what Mary had just said.

"As Cindy watched Kitty struggle to extract milk, a strange but exhilarating feeling was coming over the mother skunk. Her maternal instincts were awash with a need to replace her daughter who had not survived childbirth, and she felt a need to mother this orphan child.

"'She is so tiny and helpless,' Cindy said as she continued watching the little one trying to nurse. Moe was a bit older and able to successfully nourish himself, but Kitty was having a hard time and was not getting much milk. As Moe pulled away and Maddie stood up, Kitty immediately went to work licking the excess milk off of Moe's face.

"Cindy was lying down in the shade cast by my shadow, watching this spectacle, when a light rain began to fall. Maddie whispered to Moe that they had to go. The sky was growing increasingly dark, and the wind was picking up. Kitty started to follow the two deer into the thicket, but the brush was too dense, and the undergrowth was much too high for her to navigate.

"Cindy called to the kitty, and the frightened fur ball with the wobbly legs turned to see Cindy walking toward her. Cindy began to lick the raindrops off the tiny kitten's fur, but the rain started falling harder, and that's when I called to Cindy to bring the kitten over to my largest branch. I explained that I have a hollow under that branch that would keep them dry until the rain let up.

"My safe house was a large storage den that had been excavated by Tommy, the white squirrel, when he was hiding food from Katie and Annie, the two chipmunk sisters. This private place was known only to Tommy the squirrel; Trey, the white rabbit who had almost been eaten by Len the coyote; Moe and Maddie; and of course, me. Each summer, Tommy would hide his winter supply of food in this hollow under my largest root so that he would have an ample store of seeds, acorns, and nuts to survive the harsh North Carolina winters. But since that ill-fated day when Tommy fell off the cliff and into the Nantahala River, the storage den had not been used to store food. It had become a safehouse for those in need of a secure place to temporarily hide or to just hang out.

"Cindy and Kitty crawled deeply into the small cave, where Cindy commenced washing the tiny cat with gentle strokes of her pink tongue. In no time, the frightened kitten was dry and no longer shivering, and she began to purr. Cindy lay down on her side next to the small kitten and offered the hungry baby some fresh, warm milk, which Kitty readily accepted. She was famished. Baby cats have small stomachs and need to eat frequently to grow into large adults, and Kitty had really only had one good meal all day. She filled her belly and promptly fell sound asleep with Cindy by her side.

CHAPTER 30

Kitty Finds a Mama

"There is no difference between humans and animals when it comes to the loss of a child. The trauma devastates the mother, and many tears are shed as the mom adjusts to the reality that her child is gone. Cindy was the mother of twins who should have been triplets. Her third child was now lying warmly beside her, a gift from God. She was whole again. As the storm raged outside, both Cindy and Kitty slept.

"'Psssst...psssst!' I whispered several hours later to my two black-and-white friends. 'Wake up! The storm has subsided, and you need to go home to the twins.'

"Cindy awoke at the sound of my voice, and she nudged her baby awake with the help of her black nose. Kitty yawned, arched her back, and was gently pushed out of the warm hollow. I lifted my branch, and a few drops of water splashed on my two guests. The sun was shining, and the forest was alive again with activity.

"Kitty wanted to chase a butterfly, but Cindy mothered her across the street and toward the direction of her own hungry twins. I watched them walking away together, their tails held high, and as they disappeared into the woods, I beamed with pride that I had helped bring these two together. Mary was proud of me too. She wanted to talk about this wonderful happening all day, long after the moon was high in the sky. The forest slept, and I finally fell asleep, but Mary just talked and talked and talked. I don't know when she finally fell asleep, but when the sun once again kissed our eastern skyline, I awoke to another blissful day on Wildcat Mountain, while Mary slept until noon.

"I didn't see Cindy for about a week after that. Moe and his mother kept coming by and asking how the kitty was doing, but I had nothing to tell them. Then, one afternoon, I was talking to Mary about how beautiful she was and how supple her needles were, and I spotted Cindy."

"What about Kitty, Mr. Fir?"

"No, Kitty was not with her, but she told me that she was fine and that the twins loved her and that they played all the time and that she was very happy.

"About a month passed—I think it was late April—and one afternoon, I spotted four black-and-white tails walking in single file across the street. They were coming in my direction, and then I recognized that it was Cindy, the twins, and Kitty. Cindy was teaching them how to catch insects, but Kitty seemed to be catching them, crunching down on them, making faces, and spitting them out. Then I saw her catch a lizard and pull its tail off. The lizard escaped into the bushes, but its tail fascinated the kitten with its lively, wiggly movement. She also chased down a couple of small mice, which she seemed to enjoy playing with, but she was not yet old enough to eat a mouse. She was still nursing on mother's milk.

"Cindy stopped to talk for a few minutes. Moe and Maddie were there too, and Cindy told us that 'Joy' was the love of her life. She'd picked the name Joy because this precious little kitten had filled the void left when her twins were born without their little sister. Cindy had chosen to adopt, raise, and love this delightful, frightened kitten.

"'Children who are adopted,' Cindy told me, 'are very special, and every time Joy nestles close to me and purrs contentedly, my heart just melts with love and joy for this child of God. I watch her play with the twins, and I see three black-and-white children playing happily together. My three children. My triplets.'"

Missy listened to me and hung onto every word. She was thinking about something, and suddenly she said to me, "Mr. Fir, my best friend is adopted, and I can't wait to tell her this story. It's just like you said, her parents love and cherish her. They're always taking her places and buying her toys, and she is a really happy girl."

"Well, Missy," I replied, "sounds to me like your story about your adopted friend is as good as my story about the adopted kitten, so let's finish by saying we are all going to live happily ever after, including your best friend."

"Missy!" called Natalie. "We have to go inside and do our shopping!"

Natalie was getting up from the bench, and Bobby, being the quintessential gentleman that he was, stood also. They were a handsome couple, Homeless Bobby with his new duds and The Princess, Natalie, in her white high-heeled shoes and yellow dress. They had talked about everything happy: Bobby's excellent life as a child growing up in Miami and Natalie's life as a stewardess in Ohio. They uttered not a single word about why Bobby chose to be homeless or the fact that Natalie was now a single parent.

As I told Missy the story of the baby kitten, "Joy," from North Carolina, I was watching joy being born on my bench at Publix, the joy of two lost and sad souls finding joy in each other. I believed that this story would have a happy ending too, but you never know for sure. *Look at me,* I thought. *I'm still homeless.*

Missy let loose my broken branch and thanked me for my wonderful story. She wrapped her tiny arms around me and said, "I love you, Mr. Fir," then she walked over to her mother, and the two girls disappeared into the grocery store. Bobby sat back down on the bench. He looked up at the cloudless blue sky of December in Florida and sighed.

"Fir," he said, "life is good!"

He didn't say anything else for a long time. He just sat there with a strange smile on his face and his arms spread out on the back of the bench.

After about thirty minutes of shopping, the McCords exited the store and stopped by to say their goodbyes. Missy ran around to me, and Natalie sat on the bench with Bobby.

"Mr. Fir, Mommy said we will be back here next Wednesday. Will you tell me one last story before Christmas? I'm still trying to get Mommy to let me take you home, but she keeps saying that we cannot afford a real tree this year."

"Missy," I said, "you come on back next Wednesday, and I'll tell you a Christmas story. OK?"

Missy jumped up in the air in excitement and hugged me tightly with both arms, being careful not to hurt my damaged branch.

Meanwhile, Natalie was talking with Bobby about the importance of him coming to the community center that Friday night.

"Bobby, we will not be open on Christmas Day, so we are serving our traditional turkey and stuffing Christmas meal next Friday, December 18. Please say you will come! And this Friday we will have all-you-can-eat spaghetti and meatballs. That's the day after tomorrow.

"Natalie, I'll be there both days; wouldn't miss it for the world. You know I love spaghetti. Will there be garlic bread? Are you going to make any of that delicious cranberry sauce for the Christmas dinner like you made for Thanksgiving?"

"We will have plenty of garlic bread, but don't tell anybody about the cranberry sauce. I'm making that just for you. We have to go now, Bobby. Missy, come along. You have homework to do."

Natalie and Missy walked slowly to their car. Missy turned and blew me a kiss. Natalie turned and waved to Bobby. They loaded their groceries into the trunk and drove off. Both of the girls were smiling.

Bobby sat on his green bench, wishing that they didn't have to leave and watching as they pulled out of the parking lot. And that's when he looked up at me and said, "It was a really good day, wasn't it, Fir? And I couldn't help but overhear your story. That was one of your best yet."

I thanked Bobby, and as he stood to walk away, I whispered, "You make a nice couple, you and Natalie. See ya tomorrow, Bobby."

And off he went, down the breezeway and around the corner.

CHAPTER 31

December 10–15
More of the Same

Every morning at 5:00 a.m., Cree arrived from North Carolina in his eighteen-wheeler with a new delivery of freshly cut trees. They were still bound in orange mesh and terrified of their new unknown. I talked to them all and did my best to appease and lessen their fears. I explained where they were and what to expect and assured them that they would all be adopted.

Kenny always came out of the store with his gloves and scissors and cut off their plastic mesh. That in itself helped with the anxiety that these new trees were having to deal with. As their branches fell and as Kenny watered them down, you could see them relaxing and adjusting to their new temporary home.

Each day, the routine was more or less the same, and I told them what to expect in the upcoming days. I, of course, was looking forward to seeing Missy on Wednesday, the sixteenth of December. Bobby came by each day and sat on the bench, and we talked. The new trees could not believe nor understand how I could talk to a human after the way we were removed from our homes in the Smoky Mountains.

Bobby spoke of his time in the military, and he talked much but said little. Both his body and his mind had been wounded in battle, but the scars were healing, and they were healing fast. I'd like to think that I did my small part in helping Bobby repair the damage that had been caused by war, but I was certain that Natalie and Missy would account for his ultimate cure.

CHAPTER 32

Wednesday, December 16

Finally, the much-anticipated Wednesday, December 16, arrived. I couldn't wait to see Missy, and I would venture to say that Missy couldn't wait to see me. Bobby arrived at about one o'clock in the afternoon dressed like a typical Publix shopper. He had on a white University of Miami Nike shirt and a pair of tight-fitting blue jeans. Bobby seemed especially proud of his like-new Adidas tennis shoes.

He strolled into the supermarket and walked proudly up to the deli to order a sub. There were several people ahead of him, so he looked at the chicken tenders and the hot mac and cheese while he waited his turn. By the time they called his number, he had changed his mind and decided to get a hot meal with two sides. The girl behind the counter scooped a pile of fresh pulled pork into a large Styrofoam container and then asked which two sides he preferred. Bobby chose the mac and cheese and turnip greens. The deli girl also put a large buttered roll on top of the container, wrapped it up in cellophane, and attached the $4.29 special sale price sticker. Bobby picked up a quart of milk and an almond bear claw for dessert. He went through the express line to check out and then headed toward the bench. Natalie and Missy would probably not arrive until 3:45 p.m., so he had plenty of time to eat and talk with me.

"You look terrific, Bobby," I commented, "and you have another new set of fine-looking duds, pardner."

Bobby unwrapped his meal and ate every single bite of food, to the dismay of the big black crow who was watching from above. Bobby got up from his seat, discarded the empty container, and returned to the bench.

"So, Fir, you like my duds, huh? I am going to see Natalie today, and I wanted to look nice. Fir, I think I'm in love. I haven't felt this way in years. By the way, how is your adoption going? Any serious families looking to buy you?"

"Well, Bobby, there was one family that came by yesterday. They had three rough-and-tumble little boys—the oldest was no more than six—and she was pregnant with her fourth child. I was looked at by the whole family for about fifteen minutes, but in the end, the broken branch did me in. They went over with Kenny to the new arrivals and bought a fresher tree."

"That's nice, Fir. I'm glad they didn't buy you!"

"Why would you say that, Bobby? I need a nice family to take me home and decorate me for Christmas. That's just not right, you saying that *you're glad*." I was feeling very angry and agitated with Bobby, and if I could, I would have clunked him on the head with one of my branches.

"Fir," said Bobby as he rose from his bench and walked over to stand in front of me. "Fir, I'm a big fan of yours; you make me happy. Every day, I awaken out there in that field behind Publix, and I look forward to my day because I will be able to sit and talk with you. You and I laugh together, we tell each other some great jokes, and you listen to my problems. You have never disrespected me because I'm homeless, and you always have nice things to say to me. And ya know what else? Missy not only likes you, but she loves you, so I'm glad you have not been sold, and that's that!"

Bobby went back to his bench and opened the quart of milk, took a three-gulp drink, screwed the lid back on, and opened the plastic container with the almond bear claw inside. "Delicious. Fir, I wish I could share this bear claw with you. It is the best darn pastry that they sell in the Publix bakery, unless you are lucky enough to find one of their flying saucers, but they almost never have flying saucers."

"What's a flying saucer, Bobby?"

"It is a big round pastry about the size of a frisbee, and it has nuts on it, cinnamon, sugar, and caramel. Some folks call it a Crispy. I'm telling you that you haven't lived until you've eaten a flying saucer. Uh, no disrespect meant, Fir, you being a tree and all."

"None taken, Bobby."

Bobby finished his bear claw and his quart of milk, got up again to discard the plastic in the trash can, and returned to his bench. We talked for about an hour and told jokes, laughed, and talked about Missy and Natalie.

"You know she works as a volunteer at the community center, don't you, Fir? And I go there every Friday night to see her. She thinks I come for the free meal, but it's really to see her, although the food *is* excellent."

About that time I spotted Natalie's car driving into the Publix parking lot. Missy was waving to me, and I waved back as best I could. Again, Natalie pulled into a parking place very close to the bench, and the two beautiful ladies hurriedly headed in our direction. Natalie was wearing a rather tight-fitting black dress with high heels. She had come straight from her office, stopping only to pick up Missy from school. She had lost some weight since the separation from her husband, and this dress really emphasized her beauty and her hourglass figure. As she sat down with Bobby and started to exchange niceties, I could see a sparkle in both their eyes. I think they were both falling in love with each other. Missy raced over to me and immediately grasped my broken branch.

"Poor Mr. Fir. I wish I could make this better for you." Missy looked up at me when she said this with those sad little girl eyes, and she just melted my heart. Then she got real happy, and a smile filled her whole face as she looked up at me and said, "It's Wednesday, Mr. Fir! Remember? You said you would tell me a Christmas story, about your last Christmas on the mountain, remember?"

"Yes, Missy," I responded, "but first, I will tell you a short story about Murphy, the town in North Carolina where I was born. Ready?"

"Ready," said Missy.

And I began to tell her the story.

CHAPTER 33

Murphy, North Carolina

"Once upon a time, there was a place in North Carolina where the animals and the Cherokee Indians lived together in harmony with nature, where the trees grew tall and there was abundant food for all to eat, and where beauty was everywhere for everyone to behold.

"That all changed one day in the early 1800s, when a road was built through the forests of Cherokee County, North Carolina. The men who built the roads brought their guns and killed bears for sport and shot deer for food. They plowed down trees, removed stumps, fenced the land, and brought in domesticated animals—cows, goats, horses, and chickens—and they rounded up all of the Indians and held them at Fort Butler until they could be taken to Tennessee. It was a sad time for the animals and for the Cherokee nation. A town was born around 1836, and it was called Huntington. Fort Butler became known as Murphy, and in 1851, Murphy was incorporated as the county seat. By the late 1800s, Murphy even had a railroad. So more people came. The land of the animals was rapidly becoming the land of man. A theater was built, along with a saloon, a hotel, and a grocery store. A five-and-dime popped up to sell cloth to the ladies and penny candy to the children. A soda fountain was installed, with round stools so that patrons could enjoy carbonated Coca Colas, ice cream floats, and sandwiches. Murphy grew, and the animals were forced deeper into the higher, mountainous terrain and away from the lush and more temperate valleys.

"But I see change as a good thing, for without man, I would not be here today, Missy, talking with you. I don't regret a day of my life. It is what it is, and the best is yet to come."

"Murphy sounds wonderful, Mr. Fir. What else can you tell me about Murphy?" asked little Missy.

"Well, I'm going to tell you about my last Christmas on Wildcat Mountain. My best Christmas ever! It was last year, Missy."

CHAPTER 34

A Wildcat Mountain Christmas

"It all started two days before Christmas Eve. Mary was talking and talking and talking, like she always did. It was early evening, and the grass eaters were grazing on the vast patches of high brown grasses, which had changed colors with the seasons from green to brown. Like huge piles of hay, the tall, sweet green blades of summer still offered abundant nourishment in the cold months of winter. The stars were beginning to sparkle in a darkening sky, and the moon was huge as it rose on the eastern horizon. It would be full on Christmas Eve. Mary wanted a party, a celebration of our life on Wildcat Mountain, a Christmas Eve gala event. Tommy the squirrel was lying on the big limb that led to his hollow, high up in the maple. He looked down from his lofty patio and hollered at the top of his voice, 'That's a great idea!'

"Suddenly, other voices were excitedly chatting with each other about the party. Maddie the deer and her now-teenage son, Moe, were running around in circles and racing through the grove, talking to the other Fraser firs about the forthcoming party. The mice, the rabbits, the possums, the bears, and even the grumpy blackbird were all excited. There was so much chattering going on that Mary's voice was almost drowned out.

"Even Len the coyote wanted to participate, and he promised not to chase any of the smaller animals.

"Bruno, the smartest black bear in Cherokee County, said, 'I will be in charge of the food.' It was agreed that he would knock down the old back door of the hardware store in downtown Murphy and take all the wire cutters so that the bears could break into the garbage cans and cut dumpster-sized holes into the fences at the county dump.

"'Humans waste so much food,' he said. 'We will have pizza, sub sandwiches, steak, pork chops, spaghetti, and all kinds of sweet things to eat. Sometimes, when I am able to get into a good dumpster, I find blueberry pies with not even a single slice removed and chocolate candies with only a small bite out of them and then thrown away. People are so dumb. They throw away lettuce, tomatoes, ham, and bread that are perfectly fresh, just a little out of date. There are always gallons of milk thrown out. I mean, a *lot* of milk is wasted by humans, so bring the kids.'

"Cindy the skunk was looking at the twins and Joy (the kitty), who were now almost full-grown. The trees were all whispering to each other about the upcoming event.

"Missy, are you listening?" I asked my precious little friend, who was, as usual, holding my broken branch.

"Oh, yes, Mr. Fir. I just love this story. I can see the animals, I can hear them talking, and it's almost like I'm right there on the mountain with you."

"Well, then, let's continue. It was agreed that the curmudgeon crow would get all the birds together to decorate me with tinsel and garland and glass and metallic decorations to reflect and sparkle from the moonlight and the starlight of Christmas Eve. The cardinals told us that there was a nativity scene on the lawn of the courthouse in downtown Murphy, and they were sure that they could bring a star or an angel to place on the top of my trunk. Every animal was committed. The mice would bring straw from the homes scattered around the mountain, the deer would gather holly branches and bring them to the gala, the possums would collect the beer and soda cans that littered the roads all around Wildcat, and each animal would be responsible for one decoration."

"Why did they choose to decorate just you, Mr. Fir?" asked Missy.

"Well, Missy, I think it's because I have the best location for a party. I'm closest to the road, and there is a soft field of grass between me and the drop-off of the cliff. I know all the trees quite well, and most of the animals too, and I'm a pretty funny tree—not funny-looking but 'ha, ha' funny. Missy, I have always enjoyed telling jokes. I make them up, and I made the trees and animals laugh. I always felt I should have been a comedian. Mary agreed with me and said that I should have been on TV, but I told her that I was too big and heavy and that I would break the TV."

"That's funny, Mr. Fir. Can you tell me a couple of jokes?"

"Sure, Missy, let me think...Oh, here's one. Where do you find a centipede with no legs?"

"I don't know, Mr. Fir."

"Right where you left him!...Ha, ha, ha, hee, hee. Isn't that a good one, Missy?"

"Yes, Mr. Fir." Missy snickered and continued to gently hold the broken branch. "Tell me another."

"OK, but this is the last one, and then back to the story, OK?"

"OK."

"Missy, what do you call a school of fish that sleep all day Monday, all day Tuesday, all day Wednesday, all day Thursday, all day Friday, and all day Saturday?"

"Hmmmmm, I don't think I know, Mr. Fir."

"A Sunday school, Missy! HEEE, HEEEE, HA, HA, har, har, hardy, har, har."

Missy was doubled over with laughter. Bobby and Natalie turned their heads to see what she was laughing about, but she just smiled at them and stuck her head back into my branches. "Mr. Fir, please tell me one more joke, just one more, *pleeeze?*"

"OK, Missy, but this is the absolute final joke. Then I return to the story, OK? What do you call a bear that likes to stand out in the rain?"

"Uhhh, I don't know, Mr. Fir."

"A *drizzle-y bear.*"

Missy giggled hysterically. "I can't wait to tell my mom that joke, Mr. Fir."

Suddenly a deep voice from around the corner said, "Ain't he a hoot?"

It was Ollie the owl, who was usually asleep high in the rafters this time of day but had been awakened by my story.

"How come you are not asleep, Ollie? You are an old coot with an old hoot, and old owls need their sleep."

"Your stories are worth losing a little sleep for, Fir," hooted Ollie. "Would you mind getting back to the story so that I can get some sleep?"

"OK, Ollie. So, Missy, we each had one vote (except for the insects, who only had an itsy bitsy vote). One vote from each animal and one vote from each tree would decide on which tree to decorate.

"There was my beloved Mary, who talked all the time. I know that she received some votes, if for no other reason than that she is so beautiful, but her nonstop racket seemed to drive a lot of the trees and animals crazy. Heck, Tommy had to wear ear plugs made out of my soft little fir cones just to sleep. Also, Mary didn't like to be touched, so she really never had a chance.

"Brutus, the Fraser fir growing behind Mary, received some votes too, and Brutus was the tallest and most majestic tree in our grove, but he didn't have the view that I had. And he was kind of stand-offish and didn't talk too much with the other trees or animals. So because of his antisocial personality and his location on the mountain, and because he was so tall, he didn't receive a lot of votes either. I heard a possum talking to a rat about how much longer it would take just to decorate a tree that big—hours and hours of extra work.

"So, Missy, most of the votes were for me, and I was honored and very proud, but from my location, Missy, you could look down into the valley and see the entire town of Murphy. It was a view to die for. Most all of the houses, businesses, churches, and trees were dressed in a light coat of freshly fallen December snow, and you could see the white water of the Nantahala River glistening and glowing in the moonlight. There's nothing like the soothing sound of running water to help one fall asleep at night or to invigorate the soul during the cool days of winter. From my spot on the mountain, you could enjoy an unobstructed view of the peaceful town of Murphy, the historic city lampposts, traffic lights turning red and green, and the tall steeples of churches of all denominations. Mine was a beautiful pastoral panorama of a typical village, like what you would find under a Christmas tree. So, Missy, I don't think they were voting for me as much as they were voting for the best location for their Christmas Eve party."

CHAPTER 35

Decorating and Catering

"Wow, Mr. Fir, this is so cool!"

"Yes, Missy, Wildcat Mountain was abuzz during the days leading up to Christmas Eve. The roadside was impeccably cleaned of litter. Piles of bottles and cans were stacked close by but out of sight of passing motorists. The bears were out in force, checking out each residential garbage can so that they could be easily opened on party night. Those with locks were duly noted so that they could be cut off by the lock-cutting devices from the hardware store. The dump was surveyed by the bears, and plans were made to cut a large opening in the rear fence the day before to facilitate the removal of food for the gala extravaganza.

"Many humans have parties on Christmas Eve, and they don't eat all the food that they prepare, so this party was going to be the eating event of the season.

"We decided to let the humans party until they could party no more, usually around midnight. That's when we would all spring into action, and spring we did. The bears broke the locks off all the secured garbage cans throughout the gated communities on Wildcat Mountain, and they did not just bring the food, they brought the entire cans. These bears were so large that each could carry four cans at a time. They each made six trips up and down the hills, until we had twenty-four cans of food and drink scattered about for our dining pleasure when the party began. Then they took off toward the dump—sixteen bears—and I couldn't believe my eyes when I saw them carrying two giant green dumpsters on their shoulders."

"Mr. Fir, bears must be very strong," said Missy. She was mesmerized by this story.

"Yes, Missy, bears are very strong, but so are the other animals of Wildcat Mountain, both big and small.

"The rats were in charge of creating decorations from the beer and soda cans that had been thrown from cars passing through Wildcat Mountain and found by the possums. With their sharp teeth, the rats could chew through anything, so they used their sharp teeth to create metallic ornaments out of the discarded beer cans. They made stars out of long strips of metal that resembled icicles and tinsel. They were magnificent artists.

"The raccoons were able to use the broken bottles found along the road to form various sizes and shapes of glass ornaments, which resembled crystal found in expensive stores. The mice and the birds had gathered many pieces of loose string both around the mountain and in the town of Murphy. The raccoons, because they had such delicate, childlike hands, were able to use this string to form loops and attach the twine to the glass and metal decorations to be hung on my branches."

"What did the bunnies do, Mr. Fir?"

"Well, Missy, they wandered throughout the mountain, gathering holly from the holly trees. They would snip off large sprigs of holly, carrying them with their front paws—what would be your arms—hop back to the grass on my left, and stack them neatly in a pile. These beautiful clusters of holly added red color to contrast with my green needles and brown cones. Most of the birds had flown south, but the cardinals and the crows stay on the mountain in winter, so they, together with the mice, started decorating me with holly. I was becoming an especially beautiful Christmas tree, Missy.

"Every job requires a leader. This Christmas party was no exception, so we chose the wise old white owl that had been living on Wildcat Mountain since he was no more than an egg in his mother's nest. Barney was his name, and he had seen it all and done it all. He was the sentry of the nights, always watching for danger and warning the animals when they were in harm's way. During the day, Barney slept, but his ears never closed. They listened and watched while his eyes slept. Barney was the quarterback of our team, the leader of the orchestra, the principal of our school, so to speak. He was the boss. He told each animal group what to do and when to do it. He told the bears when to go get the food and where to put the cans when they returned. He told the rats where the ornaments had to be stacked, and he instructed the mice and birds on how to decorate me so that I would be the most beautiful Christmas tree ever.

"The full moon was rising in the eastern sky, and the humans in downtown Murphy were beginning to settle in for the night. We could tell because lights were being turned off in the houses as the city people climbed in bed and prepared for the arrival of Santa Claus.

"Barney sent the possums into town, along with several raccoons. Their job was to bring back as much of the nativity from the town square as they could carry. They had to make several trips, but they succeeded in bringing the entire nativity, including the three wise men, the plastic animals, and the plastic likeness of the baby Jesus. Barney told all the animals that after our party and before the citizens of Murphy awoke on Christmas morning, they would all have to return the things that they borrowed. Mr. Crow—Carl, as he was known—was to go into town and bring back the most important decoration, a star, which he would place on the very top of my head. Barney had seen the star while flying through town. It was sitting at the very top of a tree decorated in the town square, so Carl was just going to borrow it for the evening. Carl flew in with about ten of his buddies, and they also borrowed many of the human-made ornaments from the Murphy tree. Carl and his friends flew high above the trees and gently placed the ornaments on the grass, as instructed by Barney. Then they flew back for one more cache of ornaments."

"What's a cache, Mr. Fir?" asked Missy.

"Well it's like a group of things, all together. In this case, another ten ornaments."

"Boy, Mr. Fir, this story is really getting exciting. What happened next?"

"Barney instructed the birds and mice to start decorating me, and he asked the chipmunks and squirrels to help. He sent the rabbits back out to see what they could find at the houses, and the squirrels who were not decorating went with the bunnies. The rabbits brought back straw, and the squirrels brought wind chimes and bird feeders. This was a big plus, because the feeders were all full of seeds, which were quite a delicacy for all of the animals.

"Barney had a family of raccoons working on a garland, which they made from string and twine tied together. The mother raccoon had used a sharp thorn as a needle and tied it to one end of the long string. She pushed the thorn through little pieces of red mulch that the rats had gathered from some of the yards of the mountain homes. When finished, the garland was a beautiful reddish color, and the crows lifted it and flew all around me from top to bottom, draping the garland over my branches. Glass icicles hung from my limbs, as did beer-can tinsel. I was becoming lovelier by the minute. Finally the human-made ornaments were perfectly placed on my branches, per Barney's instructions, and it was time for the crowning moment, when the star would be placed on my head. Carl flew high with the reflective, five-pointed star in his mouth and placed it exactly where the wise old owl said it was most beautiful.

"Everyone clapped and cheered and stared at me. I was so beautiful. I thanked all my friends, and one by one, they rubbed against my trunk, a gesture of love and friendship.

CHAPTER 36

Santa Visits Wildcat Mountain

"'Party time!' hooted the owl, and we all began to feast on the food the bears had brought and the raccoons had washed. There were plastic liter bottles of soda, which still had plenty of liquid left inside, and the raccoons carried the bottles throughout the grove and poured the soda on the ground for the trees so that it would seep down and into our roots. The bears had hung the wind chimes on the other trees, and the breezes were causing them to sing beautiful, harmonious melodies of the holidays. But before we could eat, Barney had something to say.

"'Let us pray,' he said. 'God, we give thanks to you, on this Christmas Eve, for all that you have given us. We are indeed blessed to live here, on Wildcat Mountain, the most beautiful place on Earth. And thank you for our beautiful Christmas tree, Fir. We love him very much. Amen.'

"And then the gala began. Platters made from garbage can lids were scattered all over the grassy lawn that sloped gently to the edge of the drop-off. The food had been expertly separated into meats, cheeses, breads, fruits, and pastries. There were fried chicken wings, cold cuts and lettuce, potato chips and pretzels, mixed nuts, tomato slices, and all types of fresh berries, all discarded by the humans. Some of the bread and chips were a bit soggy, but most were fresh, crisp, and tasty.

"Barney the owl must have consumed some of the adult drinks that had been found in the dumpster, for he was quite unsteady, sitting on the low branch of a nearby maple tree. I couldn't help but watch him teeter back and forth on the limb, and I was certain that he would fall off at any moment, but he didn't. He just sang with the others and enjoyed the party.

"The moon continued to rise, and the breezes continued to gently cool our mountain. A soft, light, fluffy, dry snow began to fall and left a patina of white on Wildcat Mountain. Barney led the singing of Christmas carols, and I shed a tear as we all sang 'Silent Night.' We were like a church choir, led by the unstable Barney, sitting on his perch with a stick in his hand—well, his winglike hand.

"Everyone separated into groups, and all were telling stories to each other and talking about their wives, husbands, and children. Laughter would erupt from one area, and animals from other parts of the lawn would turn their heads toward the din of laughter and laugh too, even though they knew not what they laughed about.

"By three thirty a.m., the food was almost gone, and the animals were relaxing on their backs, looking up into the starlit heavens. That's when they saw what appeared to be a rapidly moving star in the far distance. The object appeared to be growing larger and coming in their direction."

"What was it, Mr. Fir?" asked Missy as she continued to hold my broken branch in her small, warm hand.

"It was a sleigh, and it was being pulled by nine reindeer, Missy!"

"Santa Claus!" Missy loudly blurted out.

Bobby and Natalie turned their heads and looked in her direction. Missy was smiling ear to ear as she stood next to me, and she was jumping up and down with glee.

"What is it, Missy?" asked her mother.

"Oh, I'll tell you later, Mom," she said to Natalie. Then she turned her head back to me and said, "Please continue, Mr. Fir."

"Well, Missy, Santa was riding in his sleigh, loaded with bags full of presents, and he landed right there on our mountain, and his sleigh came to rest right in front of me. Rudolph spotted one of my tender cones and nibbled it off. Maddie and Moe and all the other deer came running over to talk with Dasher and Dancer and the other reindeer. Santa got out of his sleigh and started passing out gifts to all the animals, and he gave each tree a little gift too."

"What was it, Mr. Fir?" asked Missy.

"It was a little scoop of special magical fertilizer and a commemorative ornament, which he hung on each tree. I heard him *ho, ho, ho*-ing as he walked through our grove. He touched each animal on the head, wished us all a Merry Christmas, and jumped back in his sleigh, and he was off. We were all awestruck as he disappeared out of sight. What a night! The best ever, Missy."

"And then what, Mr. Fir?"

"Well, Missy, the animals all opened their gifts, gathered into small groups, and talked and laughed together for the next hour.

"Morning was on the horizon, so Barney the owl directed all the animals to return the things they had borrowed. Everyone scurried off the mountain with chimes and wise men and garbage cans and raced up and down the mountain to put everything back in place. The last thing was the dumpster, but since it had wheels, and since the adjacent road led toward town, it was easy for them to push the big green contraption back to the dump.

"Everyone was tired from the long night of partying, but my mountain was left impeccably clean. As the sun rose in the sky and replaced the moonlight of night, all the animals disappeared into the forest from whence they came. I napped all day that Christmas Day. A light snow continued to fall, and the animals were all nestled snug in their beds. Two wind chimes had been left in the trees, maybe by accident, maybe on purpose. One was of tubular metal, like small organ pipes, and when the pipes touched each other, they sounded like church bells. The other was made of stained glass and tinkled when the wind blew. We were all happy to have these chimes to remind us of the best Christmas ever on Wildcat Mountain.

"And, Missy, we all lived happily ever after."

"Missy, are you about ready to go?" Natalie was standing in front of Bobby and was shaking his hand as she called to her daughter. "Missy?"

"I'll be right there, Mom. I just want to hug Mr. Fir!" And with that, she wrapped her small arms around my branches and held me tight.

"I'll see you again after we shop, Mr. Fir. I love you, Mr. Fir."

Then she was gone. Missy and Natalie stepped into the air conditioning and quickly disappeared among the other shoppers. Bobby and I were alone again; well, not really alone. I had my sparrows, who were listening to every word of my story, and I had the other unsold trees, but Bobby and I seemed to be connected at the hip. We had grown extremely close during the last month, and we shared a lot of very personal thoughts.

"I think she likes you, Bobby. I mean, there seems to be a special energy between you when you and Natalie are together. Do you feel it, Bobby?"

"Yes, Fir, I feel the love, but only time will tell if Natalie and I will have any future together."

CHAPTER 37

The Water Blaster

The sparrows were chattering among themselves while Natalie and Missy shopped, talking about the last Christmas on my mountain and about how all the animals celebrated Christmas Eve and about how the birds helped decorate me and about all the food. All three birds were talking at the same time. I never saw them so animated. The other trees talked about the party too. They had heard about the gala event through the grapevine, so to speak, but they were not Murphy trees. Their groves were scattered throughout western North Carolina and Tennessee and even southern Kentucky.

Bobby was back on the bench, oblivious to the goings-on of the world. He did not hear the sparrows talking to each other or the whispering between the trees. Bobby did not hear the honking of cars in the parking lot or the voices of excited families looking to buy a Christmas tree. All he could think about was Natalie. It was as if he were in a trance, enchanted by the magic wand of his fairy princess. Bobby was looking up at the darkening clouds in the blue Florida sky when he started talking to me again.

"Hey, Fir, it looks like rain. You think it's going to rain this afternoon?"

"No, if it were going to rain, I would know it. We trees depend on water to survive, and we have a supernatural connection with the weather. We can anticipate drought, and our roots grow deeper so that we can survive the dry months, and we can feel the humidity in the air like a barometer does so that we know when to open or close the pores in our needles, to release excess water or to keep the water we have from evaporating. No, Bobby, it's not going to rain."

"Fir, does a fish have a soul?" Bobby asked me this strange question while still staring at the low gray clouds in the west.

"Of course, Bobby, why would you ask such a question? All of God's creatures have souls, including trees. Rabbits have souls, bears have souls, raccoons have souls, sparrows have souls, and even that cantankerous crow up there has a soul. I have a soul, Bobby. Do humans have souls?" My sparrows were annoyed with Bobby and had stopped talking about the Christmas story. The big blackbird was upset that Bobby would dare ask such a question, and he started to squawk, "Caw, caw, caw."

He flew down and landed on the back of the bench and pecked at Bobby's right hand, then noisily flapped his wings as he took flight and flew up to the rafters above Bobby's head. Bobby heard a squirt, and then a wet, white splotch of goo landed right on top of his head.

Bobby jumped up, waving his arms and shaking his fist at the crow. We all silently laughed at this spectacle as Bobby went into the Publix restroom to wash his hair.

Bobby was in the men's room for nearly ten minutes before he returned to his bench, but when he sat down, I noted that he had something plastic in his hand, and it looked like a yellow gun. After cleaning his hair, Bobby had purchased a plastic water blaster, a high-powered squirt rifle, and he had filled it with water in the bathroom. Bobby had been a sniper in the military and was a crack shot. The big blackbird was still above the bench, in the same spot as when Bobby had left, and he did not notice Thornton's return. I saw what was about to take place, and I whispered to my sparrows to watch what was going to happen. In the blink of an eye, Bobby aimed at and shot the huge crow with a massive burst from his water rifle. The bird was drenched and angrier than I had ever seen him. He looked down at Bobby with his head cocked and glared at him with his big, black eye, and it was obvious that he was saying, "This is not over!" Then he flew away.

Natalie and Missy completed their Wednesday shopping and exited the supermarket with their usual buggy full of groceries. As they walked by Bobby, Natalie saw that her friend had combed his hair and that it was still rather wet. She also saw the water blaster. "What's going on, Bobby?" she asked.

"I'll tell you all about it this Friday, Natalie."

Missy ran around to say goodbye to me, and she held my branch until she was called by her mother.

"Missy, I bought you a water blaster, if your mom will let you have it. Natalie?"

"Sure, that's real nice of you, Bobby, but you shouldn't be spending your money…"

"It was on special, Natalie. If it was any cheaper, it would have been free."

"Thank you, Mr. Thornton," said Missy. "We'll see you next Wednesday, OK?"

"OK, Missy. See ya this Friday, Natalie." Then the McCords loaded their groceries in the trunk and drove away.

CHAPTER 38

Friday, December 11
Spaghetti and Meatballs

"What happened to your eye, Bobby?" I asked when Bobby returned from the community center on Friday night around 11:30 p.m.

Bobby sat down on the bench, sighed, and turned his head to look at me. "I was mugged, Fir. Can you believe that? I was bloody mugged."

"By who? Or should I say by whom?" I asked in a most concerned whisper.

"Three young punks, Fir. One of them had a baseball bat. I was just sitting on the bench over at the community center, minding my own business, when these three teenage boys approached me. One grabbed me from behind, and the smaller of the other two swung a baseball bat at my head. I was able to lean forward, which brought the other boy's head into direct contact with the bat. I suffered a glancing blow, but the kid behind me was knocked unconscious by the bat. Two of the boys were on my bus last week and were hassling an old woman. I threw them off the bus. I guess that they were trying to get even, Fir. Fortunately, there was a patrol car at the community center, and the two officers on duty saw the whole thing. I wrestled one of the two boys to the ground, and the third boy was chased down by a large police dog. He was pretty badly bitten."

"How old were these boys, Bobby?"

"Oh, I'd say about sixteen or seventeen, maybe older, but they were full-grown boys. Punks, Fir. Hooligans. Bullies. Kids who cause trouble in school and bully the smaller kids. Kids who go to school but do not pay attention to the teachers. Kids who are disruptive in the classroom. Kids who do not do their homework. Kids who will one day end up in jail.

"That's what happens to the bullies when they grow up, Fir, they end up in prison. Bullies steal from other kids, they litter, they push people around, but tonight, they tried to push the wrong person around. I was the wrong man for these boys to try and hurt. There is always someone bigger and meaner and stronger in this world, and eventually the bully will meet that person and find himself on the short end of the stick. Tonight they found themselves on the short end. They messed with the wrong man."

"Are you sure that you are all right, Bobby? Your right eye is pretty swollen, and you are dripping blood. Your new pants are torn, and your shirt is ripped too."

"Yeah, Fir, I'm fine. I'm just glad that this happened after I left the community center. I had such a good time tonight. This evening was really special, except for those thugs and tearing my pants and all. Anyway, here I am, and here you are, and we are both enjoying each other's company. It doesn't get much better than this, does it, Fir?"

"No, I guess not, Bobby, but I'm still not adopted."

A light mist had started to fall in the parking lot, and small puddles were beginning to form in the low spots. I looked down at the river of rainwater that had collected at the base of my trunk. An early-winter cool front was moving through south Florida and would be dropping the temperature into the midfifties over the next few nights. Bobby welcomed the rain, and I was always happy to see pools of water forming in the breezeway. You can never have too much hydration if you want your needles to stay supple and soft.

Bobby daubed at the abrasion over his right eye. The paramedics had closed the wound, but a bit of blood was seeping from the bandaged eye, and quite a lump had formed underneath the bandage.

"Bobby, could you move me just a bit so that I can stand a little straighter, and maybe put my trunk right in the middle of that large accumulation of water over there by your bench?"

"Sure, Fir." Bobby got up and walked over next to me, reached in, grabbed firmly ahold of my trunk, and lifted me into the air. He aligned my trunk perfectly so that I would be able to drink to my heart's content, careful to set me down so that my broken branch faced the wall. That way customers would see my best side.

Then he went back, sat down, and proceeded to tell me about the spaghetti and meatballs dinner. "It was a wonderful evening, Fir. Natalie helped prepare spaghetti and meatballs, and then after we all finished eating, Natalie and several of the volunteers carried in a birthday cake with candles ablaze all over the top of the cake. She set the cake down on my table, and everybody in the room stood and sang 'Happy Birthday' to me. I was so emotional that tears were streaming from my eyes. Paul, the man with the deep voice who always sits in the back of the room, stood and kept saying, 'Speech! Speech! Speech!'

"So I stood up and looked at all my friends staring up at me and thanked them for thinking of me on my birthday."

"But how did they know it was your birthday, Bobby?"

"Well, that's a good question, Fir, and it seems that someone here at Publix has a big mouth. Now, I'm not mentioning any names, but he kinda looks like a Christmas tree, and he has a broken branch, and his name is Fir! Do you have any idea who that might be, Fir? Wait a minute. Your name is Fir, isn't it? *And* you look like a Christmas tree, don't you? And don't you have a broken branch? You know, Fir, they say that if it looks like a duck, and if it walks like a duck and quacks like a duck, it must be a duck."

"But I don't know anyone at the center, Bobby. I didn't tell anyone that it was your birthday, except Mis…"

"So…Missy knew it was my birthday, huh, Fir?"

"Uh…yes, I told her last Wednesday. It just kind of slipped out, Bobby. But you know, I'm glad I told her. And I'm glad she told her mother. And I'm glad that they baked you a cake, and I'm glad that everyone sang 'Happy Birthday' to you, Bobby. How was the spaghetti and meatballs meal?"

"Outstanding, Fir. Natalie's recipe again. Lord, can that girl cook. She's really a fine woman, Fir. I…"

"You like her a lot, don't you, Bobby? You light up when you talk about her. So tell me about the meatballs."

"Well, as I said, Natalie was using her recipe. Actually, she said it was her mother's recipe, but boy, did I eat a lot of meatballs. Each one was about the size of one of your sparrows."

The little birds were wide awake and listening to every word but started angrily chattering when Bobby compared *them* to meatballs.

"I'm sorry, guys, I didn't mean to get you upset. I would never eat spaghetti and meat-sparrows. I was just comparing their size to your size. And the meatballs were brown like you guys."

The sparrows settled down and started to preen my needles. As Bobby continued his story, they cocked their heads in his direction.

"Now where was I? Oh, yes! Paul wanted a speech. So I stood up, and they all started to sing to me. They were singing 'Happy Birthday' to *me*. It watered my eyes, Fir. After they finished their song, I said, 'Let's make this a birthday party for all of us.' So we sang again, and this time we each put our own names in the song. The kids loved it. Publix donated a huge sheet cake, and they also donated birthday presents to all of us homeless people."

CHAPTER 39

Food Fight

"Bobby, why are you homeless?"

"Good question, Fir. I guess I just lost my way. Somehow I got lost in the forest of life. I walked and I walked through the woods, but everything looked the same. There were no signs, no paths or trails, and the canopy above was so thick with foliage that I could not see the sky. I knew not whether I was walking north or south, east or west. I was lost. There were no people, no houses, no birds, and no noise, save the crunching of leaves and sticks beneath my feet. I do not know how I found myself in this world of aloneness, but when you arrived in Lake Worth, and then Missy and Natalie, it was like coming to a paved road that led me out of the darkness and into the sunshine."

"So you are going to be all right, aren't you, Bobby?"

"Yes, I'm going to be fine, and so are you, Fir. We are both in the sunshine, and we are both going to have a very merry Christmas."

"Now let me tell you about this crazy evening at the community center."

"Yes, Bobby, you said that there was a cake with candles and that everybody sang 'Happy Birthday' to you and then 'Happy Birthday' to themselves…"

"Right, Fir, well, we were still eating spaghetti and meatballs when they set the cake down. I asked the kids to all gather around the cake and make a wish and blow out the candles. Faster than a speeding bullet, all the kids in the center rushed over to my table. Natalie was sitting next to me and wore her beautiful smile as she joined in on another chorus of 'Happy birthday to Bobby.' I looked at her, and I watched her eyes sparkle as she held my hand and kissed me on the cheek.

"We were just about to cut the cake when Paul, the big guy in the back with the deep voice said, 'Hey, Bobby, you gonna eat the rest of those meatballs on your plate?'

"Well, Natalie had been very generous with my plate of food, and I still had about half of my spaghetti and four good-sized meatballs left. I don't know what came over me, but I looked at Paul and said, 'No, would you like them?'

"Paul said, 'Sure would,' in that deep, deep voice of his, so I picked up a meatball in my hand and threw it at Paul, hitting him right between his eyes. I used to be a pitcher on the high school baseball team, and I think I threw my fastball. That meatball went splat and broke into about six soft pieces as it shattered against Paul's forehead. It left a big, round circle of spaghetti sauce dripping into his eyes. Big Paul arose from his seat and started walking with long strides directly toward me. He had his plate of half-eaten spaghetti in his right hand. And I don't know if I mentioned it before, but Paul is about six feet, six inches tall, and he can be meaner than a junkyard dog."

Concerned, I asked, "What did he do to you, Bobby?"

"Well, he stood next to me and lowered his plate so that it was close to mine. I thought he wanted my three remaining meatballs, but then he said, 'Happy Birthday, Bobby, I've brought you a gift!' And with that, Paul dumped his whole plate of remaining spaghetti onto *my* head. Strands of spaghetti and red tomato sauce dripped down my smiling face and onto my new white polo shirt. Everyone in the room was stunned, and it became really quiet as everybody stared at Paul and me and wondered what would happen next. That's when I started to laugh, and Paul started to laugh, and all hell broke loose in the dining hall.

"An old gray-haired fella named Larry yelled, 'FOOD FIGHT!' and the spaghetti and meatballs began to fly across the room. Natalie got hit in the left ear just as she was starting to stand up to try and prevent the disorder that was about to take place. But she was too late. I watched the sloppy wad of pasta hit Natalie, and I broke out in a big smile. I then zeroed in on the person who had connected with Natalie's face. I picked out a meatball, wound up like a major-leaguer, and let 'er rip. The meatball hit Larry squarely in the mouth just as he had started to laugh at the mess he made of Natalie. The meatball actually flew into his mouth and made Larry temporarily gag, and then he choked, coughed, and splattered the meatball onto those sitting at his table.

"The kids seemed to be having a ball—no pun intended. Kids don't eat enough to satisfy their parents anyway, so most of the children had full plates, and they were hurling their dinners at each other as if this were a food-fight fun festival. Everyone was a participant in the fun night at the community center, except for a few of the more hardened and stoic mothers. There were also two grumpy old men who did not seem particularly happy, but all in all, this was a night to remember.

"Strangely enough, the cake was spared and only suffered slight discoloring here and there, but after about ten minutes passed, things settled down, and Deep Voice Paul stood and in his bass voice said, 'This is the most fun I've had in fifty years.'

"Everyone applauded, and when the high fives and laughter subsided, Paul continued, 'I want everyone to stick around and clean up this mess after we have our cake.'

"And we did, Fir. We made that dining hall spick-and-span before we left. We cut the cake and sang happy birthday to us again. Natalie passed out the presents, and we all hung around until almost nine o'clock washing walls, tables, and dishes. We mopped the floors and all became closer friends than I think we ever were before this special night at the community center.

"Well, like I said, we began to leave at about nine o'clock. Many of the little ones had already fallen asleep, and Natalie and I were the last to leave. She locked up the center, and I walked her to her car. After she drove off, I went over and sat on the bench out front before walking back here to see you. I could tell it was going to rain. I could smell it in the air, but the stars were still twinkling, and the cloud cover was just rolling in. I could still see the moon, and I just wanted to sit for a few minutes and reflect on this wonderful night. And that's when the bad boys came out of the darkness, Fir."

CHAPTER 40

Friday, December 18
Christmas Dinner
Off to the Center to See Natalie

They say that you are lucky if you find five good friends in a lifetime. Bobby had found three in a matter of one month: me, Missy, and Natalie. Bobby felt blessed to have found such wonderful friends, but Natalie took the friendship to a new level. She had captured his heart. Bobby had fallen in love with Natalie, and Natalie was equally enchanted with Bobby.

As if Tinker Bell had dusted the two beautiful human beings with pixie dust, Bobby and Natalie were walking on clouds and consumed by a need to see each other, to sit, to talk, to touch, to hug, and maybe even to kiss. Friendship is great, but nothing in the world compares to love.

And I was pretty darned lucky too, in spite of my present predicament—you know, being stuck on this breezeway for so many weeks. I had enjoyed many, many friendships in Murphy, North Carolina, some who were close, others who were closer. They shared their problems with me and came to me when they needed advice and counsel, but only my Mary was a *close* friend, someone who was always there to watch my back. She was, as they say, the person (or tree) that you would want in your foxhole when it's you against the world. A real, true friend, my Mary, and I loved her, my dear, dear Mary.

Missy, too, had become one of the most special friends that I would probably ever have, even though she was not a tree. Of that I was sure, and then there was Bobby Thornton, the ex-military homeless guy. He and I had a very magical relationship, and although I often got pretty mad at the man, I really did love him. He was really special, just like Missy. And then there were my sparrows. But I'm wandering again. I tend to do that, so let's get back to my story.

It was Friday night, December 18, one week before Christmas, and Bobby and I were pretty much alone. He was next to me, sitting on the bench, but his mind was somewhere else, and his heart was with Natalie.

"What are you thinking about, Bobby?"

No answer.

"Hey, Bobby, what are you thinking about?"

Again, no answer.

I felt a breeze suddenly rush through the breezeway, so I fluffed up my needles and extended my branches like a sail, and I was pushed by the wind just enough to teeter and fall onto the bench where Bobby was sitting.

"What the heck is wrong with you, Fir?" Bobby angrily blurted. "You almost hit me in the head."

"Well, he speaks! Ol' Bobby Baby hasn't lost his voice after all. I thought that maybe the bump on your head had caused you to lose your voice. You didn't seem to hear me either, Bob. You don't mind me calling you Bob, do you? Or maybe Robert? Or Sarge?"

"No, Fir, call me whatever you want, just don't call me late for dinner. Ha, ha, ha. Oh my goodness, I've been sitting here for almost an hour. I have to get to the community center for their annual Christmas dinner. Natalie said they decorate the center with garland, and they have a seven-foot tree, decorated with lights and bulbs and strands of popcorn and an angel on the top, and she said that she decorated it all by herself. Natalie said that Missy made the popcorn garland that is strung around the tree...What's wrong, Fir? You seem sad or something. Did you hurt yourself when you fell against my bench?"

"No, Robert, I just feel alone. I'm depressed. *Why couldn't I have been the tree at the community center?*"

Bobby could see tears of pine sap dripping from my eyes. The sparrows were all huddled together, close to my face, offering me comfort and wiping the sap from my eyes. Bobby arose from the steel bench and walked around to where I had fallen. He reached in and grabbed me by the trunk, careful not to disturb the three sparrows, and carried me to a spot where there was ample water still making a puddle in the breezeway. Then Bobby set me down and did something that he had only seen Missy do. Bobby wrapped his arms around me and said, "I love you, Fir. You are very special to me. Don't be sad. Everything's going to turn out just fine. You will be adopted and live happily ever after, just like your stories." Then he hugged me tighter and returned to his bench, where he sat down.

"And, Fir, the tree at the community center is plastic. It's artificial. It's not real. They use the same plastic tree every year. If you were the tree at the center, you would never have lived or loved or had dear friends like me or the animals on your mountain."

It was 6:00 p.m., and Bobby wanted to be at the center no later than seven. The weather had changed, and the temperatures were now in the sixties. Bobby carried a sweater, which he would wear as he walked back to Publix after this evening with Natalie. Bobby almost always stopped by to visit with me before going to the field he had made his home. Bobby and I had become very dear friends, and we would talk and laugh and even cry as we discussed the world as it is and the way we each thought it should be. But Bobby would always end the conversations by saying, "It is what it is, Fir." Then he would up himself from the bench and disappear around the corner.

But tonight, Bobby was anxious to get to the center to enjoy a holiday evening with Natalie. He had daydreamed on the bench of candlelight and soft music, a table for two, and wine glasses of crystal clinking together as they toasted their love for each other. I talked and talked, just like Mary had done on Wildcat Mountain, but Bobby heard nothing. He was immersed in his thoughts of this wonderful woman, Natalie, transported to a fantasy world where he hoped to enjoy his happiest evening ever.

So Bobby looked at me with those glassy eyes of a man in love and said, "See you later, Fir; it's Natalie time." And off he went toward the bus stop on Lantana Road. In less than five minutes, Bobby was sitting comfortably in the front seat of the bus, next to a new driver, one he had never seen before. They introduced themselves, exchanged small talk, and Bobby told him that he needed to get off at the community center.

As he stepped off the bus, Bobby thought he saw Natalie standing outside the dining hall. As he neared the flowered area of benches in front of the community center, the same place where he had been attacked by the bad guys the week before, he waved to Natalie. She waved back and quickstepped her way to the benches, where she opened her arms and gave him a tight hug.

Natalie had been crying, and her tears soaked through Bobby's shirt. She was also trembling and unable to speak. Bobby asked her what was the matter, but she only held him tighter. Bobby patted her on the back and stroked her long, black hair. They stood by the benches for several minutes before Natalie was able to talk. She and Bobby looked into each other's eyes, and Natalie broke down and started to sob. Bobby held her tightly and spoke soothing words, "I'm here, Natalie. Did someone hurt you? Everything will be all right, Natalie. I will stay with you as long as you need me."

They sat side by side on one of the benches, four hands coupled together. Natalie's eyes were swollen and red. Her face was flushed. Natalie had been distressed for quite a while, and Bobby chastised himself for spending so much of his time blowing bubbles, daydreaming, and talking nonsense with me.

"I need to blow my nose and get something to drink, Bobby. Would you mind going inside to our table and bringing me a bottle of water? And the tissues are just inside the kitchen area."

"Sure, Natalie." Bobby carried a gift bag with nonalcoholic champagne inside, together with two plastic flutes for toasting a friendship that was quickly turning into love. Natalie had not noticed the colorful Christmas gift bag. She had her head bowed, and she had both hands over her eyes as Bobby walked into the dining hall.

CHAPTER 41

Teardrops and Kisses

Paul was still inside with the entire contingent of others, who were all concerned for Natalie. Paul walked up to Bobby and in his deep voice said, "Boy, am I glad to see you."

"What happened, Paul?" questioned Bobby.

"Well, the dining room was full, our usual turnout for the annual Christmas turkey dinner. Most of us were seated and enjoying our traditional holiday meal. Alberto and his uncle were the last ones in the serving line, and Natalie had just finished pouring a ladle of gravy over Alberto's turkey and mashed potatoes when there was a loud crash as the front door was pulled open. It was pulled so hard that it slammed against the wall outside of the building."

"Who was there, Paul?"

"That would be Glenn, Natalie's good-for-nothing, separated ex-husband. He was drunk as a skunk. He could not even walk a straight line, Bobby. He yelled at the top of his drunken voice, 'NATALIE!...NATALIE!'

"He did not see her behind the counter, so he stumbled around the dining hall, searching for her at each table. He threw empty chairs to the floor and scanned the room. Then he spotted her. Bobby, she was so embarrassed; she was mortified."

"What happened next, Paul?"

"He staggered toward her, screaming at the top of his voice, 'No child support, Natalie. Get it? Not one penny more! I'm divorcing you, and I hope I never see you and Missy again.'

"Then he threw the car keys at Natalie, the ones to their old clunker, the Chevy Caprice, and he yelled, 'And I'm taking your Lexus, the one parked outside. Have a good life!'

"Then he turned and staggered toward the door. Everyone in the room just stopped eating when this happened, Bobby. The night was turning out to be a disaster. Everybody felt so bad for Natalie. She's such a good person, Bobby. She didn't deserve this."

"So, Paul, what did you do to help Natalie? You must have done something. I know you, Paul."

"Well, yes, actually, you know me pretty doggone well, Bobby, and you know that I've never been very good at minding my own business, so I kinda *helped* him out the door, and I kinda helped him *to* his car, and I kinda helped him *into* his car. He kind of *slipped* a couple of times and fell down, and I kinda noticed that he must have hurt his nose when he *tripped* and fell to the ground. I think he slammed the car door on his fingers too, 'cause he was really screaming when he drove off, and he seemed in quite a hurry to leave the center."

"Paul, tell everyone that I'll be outside with Natalie for a few minutes, and ask them, please, not to leave. We will be in shortly."

Bobby walked across the room to the kitchen to find a box of Kleenex tissue for Natalie. All eyes were fixed on Bobby as he grabbed a bottle of water and left the dining room. You could almost hear a pin drop. Only an occasional sniff or a cough could be heard in the large dining room. Nobody was eating. Bobby closed the door behind him and returned to the bench where his dear Natalie sat, her heart broken by the events of the evening.

Bobby loosened the cap of the plastic water bottle and handed it to Natalie. She was no longer crying but was staring off into the darkness of a moonless night. She grasped two tissues and wiped her eyes. She then blew into the tissues to clear her nostrils, and a kind of snorting sound came out of her nose. This made her chuckle, and Bobby couldn't help but snicker. He embraced her and told her that she would be all right. Bobby then lifted her hand and kissed it gently with his soft lips. "You are very special,

Natalie. You are loved by the hundred people in that room," and he pointed toward the dining hall. "Let's go inside and eat turkey, sing carols, and enjoy this Christmas celebration that only you have made possible for all of us."

Bobby and Natalie arose from their bench and walked hand in hand toward the front door. Natalie abruptly stopped and turned to face Bobby. "I'm so embarrassed, Bobby. I don't think I can face anybody. I think I should just go home. I need a good cry, Bobby."

Bobby wrapped his arms around her and held Natalie close. He could smell the sweetness of her perfume and the fresh aroma of shampoo in her hair. He whispered into her ear, "Natalie. You are better off without Mr. McCord. You need to be with those who love you, and everyone in that room loves you, and Natalie, I love you. By the way, did I tell you how beautiful you look tonight? Even when you snort?"

"No, but I think you are beautiful too. To me, you are the most beautiful human being I think I've ever met."

Bobby again held her closer, lifted her chin with an index finger, and asked her if she was ready to go inside. She took one last gasp of breath and headed toward the door.

CHAPTER 42

Holly and Richie

When Bobby left the community center, it was well after 10:00 p.m., and the temperatures outside had already dropped to fifty-two degrees. Bobby was very happy to have worn a sweater. Natalie was holding Bobby's arm as they walked toward the tired old Caprice that Glenn McCord had left in the parking lot. She was hopeful that it would start. Glenn had a history of being mean spirited, and it would not have surprised Natalie if the spark-plug wires were pulled or the distributor cap tampered with, but one turn of the key started the eight-cylinder Chevrolet. Even though the car was old and rusty, the Caprice had always been dependable transportation. Natalie offered Bobby a ride back to Publix, so Bobby jumped into the passenger seat for the short trip back to where I anxiously waited to hear about his evening.

Bobby invited Natalie to sit on our green bench and talk for a while, but sadly, Natalie had to decline. She had to hurry home to Missy, who was being babysat by the sixteen-year-old next-door neighbor's daughter, Melissa.

Bobby was euphoric as he settled onto the bench. We watched Natalie drive away, and that's when I asked, "What's with the rusty old car?"

"It's a long story, Fir, but you and I have all night, don't we?"

"Uhh, maybe you do, Bobby, but I need my beauty sleep. I still need to be adopted, and sleep helps me regenerate my supple Fraser fir essence. Five of these trees that Cree delivered this

morning were sold today; that's a credit to Kenny and to rehydra-
tion and to plenty of restful sleep. Those trees were so sick that all
they did today was rehydrate and sleep. In fact, the new ones that
were sold were still asleep when they were being tied to the roofs of
their respective cars. A little sleep wouldn't hurt you either, Bobby.
Are you aware that you have red stuff all over your face, your lips,
and your shirt? Have you been involved in another fight?"

"Yeah, Fir, it was kind of a fight. I was fighting Natalie off me
all night. She just wanted to kiss me and kiss me and kiss me. That
red stuff all over my face is her lipstick. Fir, I think I lost the fight.
Wow, what a night. She loves me, Fir. At least I think she loves me.
No, I know she loves me. I think that we should talk about this
tomorrow, Fir. You're tired, I'm tired, and in all candor, I'm cold.
This sweater is just not keeping me warm. I'm shivering, so I think
I'll call it a night—that is, if it's all right with you. Tomorrow is
another day, OK, Fir?"

"Sure, Bobby. I, too, have had a most stressful day and need
to decompress. You know what I mean? Rest and get my thoughts
together? Sleep and drink as much water as I can so that I will look
my best for tomorrow?"

"Yeah, I get it, Fir," Bobby yawned like a lion in the wild, and
then he stood and stretched his arms high in the air, all the while
clenching his fists. Bobby was loosening up for his evening walk
down the breezeway, where he would disappear into the wooded
area behind Publix.

It was almost 11:00 p.m., closing time for Publix, and a customer walked out of the store with Kenny to look at Christmas
trees. There were not many of us left, so I really perked up as
Kenny approached me. He was wearing a red-and-black plaid long-
sleeved shirt and was also wearing his leather gloves. He reached
in and grabbed me by the trunk, careful to display only my perfect
frontal view. The overhead fluorescent lights seemed to make me
glow a silvery gray, as if I were reflecting moonlight on my mountain. I fluffed and stood tall. Every needle stood at attention as this
young couple stared at me.

"What do you think, Holly?" asked the red-haired man as he cocked his head while stroking his beard with his right hand.

"I think this is a beautiful tree, Richie," she replied, "but I wonder if you can turn him around so that I can see the other side?"

Kenny complied and rotated me so that she and Richie could see my back side.

"Oh my gosh, Holly, he looks like someone blasted him in the behind with a shotgun. Look at the size of that hole. An entire branch seems to be missing."

Richie turned and headed toward the other trees, leaving Holly and Kenny alone, standing by the bench.

"Richie, we could put him in the corner, where his broken limb won't show. He really is beautiful, Richie."

Bobby had sat back down on the bench, watching, blowing bubbles, and listening to every word.

"Ma'am," said Bobby, "those other trees are more beautiful than this ol' broken down pile of wood, and besides, he been here so long that his needles are all falling off. But truth be told, all these trees were delivered about a month ago, so you ought to think long and hard about this before you take one home."

Holly looked Kenny square in the eyes and demanded to know, "Is that true? Is this an *old* tree? Are all these trees *old* trees?"

Kenny stuttered and stammered as he looked down at Bobby, then at me, and then at the other trees.

"Uh, errr, uh, yes, ma'am, these trees were delivered several weeks ago, but I take good care of them. I give them plenty of water and spray them down five times daily. They're really kinda like brand-new, fresh trees."

"Richie! Richie, let's go home. We can look tomorrow, when there is more light. Besides, I think these trees are all too old and dried up. Let's go home."

Holly hurried her way over to Richie, who had just picked up another tree, which he was inspecting from top to bottom and front to back. She grabbed him by the arm, escorted him to the car, and they drove away.

"DUDE," I yelled at Bobby. "WHY DID YOU TELL HOLLY THAT I WAS LOS-
ING MY NEEDLES? Why did you say what you said? What the heck is
wrong with you? I thought you were my friend. I'm *not* dried up.
Kenny gives me tons of water every day. My needles are as supple
and soft as when I was on Wildcat Mountain."

My outburst awakened the sleeping sparrows and all of the
other critters who lived in nooks and crannies all around the Publix
breezeway. Kenny had taken off his gloves and green apron and
gone back inside the store. It was now 11:00 p.m., and the locks
clicked on the doors. Publix was closed. One by one, the cashiers
inserted their cards into the time clock and punched out. Then
they were escorted to the service door, which was unlocked by
the assistant manager, Mark Wilson. The cashiers all knew Bobby,
who was sitting in his usual place and blowing huge bubbles. They
all liked Bobby, and as they passed him on the way to their cars,
they commented on the massive size of his bubbles and bid him
a good evening. The remaining employees in the store were busy
straightening up and involved in minor cleaning activities that
would make the Publix presentable for opening the next day. As
the various workers exited the store and filed past his bench, each
exchanged pleasantries with Bobby. It seemed that everyone knew
and liked this bubble-blowing homeless man.

But the entire time that Bobby was making small talk with the
Publix people, I was seething. The three little birds could feel
my limbs quiver and shake as I became more and more stressed
and agitated. These sparrows clung tightly to their tiny branch as
the vibrations intensified. They felt as if at any moment, I might
explode into millions of tiny pieces, splattering them onto the
Publix wall or the ceiling or hurtling them into the darkness of the
upper atmosphere. So to try and settle my agitation, they started
softly talking to me to try and get me to relax.

Eddie, the oldest of the three sparrows, started singing a soft
melody, like a lullaby, to try and calm me down. His two brothers
joined in, and the soothing, songlike harmony of these three dear
creatures slowly melted the tension that had me so irritated.

Mr. Wilson was the last to leave, at about midnight. The lights went off, and the store was dark except for the illumination of the cash registers inside and the covered area outside, where the Christmas trees and benches were located. Mr. Wilson touched Bobby on the shoulder as he passed the bench, said, "Good night, Sarge," and walked briskly toward his car. He was holding his cell phone to his left ear and laughing about something said or done that day. He started his car and drove off into the darkness.

CHAPTER 43

Saturday, December 19
The Coot

Bobby awakened to the sound of a screeching coot, the same one that awakened him each and every morning at precisely the time that the sun peeked above the eastern horizon. A coot is a small, aquatic bird that nests in the grasses that grow in the shallows of lakes and canals. Coots are black with red bills and are about the size of a guinea pig, with wings and webbed feet. But this coot thought he was a rooster, and at the break of dawn each day, he would begin to screech, a high-pitched, bloodcurdling noise that would penetrate Bobby's slumber and make it impossible for sleep to continue.

Most days, though, Bobby didn't really mind. He had always been an early riser, and besides, he loved watching the sunrise reflect off the lake the coot called his home. The caterwauling of this waterbird was especially loud and annoying, though, this particular Saturday morning, so Bobby climbed out of the warmth of his sleeping bag and slipped into his tennis shoes. He rubbed his eyes, yawned, and crawled out of his camouflage-colored tent. Bobby stood, stretched his arms high above his head, twisted his body back and forth, and then tried to locate that noisy coot. He casually walked toward the lake, suddenly noticing for the first time since he had awakened the cool air, which was like white powder blowing from his mouth. He would learn later that, indeed, a record-low temperature had descended upon Lake Worth. His shivers became shakes, so he about-faced and returned to his camp for warmer clothes. Bobby layered himself with another shirt and his wrinkled sweater, which he had worn the previous night. Bobby then reached into his fanny pack for several pieces of gum and returned to the lake to look for the coot.

A large old oak tree grew stately and majestic near where he stood. The location of this tree was such that he could sit at its base and lean up against the huge trunk and enjoy each morning's sunrise and be warmed by a slowly rising sun. Bobby sat, crossed his legs, maneuvered his back until he had found the most comfortable backrest, and began his search for the little squawker. He could hear the dissonant blurts of noise but could not see the bird. Other wildlife were out and about, searching for food or resting after successfully catching something to eat. He watched a gray squirrel twitching its nervous tail and chewing on a juicy acorn. Monarch butterflies were drinking nectar from the many flowers growing wild in Bobby's field, and a snake bird was trying to swallow a fish he had just speared with his razor-sharp beak. But the coot was not to be seen. This had become a daily ritual for Bobby. He knew the coot was there, and he heard the bird squawking, but he could never seem to locate him. This morning, it seemed, would be no different. Bobby chewed his gum and began to blow small bubbles.

The jagged edge of the oak tree's bark was irritating the middle of his spine, so Bobby shifted his weight a bit and found a more comfortable spot to rest his back against the tree. He also adjusted his sitting position so that his backside was between two large roots. Bobby felt as if he were resting in an easy chair. He pulled his knees up close to his face and laid his chin on top of his arms, which were wrapped tightly around his legs.

CHAPTER 44

The Homeless Puppy

Unbeknownst to Thornton, an uninvited guest had sat down next to him and was looking alternately up at this strange human and out at the noise coming from the lake.

A splinter had become embedded in Bobby's right index finger, and because he was so engrossed in trying to remove the festering piece of wood, he did not notice the floppy-eared puppy sitting on his left, intently watching him pick at his splinter. The coot continued to disrupt the peaceful silence of the morning, and each time it would bleat, both Bobby and the dog would turn their heads and search for the origin of the awful noise. It was humorous to see the two heads bobbing and weaving in the same direction, as if they were watching a ping-pong match. Finally, Bobby was successful at extracting the sticker from his sore finger, and he tossed it aside, pleased with his surgical success. That's when he spoke. "Wow, I thought I would never get that splinter out."

And as Bobby yelled, "EUREKA!" the shaggy puppy excitedly yapped, "ARF!"

Bobby was startled, and he jumped at the unexpected sound. His sudden movement frightened the puppy, which retreated to a safe distance from this stranger.

Turning his gaze from the pond to the bushes near where the small dog was now sitting, Bobby stared at a raggedy, camel-colored, skinny pup who couldn't be more than two months old. The dog was obviously homeless, which meant he was a kindred

173

spirit to Bobby, who was also searching for a new, better reality. For several minutes, these two homeless strangers just stared at each other, sizing each other up, neither daring to venture closer to the other.

Various studies over the years have concluded that a dog's sense of smell is anywhere from forty to ten million times better than a human's, so when a waft of leftover turkey and dressing floated on a breeze from Bobby's tent, it aroused hunger pangs in the small dog. His black nose directed the small pup toward the camouflage tent, where he began to sniff and search for leftovers from last night's Christmas dinner. Bobby knelt down and softly called to the puppy, who was now circling the tent with his nose to the ground, tail wagging, and busily trying to gain access to the tent that harbored the food, which the puppy so desperately needed. It had been two days since he had eaten, and that was only a half donut, which he had stolen from a crow in the breezeway.

Bobby arose and approached his tent. As the pup further distanced himself from his new acquaintance, he kept his eyes on every movement that Bobby made, ready to run if he detected danger. But this human did not appear to be a threat, so the dog sat near a bush and watched as Bobby entered the tent and quickly exited with an aroma-filled bag of food. Bobby knew that the best way to befriend an animal was with something to eat, so he carried the bag of leftovers that Natalie had given him the night before, sat back down under his large oak, leaned against the trunk, and opened the paper bag. The noise of crisp paper and metallic tinfoil did not go unnoticed by the brown pup. The small dog watched every move that Bobby made, listening with flickering ears and sniffing the wonderful scents coming from where Bobby sat. All of the pup's senses were aroused. He was salivating, staring at Bobby's every movement, and rapidly wagging his tail. This puppy was on full alert. Bobby pulled loose a small piece of turkey and laid it down next to where he sat, carefully avoiding eye contact with the dog. The puppy's eyes followed every movement of Bobby's hand. Next, Bobby pulled a piece of turkey from the large drumstick and placed it into his mouth. He chewed loudly, smacking his lips, and then pulled off another piece, which he tossed toward the dog, again not making eye contact.

"I think I'll call you Turk!" blurted Bobby as he manipulated the turkey leg and removed several more pieces of dark meat. "Sure seems appropriate to me. What do you think, Turk?"

The puppy inched his way toward Bobby, being guided by his nose to a slice of turkey that had been tossed toward the bush.

Not once did the puppy take his eyes off of the man sitting under the tree looking out onto the sparkling lake. It was as if Bobby had totally forgotten about the dog. But Bobby continued to talk softly to Turk and toss chunks of turkey toward the ravenous pup. The meat was not being chewed but rather swallowed whole, and each piece landed a bit closer to Bobby, forcing Turk to inch his way closer and closer to the source of the food. It did not take long for the hungry Turk to find himself standing adjacent to Bobby, gobbling down large pieces of turkey and stuffing that had been piled high next to Thornton's left leg. Bobby had been talking nonstop to Turk in soft, gentle tones, assuring the small dog that the two homeless boys would soon become very close friends.

CHAPTER 45

The Dog Has Fleas

And so it was, as if it were meant to be, that these two very different creatures were soon snuggled together and searching in vain for the owner of the screeching, ducklike sound, who was hidden by water plants growing in the shallows. Turk was licking Bobby's face with his warm, wet tongue, and Bobby was scratching the swollen belly and behind the floppy ears of his newfound friend. Between Bobby and his puppy, they had consumed almost a half pound of meat and another quarter pound of stuffing. Little did Natalie know that this would indeed be a "doggie" bag when she filled it so full of leftovers from the annual Christmas dinner.

Bobby's eyes started to flutter as he leaned back against the old oak, which was now bathing Bobby and Turk with intermittent shadows of shade. He held Turk in his arms, and as the morning sun warmed the cool breezes blowing off the lake, soon they were both sound asleep. They couldn't have been in dreamland for more than fifteen minutes when Bobby began to scratch. His entire body seemed to be itching, and little Turk was scratching at his own ears with a pistonlike motion of his rear leg. Bobby's eyes opened wide, and he quickly realized that the soft bundle of love that he held in his arms was infested with fleas. And now Bobby was infested. There was only one thing to do, and that was to disrobe as quickly as possible and make tracks for the lake. Careful not to frighten the puppy, Bobby gently set Turk down on the ground and began to take off his clothes. He removed his shoes and socks, his sweater, and the new slacks that he had slept in last night. Everything but his underwear was left in a pile by the tree, and he quickstepped to the lake, where he dove into the chilly water. In a way, it was refreshing, but if he had his druthers, Bobby would have been enjoying a warm shower right then instead.

Turk just stood by the tree, watching Bobby splish and splash in the water, wondering what had gotten into his new friend. *This is one crazy human,* thought Turk, *but he sure seems to be having fun out there.* The puppy briefly considered joining Bobby in the cold water, but a flea was feasting on his hind side, so he twisted his head and started chewing at the bite area, which was on the top of his back, next to his tail. After successfully destroying the flea, Turk turned his head back toward the water, where Bobby was doing something to his head that was causing his hair to turn white and bubbly. Then he heard the coot screaming like crazy, and he saw this small black bird with puffed feathers seemingly walking on water, wings flapping, headed right toward Bobby's eyes. Bobby saw him too, just in time to backhand the coot like a tennis ball being whacked over a net. Bobby had swum too close to his nest, and the coot was simply protecting his family. Fortunately, the coot was unhurt and returned to his nest, where he squawked even louder than before.

Bobby's teeth began to chatter after about fifteen minutes in the water, and he knew that the insects that had been chewing on him could not possibly survive for fifteen minutes underwater, so he exited the lake and headed for his tent. Turk followed, hoping for some more leftovers and happy to have found someone nice to share his life with. Bobby crawled into his canvas shelter and zipped the opening shut. This confused Turk, who began to yap. He wanted to go inside with Bobby, but Thornton had other plans for the pup.

Quickly, Bobby changed into dry clothes, grabbed a small rope from inside the tent, put on his tennis shoes, and exited his shelter. He put the rope around Turk's neck, and they began their walk to Walker's Veterinary Clinic on Lake Worth Road. Walker's was open all day on Saturdays for folks who have pets that don't get sick on Monday through Friday. They also had a rookie veterinarian who worked on Sundays, just in case an animal became ill on the Lord's day. But first, they would stop to see me. Bobby wanted to show me his newfound friend. He didn't know that Turk and I had already met.

The last Saturday before Christmas was about as perfect as a day could be: not a cloud in the sky, virtually no humidity, temperatures not expected to rise above seventy degrees, and two friends walking together tethered by a white nylon rope. Bobby stowed his belongings in a secure hiding place, the trunk of an old rust bucket of a car left abandoned years ago near the lake. It had once been a shiny red Chevy with multiple layers of paint and a clear coat to enhance its glossy exterior and protect it from the elements. But Father Time and neglect had not been kind to this old car. So there it sat, tires long since removed, as were all other items of utility to vehicles that were still on the roads and highways. Each morning, Bobby would disassemble his campsite and hide all traces of his presence before departing his field to embrace the adventures of a new day.

Bobby never walked in the same direction to or from his home in the woods. He did not want to blaze a trail that would alert someone with ill intentions to where he settled down for the night. Although his possessions were scant, they were of great value to Bobby, and he took great care to keep them well hidden. But this morning, he had a new prized possession, and he wanted to show it to his best friend, me, so he headed toward the breezeway with his buddy Turk in tow.

Turk took the lead as they headed west toward Publix, zigzagging in every direction so as not to miss a single smell. Turk kept his nose close to the ground, and when he noticed a whiff of rabbit, mouse, or feral cat, he would pull at the rope and try to run in the direction of the odor, but Bobby tugged back, and Turk would be forced to stay on course. They rounded the corner of the breezeway and walked down the long, covered corridor leading toward Bobby's bench. Turk spotted me and started to bark as if he had just recognized an old friend. The puppy was gurgling all kinds of happy-sounding noises as they approached. Bobby thought that the rope was too tight around Turk's neck, and as he sat down on the green bench, he reached for the loop so that he could loosen his makeshift leash.

"How are you doing, Bobby?" I inquired as I looked at the rope and the puppy attached to the other end. "I see you have a new friend." I was smiling ear to ear. (Of course, you know trees don't have ears, don't you? Wanna bet?). My grin extended around half my trunk.

I was so happy to see Bobby and the puppy together. Bobby did not realize that it was me who had sent the puppy into the wooded area behind Publix. I and the other trees had been hiding Turk from the dogcatcher for the past three days, but as the trees were being sold to Christmas shoppers, hiding the thin, brown, scraggly dog had become increasingly difficult.

Bobby noticed the smile on my trunk and said, "You've met my puppy, haven't you? You two guys know each other, don't you?"

Turk became yappy and pulled hard on the rope leash. I started to laugh. "Yes," I excitedly said. "We have been very close friends for the past three days, Bobby."

CHAPTER 46

Introducing Harry the Dogcatcher

All the trees started to whisper loudly to one another, each talking about something out in the parking lot. Bobby had never heard any voice but mine, but suddenly, he was hearing the chatter of this small forest of Christmas trees, all talking at once.

"Shhhh!" I said. A hush wafted over the breezeway. The warning sounds of Carl the crow echoed off the walls and ceiling, "Caw, caw, caw." That was his alert that the dogcatcher was back. I told Bobby to hurry away from there with Turk, as fast as he could go, before the animal control officer could catch and take the puppy away. Bobby picked Turk up, put him under his clean shirt, and hustled off toward Jog Road, hiding behind me and the other trees so that he would not be seen by the animal control man. The veterinarian's office was not far away, and Bobby wanted to get Turk checked out by the doctor, deflead, and fattened up. Although he would love to keep Turk, he had decided to make him a Christmas present for Missy—that is, if it was OK with Natalie. Bobby knew that the vet would make Turk fat and fluffy and warm and fuzzy by the time Christmas Eve came around, and he knew that Turk would fill the void left by the loss of Sammy, her bulldog.

I had watched this officer before. I knew how he operated. He was dressed in a pair of black trousers and a white short-sleeved shirt, and he wore a pair of black Brooks running shoes, and he was fast, as fast as any dog that I had ever seen. His name was embroidered on his shirt. "Harry," it said; what a perfect name for a man who runs around all day chasing furry creatures for a living. He had a silver Palm Beach County Animal Control badge, shined and brightly polished, proudly displayed on the left side of his starched white shirt.

Harry carried a sturdy pole with a loop on one end for capturing animals that were running loose, lost, forgotten, scared, hungry, and homeless. He would lure the unsuspecting dog to him by offering tasty treats and speaking to it in a soft, calming voice. His capture method had been perfected by years of experience and was really quite simple. He would crouch down on bended knees, smiling and extending irresistible-smelling food to the unsuspecting animals. If you are having trouble trying to picture this device, try drawing it on a piece of paper. First, draw a long straight line… this is the pole. Next draw a big circle at the end of and touching the end of the pole…this is the rope. Next, pretend that that circle is a face with no eyes, no nose, and no mouth. Now, draw only the nose…this is the treat. If Harry extended his pole toward the wary animal and held it up at the level of the dog, the looped end would resemble a giant mouth, and most animals would be frightened by the prospect of being eaten. But if you lay the trapping device on the ground, the threat goes away, and when the looped end was laid on the ground, the dog felt less threatened by the pole and more interested in the treat.

The keen noses of most hungry homeless dogs are attracted to the smell of an easy meal, which is why the officer placed the tasty food inside the loop. The watchful eyes of these easily spooked animals rarely looked away from a source of potential danger, so the pole distanced the danger from the dog. Once the animal realized that he was a safe distance from the man, he could concentrate more fully on what he needed and wanted the most: *food.*

The fact that the man was far enough out of reach, separated by a pole, was interpreted by the dog to be a human who seemed to pose no serious threat to the dog. Each time the dog would grab the tasty food, he would quickly retreat several more feet from the loop, chew and swallow the delightful food, and then look at the man to see if there was more. The dogcatcher would reload his loop with a second treat and repeat the procedure, all the while speaking soothing, soft, musical words such as, "Good boy, good doggie." By the third time that a treat was placed onto the loop, the dog would have become trusting, and as the man remained crouched, extending the pole with the loop armed and ready, he would capture the dog with a quick movement of the loop around the neck of the dog. The dog would try to pull away, but this only tightened the loop around its neck. Some dogs would yell and scream, jump and twist, and try to bite the man, but it was useless, because the pole kept the man away from the dog and the dog away from the man. That's what had happened to Turk's mother, brothers, and sisters, but I had told Turk to run into the woods, so he was not captured by the dogcatcher, but the officer saw him running down the breezeway and knew that there was still one pup on the loose. For that reason, the man with the pole was driving around the Publix parking lot three times a day in pursuit of the missing pup. That's why I had finally suggested that Turk go into the woods and find Bobby.

CHAPTER 47

Shots Fired

However, today would not be Harry's lucky day. I watched Bobby running through the parking lot, dodging cars as he passed the Home Depot. Turk had been scratching Bobby's belly, and the fleas were feasting on Bobby's soft tummy, so Bobby was now carrying Turk in his arms while he and his dog were escaping the big, bad dogcatcher. Harry was looking under all our branches and scanning the parking lot for clues that would lead him to the motherless puppy. Harry was very good at his work, which explains why he had been the number-one animal control officer for ten years in a row, no matter that Palm Beach County has only had one dogcatcher for the past ten years. Harry spotted Bobby and Turk just before they rounded the Home Depot and headed north on Jog Road. The chase was on. Bobby was running and scratching and scratching and running as Harry jumped into his truck and sped after him. Publix has six stop signs in front of the store, and Harry had to slow down for pedestrians at three of the stop signs. He was honking his horn, waving his arms, and yelling angrily at all the Christmas shoppers.

"Slow down!" yelled an old man with gray hair.

"Young man," screamed his elderly wife, "you need to take a pill; you almost hit my husband." She pointed her index finger at the stop sign and continued, "Do you know what this red sign means?" Then she saw the logo on his truck and reached into her purse for her glasses. She was blocking his way for about three minutes, and Harry was having a hissy fit. He was pulling at his hair with both hands, screaming at the top of his voice for her to get out of his way. She was looking for her spectacles, a pencil, and paper. When Harry realized that she was going to write down the information painted on his truck, he quickly put his vehicle in first gear, turned his steering wheel hard to the left, and took off around the couple in hot pursuit of Bobby and Turk. He went through two stop signs, barely missing a young family and a teen on his skateboard. Fists were waving, and loud voices hollered at Harry as his tires bounced off curbs and his horn screamed the high-pitched beeps that come from horns installed in fuel-efficient trucks imported from Japan.

Harry was obsessed. When he took the dogcatcher oath, he swore to capture all stray dogs that were running loose in the City of Lake Worth, an oath that Harry took very seriously.

As Harry exited the Home Depot parking lot, he spotted Bobby running down Jog Road, heading north. Harry sharply turned his steering wheel to the right and punched his accelerator to the floor. The small white truck lurched forward and nearly collided with a white Nissan, which had slowed to turn into the shopping center. Harry's vehicle was on two wheels as he made the turn onto Jog, and his tires were screeching. Harry briefly lost control of his small truck as he made his turn, and he sideswiped a Honda minivan that was in the left lane. Pedestrians in the parking lot were on their cell phones, dialing 911. The woman in the blue van into which Harry had smashed applied her brakes and came to a sudden stop in the middle of Jog Road. Harry had carelessly sideswiped her Honda, and now he was leaving the scene of an accident. The outraged animal control officer was in hot pursuit of Bobby and the puppy. The chase was on. Harry seemed to be in a trance, oblivious to the fact that he had caused an accident and almost run over shoppers.

Meanwhile, Bobby was looking over his shoulder as he ran north at full speed. He spotted the dogcatcher and immediately took evasive action, running at a full gallop across Jog Road to the median and then crossing the two southbound lanes so that he could disappear into the Fountains golf course, which ran parallel to Jog Road.

The Fountains is an adult community that is gated and extends from Lantana Road on the south to Lake Worth Road on the north. Three- and four-story condominiums line the western side of the fairways, and tall, closely bunched Arica palms act as a dense, almost impenetrable fence on the eastern side to ward off outsiders. It is a truly secluded, members-only golf community, and the Fountains takes their privacy very seriously. Guards at the security entrances are armed with loaded weapons, and there is no tolerance for guests seeking entry who have not been duly authorized in advance by owners.

Bobby, however, was on foot, and he managed to hide among the bushy Arica palms that densely lined the eastern boundary of the golfing community. These palms buffer the road noise on Jog Road, and they keep nonresidents out.

Harry spotted Bobby running toward the palms and turned his steering wheel to the left, crashing hard against the concrete curbing of the median. The front of his truck leaped into the air and bounced onto the southbound lane. He was thirty yards from Bobby. Sirens were everywhere. The Boynton Police Department, the Palm Beach Sheriff's Office, and the City of Lake Worth Police Department had all dispatched cars. Bobby was in deep trouble, and he knew it. He could hear the sirens coming from all directions, and Harry was closing in. Bobby tried to get through the palms, but they were just too dense. They acted as a security fence to keep the unwanted from entering onto the sacred grounds of the Fountains.

Harry's truck crashed into the palms, barely missing Bobby. Harry leaped out of his vehicle and pointed a pistol at Bobby just as four police cars screeched to a stop behind Harry's truck. Bobby was cornered.

"Hands up!" shouted Harry as he held his gun in both hands, directing the barrel at Bobby's chest. "Down on the ground! You're under arrest! You have the right to remain silent…"

Bobby did as he was told but only put one hand in the air. The other hand was inside Bobby's jacket, holding Turk. Harry thought Bobby had a weapon and fired, and Bobby fell facedown on the ground.

PART TWO

CHAPTER 48

The Getaway

Several shots rang out, and Bobby tumbled facedown to the ground. Harry immediately jumped on his back, placed a knee onto his spine, and reached for the arm that was loosely hanging at Bobby's side. Harry was reaching for his handcuffs, which were supposed to be in his cuff case on his duty belt, but he had forgotten to wear his duty belt, so he did not have his cuff case and thus, no cuffs. He had tried to reholster his gun but had missed the holster, and his weapon had fallen to the ground. Actually, dogcatchers were not issued guns or duty belts or handcuffs, so Harry was now impersonating a police officer.

That's when all the other police attacked and wrestled Harry to the ground. One officer stepped on Harry's hand and then kicked the gun away as two other cops cuffed the screaming Harry. "You got the wrong guy!" yelled Harry, but no one could understand his utterances, because one officer had a knee in Harry's back and another was pushing his head facedown into the ground.

Bobby, seeing the spectacle of Harry's arrest, saw his opportunity to slip away. He saw the opening in the Arica palms created by Harry's truck and crawled through to the other side. The police were so busy with the writhing, twisting, kicking, and yelling Harry that they failed to notice Bobby's escape. Bobby had not been hit by a single bullet. Harry had never been able to hit a target at the police academy, which is one of the many reasons he washed out and became a dogcatcher.

Bobby took off, running north along the fourteenth fairway toward the tee box. He continued running the entire length of the five-hundred-yard thirteenth fairway, staying close to the palms so that he could hide among the arecas if the need arose. There was a group of three golfers on the thirteenth tee, ready to drive their golf balls, when they spotted Bobby running in their direction. The chunky lady who had been addressing her ball, wiggling her butt, and taking about her seventh practice swing backed away and motioned for Bobby to continue running in her direction. Bobby slowed as he approached the three older women, who were wearing very chic and neatly pressed pastel shirts, coordinated Bermuda shorts, matching golf shoes with tassels, and Pittsburgh Steeler sun visors. These girls were obviously seasonal residents of the Fountains condominium complex and clearly were from Pennsylvania. They didn't seem to mind yielding to a jogger, especially a young man as handsome as Bobby, and they were all three standing lovestruck with their mouths agape as he looked at them with his azure blue eyes.

Bobby tipped his hat, slowed his gait to a walk, and said, "Howdy, ladies. You girls are the loveliest ladies that I have ever seen on this golf course."

The women covered their mouths, looking at each other with smiles and giggles the likes of which would usually only be heard from teenage schoolgirls.

The eastern entrance to the Fountains Golf and Country Club was not far from where the ladies stood staring at Bobby's muscular physique. Bobby looked back, smiled, and again tipped his hat as he walked toward the pedestrian entrance where the guardhouse was located. Cars and trucks alike were lined up in the visitors' lane, awaiting access to the Fountains. No one could gain entry unless they had a prearranged appointment in the computer or unless a quick phone call from the guard to the owner OK'd their admittance.

Each fairway had an asphalt path leading to it, which ran the entire length of the eighteen-hole golf course. On the eastern perimeter, the path ran adjacent to the Arica palms and was used by both golf carts and joggers, although joggers were discouraged from using the paths during the daytime due to the danger of being hit by a golf ball.

Bobby was walking along the path and approaching the pedestrian gate. There was no real concern from the guards as to who was leaving the community on foot. The gate was locked from the outside, but a push on the lock-release mechanism afforded Bobby an easy exit from the Fountains. He found himself once again on Jog Road and looked to the right, noting that the flashing blue lights of half a dozen police cars were busily investigating the accident scene that had breached the Fountains' Arica palm hedges. Jog Road is a very busy north-south artery, with six lanes divided by a landscaped median. It was a miracle that Harry had not caused a multiple car accident when he was in blind and reckless pursuit of Bobby and Turk. Bobby just shook his head as he thought about how many people could have been injured by the simpleminded animal control officer.

"Well, Turk, we sure have had an adventure today, haven't we?" Bobby was looking down at the little dog and stroking his soft, matted fur as he waited on the sidewalk for the traffic to ease up so that he could cross. Turk was licking Bobby's arm with his soft, wet, pink tongue. The traffic had backed up due to the police car presence on Jog Road, so Bobby was easily able to cross between the bumper-to-bumper gridlock of cars snaking slowly in the southbound lane. Once on the median, Bobby felt a warm wetness on his right forearm, the arm carrying Turk. Turk let out a sigh and looked up at Bobby with his brown doggy eyes and what appeared to be a smile on his face. Bobby looked down into those lovable eyes of the little pup and smiled. He put Turk onto the grass of the median and held tightly to the rope leash. Turk sniffed the grass and the shrubs and then started barking at a large, curly-tailed lizard that was almost as large as a small brown banana. Turk had never seen one of these creatures before, so he kept his distance. Bobby laughed at his little dog, who was so much larger than the lizard but yet seemed fearful of getting too close to this strange, snakelike reptile. Bobby wiped his arm on a white handkerchief that he carried in the rear pocket of his jeans and made a mental note to not blow his nose on that hankie until it was washed. He then picked up the puppy, looked to his right, and, seeing no traffic in the northbound lanes, crossed the road.

The veterinarian's office was located in a freestanding one-story building on the corner of Jog Road and Lake Worth Road, one of the outbuildings that was part of the Winn Dixie Shopping Center. Dr. Walker had purchased the building two years earlier and had completely remodeled the structure. It had been a Denny's restaurant but now was architecturally reconfigured into a veterinary hospital and boarding facility. It was a walk-in clinic for animals. Dr. Walker was an aging veterinarian with silvery-white hair, dark horn-rimmed glasses, and a limp. His son, Gabriel, was also a veterinarian, having studied at the University of Florida, along with his twin sister, Jordan. The two Walker siblings graduated top in their class and had the same love for animals as their father. The general consensus in Palm Beach County was that if you had a sick or injured animal, you took that animal to Walker's. They were the best, and that's just what Bobby was doing; even though Turk was not sick or injured, he needed a full check-up, shots, flea treatment, a bath, a much needed grooming, and lots of food to fatten him up.

Bobby skipped across the three northbound lanes, singing "Grandma Got Run Over by a Reindeer" as he made a beeline for Walker's Veterinary Clinic and Resort. Bobby had outsmarted the dogcatcher, and in a few minutes, he would be purchasing a red collar for Turk and completing the registration process. The plan was coming together. Bobby was almost giddy as he approached the front door of Walker's clinic. He could just visualize Missy's face as he handed her the heavy box wrapped in red-and-green Christmas paper and tied shut with a big red ribbon. Turk would be fat and fuzzy. He would be yapping loudly inside the box. And when she untied the bow, Turk would jump into her arms and give her a big, wet, slurpy kiss, right on the lips.

CHAPTER 49

Saturday, December 19
Walker's Veterinary Clinic and Resort

Walker's Veterinary Clinic and Resort is a Disneyland for dogs, situated on a five-acre plot of land in Lake Worth. "The Resort," as it is known, offers "Doggie Day Care," pampered boarding, an Olympic-sized doggie swimming pool, state-of-the-art surgical facilities, a grooming spa, licensed dietitians, certified nutritionists, dog psychologists, and even psychic mediums who can help owners communicate with their animals. There is also a pet cemetery, a pet crematorium, and memorial chapels for owners of their dearly departed best friends. No expense has been spared by the Walker family in affording only the best of care to the canine world.

The resort has posters everywhere:

"Love Thy Dog."
"A House Is Not a Home without a Dog."
"A Happy Dog Is a Happy Home."
"Ring Bell and Run. Our Dogs Need Exercise."
"Do unto Your Dog as You Would Do unto Yourself."
"I Love Dogs! It's Humans That Annoy Me."
"Have You Hugged Your Dog Today?"
"All You Need Is Love…and a Dog."
"There Is No Limit to How Much Your Dog Will Love You."
"Caution: Dogs Can't Hold Their Licker."
"Your Dog Will Love You in Spite of Yourself. Return the Love."

Bobby felt the energy of this place. He felt the love. The reception area was a rainforest of tropical plants. Bobby listened to the peaceful sound of water trickling off river rock and tumbling into ponds, and his eyes tried to locate the source of the water, which seemed to emanate from granite near the ceiling and cascaded down the jagged rock wall. At the base of this cairn of stones was a large pond that welcomed each droplet of water as it tumbled and splashed its way down to the waiting pool. The room was massive, and each corner had a unique, soothing water feature, one made of coral rock, a second of granite, and a third of limestone. Each waterfall had a pond with large, multicolored koi, golden fish swimming in circles and begging for food. A small bag of fish food was available for purchase for three dollars. Then there was the vertical ceiling-to-floor slab of polished marble. Crystal-clear water sheeted from the top like a curtain of white water cascading down a waterslide and into a pool. It was spellbinding, as if the sheer descent of water were sliding down a slippery slope of shimmering, iridescent glass. Again, like the other waterfalls, a sudsy landing into a misty pond was the final destination for the water that had traveled so deliberately down the dense stone. The room was awash with ferns, orchids, bromeliads, birds of paradise, bamboo, and other tropical and aquatic plants, including lily pads floating in the ponds.

There was a mystical, spiritual feeling of peace and tranquility that punctuated these hallowed walls. Although speakers were not visible, music filled the air with melodious soundscapes of birds happily chirping, waves gently breaking on beaches, and wind blowing through trees and bushes.

An older woman with graying hair stood at the counter behind a computer monitor. She was wearing reading glasses, which balanced precipitously close to the end of her nose, and she was engrossed in a book that explained the spiritual and psychic powers of dogs. This was required reading for all newly hired employees. She looked up and greeted Bobby with a smile and a curious look at the skinny little dog straddled over Bobby's right forearm. She was wearing a name tag that said, "Sharon."

"What have we here?" she asked as she reached out to pet the puppy's small, brown head. Turk watched her every move but detected no threat, so he checked her out by sniffing at the approaching hand. Her fingers softly touched the top of his head and scratched the itch behind his left ear. He thought, *How did this lady know I had an itch behind that ear?* Turk lifted his head and licked her arm. They were friends.

Bobby explained to the lady what needed to be done to Turk to transform the skinny, scruffy fur ball into a soft, fluffy Christmas gift for a little girl. Bobby told Sharon that the raggedy puppy's name was Turk and that his name was Bobby Thornton. They discussed money, and Bobby reached into his pocket. He placed a pile of green paper on the counter, handed Turk to the lady, and headed toward the door.

"Mr. Thornton, don't forget to pick Turk up by three p.m. on Christmas Eve. We will put him in a small, portable doggie carrier for you, OK? The kennel has a handle so that you can easily carry him out to your car."

Bobby didn't tell the lady, Sharon, that he did not have a car, but he thought a carrier would be a good idea. He could wrap it up with green-and-red paper with Turk inside.

"Don't forget that I will need a good leash and a red collar that won't come off. And make sure that he smells kinda perfume-y, OK? And no fleas, all right?"

Sharon cocked her head and said, "Mr. Thornton, this is Walker's! No dog leaves this resort without being in perfect condition. He'll look like a show dog!"

"Thanks, Sharon. I'll see you on the twenty-fourth."

CHAPTER 50

December 19
"Psssst, Psssst, Kenny?"

Bobby was as happy as a cold booger in a warm nose. His escape from the dogcatcher had been successful, his dear puppy was in good hands, and soon he would be back on his bench talking with me. I knew all about the escapades of Bob because Carl the crow had watched Bob and Turk's great adventure while flying high in the sky over Home Depot, while sitting in trees at the Fountains Golf and Country Club, and from his favorite perches on top of concrete light poles. Also, as you know, we trees can talk, and we do. We talk to the bushes, to the grass, and to each other, so our grapevine extends all over, and on this afternoon, Bobby and Turk and that Loony-Toon dogcatcher were the talk of the town. My sparrows were out and about, watching and laughing and cheering Bobby and Turk to the finish line. The sparrows returned first and told me the whole story word for word. Their chatter and laughter went on and on, as did the noise from all the unsold trees on my patio. I was especially delighted that Bobby was returning to the bench. Carl said it might take a while, though, because Bobby was walking kind of slow and singing some Christmas carols as he headed back to Publix. I was anxious to see him. We needed to finish our stories. He had started telling me about Natalie and the Christmas dinner at the center, and I had been telling him about a family who went picnicking on Wildcat Mountain.

It was late afternoon when Bobby arrived at the bench. I was quite agitated by the time he arrived. I liked Bobby more than any human I had ever known, except for maybe Missy, and I was upset that so many Christmas shoppers had passed me by on this, the last Saturday before Christmas.

"Well, Fir, there are only six more days until Christmas. Do we count today? Hmmmm, I don't know. Do you count Christmas Day? Nah. Let's see, today is Saturday. If we don't count today and we don't count Christmas Day, which is next Friday, there are... uh...Sunday, Monday, Tuesday, Wednesday, and Thursday." Bobby started counting out on his fingers, "One, two, three, four, five... That's it, Fir, only five more days." Bobby looked up at me with a big smile on his face, as if he felt he deserved a gold star or something for solving a simple math problem. For the first time since I had met Bobby, I was looking at him with disdain. I was not a happy camper, and yet Bobby seemed so incredibly elated about everything. I thought, *How can a homeless man with so little be so happy about so much?* He reached into his pocket to retrieve some Double Bubble gum and came up empty, just as a Mexican couple stood in front of me and started smiling at each other and talking rapidly in Spanish.

Bobby had taken three or four steps toward the Publix entrance to buy more gum, but he did a quick about-face and returned to the bench. Bobby did not sit down, but he did something that blew me away—he started talking to the Mexican couple in Spanish. "*El arbol no esta bien. Es viejo y cansado, y el otro lado del arbol esta roto. Mira.*" And then he came over to me and turned me around to show them my broken branch. The man and his wife and their three children walked over to another tree. They called Kenny, who lifted my friend Butch and, after securing him in an orange mesh sleeve, tied Butch to the top of their car.

What just happened? I thought. Bobby had just ruined my sale to that nice couple. I had just gone from sad to mad, from wallowing in my own self-pity to furious, and all of my anger was directed at Bobby. But he was oblivious to my pathetic emotional meltdown, and he about-faced and headed into Publix for his gum. I stood there and seethed. Bobby had left me against the wall with my backside facing the world. My broken branch and gaping hole were on display for all the Christmas tree shoppers, and no one seemed the least bit interested in looking at me, much less buying me and taking me home.

Kenny returned to the patio and reconnected the hose so that he could rehydrate us while at the same time washing off all of the dried brown needles that had dropped from our branches. He sprayed water all over each tree, and when he came to me, he became upset that I had been turned in such a position that my broken branch was my most prominent feature. Kenny also noted that I was leaning precariously against the wall and in dire peril of falling down.

"What the…? What happened to you, little fella?"

"LITTLE FELLA?" I yelled. "How dare you? I'm seven feet tall! How tall are you?"

I don't know what made me blurt out to Kenny that way. I had never spoken to any of the humans besides Bobby and Missy, and Kenny was always so good to me, and here I was yelling at him. I think I was still mad at Bobby and taking it out on poor Kenny.

Kenny jumped back, and I almost fell to the ground. Hose in hand, he sprayed fresh water on me, and then he surprised me with what he said next. "I thought you could talk! I knew it! I've been hanging around you a lot lately, and I thought I heard you talking to that little girl the other day."

"Missy? Her name is Missy, but I'm very particular in whom I talk to."

"Oh yeah? I hear you talking to that Loony-Toon homeless guy who sits on the bench and blows bubbles all day. So how can you say that you are particular about who you talk to?"

"Bobby? Bobby is not a Loony Toon, and you better not let him hear that you called him a Loony Toon. He is a war veteran. He served in Iraq and Afghanistan, and I think he is Special Forces or Green Beret or something like that."

"Golly, Mr. Tree, I didn't mean nothin' bad. My dad is a veteran. He was a navy SEAL. Please don't tell your friend Bobby nothin' bad about me. I just see him acting a little goofy sometimes, and I thought…"

"Shhhh, here he comes now, Kenny. And my name's Fir. You can call me Fir. And by the way, how tall are you, Shorty?"

"I'm six feet, six inches tall, Mr. Fir, and I play basketball for Santaluces High School. You were just tilted sideways against that wall, so you did not look to be seven feet tall. Mr. Fir, seven feet is really tall! You are a giant of a tree, OK?"

"OK, Kenny, and it's just Fir, not Mr. Fir. Mr. Fir was my father, and he's about *fourteen* feet tall, so don't mess with him."

Bobby slowly ambled toward the bench, chewing vigorously on his mouthful of bubble gum. He looked like he was sucking on a softball and trying to chew the cover off. Kenny straightened me up and turned my bad side toward the wall. I whispered to Kenny in a whisper that only he could hear, "Pssssst, Kenny. Psssst, Kenny!"

Kenny came close and stuck his head in among my branches like he was looking for a bug or something. My sparrows were together on a higher limb, watching and listening to all that was going on. Kenny looked silly with his head inside a Christmas tree and his butt sticking out, bobbing and weaving for the whole world to see. Everybody who walked by pointed and chuckled at the funny-looking bag boy with his head in a tree. Kenny was looking for my mouth, but everyone knows that trees don't have mouths. "Hee, hee, hee."

"Kenny," I whispered, "don't tell anybody that you talk to trees. They'll think you're daft. They'll think that you are a Loony Toon."

With that, Mr. Kemp came walking by after punching out for the day. He noticed all the customers laughing at the tall bag boy with his head inside a Christmas tree, and he yelled in Kenny's direction, "Kenny! Kenny, what the heck do you think you're doing?"

Kenny backed out of my branches and stood tall and at attention as he looked down at the shorter Mr. Kemp.

Kenny stuttered as he searched for an answer for his boss. "Er, er, uh, I was trying to find a, uh, uh, a piece of bubble gum that Mr. Bob threw to me. I missed the piece of gum, and I think it went into this tree."

CHAPTER 51

"Kenny, I Hate Rap!"

Bobby was sitting on the bench, chewing the five pieces of Double Bubble and grinning from ear to ear. "That's right, Mr. Kemp, would you like a piece?"

Before he could respond to Bobby's offer, Bobby stood up, reached in his pocket, and tossed a rectangle of gum in Mr. Kemp's direction. Kemp tried to snag it out of the air, but he missed, and the piece of Double Bubble came to rest under one of the other trees.

"Thanks for the offer, Bobby, but I've just had some dental work done, and my dentist told me not to chew gum or eat apples until the work is completed."

"That's funny, Mr. Kemp. You're the produce manager, and you can't eat apples."

A big smile came over Kenny's face. I was laughing my needles off, and, quietly, even my sparrows were snickering. Mr. Kemp seemed to turn a light shade of red.

"Well, I have to be on my way. You have a good day, Bobby, and Kenny, why not give that tree a drink of water and keep your head out of its branches?" Mr. Kemp turned and headed toward his car, the crowd dispersed, and Bobby blew a very large bubble, which popped all over his face.

"Thanks, Mr. Bobby. You just saved my bacon!"

"Think nothing of it, Kenny. Sometimes a man's bacon needs saving. You are good to Fir, and he likes you a lot!"

"He likes you a lot too, Mr. Bobby, but he told me that you sometimes irritate him."

"What are you talking about, Kenny? You and these trees been talking to each other? You on drugs, Kenny, or what? What exactly did this tree say to you?"

"The tree, Mr. Bobby, told me his name is Fir. He told me that he talks to you and that you talk to him."

"Kenny, you are a pretty tall young man. You play basketball or football?"

"Both, Mr. Bobby."

"Stop with the Mr. Bobby stuff, Kenny. I am just plain ol' Bobby. Anyway, I think you've been hit in the head too many times. Trees can't talk, Kenny." And with that, Bobby blew another large bubble, stretched his arms out on the back of the bench, and smiled at the blue sky above.

Bobby and I watched Kenny as he twisted the nozzle onto the end of his black hose so that he could once again mist us trees. Although he had just misted us, Mr. Kemp told him to do it again, so he was doing it again. He had learned that from his dad, the retired navy SEAL. "Always follow orders, son. *Never* have to be told twice to do something that you were told to do the first time."

As he stood in front of me, misting my needles, I listened to him singing—if you can call it that. Some kind of teenage jibber-jabber. Rap, I think it's called. Yes, he was listening to rap, and I hate rap. Rap is an abomination and should not be called music.

But Kenny obviously liked it, and because he was wearing earbuds, he was oblivious to the fact that he was singing loudly enough to be heard by everyone walking in and out of the store or sitting in the breezeway. His mouth was going a mile a minute as he loudly sang along to the music he was listening to:

"I'm gonna walk into a red brick wall, and hit my head and fall, fall, fall.

I'm gonna slip on a 'nana peel, and hit my head and bruise my heel.

Don't ja fall down and bust yer head, cause you'll end up in a hospital bed.

Don't ja hit that wall you nut, cause you'll bang yer head and fall on yer butt.

Don't do nutting to make you cry like sticking yer thumb into yer eye.

Don't eat food that make you fat, feed it to the crows and feed it to the rats…"

Kenny was in his own world, listening to that God-awful music and *rapping* along with the goofy guy who wrote it and singing those inane lyrics. Bobby and I were getting irritated, but the misty water Kenny was spraying on me sure felt good.

"Hey, Bobby, are you listening to this crappy rap that is coming out of Kenny's mouth? Did you ever hear anything so awful?"

I watched Bobby blow another bubble, stand up, and start walking down the breezeway toward his corner. He looked back at me and said, "See ya tomorrow, Fir. I can't stand that rap stuff either, and I'm going home. I've had enough. I'm leaving. Too bad you don't have legs. You could come with me. We could finish our stories. See ya, glad I not be ya." And then he turned the corner and headed toward the field where he lives, leaving me behind with this wannabe rapper.

And that's pretty much the way Saturday went. Shoppers in and out of the store, couples with rambunctious kids, people lifting me and turning me and throwing me down when they saw my broken branch. Kenny continued to chirp like a wounded bird, but every time he saw me on the ground, he would pick me up. He didn't talk to me, but he did stare at me a lot. I didn't talk to him either, but he wouldn't have heard me anyway with those earbuds that he was wearing. My sparrows flew over to another tree near Publix, where the speakers were playing Christmas music.

Cold fronts routinely move through Florida all winter, but South Florida only gets the tail end of the fronts. Ohio, Michigan, Wisconsin, and New York are blasted by freezing ice and snow, blizzards, and skies so gray that you can't see the sun for weeks. I could see the clouds rolling in, and I knew that we would have a little wind, then a couple of hours of rain, and afterward, the temperature would drop down into the fifties. *Brrrrrr.* Ha, on my mountain in Murphy, the temperature would be in the teens, and all living things would be shivering, except for me. I'm a Fraser fir. But not here in Lake Worth; you know, this was not such a bad place to live after all, if only Kenny would shut up and someone would adopt me. *Oh well,* I thought, *I'm going to sleep.* The wind blew, the rains came, the store closed for the night, and I dreamed of white bunnies, spotted deer, and beautifully colored wildflowers in Murphy, North Carolina.

CHAPTER 52

Sunday, December 20
Coot Wakes Bobby

Sunday morning was cool—not cold, but cool enough that Bobby zipped up his sleeping bag and cocooned himself inside like a caterpillar waiting to emerge as a butterfly. Bobby was dreaming of Natalie, Turk, and Missy and Christmas carols, when he was abruptly awakened by that squawking coot. Bobby knew it was eight o'clock, because this same routine awakened him every morning. He wished that he could roll over and fall back asleep, but he knew it was futile with all that racket outside, so he climbed out of his tent and walked over to the oak tree where he'd first met Turk. Bobby sat down, leaned against the mighty oak, and reflected on the beauty of this world. He looked out at his sparkling lake, the sun slowly rising on the distant horizon, and its reflection on the placid water. He watched bushy-tailed squirrels chasing each other up and down and all around the tree where he sat. Birds were chirping the melodies of morning, and white wading birds were walking the shoreline, with their long yellow legs bending backward and their needle-nosed beaks stabbing small fish for breakfast. An omnipresent breeze was blowing off the lake, but this morning he also smelled the salty, fishy odors of the Atlantic Ocean, which was only about ten miles to the east of his waterfront campsite.

Although seagulls are saltwater beach birds, these scavengers frequented the dump sites, lakes, and almost anywhere near the coast where an easy meal was to be found. As Bobby leaned up against his crusty old oak tree, soaking up the warm morning sun, he watched several white gulls ripping the flesh off a dead fish on the other side of his lake.

These voracious, selfish birds fight each other for a fish that is much too large for any one of them to consume, but I guess that is their nature, he thought, shaking his head.

A graceful brown pelican circled his lake, searching for an unsuspecting fish, and when it spotted its prey, the pelican dove head first like a missile, wings held close to its sides, into the cold water. The fish never knew what hit it.

"Pow! Wow! He was pelican chow. Now...and how!" Bobby chuckled at the rhymes he made. "How now, brown cow!"

Bobby watched the pelican disappear under the water only to resurface and float like a duck, with a large fish in its pouch. He thought, *What an incredible display of fishing prowess.* The pelican swallowed its fish whole, and Bobby watched the large lump in the pelican's throat gradually disappear as the fish swam downstream to the pelican's belly, never to be seen again.

Seagulls and terns are ever present in the skies of Lake Worth, as is an occasional pelican—all saltwater birds. But the coot is a freshwater bird; this was his lake, and he wanted everybody to know it. So he continued to blow his horn as if he were the bugle boy at boot camp in charge of waking up the troops. But Bobby was not in the army anymore, and he could sleep as long as he liked but for that darned black waterbird.

Bobby rose and stood on his tippy-toes, trying to locate that noisy fowl, but as always, the coot was somewhere behind the bulrushes, obviously hiding and successfully avoiding Bobby's watchful eyes. Bobby walked over to the water and stuck his toe in to test the temperature. "Yikes," blurted Bobby. "That water is freezing." He picked up a couple of pebbles and threw them in the direction of the coot, but this only made the bird squawk louder. Bobby returned to his tent and began the process of tearing down his campsite. He rolled up his sleeping bag, put his dirty clothes in a duffle bag, stowed all his things in the rusty old car, and headed to the laundromat.

CHAPTER 53

Sunday, December 20
Rose's Laundromat

Today was Wash Day. With his duffel bag over his shoulder, Bobby headed toward the Publix shopping center, where Rose's Coin Laundry was located. Rose was anything but a rose. She had spent much too much time in the sun, and her skin was dark brown, hard, and waxy, like that of a lizard. Rose was an older woman, probably in her sixties, maybe older, maybe younger, but too many cigarettes and too many adult drinks had caused her to look much older than she probably was. Rose had not taken care of her teeth; I'm not sure, but I think she only had three or four good ones left in her mouth. She coughed a lot because of the years of smoking cigarettes, but every time she would start to cough, she would light another cancer stick—that's what Bobby's dad called cigarettes when Bobby was a boy. His father would say, "Now, Bobby, don't ever let me catch you smoking one of those cancer sticks, 'cause if the cancer don't kill you, then I'll whoop you to death." Bobby's dad didn't mean it about whooping him to death, but he said it to scare him. And it worked. Bobby never smoked or did drugs, because his dad had warned him of the consequences. Bobby looked at Rose, sitting in her wooden chair next to the Coke machine, coughing and looking all around the laundromat, but he quickly turned away when she spotted him.

"Bobby, how the heck be ya?" Rose was from some podunk town someplace where they didn't have indoor plumbing, and

Bobby swore that she never went to school. But she was reasonably nice, although somewhat cranky, a woman who complained about almost everything and who talked and talked and talked but never really said anything. Bobby told me that he didn't believe that she ever took a breath when she talked, except to take a drag on her cigarette. But Bobby said that she was a pretty nice ol' gal in spite of herself.

"I'm fine, Rose. How are you doin'?" Bobby knew that was the wrong thing to ask her because she would start her nonstop answer, so he cut her off before she could respond. "Which are your best two machines? I am in a hurry this morning. I am going to try and go to the Baptist church over on Military Trail for the morning service."

"Number two for washing and number sixteen for drying, Bobby. Do you need any soap or quarters?"

"Yes, ma'am, here's a ten-dollar bill. Give me fifty quarters."

"Bobby, I wasn't born yesterday. Everybody knows there are only thirty quarters in a ten-dollar bill." And with that, she gave him thirty quarters and stuffed his ten in her pocket.

Bobby knew that Rose had kept ten of his quarters, but he didn't mind. It was a kind of game she played with Bobby. Sometimes she even gave him fifty quarters for a ten-spot. Rose went back to her chair and grinned. She did not make eye contact with Bobby, and he did not have to listen to her incessant talking while he washed and dried his clothes. That in itself was worth ten quarters.

Forty-five minutes later, Bobby had all his clothes clean and neatly folded, and he looked back to say goodbye to Rose as he walked out the door. She was still grinning. She thought she had pulled a fast one on Bobby.

It was quickly approaching 9:45 in the morning, and church services started at 10:45 a.m. He should have just enough time if he hurried. Back to the rusty old car to hide his clean clothes, a quick hike up the road to the community center for a shower and a shave, and a change of clothes, and then off to the First Baptist Church on Military Trail. Bobby had rented a locker at the community center, where he kept his cologne, aftershave, razor, toothbrush, comb, deodorant, and mousse, which were used for his personal hygiene. The center also had hot showers and toilet facilities for use by Lake Worth's homeless population, and best of all, it was around the corner from First Baptist. Bobby looked spiffy. He stowed his dirty duds in his locker and would return for them later, after worship services.

CHAPTER 54

Sunday, December 20
First Baptist

B obby had purchased a used "no-name" watch at the thrift store, and as he glanced down at his wrist, he noted that it was approaching 10:15 a.m. He would have to hurry if he wanted a seat. According to the Bible, as best as Bobby could recollect, Sundays were supposed to be a day of rest, and Bobby usually took that literally—to mean lounging around and doing nothing. But today, this Sunday, the Sunday before Christmas, something was driving him to attend services at the First Baptist, where Reverend Moore was the young, motivational pastor. Josh Moore, a good ol' boy from North Carolina, was married with two ruffian little sons, Harry and Doug, ages six and eight, respectively. Carolyn was the preacher's wife, and although she was a bit on the plump side, she was absolutely gorgeous, with skin of alabaster and a sparkle in her eyes that most surely came from the heavens itself.

Bobby secured his locker and high-tailed it out of the community center, which was no more than two blocks from the church. He could hear the bells ringing and knew that he must hurry. First Baptist had an excellent choir, and today Carolyn, who doubled as music director and preacher's wife, would lead the choir in presenting the annual musical Christmas pageant. Children would be dressed as kings and shepherds, and Carolyn would sing a solo, "O Holy Night." The sanctuary would be filled with her angelic voice, the subtle harmonic hum of the choir, the darkening effect of lights dimming inside the church, and the single spotlight that would appear from above and shine brightly on Carolyn like the light from a single star. Bobby had attended the pageant last year and was spellbound by the beauty of Carolyn's hymn and the effect that her song had on his inner being. He had been mesmerized and, at that very moment, touched by an angel.

He knew that he must not be late, so he stepped up his pace as the church bells rang in the distance. Bobby could see cars turning into the parking lot, with traffic being directed by a police officer, with the blue lights of his patrol car flashing. Bobby was thankful that he did not have a car to park. He jogged straight toward the church, then slowed to a walk as he approached the steps leading up to the main building. Men and women were milling around, dressed in their "go to church" clothes and chatting with each other; wives in new Christmas dresses were hugging each other, and husbands in suits were giving high fives to their buddies. Impish young boys were running in circles around their dads while little girls in beautifully frilly outfits clung tightly to their mother's legs. Pastor Josh and Carolyn were standing next to the open double doors, welcoming their flock to the Sunday service and directing them inside, where they would be seated by the ushers.

Bobby quickly climbed the seven steps and took his place at the end of the receiving line, and that's when he heard a familiar voice call out his name.

"Mr. Thornton?"

Bobby looked down, and there, standing right in front of him, was Missy, in a brand-new red dress that flared out at the knees. She had a red bow in her hair and was wearing black patent-leather shoes, and standing right next to her, with a big smile on her face, was none other than Natalie. "Well, as I live and breathe. Is that you, Mr. Thornton? Merry Christmas." Natalie moistened her lips and tossed her head to the side to reposition hair that had fallen into her eyes.

Bobby was so excited to see Natalie and Missy that he was stammering his words. "Yeah, yes, uh, it is me, Ms. McCord. Uh, Ms. McCord, please call me Bobby, and Merry Christmas to you and

Missy." This was kind of a game that they were playing for Missy's sake. Missy was totally unaware that they had been meeting at the community center for the past month and that they had become quite fond of each other and had been on a first-name basis with each other for the past month.

Missy looked up at Bobby and asked, "Mr. Thornton, can you sit with us—that is, if it's all right with Mommy?"

Natalie's eyes met Bobby's, and they smiled at each other.

"Yes, sure, Missy, that would be fine, if Mr. Thornton isn't with someone and he would like to sit with us. Mr. Thornton...uh, Bobby...would you like to sit with us?"

"I'd love to, Ms. McCord, uh...Natalie."

The receiving line began to move again, and Natalie placed both hands on Missy's shoulders so that she would be single file in front of her mother.

Mr. and Mrs. Compton, an elderly couple who both walked with canes, were in front of Missy, shaking hands with Carolyn and the preacher and talking about all the changes they had witnessed at First Baptist. Natalie took her right hand off of Missy's shoulder and turned to locate Bobby. Her fingers brushed against Bobby's hand, sending a shudder up and down his spine. He felt flushed, and his heart began to race, and then a breeze blew the soft, sheer fabric of her yellow dress against his hand. Just as he was trying to collect himself, she grasped his hand with hers and whispered softly into his ear. The warmth of her breath was almost too much for Bobby to bear.

"Me too, Natalie. Me too."

People in their eighties don't move very fast, and they just love to meander and talk with old friends, but once the Comptons were ushered to their pews, the line moved briskly. However, most of the worshippers had bypassed the logjam that had developed at the top of the steps, and rather than shake hands with the pastor, they circumvented the receiving line and sought out the few remaining places to sit. Missy, Natalie, and Bobby were welcomed and hugged and were ushered to the last three seats in the last pew. Pastor Moore and his wife made their way into the sanctuary, where the choir was already singing Christmas carols. Hymnals were open; parishioners were singing; the warm, warbling organ music vibrated and hummed; and the piano tinkled and resonated with the melodies of the holidays. Carolyn took her place as music director and led the next Christmas carol, "Joy to the World," after which the church grew silent as Pastor Moore approached the pulpit.

"Good morning! Welcome to First Baptist! We are so happy to have you here today as we celebrate this most wonderful time of the year, the birthday of our Christ. Our pageant will begin shortly, but first I need to ask that all our little helpers please come down to their designated areas to gather and put on their costumes."

Bobby watched Missy stand and ease her way past the ten or so people sitting between them and the aisle. She then hurried toward the front of the church, where the other children were disappearing behind huge canvases to don their costumes. Several members of the church were talented artists, and they had painted a mural of the streets of Bethlehem and the manger where the Christ child would be born. The canvases were eight feet tall and depicted the deserted streets of the city and the stables where Mary and Joseph would spend the night, where Mary would give birth to the baby Jesus.

The lights dimmed, and a single spotlight illuminated Carolyn, who stood alone, clad in her choir robe. The sanctuary grew deathly silent as the organ began to play the prelude to "O Holy Night," and the children, dressed like winged cherubs, surrounded Carolyn Moore as she sang like the angel she was.

"O holy night, the stars are brightly shining…"

Natalie reached over and gently held Bobby's hand. She turned to her right and whispered in his ear, "I'm so glad you're here, Bobby,"

She squeezed his hand, and he gently squeezed back. Bobby so hoped that she would not let go. Natalie nestled herself closer to Bobby and twice laid her head on his shoulder as Carolyn sang her first solo.

When she finished, Pastor Moore, who stood at the podium on the left side of the stage, asked that the congregation stand so that he could lead them in prayer. "Thank you, oh Lord, for bringing us all together on this, the last Sunday before Christmas Day... Amen."

CHAPTER 55

The Pageant

Bobby was thankful, more thankful than he had ever been before in his entire lifetime. Thankful to be here today with Natalie, thankful for having met Natalie, and thankful that Natalie cared for him. Bobby said a prayer of his own and thanked God for Natalie. The pastor finished his prayer, and the pageant began.

Bobby focused on the stage and saw Missy carrying a small, life-like doll in swaddling clothes. She knelt next to a manger, where she laid the Christ child. Kings, shepherds, and wise men brought gifts while the choir sang songs of joy and adoration. Angels with feathered wings surrounded the baby Jesus, and the choir sang "Joy to the World." A single spotlight shone down from the ceiling on the newborn king, and the pageant ended with everyone joining in and singing "Silent Night."

A Baptist service always ends with the preacher inviting anyone in attendance who may have been touched by the Holy Spirit to come down and offer their profession of faith. Visitors are welcomed to join the church, and the choir sings the invitational hymn "Softly and Tenderly," "Wherever He Leads I Go," or "Just as I Am."

An invisible tap on his shoulder and an overwhelming warmth in his heart called out to Bobby, who stood and made his way down the aisle to talk with Pastor Moore about joining the church. Natalie was awestruck, with tears of joy streaming down her face as she watched her man rise from his seat and begin his slow walk toward the town of Bethlehem, where the children still quietly sat. Dr. Moore, the deacons, and Carolyn all greeted and hugged the radiant Bobby Thornton. Josh introduced Bobby to the congregation and asked everyone to come up front and meet this fine young man who had asked to be part of the First Baptist family. The preacher said one last prayer and thanked God for bringing Bobby to be baptized and to be born again. Although the service was over, Bobby shook hands with and was welcomed by hundreds of members, strangers who would become future friends.

Missy ran up to Bobby and tugged at his sleeve. "Mr. Thornton, Mr. Thornton, you're just like Mommy and me now!"

Bobby looked down at little Missy, who was still wearing her costume from the pageant, and tilted his head sideways, puzzled by what she meant.

"We're all Baptists now, Mr. Thornton!" A massive smile had erupted on her face, and she extended her arms to give Bobby a congratulatory hug. Then Natalie opened her arms and embraced Bobby with a very special, warm hug of her own.

Missy slipped her small hand into Bobby's, Natalie grasped his other hand, and with Bobby in the center, flanked by his two girls, they walked down the aisle toward the rear of the church.

"How about some lunch, Bobby? Are you hungry, Missy?" Natalie wanted to celebrate. "The Country Inn is just up the road on Military Trail, and they serve the best fried chicken and biscuits in Lake Worth."

Missy looked up at her mother and said, "But Mommy, you said we could go to Publix after church and that we could sit on the bench and share a sub and that I could look at the Christmas trees. Please, Mommy, please, please?"

"But, Missy, this is a very special occasion. Bobby has joined First Baptist today, and we need to celebrate."

Missy began to sulk. She was no longer holding Bobby's hand, her face was splotchy, and her eyes were red and moist. She wanted so much to see *me* and to talk and to tell me about Bobby joining the church and maybe even hear another story. But Missy was a very mature little girl for her age, and she knew that her mother was right, that they should celebrate at the Country Inn. She looked up and said, "OK, Mommy, OK."

Bobby looked into Missy's blue eyes, but the happy, smiley face had disappeared. The whites of her eyes had turned a pinkish red, and her little girl giggles had gone away.

Natalie grabbed Missy's hand, and they headed toward the old Chevy Caprice. Natalie's other hand was discreetly holding Bobby's fingers, but Missy didn't notice because she was holding her head down and kicking rocks through the parking lot.

Missy slowly opened the creaky rear door and climbed into the back seat. Natalie sat behind the steering wheel, fastened her seat belt, and turned toward Bobby.

Bobby looked at Missy, Natalie's beautiful little girl in the red dress, sitting quiet and forlorn in the back seat. Her disappointment was chilling. The Chevy felt cold inside even though there was no AC. Bobby decided to try and change that, so he looked into Natalie's eyes, leaned over, and whispered into her ear, "How do you feel about splitting a sub at Publix, Natalie? They have a chicken tender sub that is to die for, or if you so prefer, it being Christmas and all, we could share a Boar's Head turkey sub. It's such a beautiful afternoon, Natalie. We could just sit on the bench and talk, maybe hold hands when Missy's not watching, and enjoy the sweet smells of the Christmas trees. What do ya say?"

Natalie looked back at her daughter sitting in the back seat. Missy was fiddling with her fingers and wearing the disappointed face of a child with a broken heart.

"Missy? Bobby wants to know if we could go to Publix for a sub instead of fried chicken at the Country Inn. Would you be upset if we didn't go to the restaurant?"

The creases in her forehead became smooth, her frown transformed into a smile, her blotchy face cleared up almost instantly, and her tearful red eyes showed no signs of sadness.

"Oh, Mommy, that would be wonderful. We can go to the Country Inn next week after church, OK?" She fastened her seatbelt, brushed the windblown hair out of her eyes, and smiled affectionately at Bobby. "That's a really good idea, Mr. Thornton, and we can see Mr. Fir."

Natalie looked over at Bobby as he was buckling up, raised her eyebrows, and whispered, "I just don't understand this fixation she has with that tree."

Bobby turned his head, wiped his brow, peeked back at Missy, and winked at the little girl in the red dress. "Well, Natalie, Fir is a special tree. Maybe I could buy him for you? What do you think?"

"Oh, yes, Mommy, and we can take him home today, put him by the picture window, and decorate him this afternoon."

"No, Missy, I told you that a fresh tree is just not in the cards this year. We have a perfectly good artificial tree in the garage, and besides, Mr. Thornton cannot afford to be buying us a Christmas tree that we really don't need. So enough about this 'Mr. Fir'!"

Natalie turned the key, and with no hesitation, the Chevy Caprice came to life with a thunderous roar. She backed out of her parking spot on the grass, turned left onto the asphalt driveway, and then turned left again onto Military Trail.

Bobby Thornton had a way of turning sadness into happiness, frowns into smiles, and forehead creases into smooth skin. He again peeked into the back seat, because he too wanted Natalie to take me home to be Missy's Christmas tree.

I wanted nothing more.

Missy sat there, happy on the one hand to be going to Publix but sad that her mom was so adamant about not buying me. Bobby broke the icy silence by changing the subject.

"Missy, you know the Christmas Carnival over at Saint Matthew's Catholic Church? How would you and your mother like to be my guests tomorrow night? You know that tomorrow is the last night of the carnival, don't you? And I just happen to have four free passes for unlimited rides, so you can bring a friend if you like… that is, if it's all right with your mom."

"Well…uh…I guess so, but Bobby," said Natalie, "I have to work until four thirty p.m. on Monday, and I absolutely must be home by seven p.m." As Natalie turned left onto Lantana Road, she whispered to Bobby, "My attorney and Missy's dad are coming to the house to sign some important papers. Can we meet you at Saint Matthew's at five p.m.?"

"No problem, Natalie. I'll meet you at five o'clock, and we'll stay until six thirty, OK?"

"Mommy? Who should we ask to go with us? Mr. Thornton said he has four tickets."

"That's totally up to you, Missy. You think about it, and we can make some calls when we get home this afternoon."

Missy sat in the back seat, smiling and thinking about whom to invite. She looked out the window at cars passing in the opposite direction. She looked to the right and saw her elementary school and started thinking about classmates she could ask. She thought of Mrs. Williams but dismissed that idea when she remembered that Mrs. Williams got tired easily and didn't like to walk too much. She told Missy that her legs get tired. Then Missy blurted out, "I've got it, Mommy. I'll invite Mr. Fir!"

Natalie almost ran off the road. She turned her head toward Missy and gave a hard stare at her daughter.

"Just kidding, Mom. Don't have a hissy."

Natalie turned right into the Publix parking lot, and that's when I spotted the old faded Chevy Caprice with my favorite people inside.

Missy was jumping up and down in the back seat at the prospect of talking with me and maybe listening to one of my stories.

"What are you so happy about, Missy?" Natalie asked.

"Talking to Mr. Fir, of course, Mom. He is so interesting to talk to. I just love him to bits, Mommy."

Natalie shook her head as she thought of a talking tree. But as she thought about the way that Bobby had put out the fire of sadness in the back seat, she had nothing but adoration for Bobby Thornton, the newest member of First Baptist and her own personal fireman. This man gladdened her heart.

Missy was now chattering happily with Bobby about rabbits and possums and deer, and Bobby was laughing about a skinny mountain man who was scared off by a bear. *What incredible imagi-nations,* Natalie thought as she drove up and down each lane look-ing for a parking space.

The old Chevy wasn't much to look at, but the engine purred like a kitten, even though the odometer read 269,412 miles. Synthetic oil changes every five thousand miles and regular maintenance of the hoses, belts, tires, and brakes made her a very dependable car, but she *was* tired, and little things like knobs, straps, torn uphol-stery, and a broken power-window switch made her appear to be ready for the junk heap. Natalie was happy that this was a cool day, because just last week, the air conditioner had quit working, and the mechanic said it would cost over six hundred dollars to repair. Yes, the Caprice was growing old and tired. Her headliner was sagging, and the once-golden gloss of a paint job was now rusty brown, weathered by the wind, burnt by the sun, and faded by Father Time. Natalie glanced over at Bobby as she began search-ing for a place to park, and she murmured an apology for the con-dition of her car. "I'm glad it's not hot today, Bobby. My AC is not working. I wish you could roll down your window, but the window thingamajig is broken." And then she began to cry.

Missy extended her arms and touched her mother on the shoulder and said, "Don't cry, Mommy, this is a wonderful car. It's like Mr. Fir! Mr. Fir is a beautiful Christmas tree. He just has a broken branch. We don't need air conditioning or a new window thingamajig."

Bobby gently grasped Natalie's hand and said, "I can fix the broken switch, and I can repair your air conditioner too. I'm pretty handy when it comes to cars, Natalie. I'll have this Chevy looking like new in no time."

And then she slowed, as she spotted a car pulling out of a space not far from the store. The Caprice pulled in, and Natalie turned off the engine.

CHAPTER 56

Sunday, December 20
A Car Almost Runs Over Missy

I was leaning up against the wall where Kenny had placed me that morning when I saw Natalie's clunker of a car come rolling to a stop in a Publix parking space. I watched with interest as three doors opened and my sweet little Missy, her mother, and of all people, Bobby Thornton, climbed out of the car and walked in my direction.

Five stop signs slow down traffic that otherwise would be colliding with shoppers in the Publix. Pedestrians have the right of way in parking lots, but not all drivers obey the rules of the road. A white Dodge pickup truck came barreling past the Publix breezeway, ignoring the stop signs and forcing shoppers to stop walking to and from the store so as to avoid being hit. Missy spotted me and broke loose from her mother and started to run toward the bench. She was on a collision course with the white truck. I yelled as loud as I could, but as I told you before, trees whisper, so she could not hear me.

Bobby saw what was about to happen and bolted toward where Missy was about to get hit. I never saw a human run so fast, like a sprinter on a track team or a deer in the forest. Bobby grabbed Missy by the left arm and jerked her backward just as the truck sped by, oblivious to the fact that he had almost hit a little girl.

Natalie was running too, and when she caught up with Bobby and Missy, all she could do was cry and hug her beloved daughter and beloved Bobby.

"Missy, don't ever do that again! You almost got run over by that truck." Natalie kneeled down and held her little girl and tried to allay her fears. Missy was scared, and because Natalie was crying, Missy was crying too.

"I'm sorry, Mommy," Missy sobbed. "I just got so excited when I saw Mr. Fir that I wanted to run to him as fast as I could and give him a big hug."

Natalie picked up her daughter and held her close, grateful that no harm had come to her precious child, and carried her through the parking lot to the green bench.

I watched as Missy was kissed and hugged by Natalie. A perfect world existed on my patio. All was right with the world.

Then, without warning, Missy pulled free and was hugging me. *Wow, this is going to be a great day,* I thought.

CHAPTER 57

Sunday, December 20
Fir and Missy, before the Picnic

Missy's crying had stopped as she wrapped her arms around me. Her embrace was soothing and seemed to energize me. All my angst and worry seemed to dissipate from my body. My sparrows flew down from the oaks, where they had been hunting for bugs, and settled in on their favorite branch. They too loved Missy, and they too felt the energy from her small body soothing their little feathered souls. Missy peeked behind me and located my broken branch and held the two pieces together. The branch was broken, not broken off, and when she held the two parts together, I was able to infuse nutrients into the end that dangled and drooped. I transferred water and food, minerals, and electrolytes to the entire broken limb. The needles perked up almost immediately, and the pain of the break seemed to totally disappear. I smiled at Missy and admired her beautiful red dress.

"Missy, you look so beautiful. Is that a new dress? I've missed you. Are you going to be able to stay for a while? Isn't this a beautiful day? Why is Mr. Thornton with you? Are you still coming to Publix on Wednesday, and are *you* going to tell *me* a story?"

"So many questions, Mr. Fir. You asked so many questions that I can't remember them all."

"Well, let me ask them one at a time. I've missed you, and I just have so much to talk about. Where have you been, and what have you been doing this morning?"

"That's not one of your questions. You just added another."

"Sorry, but you look so beautiful, so dressed up, that I want to hear about your morning, Missy."

"OK, Mr. Fir. Mommy took me to the First Baptist this morning. We go there every Sunday, but this Sunday we had a Christmas pageant, and we met Bobby there, and he sat with us in the rear pew."

"What's a First Baptist, Missy, and what's a pew?"

"Mr. Fir, you don't know what a First Baptist is? Didn't they teach you anything in North Carolina?"

"Missy, I was born and raised in the country, on the side of a hill, and all I ever saw were other trees, bushes, and animals. Oh, yes, and an occasional country boy that would come walking through my grove with a gun or a bear trap. I saw cars driving down the road next to me, but I have no clue what a First Baptist or a pew is."

"Oh, yeah, I forgot that you are a tree." The sparrows were looking back and forth at me and Missy as we talked, as if they were watching a ping-pong match. I think they were getting a kick out of our conversation, because I heard them snicker more than once. Birds can fly, so they knew about First Baptist, but I really don't think they knew what a pew was.

"Mr. Fir, First Baptist is the church that Mommy and I attend, and a pew is the long wooden bench that we sit on inside of the church."

"Oh," I whispered, "and what else do they do in churches, Missy?"

"Another question—you have so many questions. Mr. Fir, you know your mountain in North Carolina? You know how beautiful it is when the sun rises and the sky is blue and the breezes blow gently and the birds sing? Do you remember how peaceful you felt when you watched the flowers bloom and the animals play? That's what church is. It's a beautiful place to go on Sunday, a place where there is friendship, peace, tranquility, and happiness. Mommy takes me to church every Sunday. I see my friends from school, and we play outside while Mommy talks with their moms, and when we go inside, we all sing songs, just like the birds on Wildcat Mountain. Sometimes, my friends and I start giggling and my mom has to shush me. As the sun reflects through stained glass windows, the rays of light bathe our church in the colors of a rainbow, just like a garden of flowers. It's so beautiful, Mr. Fir, and the preacher always tells us interesting stories, and he talks about all the nice people in the world. He talks about heaven, and he talks about our souls, that special spirit that makes each of us unique. That's what a church is, Mr. Fir."

"Wow, Missy, I wish I could go to church with you. It sounds wonderful."

"It is, Mr. Fir, and…"

CHAPTER 58

Sunday, December 20
Publix Picnic Subs

"Missy," called Natalie, "we have to go inside Publix and get our subs."

"OK, Mommy, I'll be right there. Just let me say goodbye to Mr. Fir."

Natalie looked over at her daughter, who was whispering to me—that tree with the broken branch. She bent down and picked up a piece of trash that someone had thrown on the ground, looked at Bobby, and mumbled, "People are slobs, Bobby. They think the world is their trash can."

Then Bobby joined her in picking up discarded trash from the breezeway and dropping it into the receptacle. Missy scurried around the bench and had started picking up cigarette butts when she spotted a shiny new quarter.

"Mommy, I found a quarter. Look!" She proudly showed Bobby and Natalie her twenty-five-cent coin, threw the cigarette butts in the garbage, and joined her Mom and Bobby.

Publix provides sanitary wipes as you enter their store, so Natalie handed one each to Missy and Bobby and instructed them to clean their hands. She grabbed a buggy, and the three soulmates entered the air-conditioned supermarket. They proceeded to the deli, where they ordered two subs and chicken tenders for Missy. While the subs were being loaded up with mayo, lettuce, tomatoes, onions, Swiss cheese, and ham, Bobby walked over and picked up a gallon of sweet tea and three cups. When they walked through the checkout, Bobby wanted to pay for the food, but Natalie insisted that she pick up the tab. After all, this was Bobby's *special day*.

"OK, Natalie, but under one condition," insisted Bobby.

"And what would that be?" inquired Natalie as she swiped her debit card.

"We have a picnic at my special place. Not on the bench, but a beautiful field of dreams not far from here."

"Do we have to drive?" asked Natalie.

"No, it's right around the corner."

So they started to walk down the breezeway. I was watching as Bobby and Missy turned and both said, "See ya later, Mr. Fir."

Natalie looked first at her daughter and then at Bobby and took a deep breath. She loudly exhaled as she thought to herself, *What is it about this stupid tree that has so captivated Missy and Bobby? It's just a tree, and a broken tree at that.*

CHAPTER 59

Sunday, December 20
Picnic on "Lake Bobby"

The little girl in the red dress held her mother's hand. Bobby walked next to Natalie and held her other hand. They headed toward the large, empty field behind Chick-fil-A, where fences and signs warned that trespassers would be shot on sight and that they would be arrested and prosecuted. The signs were large, with bold red-and-black lettering on a white background, and there was a second warning that this property was protected by guard dogs.

Natalie took pause as she stopped dead in her tracks and read the signage. She pulled Missy close and looked up into Bobby's face.

"I'm not going in there! Can't you read, Bobby Thornton? Have you lost your ever-loving mind, Bobby?" Natalie had her hands cupped tightly over Missy's ears as she read the riot act to Bobby.

Bobby was oblivious to the ranting of Natalie as he approached the rusty iron gate connected to the barbed-wire fence. Natalie continued to object, to explain in much detail why she would not go with Bobby, and to protest his attempt to unlock the gate. Bobby had reached deep into his pocket and retrieved some sort of device that obviously allowed him to pick the very large lock attached to a very large chain.

"Shhhh," beseeched Natalie, "you are going to attract the dogs. Bobby, someone is going to shoot us."

Natalie began to cry. Tears of fear and concern were rolling down her face, just as the lock unclicked. She looked at Bobby in utter terror, afraid to move, her feet frozen to the ground and her hands still tightly cupped over Missy's ears.

"What are you doing, Bobby?" she pleaded.

"Oh, I do this all the time, Natalie. I live here"

"You live here? So you own this land, Bobby?"

"Well, sort of. My stuff is in there," he pointed toward an area far off behind many trees and bushes, "and every night I sleep in a real nice sleeping bag under the stars or in a state-of-the-art tent if the weather is bad."

"What about the dogs?" asked Natalie.

"There are no dogs, and there are no men with guns, Natalie. It is really quite a peaceful place, and the police know that I am here, so they watch out for me."

Natalie relaxed somewhat, removed her hands from Missy's ears, and returned Bobby's smile. Bobby opened the gate just wide enough for them to squeeze through, and then he clicked the lock shut through two giant links of chain. Natalie's load was becoming too bulky, so she asked Missy to tote the chicken tenders, leaving Natalie with only the subs and her purse. Bobby was in charge of the gallon jug of sweet tea and the three cups. There was a sandy path of sorts that led from the gate entrance in many directions, as if made by animals. There seemed to be no rhyme or reason for where each path led, if indeed they led anyplace at all, but Bobby knew every inch of this land, and he was leading the girls to the same oak tree where he first met Turk. Both Natalie and Missy were getting sand in their shoes, so Bobby suggested that they remove their shoes and walk barefoot in the sand.

"There used to be stickers here, but I pulled up every last one and burned them on my campfire. Tens of thousands of years ago, maybe hundreds of thousands of years ago, the entire southern part of Florida was underwater. That's why you have all this sand, Missy. See that big oak tree over there?" Bobby waved his hand at a massive tree on the other side of some bushes. "There is a beautiful lake over there, and it even has a white sand beach area. The water is clean enough for swimming, but it's too cold today. Besides, we don't have our bathing suits."

Missy was getting excited as she navigated the path. She could hear ducks quacking in the distance, and she could see squirrels chasing each other around the trunk of the mighty oak. Natalie took a deep breath and slowly exhaled.

"Bobby, this is where you live? This is just breathtaking." Natalie's mouth was open as she scanned this panorama of verdant bushes, wild Florida flowers, giant oaks, and the shimmering ripples of the blue lake. "I'm awestruck, Bobby, just awestruck."

"Mommy, can I go down and walk in the water?" asked Missy, looking up at Natalie with pleading eyes.

Bobby warned Natalie that they could only walk out about ten feet or so, because then it got deep pretty quickly.

Natalie and Missy dropped their shoes next to a large, benchlike log and ran to the lakeside, where both enjoyed walking in the cool water along the bank. Meanwhile, Bobby ambled over to the rusty old Chevrolet Nova, lifted the trunk, and retrieved a brown blanket for their picnic. As he returned to his mighty oak, Bobby spread the blanket on the ground, smoothed the corners, and leaned back against the trunk to watch his girls frolic and laugh. Noticing some ants on their bags, Bobby called to Natalie, "Nat, I think we should eat this food so the ants don't get to it before we do."

And so it was, as Bobby would later tell me, one of the best days of his life. They ate their subs and chicken tenders, drank tea, and lay on the blanket, looking at puffy white clouds floating in an azure-blue sky. They laughed at squirrels chasing each other from limb to limb in the hundred-year-old oak that shaded them from the sun. They were refreshed by the cool breezes blowing from the southeast, and they were entertained by waterbirds splashing and fishing in the glistening waters of Bobby's lake. The coots squawked but remained hidden, the mallards paddled close to shore but were wary to come close, and a solitary osprey circled overhead, looking for fish swimming carelessly near the surface of the lake. Indeed, this was a day of total bliss.

Missy spotted two rabbits that were eating tender shoots of grass near their blanket. She pointed and then brought a small finger to her lips to shush everyone, so the brown bunnies wouldn't be scared away. Missy spotted an odd-looking brown-and-black bird off in the distance by the lake, a strange-looking creature that looked like an old scarecrow in a cornfield.

"What's that, Mr. Thornton?" whispered Missy, pointing to the large, black bird by the lake.

"That's an Anhinga. Some people call him a water turkey or a snake bird, Missy."

"Why?"

"Well, because he swims real fast under the water when he's looking for fish, and when he spots one, he spears it with his needle-sharp beak. Actually, when he is underwater, or when he sticks his head above the surface for a gulp of air, he looks like a snake, but when he is on land, like he is now, drying his feathers, he looks kinda like a turkey. Anyway, after he spears the fish, he throws it up into the air, catches it in his mouth, and swallows it whole. Then, with his belly full, he swims over to the shore and holds his wings out to dry. See how he has all his feathers fluffed up? And look at his tail. It looks just like the tail feathers of a turkey. Poor ol' Anhinga can't fly till he's dry. Ha, I made a rhyme, Missy…*can't fly till he's dry.*"

Bobby never mentioned Turk or that he and the scraggly brown puppy met under that very oak tree where they sat. Weeks ago, Natalie had told Bobby about Missy's bulldog having been run over by a car and how it broke her little heart. When Turk serendipitously came into Thornton's life, Bobby asked Natalie if he could give the loving little brown puppy to Missy as a Christmas present. Although Natalie could ill afford another mouth to feed, she agreed to accept Bobby's offer because she knew that the loss of Sammy had left a massive void in Missy's life.

Natalie rose to her feet and began gathering what few personal effects she and Missy had brought to the picnic. "All good things must come to an end, Bobby. Missy, grab that bag of trash, and we will toss it in one of the Publix trash cans as we go to our car."

Bobby quickly interrupted, "No, Missy, it's just paper, and I can use it to start my fire tonight." Bobby rolled up the blanket and walked it over to the rusty Nova, where he placed it neatly in the trunk next to his sleeping bag. Then he returned to Natalie, who was holding her daughter's hand. He held her other hand, and they began their walk back toward the shopping center. When they arrived at the chained gate, Bobby again reached into his pocket for the tool that he had previously used to pick the lock. In seconds, the gate was swinging open; then he relocked it, and the three happy campers were back in the breezeway, walking toward my bench.

I was lying on my side, where an inconsiderate customer had roughly thrown me to the pavement earlier in the afternoon. The entire time that I lay on my side, not a single shopper had given me so much as a glance. The first thing Bobby did when he saw me was pick me up and water me down. Boy! Was I thirsty! Missy wrapped her small arms around me and said she would see me Wednesday. I reminded her that it was her turn to tell me a story. The girls hugged Bobby and thanked him for a wonderful day, got into their good ol' reliable Caprice, and drove away. Bobby found Kenny and dressed him down for not being especially watchful of me and for not keeping me hydrated, and then Bobby sat down on the bench.

CHAPTER 60

Monday, December 21
That Blasted Coot

A chill was definitely in the air as temperatures in Lake Worth hovered around thirty-nine degrees, a record low according to Bill Gunter, the local Channel Seven weatherman, but Bobby was warm as toast, nestled snugly in his sleeping bag. He was lost in dreamland, having fallen into a rabbit hole where Natalie was the princess of Wonderland and Bobby was the prince whom she would soon marry. Bobby was deeply asleep in this fantasy world of colors and sounds, with birds singing and butterflies fluttering among the sweet scent of flowers, snow-capped mountains, and verdant valleys. A small, white, steepled Baptist church sat on a hill, and standing on the veranda, waving, was Natalie, dressed in a wedding gown, her eyes focused on Bobby as he approached the steps. Organ music was playing inside the church, "Here Comes the Bride."

"HONK, HONK, HONK, QUACK, QUACK, QUACK!"

Suddenly Bobby's dream was popped like one of his chewing gum bubbles by the squawking sounds of the black coot that lived in the bulrushes. Although Bobby had seen this floating alarm clock only one other time, and that was when Turk had watched the mysterious waterbird attack Bobby, he could almost set his watch by the screeching honks and bleats that echoed from behind the cattails each morning. It was always at 8:00 a.m.

Oh no, Bobby thought, *not now! Not in the middle of my blissful dream!*

Bobby tried to block out the squawking racket of that water-bird by stuffing himself deeper into his sleeping bag. He stuck his fingers in his ears, but it was of no use. He was now wide awake. Bobby rubbed his eyes with the palms of his hands as he desperately tried to remember every detail of the rapidly fading dream.

Most dreams evaporate quickly. Why, exactly, I'm not sure, but some dreams stay with us forever. I once dreamed that I was a giant redwood on the coast of Northern California. I was thousands of years old, tall and stately, and enjoyed views of the Pacific Ocean to the west and the Rocky Mountains to the east. I was the most majestic tree in the United States of America and had been home to generations of flora and fauna ecosystems my entire life. But one day, my world literally came crashing down. The skies turned black, and a horrific storm blew violently throughout the forest, the likes of which I had never seen. Bolts of lightning exploded like bombs bursting in the air, and suddenly I was hit. I could feel myself falling, and as I crashed to the ground, I took many other trees with me to their graves. It was just a dream, but it was so real that I awoke in a cold sweat on Wildcat Mountain. The wind was blowing, the skies were dark, and the rain was falling, just like in my dream, but I was a Fraser fir, and I was on Wildcat Mountain. I was not a redwood in California, and I was not hit by lightning. It was all a dream, nothing more, just a dream, but a dream that I never forgot.

Bobby's dream was evaporating, maybe because his mind was focused on the irritating sound of the coot and his anger toward the black bird for awakening him from his peaceful sleep.

"I'm gonna kill that coot," Bobby screamed. "You are dead meat, coot!"

Bobby was so angry that he jumped out of his sleeping bag and tried to stand up. He had forgotten that he was in a tent, so when the tent collapsed, Bobby found himself entangled inside, unable to locate the zipper and rolling down the bank toward the lake. Bobby was enraged, furious that he had been so abruptly awakened by that rooster-wannabe coot, and the more he fought to get out of that tent, the faster he rolled. Suddenly—splash!—he was sinking in the cold water of Lake Bobby. His military training immediately kicked in, and he reached in his pocket for the small knife he carried everywhere. Bobby's dad had long ago told him to always carry a small knife for emergencies, like cleaning your dirty fingernails or removing a splinter. But this was no splinter. He was trapped in a sinking tent. With lightning speed, Bobby slashed at the canvas and extricated himself from his blue sleeping quarters. He was soaking wet and cold, and his head was throbbing from the incessant honking of the coot. His tent was ruined, and all he could think of was killing that coot.

Little did he know that this coot had just become the father of three, and he was quacking as loudly as he could quack to let everyone know how proud he was to be a daddy. Bobby had only once seen this little black bird and had no idea that he even had a mate.

Just as Bobby had cut himself free of the tent and sloshed his way back onto the bank, the coot family of five emerged from behind the bulrushes. Papa Coot was in front, followed by three tiny black babies, with Mama Coot holding up the rear. The two adults were honking, and the little ones were squeaking. They paddled like ducks, all in a row, and then disappeared behind the water plants growing to the right of where Bobby's tent had sunk.

Bobby sat near the water and reflected on what had just happened. He knew that he had been dreaming, but for the life of himself, he could not remember the dream. Bobby was shivering. It was a cold morning in South Florida, and the unexpected dip in his lake had made Bobby's number-one priority a warm fire. His clothes were wet, and the wind was blowing briskly from the north. Bobby jumped up and high-tailed it toward the old rusty Chevy where he kept his clean clothes and other personal effects, including matches. He quickly stripped off all his clothes and layered himself in dry underwear, T-shirts and a sweater, and a clean pair of jeans. He put on dry shoes and socks and a warm coat and dried his hair with an old white towel. He grabbed some matches and started walking back toward the old oak tree. On his way back to his campsite, he picked up some twigs and large pieces of wood with which to start a fire. Bobby took pride in keeping his area clean and neat, so when any trash, bottles, or debris found its way into the reserve Bobby called home, he would pick it up and drop it into an old metal garbage can he kept in the brush. This came in handy when he needed to start a fire, because there was plenty of paper inside the can. Bobby lifted the rusty lid and grabbed a few sheets of newspaper. He lit a piece, put twigs on top of the burning paper, then larger sticks and a small log, and soon he was being warmed by a blazing fire. Bobby had been a Boy Scout while growing up, so he knew to surround your fire with rocks and build it in an open area away from any combustible brush.

Bobby laid out his wet clothes on the palmetto scrub that surrounded his camp and planned his day. He would have to go to the bank to get some cash, although he mostly used his debit card for purchases. He would then stop by the Metro PCS store and inquire about buying a cell phone. This was his prime objective today. Bobby wanted to be able to talk to Natalie and text her and search the web like everyone else seemed to be doing these days. Bobby had mentioned to me more than once that everybody seemed to have a phone growing out of their ear. Some folk, he would say, would probably need surgery to remove the phone from their head. I thought that was kind of funny, but he was right. Anyway, Bobby wanted to call Natalie and see if they could have lunch together, and of course he wanted to sit for several hours on the bench and talk with me.

So, warmed by the fire, with wet clothes drying in the Florida sun, Bobby heard his stomach growl and realized that he had not eaten any breakfast. He looked at his watch and noted that it was already five minutes past nine. Bobby knew that he must hurry in order to complete all the tasks on his to-do list, so he quickly put out the fire by pouring ample lake water over all the burning embers until there was nothing left but charred sticks. He then covered the remains of his fire with sand, put the rocks back where he had found them, and swept the area with a bushy branch to hide any traces that anyone had camped in this area last night. This was Bobby's daily routine, and save for the squirrels, birds, and lizards who made this their home, there was no sign that a human had ever been there.

CHAPTER 61

Monday, December 21, Morning
Chase Bank

B obby set out for the Chase Bank that was on the other side of Lantana Road. There, he would withdraw four fifty-dollar bills, which would be Christmas gifts to four of his neediest friends. It was good to be retired from the military and have a guaranteed pension for the rest of your life, but not a day went by that Bobby did not give thanks to his country for this benefit given to all retired veterans.

He would give fifty dollars to his dear friend Paul and fifty dollars to Santo's mother so that Santo would have toys for Christmas. No child should be without a toy on Christmas morning.

A young woman named Sarah worked as a volunteer at the Salvation Army Thrift Store, and she had fallen on hard times of late. Due to the recession, she had lost her job as a waitress at the Pancake House, where Bobby ate breakfast almost every morning. Sarah had always given Bobby an extra pancake or two, extra-large helpings of hash browns, and all the coffee he could drink. She even sat and talked with him when she was not busy serving customers. Sarah began sharing her personal problems with Bobby, and his advice to her was to end the troublesome relationship with her abusive boyfriend. She finally took Bobby's advice and was now living in a women's shelter; she was not yet employed but had been interviewed twice for an opening at the Olive Garden. Sarah would receive the third fifty dollars.

Lastly, there was fifty dollars for the "Will Work for Food" man on Jog and Lantana. Michael was his name, and he worked that corner every day, in good weather or bad, on hot days or cold, rain or shine, trying to eke out a living to provide for his disabled daughter and himself. He was a veteran, just like Bobby, and although many of the panhandlers seen on street corners are alcoholics and druggies, Mike never touched a drop and had never even smoked a joint. He was a good man, just a little slow, if you know what I mean. He did not serve in the military long enough to become eligible for a pension, again because he was a bit slow. The army had given Mike an honorable discharge instead.

One day when we were sitting together on the bench, he told me about the woman he married while in basic training at Fort Benning, Georgia. Her name was Gladys, and they had a child who was born with Down syndrome. Gladys blamed Mike for their daughter's disability. She assumed that because Mike was slow, her daughter's mental impairment was his fault. One night she told Mike she was going to the store. Gladys never came back home. When he went to bed that night, he found her suitcase and clothes were gone. She had deserted them. Ever since that day, he had loved, cared for, and tended to his child's every need. She was now seven years old and in the special needs program at Missy's school. Missy told me all about Phyllis—how nice she is, how loving, how generous, and that they eat lunch together and share each other's sandwiches.

Fifty dollars, maybe more, would also be withdrawn for Bobby's personal use. He had gum to buy and needed tips for the waitresses, and if he saw a good deal at the thrift store, they usually only accepted cash, so he had to make sure that he had fifty one-dollar bills, which he always carried in his left pocket. This was another life lesson learned from his father.

"Bobby," his dad had said, "always have twenty dollars in your wallet for emergencies. You never know when you might need a buck." Well that was twenty-five years ago. Today, a man needed fifty dollars in his pocket for emergencies.

Bobby went inside the bank and approached the counter where customers stood to fill out their deposit and withdrawal slips. Bobby had his account number memorized, so it was a snap to complete his withdrawal form, which included the extra fifty dollars in cash. He could have used the ATM machine, but he felt that machines replace people, so he refused to use them. He did not want any of the nice tellers at Chase Bank to be replaced by a machine.

As he stood in line, awaiting his turn, he was making small talk with a little old woman with gray hair. She said that Bobby looked just like her grandson. She told him how handsome he was and how much she loved banking at Chase. She pointed to the coffee machine and said, "Mister, I come here every morning, and they always offer me a free cup of fresh coffee."

Then he heard his name called. It was Christina, arguably the most pleasant teller of all the pleasant tellers. As he handed his withdrawal slip to Chris, he said, "Oh my, I've changed my mind. I need an extra thirty-nine-ninety-five in cash."

Chris said, "No problem, Bobby. Just initial here where I made the changes, and I'll give you two-eighty-nine-ninety-five."

CHAPTER 62

Monday, December 21, Morning
Cell Phone

Next Bobby had to buy a phone, so he scanned the strip stores on the south side of Lantana Road. He knew there was a Boost store somewhere in this center, because he was always watching this guy dressed like a chicken flipping a "Boost Cellular" sign in the shape of an arrow. Bobby placed his hand over his eyebrows to shade the sun, and that's when he spotted the cell phone store, where the old Radio Shack used to be. He looked at his watch: 0930, military time, and since he was on Jog Road, Bobby jogged from the bank to the Boost store. If the chicken man had any good deals or packages better than Metro PCS, Bobby would purchase his phone from Boost. After all, Metro PCS did not have a chicken with a cardboard sign, and that chicken had some skills. He could flip the sign, twirl it, dance with it, and even do backflips without ever dropping the sign.

A tall, skinny youngster with a pair of horn-rimmed glasses met him at the door. "Good morning, sir," he said to his first customer of the day in a high-pitched voice. "May I help you?"

"No, I just came in for the air conditioning," responded Bobby.

"But, sir, it's forty degrees outside. Surely you can't be hot."

"I was just kidding, son. I'd like to know what kind of deals you guys have. I see that chicken outside every day with his Boost sign pointing toward this store, and it says, 'FREE PHONE.' So I thought I'd stop by for my free phone. Would you give me a red one?"

"No, no, no, you misunderstand the sign. You only get a free phone if you sign up with Boost, sir, and…"

"But isn't that false advertising, son?" interrupted Bobby. "I thought I would stop here for my free phone and then go across the street and sign up with Metro PCS."

"No, no, no, it doesn't work like that, sir. Let me…"

Again, Bobby interrupted. "I'm just playing with you, kid. I know how all this works. Can you just give me the basics? Must I sign a contract? How many free minutes do I get? Do I get unlimited texting? What type of free phone do I get? Is it a smartphone? How much does it cost per month? And does the phone work in North Carolina?"

The youngster, Herman, exhaled, slumped his shoulders, and smiled at Bobby. "I knew you were kidding all the time."

Herman ran a quick credit check on Bobby, collected a deposit, helped Bobby choose an easy-to-remember phone number, gave a quick tutorial of the iPhone, and shook Bobby's hand. "Sure am glad you stopped by, Mr. Thornton. If you have any problems using your phone, just go see the chicken out there by the road. His name is Bubba. But don't make fun of him. He's real serious about his job and very sensitive about his appearance. I'm going to repeat what I just said, 'Don't make fun of Bubba.' Bubba is six feet, seven inches tall, and he gets real mean when he's been drinking…"

Bobby was getting ready to hand the phone back to Herman, when he saw the tall, skinny, stork-like salesman smile. "Got ya, didn't I, Mr. Thornton? I was just kidding, but if you need any help with pictures or setting up your address book, stop by any time. I'm here every day. And as for Bubba, he's cool. Sometimes he comes in here and I go out there, but we never go near that Chick-fil-A, across the street, if you know what I mean. Ha."

They shook hands again, and Bobby looked at his watch. It was 10:10. Biscuits Plus was on this side of Lantana Road, and they made the best biscuits in Lake Worth, so he jogged over to see what was on special. His stomach had been growling all morning, and Herman had made fun of the noises more than once and even offered Bobby a donut to silence the beast in his belly.

Bis-Plus, as Bobby called it, had a "buy one egg-and-cheese biscuit, get one free" special, so he got one with sausage and one with bacon. The meat was free too. He found a table by the window where he could sit and study his new phone. He could see Publix across the street, and he saw me standing where I always stood, next to his green bench. I was enjoying the cool weather, and Kenny was connecting the hose for our morning drink. I had watched Bobby all morning. I saw him jog across busy Lantana Road and stop by the bank, but then I had lost him until I saw him go inside the Bis-Plus. I was hoping he would stop by for our morning chat. I was in one of my depressed moods and desperately needed to talk. My spirits were low, and I was not feeling well at all.

Bobby knew that Natalie worked at the Homes Depot, a local real estate office that had been sued several times for using a name similar to Home Depot, but their signs were red, white, and blue, not orange, and they specialized in selling homes to veterans, so the suit was finally dropped. He had her card in his wallet, but as he fished it out, it slipped from his hand and fell to the floor. As he bent over to pick it up, he noticed a pair of white high-heeled shoes, two gorgeous legs, and a sexy hand picking up the card. It was Natalie.

"Natalie!" blurted Bobby. "I was just getting ready to call you. Won't you sit down…uh…have a seat…uh…join me? Could I buy you a cup of coffee? Have an egg-and-cheese biscuit. I have two of them. They had a special. God, it's so good to see you, Natalie. You're always on my mind."

Natalie sat down and said, "Me too, Bobby. I've been thinking about you a lot too. Missy and I really enjoyed the picnic Sunday. Missy wants to do it again. I don't have time to sit and talk. The boss sent me down for a cup of coffee. Our coffeemaker is on the blitz, and he said he is going to buy one of those new K-cup machines for the office. They say that's the only way to go anymore. He is going to use the honor system, and anyone who wants a cup puts a dollar into the kitty, which will pay for the machine and the K-cups too. Look, I have to go, but could we split a sub today at Publix? I get an hour for lunch, and I could meet you on the bench."

Bobby couldn't believe his ears. "Sure, Natalie. What do you want on your sub?" They agreed to leave off the pickles, hot peppers, onions, and olives. Anything else was fair game.

Natalie stood up and gave Bobby a kiss on the cheek. "You need a shave. See you at one." She turned and sashayed her way to the counter to purchase a cup of coffee, and as she walked away, Bobby couldn't take his eyes off her hourglass figure with the wiggle when she walked. Natalie paid for her coffee, turned to wave goodbye to Bobby, and then exited the building. Bobby finished the sausage-and-egg biscuit, put his "get one free" bacon biscuit in the white sack, and followed Natalie out of the Bis-Plus.

As Bobby watched her drive away, he noticed that her Chevy was coughing and sputtering. *That's not good,* he thought. *Maybe I should give that car a tune-up. I could fix that broken window mechanism at the same time. Yep, I'll offer to work on her old Caprice when she meets me for lunch.*

CHAPTER 63

Monday, December 21, Morning
Passing Out Fifties

Bobby scanned the corner of Jog and Lantana. Mike was standing on the concrete median with his "Will Work for Food" sign—and be it known that not only would he work for food, but he was often offered jobs to do day labor, which he never turned down. Bobby crossed the eastbound lane and hollered to Mike, "Hey, Mike, how you doing? I've got something for you." As Bobby approached Mike, he extended his right hand with the fifty-dollar bill inside, shook hands with his dear friend, and said, "Merry Christmas, Mike."

Mike opened his hand, and his eyes began to water. He hugged Bobby tightly and then quickly looked away so that Bobby would not see that he had teared up. Mike thanked Bobby profusely and hugged him again, this time tighter than before.

"I'm so grateful, Bobby; thank you. You've just made my daughter's Christmas very special. I don't know what to say."

"No need to say anything, Mike. You are my dear friend, and I love ya, man." He handed Mike the bacon, egg, and cheese biscuit and said, "Enjoy, buddy! Compliments of Bis-Plus. I ordered one, and they gave me two. What a country! Hope you like bacon."

Mike hugged Bobby a third time, teared up again, shook hands with his homeless pal, and reached into the Bis-Plus bag for the hot bacon biscuit.

Mike had the breakfast sandwich in his left hand and was taking a bite, when a car in the left turn lane stopped for a red light. An attractive older lady wished Mike a merry Christmas and handed him a five-dollar bill. "God bless you," she said.

"And God bless you, ma'am," responded Mike. "My daughter and I are most grateful for your generosity." Then the left-turn arrow turned green, and she drove off.

Bobby had completed three of the tasks on his to-do list, four if you count contacting Natalie for lunch, but his running into Natalie at Bis-Plus was kind of like fate. Sometimes I think that things happen for a reason. We don't always understand why or how things happen. Serendipity? There is that word again: seren-dipity, fate. Maybe some things are just meant to be, like things are prearranged to work out a certain way or like fate causes things to happen for some unknown reason, maybe for the greater good. Maybe that's why Bobby ran into Natalie at Bis-Plus. Maybe that's why I got cut down in North Carolina and brought here to Lake Worth. Fate. Serendipity. For the greater good. I don't know, but I sure have met some terrific friends here in South Florida. When you stand in one place all day, you have lots of time to think about lots of things.

Bobby says my deep thinking is philosophical. I asked him what that meant, and he said that people are always trying to figure out why the world is the way it is, why people do what they do. And philosophy is the ideas or explanations that people dream up to explain the things that they do not understand. I had to remind him that all living things, like trees and sparrows and skunks and bears, have souls and can think, and maybe trees and birds and all living things ask the same questions and dream up answers to these ques-tionable questions. Maybe I am philosophical. I'd like to think that I'm here in Lake Worth because some lonely family needs me. I'd like to think that my life has always had meaning. I'd like to think that I'm part of this earth because I'm part of the greater good.

Just as I was standing there being philosophical, Bobby jogged over and sat down on the bench. He crammed about another five pieces of bubble gum into his mouth and started to chew. He did this all the time, and I knew better than to try and talk to him until he had chewed all the juice out of the gum. Many times I listened to him try to talk when he was chewing a wad of gum, and it was like trying to understand someone who talks with a baseball in their mouth. Kind of like listening to those mountain hillbillies talk to each other when their mouths are full of chewing tobacco. Forget about it! You can't make heads or tails out of what they are saying. It's like they are speaking another language. So I just stood there being philosophical. I had been watching Bobby all morning, and I knew that he was on this earth for the greater good. I thought that fate had brought him to Natalie and that it was serendipitous that they ran into each other that morning at Bis-Plus.

"How ya doin', Fir?" Bobby blurted in an easy-to-understand voice. "Ya been sold yet?"

"What a dumb thing to ask, Bobby. If I had been sold, I wouldn't be here now, would I?"

Bobby took off his blue jacket and laid it on the bench. The Florida sun was bathing Lake Worth in warmth, and the temperature was already up to fifty-nine degrees. The weatherman predicted a high of sixty-eight.

Bobby pulled out his new red cell phone and said, "What's your number, Fir? I'll put you in my address book. Let's see, Herman said touch the phone icon, then contacts, and then hit the plus sign. Now, how do ya spell Fir?...F-U-R?"

"You're real funny, Bobby, a laugh a minute. And I don't have a phone number. You know that."

"I know, Fir, I'm just funnin' with ya. I'm also practicing so that when I see Natalie for lunch, I can get her phone number. But you know what I could do? I could get you a free cell phone at Boost. Herman said they have a family plan, and I could tell Herman that you are my brother, Fir Thornton. You like that? Fir Thornton. Sounds like a plan, Fir. What color you want? Green? Or maybe brown to match your trunk?"

"You're in rare form this morning, Bobby. I saw you go into the Bis-Plus. And I saw Natalie go into the same fast-food joint just after you went in. You two maybe are meeting on the sly?"

"Oh, no, Fir. She was just there buying a cup of coffee for her boss. Seems their coffeepot broke, and…"

"Sure, Bobby. The old office-coffeepot-broke-down trick. If you expect me to believe that, I suppose you have some bridge in the desert you'd like to sell me."

"Let's get back to the phone, Fir. Seriously, I can get you a phone with your own personal cell phone number. That way, anytime we want to talk to each other, we just dial each other's number."

"Bobby, don't be foolish. I have no fingers. I can't dial a phone."

"No, but you have three sparrows. I could set up a speed dial so that one peck of their beak would dial my number. And I can show them how to answer a call with one peck of their beak. It would be a snap."

"But, Bobby, what if someone steals the phone?"

"Good question, Fir. That's why I asked if you wanted a green phone or a brown phone. I can disguise the phone so that it will appear as a trunk or as a green limb with green pine needles. Think about it and let me know."

CHAPTER 64

Monday, December 21
Mona

As Bobby sat in the middle of his green bench, with both arms spread out onto the backrest, golf ball–sized bubbles exploding on his lips, and his eyes staring blankly into nowhere, a little old lady tapped him on the shoulder.

"Excuse me, sir, is this seat taken?" she asked. Her name was Mona, and she was a seventy-two-year-old, slightly plump widow whose husband had just passed in November. Mona had never worked outside the home, but since her husband's fatal heart attack, she was having difficulty paying her bills. Publix had hired and trained her to be a part-time cashier. As coincidence would have it, Mona was born in Murphy, North Carolina, but had moved to Florida in 2008 due to breathing problems attributed to asthma and allergies. Her doctor suggested the subtropical salt air of Florida or the dry desert air of Arizona. Obviously, she chose Florida.

I perked up when I heard her tell Bobby that she was from Murphy. We were kindred spirits. I listened intently as she talked of the river walk that she took every day when she lived in Murphy and about how she missed the changing seasons. I was so tempted to engage this woman in conversation, but she seemed frustrated by the challenges of working for the first time in her life, and Mona looked tired from standing on her feet for such a long time.

One thing that was immediately apparent to me was how attractive she looked. Her hair was impeccable, looking as if she had just come from the beauty salon; her nails were polished and neatly trimmed; her face was perfectly adorned with makeup, as if she were a movie starlet; and her clothes were neatly ironed. Each Publix cashier wears a lime-green vest over his or her blouse, and this vest seems to afford the employee a touch of class that he or she might not otherwise have. But Mona had class. That was immediately clear from the pride she displayed in her appearance and the eloquence of her speech.

Mona and Bobby spoke of nitnoy stuff like the weather, the traffic in Lake Worth, and the noise. "Murphy was so peaceful," said Mona as she watched Bobby blow an extraordinarily large bubble, and then she looked at her watch. "I have to go Mr....uh, Mr....I'm sorry, but I don't know your name."

"Just call me Bobby. I'm Bobby Thornton, but please, just call me Bobby."

Mona arose from the bench, extended her right hand, and said, "I'm Mona Williams. Pleased to meet you, Mr. Thornton."

"No, no, no! It's Bobby! Please, just call me Bobby."

"OK, Bobby, I'm sorry that I have to leave, but my break is over. I have to go back and learn this cashiering stuff. It is so difficult. You have to weigh bananas and put in the correct codes for everything. You have to help people with their credit cards, debit cards, and gift cards. Half the customers don't know how to slide them, and then there are those coupon people. Bobby, I don't think I can do this job."

"Mona, you'll do fine. Just don't try to learn everything at once. One thing at a time. One customer at a time. Kinda like my friend who had a drug problem. He went to a rehab center, and they taught him *one day at a time*, and he has been drug free for five years now. He just got his five-year chip, and he was so proud."

"Thank you for the advice, Bobby. I'm going to go in there and check out one customer at a time. Thanks." And Mona turned and walked through the double doors and returned to her cash register.

CHAPTER 65

Monday, December 21, 12:00 Noon
Fir Needs Advice

"That was really good advice you gave Mona. I wish you could give me some good advice, Bobby, or should I call you Mr. Thornton, like Mona called you?"

Bobby was looking up at the rafters and watching people walk by. He did not seem to hear me.

"Mr. Thornton, do you have any good advice for a depressed Fraser fir with a broken branch, one that nobody seems to want for their Christmas tree?" I whispered to Bobby, who was relaxing on the bench.

"Mr. Thornton?" I whispered again, only this time louder.

"Did you hear what I said?" I *yelled* at Thornton.

Bobby looked up at me and said, "Keep the faith, good buddy. Just keep the faith. We are all on this earth for a purpose. Just go with the flow. Keep smiling, enjoy my company, and have faith that everything will be OK." Bobby had finally answered, but he was chewing on a loose fingernail and not looking at me as he spoke.

"By the way, Fir, Natalie is coming over at one o'clock. We are going to share a sub."

"Is Missy coming?" I asked.

"No, Natalie is at work right now, and she gets a lunch break from one to two p.m. I ran into her at the Bis-Plus this morning across the street, and—listen to this—she asked me if we could eat lunch together. She wanted to split a sub with me, right here at Publix, on this green bench."

"She seems to like you very much, Bobby. It sounds like your relationship has become more than just a friendship."

"Yes, Fir. Remember this past Friday night, the night that Natalie drove me here in that old Chevy Caprice? I don't think I told you everything that happened at the community center that evening."

"Yes, Friday night, of course I remember. You were driven back to Publix in that old, bucket-of-bolts Chevy that Natalie owns, right?"

"Right, her ex-husband, Glenn, took the Lexus."

"And he left the old Chevrolet for Natalie. Hmmm, I see."

Bobby recounted the entire evening as I listened intently. I was appalled that anyone could possibly be so mean and hateful, so insensitive and mean spirited, as this man, Glenn, had been to Natalie. Bobby told me how badly he embarrassed Natalie and how when Bobby finally arrived at the center, Natalie was outside, alone and crying. Bobby told me that he and Natalie sat together on one of the benches outside the dining hall, and he held her close and comforted her. Bobby related to me the details of how Missy's dad had come to the center, uninvited, unexpected, and drunk—sauced, loaded, plastered. He was so inebriated that he could hardly walk. He threw open the door to the dining hall, tossed chairs all over the floor, insulted and screamed at Natalie, told her no more child support for Missy, and then he stole her car. And all this happened before Bobby even arrived at the center because he was sitting here, talking with me, chewing gum, and blowing bubbles. Bobby also told me about how Paul had *helped* Glenn out to his Lexus, with Glenn tripping several times, falling down, breaking his nose, and slamming his fingers in the door before driving off.

"Holy moly," I said to Bobby. "Good thing that Paul guy was there to help Missy's father, or he might have really hurt himself. Wow, he kept falling down? And he broke his nose. Whew, he must have fallen flat on his face. He was really lucky to have Paul there to keep picking him up. How do you slam the car door on your hand? What a putz."

"Yeah," answered Bobby, "he was lucky Paul was there, and yes, he is a putz. But you know what, Fir, those people at the center really love Natalie, and if I'm repeating myself, I apologize, but nobody left, and when I was finally able to convince her to go back inside, all she got was hugs! From everyone. The dinner went on as if nothing had ever happened. We sang Christmas carols, opened gifts, and do you want to know the best part?"

"Absolutely, Bobby; don't stop now."

"Natalie and I found each other that night. I mean, our relationship was elevated to a new level. I think we were already in love, but after what happened at the center on Friday, we both knew we were in love.

"So, Fir, that's what happened Friday night." Bobby leaned back on the bench, spread his arms out on the backrest, and let out a deep sigh. "Fir, watching Natalie cry Friday night broke my heart. I held her. I hugged her. I was angry. I was sad. I was an emotional train wreck. But Fir, she was the one who had suffered the hurt, yet I, too, was feeling her pain. She is so dear to me, Fir, and I don't ever want her to suffer like that again. I want to protect her. I need to protect her. Does that make any sense at all to you, Fir?"

"Bobby, we all need someone to hold us when we are sad, to care about our pain when that pain hurts so bad, to hug us when we are so incredibly anguished. That's what you and Missy have done for me, and I thank you more than I can say. You've made it possible for me to continue living. You have given me hope. You have always been there for me, and I am so grateful...You always say, 'Keep the faith, Fir!'"

"Well, Fir," Bobby went on to say, "there is only one thing I can say about that."

"And what's that, Bobby?"

"Keep the faith, Fir."

CHAPTER 66

Monday, December 21, 12:45 p.m.
Natalie and Bobby Share a Sub

Bobby looked down at his watch and noted that he had been talking for forty-five minutes. Realizing that Natalie would be there in fifteen minutes or so, he jumped up and headed toward the Publix entrance but stopped about halfway to the doors to tell me he'd be right back. I knew that he had to go inside and buy a sub. He stopped at the dairy cooler for two small bottles of milk and then the bakery for two scrumptious almond bear claws. The sub and the bear claws were on sale, so he saved $2.61 by buying the Publix-brand deli meat sub and the discounted bakery items. Saving money always delighted Bobby. He absolutely despised paying full price for anything, and when he saw the opportunity to make a deal, he made the deal. That's one reason why he always carried fifty dollars in his pocket.

Bobby saw his new friend Mona at register number seven, so he hoofed it over to her checkout line, even though there were three buggies full of groceries in front of him. He patiently waited his turn, watching Mona's trainer and observing how Mona interacted with the customers. She was good! Bobby wondered why she had so much angst, why she was so hyper about her new job. She was doing just fine, but just as Bobby was mentally praising Mona, she had a meltdown. Her mind couldn't seem to process what kind of fruit needed to be weighed. Her trainer showed her the chart and pointed to the pictures. She then showed Mona how to key in that number so that the computer would weigh and price that item into the register. Mona listened and watched everything her young teacher said, but for some reason, it was just not sinking in. Mona started to cry. Everyone felt bad for the little old lady, everyone but the grumpy old man in front of Bobby. He started yelling at her and saying mean-spirited things. Bobby tapped him on the shoulder, tightly grasped his arm, whispered in his ear, and watched him apologize to Mona. The grump then backed his buggy out of the line, abandoned his groceries, and ran out of the store. Mona regained her composure, completed the transaction like a pro, and greeted the next customer with a smile. The lady now in front of Bobby was a slam dunk for Mona, and then it was his turn.

"Good afternoon, Mr. Thornton. Did you find everything that you were looking for?" Mona was on top of her game. Her supervisor just beamed as she noted that Mona not only used the correct salutation and asked the scripted question but also addressed Bobby by his name.

"Yes, ma'am," Bobby smiled at Mona as he answered. Bobby looked at her name tag as if he did not know her first name. "Mona? Is that your name? How do you use this debit card machine?"

Mona reached over and showed Bobby where to slide the card and then asked him if it was debit or credit. Bobby said, "Debit." Mona then asked if he wanted any cash back. Bobby said no, and the transaction was completed without a hitch.

Bobby returned to the bench just as Natalie was parking her car. I watched them wave to each other, and I couldn't help but notice the aura of happiness that surrounded both Natalie and Bobby. They were excited to see each other and to spend time together, even if it was only an hour sharing a sub sandwich.

It's funny how one person can impact a lonely person's life. One friend. One loved one. Loneliness is a sickness that has a cure, and the cure is the love and friendship of another person. Despair is another sickness, and the cure is finding a reason for living. Sadness, misery, and fear can all be cured by the friendship, love, understanding, and companionship of another caring person or even a magical Christmas tree.

Bobby and Natalie ran toward each other like two lovers in one of those black-and-white, old-time movies. Bobby lifted her off the ground, spun her around, and hugged her tight. *Wow,* I thought, *these two people have come a long way.*

For forty minutes of smiling, laughing, touching, holding hands, and of course, eating their shared sub, I listened to Bobby tell her things that he had never told me, and I listened to Natalie talk about the love of her life, Missy.

Time flew by, and Natalie had to return to work. Bobby arranged to have her stop by the store on Tuesday at 0830 military time so that Bobby could drive her to work. He would keep the car all day Tuesday, tune up the Caprice, fix the broken window mechanism, and repair anything else that was not functioning properly. They also reminded each other to meet at the Christmas Carnival at 5:30 p.m. tonight. Natalie asked Bobby if he needed a ride, but he said that his buddy Nick was picking him up. Nick had provided Bobby with the free passes.

At 1:45 p.m., Mona came out of the store and saw Bobby and Natalie chatting on the bench. They had not noticed her watching them enjoy each other's company.

Natalie had only taken three bites out of her ham-and-cheese sub, and Bobby had not even opened his. The bear claws and the milk had not been touched. These two young people were too busy frolicking in their own world to notice any goings-on around them. I may as well have been invisible, and Mona, had she not tapped Bobby on the shoulder, would not have been seen.

"Hi, Mr. Thornton, did you find everything that you were looking for?" Mona chuckled as she looked at Bobby and then at Natalie. Then Mona cocked her head to the left and placed her thumb under her chin.

"Hi, Mona Williams, I'd like to introduce you to Natalie McCord, a dear friend of mine."

The women recognized each other immediately and shook hands.

"I know you," said Mona. "You live on Banyon Way, across the street from me. You have that adorable daughter who I used to see playing with that bulldog puppy, and I always see you pushing that lawn mower on weekends. You have the prettiest yard in the neighborhood."

"Thank you, Mrs. Williams, but I think that your lawn and the way you keep your property are right out of *House and Garden* magazine. I didn't know that you worked for Publix."

"Mrs. McCord, I'm just learning the ropes. I lost my husband recently, and he always took care of the yard…and…and, well, he took care of everything else too. Now that I'm alone, I'm trying to do the best I can, but everything is so expensive, and all I have is my social security."

"I know what you mean, Mrs. Williams. I'm a single mom right now, and so it's just me and Missy trying to manage as best we can."

"What happened to the bulldog? I haven't seen him around lately."

Natalie looked at the ground and told Mona that he had been hit by a car. She then looked at her watch and started waving her hands in the air. "Oh my gosh, I have to get back to work. Mrs. Williams, I'll stop by after work, and maybe we can talk."

"Oh, that would be wonderful. Bring your daughter. I'll have milk and homemade cookies, and you and I can have tea or coffee. Six p.m., OK?"

"Well, six is not good for us. We are going to the carnival at Saint Matthew's from five to six thirty, but if you don't mind watching Missy for about an hour, I can bring her over at about six thirty this evening, and then I will join you at about seven thirty. My attorney and my ex-husband are coming over at seven o'clock sharp so that Glenn can sign some important papers, and I would prefer that Missy not be there."

"That sounds great, dear. I will prepare the cookie dough, and when Missy comes over, she can help me roll it into little balls and put them on cookie sheets. By the time you get to my house, we'll be taking them out of the oven."

Natalie said, "Sounds like a plan, Mrs. Williams. We'll see you this evening. It'll be great."

And with that, Natalie raced to her car, waved to Mona before she got in, blew a kiss to Bobby, and drove away.

CHAPTER 67

Monday, December 21, Afternoon
The Tent

All three of us watched as Natalie pulled out of the parking lot. Mona stood there next to the bench, smiling at Bobby. "You've got yourself a real nice girl, there, Mr. Thornton."

"*Bobby*—please, Mona, call me Bobby, or I'll have to start calling you Mrs. Williams!"

"I'm sorry, Mr. Thor—er, Bobby. Do you mind if I sit down for a few minutes? My feet are killing me. I wore the wrong shoes for this job. I'm getting too old to wear heels, even pumps like these. Tomorrow, I will wear tennis shoes."

"Are you hungry, Mona? I have a half a ham and cheese sub that has not even been taken out of the sack. Natalie hardly touched hers, so I'm going to finish it. We could kinda break bread together and get to know each other."

"Sure, I could eat." Bobby handed her the sub, and Mona neatly peeled back the wrapper to expose the top half of the sandwich. "Looks good, Bobby. All the things I like, Swiss cheese, spinach, tomatoes, lettuce, and mayo. Did they put salt and pepper on it?"

"No, but I asked them to put mayonnaise on both buns, Mona. That way, the bread is not so dry and brittle. I'm sorry about your husband."

"Thanks, Bobby. He was too heavy. I was constantly telling him to lose weight, but he loved to sit in front of that TV and eat potato chips, and Fred would eat a pint of ice cream every night.

He was outside mowing the grass when he started experiencing chest pains. He came inside, sat in his favorite chair, closed his eyes, and never woke up. He was a good guy, and I miss him, but we have to go on. I can't sit and wallow in self-pity. Bobby, why are you homeless?"

"Boy, you get right to the point, don't you, Mona?"

The whole time that Bobby and Mona were talking, they were ripping off large bites of their ham and cheese subs and chomping away. Bobby looked at Mona and said, "Mona, it's a long story, and one day I will tell it to you, but not today. I have to go to the sporting goods store for a new tent. You're going to see Natalie this evening, right?"

"Yes." Mona watched Bobby rise from the bench. He handed her the plastic bag with the milk and bear claws. Could you give this to her? Tell her I'll see her late this afternoon and to enjoy these pastries with Missy, OK?"

Bobby looked at me and waved. "See ya later, Fir. I'll stop by after the carnival, around seven p.m., and we'll talk some more."

Mona turned her head to see who Bobby was talking to but saw no one. She shrugged her shoulders, got up, and walked out to her Toyota.

<hr/>

Bobby walked into the sporting goods store on Congress Boulevard, a massive store as large as a supermarket. Never in his life had he seen so many shoes or people trying them on. This place was a madhouse.

Ah, Bobby thought, *last-minute Christmas shoppers.* Everything in the store was discounted, and the building was packed with people. Shoppers had buggies piled high with golf clubs, basketballs, sporting apparel, hockey sticks, ice skates, and swimming gear. If it could fit in a cart, these wacko shoppers were grabbing and stuffing everything they could into their buggies. The racks and shelves of Sports Depot were rapidly being depleted of merchandise.

What gives, here? thought Bobby.

A youngster with a blue shirt and an employee name tag was walking in the opposite direction, so Bobby grabbed him by the arm, stopping him in his tracks. "What's going on, young fellow?" Bobby looked down at the teenager's name tag and smiled. "Bob—that's my name! Bob, why are these people all acting like they've gone crazy? They're literally fighting each other for all the merchandise."

"The store is going out of business, sir, and today is the last day. Everything must go. Up to ninety-percent-off discounts," said Bob to Bobby.

"Hot dang, that means I'm gonna get a good deal! Where are the tents, Bob?"

The young man pointed to the rear of the store. "Over there, behind the bikes, if there are any left, Bob. Bob, could you please let go of my arm? I have to open another register. You're kinda hurting my arm, Bob."

"Sorry, Bob." Bobby released the lad's arm and started to run toward the rear of Sports Depot. He spotted the tents, but only one was left, a very expensive Kelly Trail Logic, a two-man tent that had a sticker price of $299.99. He spotted the teal-green tent at the same time as a big dude running from another direction. Bobby dove on top of the tent and claimed his prize. But Godzilla, the huge camper man, dove on top of Bobby and tried to wrestle the tent from his arms. Little did this big monster of a man know that he had a tiger by the tail, and before the big guy knew what hit him, Bobby was in sole possession of the tent and the big fella was lying flat on his back with his eyes closed. Bobby ran to the front of the store just as the other Bob was opening his register. As luck would have it, Bobby was Bob's first customer, and the tent was reduced to thirty dollars, 10 percent of its original price. Bobby swiped his debit card and cheerfully left the store, chewing six pieces of Double Bubble and running in circles like a happy little boy.

CHAPTER 68

Monday, December 21, 4:30 p.m.
Christmas Carnival at Saint Matthew's

Bobby carried his bargain tent to the bus stop, where he would sit, chew gum, and blow bubbles until his bus arrived. He kept looking into the large plastic bag that held his tent, and he studied the receipt, which clearly showed the original sales price of $299.99. He was overwhelmed with joy at having made such an outstanding purchase. There is that word again—it was *serendipitous.* He was in the right place at the right time, and thanks to that noisy coot, Bobby was now the owner of one of the finest tents sold in these sporting goods stores. *It was meant to be; fate*—serendipitous! he thought.

Bobby thought about the big guy who had tried to wrestle the tent from his grasp and hoped that he was OK. "Yeah, I'm sure he's all right," he said to himself. "He was a big guy and probably just got worn out as he wrestled with me. He was probably just lying there with his eyes closed, resting his tired self after the tussle with ol' Bobby Baby."

Bobby smiled, blew another bubble, and thought of all the other men who had rested with their eyes closed after they messed with Bobby. His career in the military had prepared him in the art of self-defense, and many a man, big and small, had grappled with Bobby at one time or another and wished that they hadn't. Many, many of them had closed their eyes and rested afterward, just like the gorilla at Sports Depot back in the tent department.

No more than five minutes had passed when the bus pulled up, the doors opened, and Bobby climbed aboard. Bobby got off at the Chick-fil-A, which, like the Publix Supermarket, was adjacent to the large tract of undeveloped land where Bobby lived, all of it fenced by seven-foot-high chain link with barbed wire on top. Bobby walked about two blocks to the gate, where he would pick the lock, walk through the sandy brush toward the old car that contained all of his possessions, and stow his new tent in the rusty old Chevy Nova's trunk. Bobby had installed a new lock on the trunk of the long-abandoned car. He carried the key in his pocket, with a few other keys that he needed from time to time. Because of the scrub palmetto and the plants and trees growing around the Chevy, it was almost impossible to see the car at all unless you knew it was there.

With the tent safely locked in the trunk with his other possessions, he headed back toward the gate, stopping only once to look at the lake and the giant oak where he, Natalie, and Missy had picnicked the day before.

Nick's shop was only six or so blocks away, so Bobby resecured the gate and started his walk toward Nick's Auto Air Repair shop. Nick and Bobby had served in the army together and were old buddies, going all the way back to high school.

They had agreed to meet at his shop at 4:30 p.m. and ride together to the Christmas Carnival, but first, Nick would have to stop by his house to pick up his wife, Theresa, and their seven-year-old daughter, Tami.

Nick was a devout Catholic and a big contributor to the church, so Saint Matthew's had given him ten free tickets for this wonderful annual Christmas event.

Natalie had arranged for Missy to spend the day with her dear friend and next-door neighbor, Roberta, a single mom who taught English at Palm Beach State College. Her daughter, Sarah, attended the same elementary school as Missy, and the two girls had been playmates and best friends for what seemed like forever. They were two peas in a pod, as close to being sisters as two girls could be without having the same parents, which meant they would sometimes quarrel with each other, but most of the time they just enjoyed each other's company and had fun. Roberta was absolutely delighted to watch Missy while Natalie worked. A special bond had developed between Natalie and Roberta from that first day when they had each moved into their brand-new homes in Lake Worth Dunes, a cookie-cutter development around the corner from Publix. And their daughters were the beneficiaries of this friendship, having also become best friends, so it was a win-win-win-win for all four of the girls. And the icing on the cake was that Sarah would be Missy's guest that night at the carnival and would be given the fourth free pass.

As the day progressed, it became clear to Roberta that neither daughter was absorbing anything from their lessons. They were too focused on the carnival, and when Roberta realized that it was futile to try and teach these girls anything, she just left them alone to play and to be giggly little girls.

CHAPTER 69

Monday, December 21, about 7:00 p.m.
Fir Is Sick

"Hi, Bobby, where have you been?" I did not feel well as I inquired into Bobby's whereabouts.

"I had to buy a new tent, Fir. I took the bus to Congress and Old Boynton Beach Boulevard, and boy, did I luck out. The Sports Depot is going out of business, and I got the last tent in the store, and afterward, I met Natalie and Missy at the church carnival, where we had a fabulous time, and…what's wrong, Fir? You don't look so good."

"I need some food, Bobby. I need minerals. Would you be able to go over to the garden area at Home Depot and buy me some fertilizer?"

"Sure, Fir, I'll be right back." Bobby jogged across the parking lot, zigzagging between cars, and entered the store through the garden center of Home Depot. Nobody was shopping for plants or mulch or much of anything that was kept in the garden area, so Bobby was in and out in a jiffy. He had asked the checkout lady what type of fertilizer or plant food would be good for Fraser firs. She had no clue, so he asked about evergreens, but she didn't know that either. Finally, realizing that he had a smartphone and recalling that Herman had shown him how to search the World Wide Web, he accessed the internet and looked up "fertilizer for evergreens." POW, just like that, he had his answer:

"What to use?

"A complete fertilizer that supplies nitrogen, phosphorus, and potassium, such as 10-8-6, is often suggested. This formula can vary somewhat, but usually the nitrogen content (the first number) will be higher than the phosphorus (second number) or potassium (final number)."

Bobby was reaching for his debit card when he realized that he needed a bucket, so he ran over to the hardware section and grabbed a shiny metal pail. He raced across the parking lot and back to his bench. Then it became apparent that he still needed water. Bobby ran inside Publix and bought two gallons of spring water. Upon exiting the store, he ran to the bench and began pouring water into the bucket.

I was in dire straits; my needles were limp and dreadfully close to falling off. I held onto them with every ounce of strength that I could muster. The stiff, woody part of my trunk that proudly holds the star or angel was badly listing to the left, and my branches had all drooped, the lower ones touching the concrete pavers. I was hallucinating and unable to think. My eyes were blurred and my speech impaired. I watched through glassy eyes as Bobby poured the fertilizer into the pail of water and stirred it with his hand. He had tears in his eyes as he lifted me into the air.

"I'm sorry, Fir, I'm so sorry. Please don't die. You are my best friend." People were walking past, looking at him as if he were nuts. They were giving him a wide berth and avoiding eye contact. They were whispering in each other's ears and pointing at Bobby. "Fir, I love you, man. Hang in there, buddy. I'm almost there." Bobby lifted me with his right hand and set the bottom of my trunk into the bucket. That night, I drifted in and out of consciousness. Bobby was there with me every moment. He never left my side.

Darkness comes early in December, around 5:30 p.m. December 21 is the shortest day of the year; winter solstice, it is called. My sadness and despair had made life not worth living, and I welcomed the darkness. I remembered December 21 on my mountain. I had hated the long, black night, but when the sun peeked above the horizon on December 22, I always knew that spring and summer were right around the corner and that my flowers would be back and my birds would sing again. Most of my friends would be asleep for the winter, or had gone south, so I had been virtually alone in the winter. Oh, I'd had all the other trees, and of course Mary, but there is nothing like the warmth of a bird sitting on your limb or a butterfly resting its wings and sniffing your cones or the cold nose of a fawn nibbling at your tender shoots.

As I slept through the night, I dreamed of my mountain. When I would awaken, I could hear Bobby talking to me. He was my strength. And my sparrows—they, like Bobby, never left my side. Bobby had asked Kenny for the hose so that he could keep me hydrated. Tuesday morning brought warmth and sunlight. I opened my eyes, smiled at Bobby, lifted my branches, and straightened my spine. I was back. I did not lose a single needle that night. I thanked Bobby for his love and affection, and I told him that I would be all right. He ran over to me and gave me the best hug of all time. There is nothing like a dear, faithful friend. *Nothing*.

CHAPTER 70

Tuesday, December 22
Bobby the Mechanic

At 8:30 a.m., 0830 military time, Natalie eased her car to a stop right next to the green bench where Bobby sat. Bobby's eyes were closed, his head was leaning back as if he was looking up at the sky, his mouth was open, and he was snoring. Bobby was sound asleep.

All night, Bobby had nursed me back to health. I was still very sick, but with the infusion of minerals and nutrients into my body, I was feeling ever so much better. I was asleep, too, when Natalie drove up, but when she exited the car and slammed her door, both Bobby and I nearly jumped out of our skin. Bobby asked Natalie to let him quickly run into the store, where he located Kenny. "Kenny, Fir is very sick. I was with him all night and have him on vitamins, minerals, and healthy food. Will you watch over him today and *not* allow anyone to move him from the spot where he is resting?"

"Sure, Mr. Thornton. I will put a sold tag on him so that nobody will even look at him. When will you return?"

"I'm going to tune up my girlfriend's car and repair her broken window. I should be back by five thirty p.m., after I pick her up from work. Why?"

"Well, Mr. Thornton, I get off work at four thirty, and I don't want to get into any trouble for having a sold tag on Mr. Fir. You know what I mean?"

"Sure, I do, Kenny. I'll tell you what, if you can sit with Fir from four thirty p.m. to five thirty p.m., I'll pay you ten bucks. Would you do that for me?"

"Mr. Thornton, you don't have to pay me. I'll sit with Mr. Fir. He's special, and I don't want anything to happen to him either."

Bobby and Kenny shook hands, and Bobby thanked Kenny profusely. He gave Kenny a quick hug, turned, and quickly returned to the bench, where Natalie stood staring at me standing in a bucket of water.

"What's with the tree, Bobby?" asked Natalie.

"That's Fir, Natalie. You know, the tree Missy loves so much, the tree you won't buy her for Christmas?"

"Oh!" answered Natalie. "So what's wrong with him?"

"I'll tell you on the way to work, Natalie. Come on, you're going to be late."

Natalie started the car and looked over at Bobby. "I have to stop at Bis-Plus for a cup of coffee. We still don't have that new K-cup machine, and my boss must have his cup of java each morning or he's impossible to work with."

"Great," said Bobby as he reached into his pocket for three one-dollar bills. "Would you get me a large cup to go, black, with plenty of caffeine. I didn't get much sleep last night."

Natalie jumped out of the car without taking Bobby's money and hurried into Bis-Plus. Bobby watched as she exited the fast-food restaurant. She carried three white bags in her left hand, a weighty red purse hung from her right shoulder, her car keys were jingling in her right hand, and somehow she was still balancing a cardboard tray with three cups of coffee.

"Wow," said Bobby, as he shook his head back and forth. "I don't know how you do it."

"Do what?" asked Natalie as she started the car and backed out of her parking space.

"Carry so many things at once, Nat. I can't imagine trying to walk from inside that store, open the door, exit the building, open your car door, and sit behind the wheel all while balancing about fifteen things in bags and such. And you are walking in high heels and toting a purse that weighs about thirty pounds. It's amazing, that's all. It blows my mind."

Natalie was laughing at what Bobby had just said. "It's all part of being a woman, I guess. When you have a baby to carry around, you learn to multitask. When your child is an infant, you just take it for granted that you can do anything and everything at once... because you have to. Anyway, we're here. Take your coffee, and I bought you two sausage, egg, and cheese biscuits. They had a special for buy one, get one free. I knew you would be pleased with a good deal, and I know you love sausage biscuits."

"Thanks, Nat, I *am* very hungry. I missed dinner last night, taking care of Fir and all, so I thank you very much." Bobby was still holding the three one-dollar bills for the coffee. He reached in his pocket and pulled out four more and handed the wad to Natalie. "Here, honey, this should cover it."

"You just called me 'honey,' Bobby. Am I your honey?"

"Gosh, Natalie, I guess that just slipped out. I'd like to think you were my honey. I really like you a lot. I'm sorry, I'll take the 'honey' back if you want me to."

"No, no, Bobby. I'd love to be your honey, but you would have to be my honey too. Would you be my honey, Bobby?"

"You bet I would, Nat." Bobby jumped out of the car as they pulled into Natalie's office. He ran around to the driver's side and gave Natalie a loving hug.

Natalie looked deep into Bobby's baby-blue eyes and softly whispered, "Don't forget to pick me up at five thirty, *honey.*

"Your car will be purring like a kitten, Natalie. See ya at five thirty." Natalie went inside her real estate office, and Bobby drove off toward Jog Road. Suddenly he realized that she had forgotten her coffee. Bobby made a quick U-turn and stopped near the front door. Natalie saw him through the window and met Bobby at the door.

"Want to come in and meet my boss, Bobby?"

"Not today, Nat. I'm dressed to work on your car, my eyes are bloodshot from lack of sleep, and I haven't even taken a sip of the coffee you bought for me. By the way, here's the money for the food and drink."

"You've got to be kidding me, Bobby. You are fixing my car today. Do you have any clue as to how much money you are saving me? Nope, the coffee is on me. And so is the sausage biscuit. Enjoy. I've gotta go. Thanks for bringing my boss's coffee back. Love ya."

One more quick hug, and Bobby drove off in the direction of the Discount Auto Parts store on Jog Road.

CHAPTER 71

Tuesday, December 22
Mona Day Care

Missy was at Mona's house for the day. Natalie had dropped her off at 8:00 a.m. after serving her a bowl of Crunch Berries cereal, Missy's favorite. Natalie and Mona had lived across the street from each other for eight years but had never met. They always waved as they loaded or unloaded their cars or retrieved the newspaper or mowed the grass, but until their serendipitous (there's that big word again) meeting at Publix, they had never spoken.

Mona had become a very lonely old woman since Fred passed, and with her daughter still living in North Carolina, she found herself emotionally connected to Natalie. They seemed to have so much in common. Missy was seven years old. Mona's only grandchild, Gracie, whom she missed desperately, would turn seven years old on Christmas Day. Mona's daughter owned a townhouse in Asheville, where she, like Natalie, was a single parent and, just like Natalie, worked in a real estate office.

So today was a special day for Mona, a day she looked forward to because it would be like spending the morning with her own granddaughter. She would babysit Missy while Natalie worked. Missy was a bit older than Gracie, but they had similar features and personalities. Both girls enjoyed school, loved to read, were always asking questions about everything, and had an affinity for athletics. Neither child had ever been exposed to baby talk, and as a result, both youngsters were gifted with exceptional communication skills. But what endeared Mona the most was that their appearance was so similar. They could have been sisters, or at least so it seemed to Mona, and both girls were polite to a fault, a tribute to the excellent job their mothers were doing as parents.

Mona and Missy were sitting at Mona's kitchen table when Missy spoke. "Mrs. Williams, you sure do have a pretty house."

"Why, thank you, Missy. My husband and I brought all our furniture down from North Carolina, where we used to live. Did you know that they make furniture in North Carolina?"

"You're from North Carolina? Mr. Fir is from North Carolina. Wow, go figure?"

"Who is Mr. Fir, Missy?"

Missy was sipping a cup of hot chocolate with marshmallows while Mona was drinking a steaming mug of black coffee. They were sharing the bear claw pastry that Bobby had left with Mona the previous day, and they were playing a card game called Go Fish.

"Who is Mr. Fir, Missy?" asked Mona as she drew a card from the deck.

"He's my friend at Publix. Mommy takes me with her every Wednesday to buy groceries, and while Mommy sits on the bench and talks with Mr. Thornton, I talk with Mr. Fir."

"Does he work at Publix, Missy? I don't remember meeting anyone named Mr. Fir."

Missy started laughing as she studied her cards. She asked if Mona had any kings. After Mona said, "Go fish," Missy looked up at Mrs. Williams and said, "No, silly. Mr. Fir is a Christmas tree."

Missy lifted her cup of hot chocolate and took a drink, leaving a brown mustache on her upper lip. With her spoon, she captured a floating marshmallow and put it into her mouth. "This is really good. Do you need any groceries, Mrs. Williams? If you do, I can introduce you to Mr. Fir. He tells me some great stories about his mountain in North Carolina and all the animals that he knows. Mommy thinks that Mr. Fir is an imaginary friend, but he's not.

Mr. Fir is real, and he tells me stories, and he listens to me, and we talk to each other. Tomorrow, I'm going to tell him about Sammy and my daddy."

As they continued their card game, Mona asked Missy if she had any tens. "Go fish," said Missy, forcing Mona to draw a card from the deck. Mona's curiosity about this "Mr. Fir" was piqued, so she looked at Missy and asked if Missy would like to go to Publix. "I need to pick up a few things for dinner, and I am running low on milk. They also have some specials that I might be interested in."

"BOGOs? That's Buy One and Get One free, Mrs. Williams. Mommy loves BOGOs. Can we really go to Publix? I'll introduce you to Mr. Fir. He may not talk to you, though. He's kinda funny like that. He doesn't talk to everyone, but maybe he will talk to you. If not, could you sit on the bench while Mr. Fir and I talk? Mrs. Williams, where is your Christmas tree?"

"I didn't put up my tree this year, Missy. I just didn't seem to have the Christmas spirit, with Fred gone and all. But you know what? I'm sure enjoying your company, and I think I am getting back into the holiday mood. Maybe I could pull my tree out of the garage and you and I could decorate it?"

"Why don't we go to Publix, and you can buy Mr. Fir, and we will decorate him, Mrs. Williams. He wants so much to be adopted, but he has a broken branch, and nobody wants him. Mommy said she can't afford a real tree this year, and she says, 'Missy, we have an artificial tree in the garage.'"

"Well, Missy, I have an artificial tree in the garage too, and it is small enough that I can easily carry it into the house by myself. I can manage it alone. Is Mr. Fir a small tree?"

"Oh, no, Mrs. Williams, he is huge. I'll bet he could almost touch your ceiling." Missy pointed up and then aimed her index finger toward Mona's bay window in the living room. "He would be beautiful over there. I would help you manage him and decorate him, and I could come over every day and talk with him. He'd be so proud to stand in front of that window with his lights on and an angel on top of his head. Everyone could drive by and look at him, Mrs. Williams."

Missy asked Mona if she had any queens. Mona gave her a queen, and Missy laid down her last pair, winning the game. Mona looked up and smiled at Missy, exhaled loudly, and said, "You beat me again! Let's finish our drinks and go to Publix."

CHAPTER 72

Tuesday, December 22, Morning
Bobby Drives Nat's Car to His Field
Tune-Up, Oil Change, AC, Paint

B obby parked by the fence, got out of Natalie's car, and
reached deep into his pocket. He unlocked the double gate,
fully opening the entrance so that he could drive the Chevy onto
the gravel road that wound around to the other side of the massive oak tree. He got back into the car, drove inside, and then
relocked the gates. With the fence secure, he followed the road
to a house that was under construction. This rock road led to
what would eventually be a driveway in front of a two-car garage.
The walls of the house and the roof were finished, and there were
stacks of drywall in the garage. Men with hammers were busily
pounding on long boards that would become the inner walls of
this beautiful home on the lake. A tall man with a full red beard
approached Bobby. "Good morning, Mr. Thornton. I didn't see
your tent this morning when I unlocked your gate. Do they have
you working overtime?"

"No, Bill. My dear friend was sick, so I spent the entire night
with him, nursing him back to health. I think he's going to be fine,
though."

"He probably has one of those twenty-four-hour viruses, Bobby.
They can really suck the life out of you...make you feel miserable."
Bill extended his large hand and touched Bobby's shoulder and
continued, "Your friend is very lucky to have you, Bobby. I'm a

pretty good judge of character, and I think you are one of the best human beings I have ever met."

Bobby smiled at Bill, looked into his eyes, and thanked him for the kind words and then thought, *Boy, you should only know, Bill, that Fir is not even human, but I love him like a brother.*

"By the seventh of January, all the interior walls will be up; the windows, doors, and kitchen cabinets will be installed; and all the plumbing and electrical fixtures and air-conditioning system will be operational. I am particularly excited about having toilets and running water in this home," said Bill. "I am so ready to quit using that stinky Porta-Potty. It's like the outhouses they used a hundred years ago up in the mountains, before there was running water inside a home."

"When will they deliver the appliances and install the wood floors, Bill?" Bobby was getting antsy. He had to get started on Natalie's car, but these were questions about his new house that he needed answered.

"Your beautiful home should be ready to furnish by mid-January. I gave all my men a week off for the Christmas holidays, Bobby. Otherwise we would have been move-in ready for the New Year. I hope that's OK with you."

"Sure, Bill, no problem. All's good in the world, Bill. You take care of your employees, and your employees will take care of you. My dad used to say that about family and friends. By the way, I'll be here this morning working on my girlfriend's car. Do you mind if I use your generator once in a while?"

"No problem, Bobby. My generator's your generator. Do you need to borrow any tools?"

"No, thanks, Bill. I'm not building a car; I'm just doing some repairs and maintenance. I stopped by the self-storage and picked up my mechanic's tools on the way over." Bobby had also stopped at his friend's Auto Air Repair shop to make an appointment to fix the Chevy's air-conditioning system. When it came to understanding the ABCs of fixing a car, Bobby was as good as they come, but the more complicated things, like transmissions and air-conditioning systems, were better left to the experts. Bobby would spend the next three hours changing the oil, replacing the broken electric window motor, and tuning up the car with new spark plugs. He would also put on new belts and hoses so that Natalie would not have to worry about her car breaking down at the worst possible time…which is any time you break down! Bobby's dad had always told him that there is never a good time for a bad thing to happen.

The old, dirty motor oil dripped slowly, one drop at a time, into the collection pan Bobby had placed underneath Natalie's Chevy. The hood was up, and Bobby was busy replacing the tired, crusty spark plugs, which looked as if they had never been changed.

With all new belts and hoses installed, this Caprice was almost ready for a test drive. Bobby inserted and tightened the last spark plug and then walked around to the passenger door, where the faulty electric window motor was dangling. Bobby disconnected the wires, reconnected them to the new mechanism, and secured the motor with two machine screws. He put the door panel back on, slapped the side of Natalie's car, and said, "Done."

He looked at his watch, pulled the red cell phone out of his pocket, and called Nick, his friend at the Auto Air Repair shop down the street from Publix. Nick's was *the* place to go if your auto air-conditioning system was on the blitz, not only because he was the most dependable shop in Lake Worth, but also because he was honest, experienced, and the most reasonably priced. Nick and Bobby had known each other for twenty years. They were in the military together and had both served two tours in Iraq and Afghanistan, so needless to say, Bobby got a really good deal from Nick.

"Auto Air Repair, Nick speaking."

"Nick, this is Bobby. You got time for me right now?"

"I've got a bay wide open for you, buddy. Come on over. We'll have your air working like new in two hours, tops. See ya shortly, man."

Bobby replaced the old oil filter, tightened the oil plug, and filled the crankcase with synthetic oil. He reminded himself that he must explain to Natalie the benefit to her engine of using synthetic oil as opposed to regular oil, another of life's lessons that he had learned from his father.

Vroooom. Natalie's Chevy was purring like a kitten, or was it growling like a junkyard dog? This eight-cylinder beast of a car sounded like it could flat-out fly if it were near an airport. He pressed the accelerator several times, *vroooom, vrooooom, vrooooom,* and then he shut off the ignition.

All the noise brought Bill, the bearded contractor, out of the house to see what was going on. Bill tipped his Miami Dolphins baseball cap to Bobby, who nodded his head and gently patted the Chevy on its rear fender. "Sounds like a new car, doesn't it, Bill?"

"Maybe a muscle car, like those you see on CAR TV, Bobby. Paint that car a hot color, put on some of those big rims and twenty-six-inch tires, some hydraulics, and a rocking bass sound system, and you will have a car that any high school kid would love to own."

"Yeah, Bill, I guess I could do all that, but my Natalie is kinda conservative, and I don't think she would be very happy if I returned her car with it bouncing up and down and rap music bouncing people off the walls. So after I clean up my mess, I'm on my way to get her AC fixed, then I'm getting her Chevy painted. This is my Christmas present for Natalie."

Bill waved goodbye and went back inside the house, where the echo of pounding hammers and electric saws reverberated off the concrete walls.

Bobby pulled the red cell phone from his pocket, and the next call he made with his new phone was to Dan, the painter and owner/operator of Like-New Paint and Body, the shop next door to Nick's air-conditioning repair shop. "Hey, Dan, are you up to painting my girlfriend's car today? I'm on my way over to Nick's to get her AC repaired, so I can come next door and do the paper-work. Probably be there in twenty minutes."

"Great, Bobby, you still want the same color that you picked out last week? I've got the paint right here, Viper Red."

"Yep!" answered Bobby. "Natalie is a fox, and her car should be the Red Fox."

Bobby was beginning to feel hunger pangs as he turned Natalie's car keys over to Nick at the repair shop. "Nick, my new phone number is 561-329…uh…uh…shoot, I can't remember the number, and I need to get something to eat. I'll call you in an hour. I'm going to hoof it back to Publix for a sub."

"I've got your number here in my cell, Sarge. Remember, you called me earlier? I'll save your number to my phone, and when I'm through, I'll call you." Nick already had the hood up, had the car idling, and was testing the AC compressor with a gadget that had red, yellow, and black knobs; a small digital TV screen; and wires with clamps on the ends. "This repair will be a slam dunk," said Nick as he disconnected his device. "One hour, tops, OK, Bobby?" Nick reached into his pocket, retrieved the keys to his Ford pickup, and tossed them to Bobby. "Take my truck, Sarge, and would you bring me back a chicken tender sub? They're on sale this week for four-ninety-nine. Lettuce, onions, mayo, tomatoes, and pickles. And don't forget the salt and pepper."

Bobby caught the keys in midair, thanked Nick, and told him that he'd be back in an hour or so.

CHAPTER 73

Tuesday, December 22
Mona Takes Missy to See Fir
Iggy the Iguana

Tuesday was such a beautiful day in Lake Worth, with just a hint of a cool breeze, a soft, yellow sun climbing slowly in the southeastern sky, temperatures in the midsixties, and a sky so blue that it must surely be reflecting the sea. And then the day became even more beautiful. I saw my Missy walking toward me. She was wearing a white dress and white shoes and carrying a paper bag in her left hand. Next to her and tightly holding her right hand was Mona. They were walking side by side from the parking lot toward my bench. I was so excited that I began to shiver, even though I was not at all cold. Trees don't get cold. I was just, well, overwhelmed with excitement. Missy walked over and circled me until she located my broken branch. Her small, soft hand embraced my limb and gently held the two pieces together, and she asked in her concerned voice, "Does that feel better, Mr. Fir?"

"Yes, oh yes, Missy. When you hold my branch like that, the pain goes away. It's like magic, Missy. Thank you for coming to see me today. I've missed you so much. What's in the bag?"

"I brought you an ornament, Mr. Fir. Mrs. Williams gave it to me to hang on one of your branches. Mrs. Williams is watching me all day while Mommy works. She lives right across the street, Mr. Fir. This morning, she played cards with me, and we talked about her granddaughter in North Carolina. Would you like to meet her?"

Before I could answer, Missy let go of my broken branch and ran over to Mona, grabbed her by the hand, and pulled her arm toward where I stood. Missy looked up at me and then at Mona. "See, Mrs. Williams, isn't he beautiful? And wouldn't he look perfect by your bay window? Let's take him home, please?"

I was speechless. Could this really be happening? Was I going to be adopted today by Mona? Oh, the joy of it all. Missy and Mona and Natalie, and maybe even Bobby, would decorate me, and there would be Christmas carols, and everyone would sing and be happy, but then Mona popped my bubble.

"Oh, no, Missy, he's too big. I couldn't manage a tree that big."

"I'll help you manage him, Mrs. Williams, and Kenny will put him on your car. OK? I'll go get Kenny."

"No, no, no, Missy!" blurted Mona. "I'm an old lady, and I have to put up a small tree, one that I can manage by myself."

"You keep saying that. What does 'manage' mean, Mrs. Williams?"

Mona looked down at Missy, then squatted so that they could talk face to face. She held both of Missy's hands in hers and quietly whispered, "Manage means taking care of him, taking him off the car and into the house, finding a big enough stand to put on his trunk, standing him up in the right place, decorating him, and keeping him watered. It's a lot of work with a tree that big, Missy, and I'm an old lady. You talk to your mom about *you* buying Mr...."

"Mr. Fir is his name, Mrs. Williams. Come over here, and I will introduce you." Missy pulled at Mona's hand and led her over to where I had been standing, listening to every word. To say that I was disappointed was an understatement. My hopes were so high that Mona would take me home, but she was right. I was so big that I *would* be difficult for a little old lady like Mona to handle.

Missy again wrapped her warm little hand around my branch and whispered, the way she always does, "Mr. Fir, this is Mrs. Williams." Missy had her head inside my branches so that her nose almost touched my trunk. Then she backed out and said, "Mrs. Williams, this is my best friend, Mr. Fir." Missy rotated her eyes from Mona toward me and at the same time lifted her other hand and pointed. "Ain't he the most beautiful tree you've ever seen, Mrs. Williams?"

"Yes, Missy, he certainly is lovely."

Lovely? I'm handsome, and yes, I have beautiful features, but *lovely?* Mary was lovely. She was the love of my life, the *gorgeous* Fraser fir who'd stood by me on the mountain for seven years. I wondered where my Mary was.

Missy was tightly holding my branch when she suddenly asked me, "What's wrong, Mr. Fir? You don't look so good."

Mona, realizing that this was her opportunity to sit down and rest, slowly walked over to the bench and took a seat. The bench was large enough to accommodate three people, but there was a very large man occupying the right side, the middle, and part of the left side. This man had eaten more than his share of French fries, ice cream, and glazed donuts. He must've weighed four hundred pounds. Mona sat on the remaining part of the bench, but half of her rear end was hanging off the side. The man was eating the first of two subs that he had purchased at the Publix deli, and he was washing it down with a gallon jug of sweet tea that was on sale inside the store. Poor Mona was getting crumbed like crazy. Every time this man took a bite, brown bread crumbs flew everywhere, like sawdust at a lumberyard.

"I must be feeling better, Missy, because I am getting a real kick out of watching Mrs. Williams over there on the bench. This man is sitting next to her, eating what appears to be an *everything* sub, and pieces of the sandwich are flying all over and landing on Mrs. Williams. She's got pickle pieces, ham, cheese, lettuce, olives, and bread on her black sweater."

The man with the overactive appetite was barefoot, and one of the store rules was that everyone entering Publix had to be wearing shoes, no exceptions, so it was a mystery to me how he was able to buy two subs and a gallon of tea...barefoot.

"Mr. Fir," asked a most concerned Missy, "why weren't you feeling well? Did someone hurt you?"

"No, Missy, nothing like that." I was listening to and answering Missy while watching the drama unfolding right before my eyes. "Missy," I continued, "Sometimes you get a stomachache, right? Sometimes you get a headache, right? Sometimes, you get a cold or the flu or a rash and your mom has to take special care of you until you feel better. Well, Missy, that's what happened to me yesterday. I started feeling very much out of sorts. I was sick, and Mr. Thornton came by and stayed with me all night. He gave me medicine and took care of me until I was better. He's a real good man, Missy."

"Well, Mr. Fir, I'm glad you are feeling better, but you still look sick, so take all your medicine so that you will get well, OK? I don't want anything bad to happen to you, Mr. Fir."

"OK, Missy."

My sparrows were watching the bread crumbs fly, and they never missed an opportunity to feast on a free meal, so my three little birds flew down, landed on Mona's shoulder, and started to peck at the debris, which was all over her sweater. Slowly she turned her head to look at them, but they simply looked up at Mona, smiled, and continued to peck at the bread crumbs. They felt very safe on Mrs. Williams's shoulder because I had already told them that she was a friend of Missy's and that she is "good people."

But my sparrows were not the only critters watching big chunks of food flying off the big man's sandwich. A three-foot green iguana, who was eating the red flowers of a hibiscus bush nearby, was also watching. Iguanas are lizards that can grow up to six feet long, and they are commonly purchased in pet shops by young boys who want to raise an exotic animal in their home. These lizards are quite cute when they are small, but when they grow too big to handle, many of these iguanas are set free by their humans, and they roam through neighborhoods, eating all the flowers, fruits, and vegetables that they can find. A full-grown male iguana looks like a dragon but without the wings and the fire coming out of its mouth.

The iguana spotted the lettuce and tomatoes and spinach falling to the ground, and he slowly moved himself toward the large man eating on the bench, careful to stay close to the hedges so that he could sneak up on this fresh food source undetected. The lizard inched closer and closer, until he was within ten feet of the bench. Then, just as the big man was taking another bite and a large piece of lettuce was floating like a parachute to the ground, the iguana leaped into the air and landed in the large man's lap. Startled, the man sitting next to Mona jumped into the air as if he had just been scared by a ghost. Big, heavy people can't move very fast, but this man was booking it down the breezeway, screaming as if he had just been attacked by a grizzly bear. He left his other sandwich and the gallon of tea. Mona jumped off the bench too, but that's when Missy came to her aid. "Don't be afraid, Mrs. Williams. It's just Iggy the iguana. He's tame." And Missy fed him a piece of lettuce to show Mrs. Williams that there was nothing to be afraid of. The sparrows returned to Mona's shoulder and finished cleaning her sweater of breadcrumbs.

"How do you know about this lizard, Missy?"

"There was a picture of him in the newspaper. It seems that someone dropped him off here at Publix, and he never left. He never bothered anyone until today. I hope they don't take him away, Mrs. Williams."

Missy and I talked for a little while longer, until Mona called for Missy, who had her head buried so deeply inside my branches that she could easily be mistaken for one of my lower limbs, that is, if she had been wearing a green outfit. Missy backed out and whispered, "I'll be right back. We have to go inside the store for a couple of things, but don't you go anywhere, OK?"

I chuckled and said, "OK, Missy. I'll stay right here until you come back."

Like, where could I go?

CHAPTER 74

Tuesday, December 22
Missy and Mona Go into Publix to Shop

Missy grabbed Mona's index finger, the one you point with, and they sashayed into Publix. The automatic double doors whooshed open as they approached and then whooshed closed once they were inside, and I was alone again.

Three days before Christmas, and I was still not adopted. Three days till Christmas, and I was still leaning against this wall. I was beginning to feel that this wall would have to be surgically removed from my body if someone decided to buy me.

Yep, I was alone. Nobody was sitting on the bench. Carl the crow was agitating me with his abrasive and irritating caws while he patrolled what he thought was his turf. It was obvious to me that he was disturbed with Iggy for crossing into *his* territory and daring to eat *his* food. Methinks that Carl be afraid of Iggy, yep, that's what I think. It was as if Carl thought of himself as the big, bad wolf of the breezeway, but suddenly, there was a *bigger, badder* wolf. Because Carl was obviously afraid of the iguana, Iggy had enabled my sparrows to gorge themselves on the bread crumbs left by the large man who ran away. The ants were happy too. They were feasting on the pieces of meat and cheese under the bench while Iggy continued to munch on lettuce and spinach. The green lizard did not seem inclined to leave, and Carl the crow was furious. He was angrily flapping his wings as he hopped around the breezeway, an angry bird dancing, cawing, and pecking to scare Iggy away. But the iguana would not leave.

CHAPTER 75

Tuesday, December 22, around 1:00 p.m.
Bobby Heads Back to Publix to Visit Fir
Iggy, Mona, and Missy

As Bobby drove up to the Publix Supermarket, he noticed a very large man running down the breezeway as if he were being chased. *Hmmmm,* he thought, *I wonder what he is running from.*

Bobby did not see Missy or Mona, because they were both inside the store shopping, but he saw me. I saw him wave, and I waved back, but I'm sure he didn't notice my branch waving at his fancy truck—you know, me being a tree and all. Anyway, he was driving an absolutely gorgeous red truck, which he pulled into a parking space located at the far side of the lot.

This was his MO, you know, his *modus operandi*...or his habit, to park a long way from the store. I honestly believed that if he could park in Miami, he would have, just for the exercise of walking a long way from his car to the store.

If you are reading this book right now, you may wish to consider where you park when you go shopping, especially if you are weight conscious or maybe just a bit on the heavy side or if you don't want people banging their doors against your car and damaging your paint job. Parking far, far away from the building usually means that you will have no trouble finding a place to park, your car is less likely to get dinged, you will probably lose weight because walking is exercise, and you will save money on gas. I watch people sit in their air-conditioned cars with their motors running for up to ten minutes, waiting for parking spaces to become available close to the store.

I truly apologize for my rambling on and on about this, and I'm probably boring you, but this is one of my pet peeves...something that really bugs me...something that just ticks me off. Can you imagine sitting in a car and throwing quarters out your window? That's what you're doing when you sit in your car with the motor running. Two old geezers were talking about this the other day on Bobby's bench, and they said that AAA did a study that showed a car uses a quarter of a gallon of gas while idling for fifteen minutes. At two dollars per gallon, that's fifty cents. What a waste! Anyway, back to my story.

Bobby got out of the truck, jogged toward his bench, and sat down. The noisy blackbird quickly unnerved Bobby, so he jumped up and proceeded to loudly clap his hands, jump into the air, and chase the crow all around the breezeway. Carl finally got the message and retreated to the safety of a vertical branch, high atop a foxtail palm. Iggy, too, was affected by the clapping noise and the antics of Bobby's bizarre and unusual behavior, so he, too, made a quick lizard exit to the safety of his hibiscus bush. Bobby sat back down on his bench, crammed bubble gum into his mouth, and began to chew.

Relieved to have quiet on the patio, I greeted Bobby with renewed energy in my branches. "Hi, where have you been?" I realized too late that Bobby was incapable of talking with a wad of gum in his mouth, but I had already asked the question.

"Airkenditchin an pant shob, Fir, wat bout chew?" Bobby looked at his wristwatch and then pulled the red phone out of his pocket. "Hmmm, twelve-fifty-two, eight minutes before one." Bobby was thinking about the things he still needed to accomplish before picking up Natalie. The touchscreen of his phone had a telephone icon, and the Boost guy had shown Bobby how to set up his address book. "How hard can this be?" he mused. The screen was black. Bobby couldn't recall how to turn it on. He saw two buttons on the left side, one on the right, and a big one on the front, just below the screen.

"That's it," he said, and he pushed the third button. Ten numbered circles materialized. "Uh-oh," he mumbled to himself, "waz my pazword?" Bobby suddenly remembered his password. "NATALIE#1. How could I forget that?" He typed in his password, and the green telephone icon, together with many other icons of different colors and shapes, populated the screen. Herman had given Bobby a quick tutorial on how to use the phone and had even downloaded the iPhone Tips app, which he could access when he needed help using his phone. Herman also downloaded YouTube and showed him how to locate videos that could literally show him how to do anything from pounding a nail to adding a contact to your new cell phone.

Bobby was vigorously chewing his gum as I watched him tap the YouTube icon. Using his index finger, he pecked at the screen, and within minutes, the phone started talking all by itself. "Good morning. I'm Johnny the cell phone expert, and today I'm going to show you how to use your new Android phone. First…" Bobby jumped as he was touched by a finger tapping him on the back. He looked around and smiled at the little girl behind him. It was Missy, and holding Missy's other hand was Mona. "Hi, Missy! Hi, Mona. What are y'all doing here this afternoon?"

Mona was the first to answer as she took the seat next to Bobby on the green bench. "We came to Publix because we wanted to talk with Mr. Fir, and because I also needed to pick up a few things for dinner."

"Hey, Missy! Did you see that fat man running down the breezeway? He looked quite frightened by something."

Mona and Missy looked at each other and then started to laugh. I was laughing too, but it was only a whisper-laugh. Mona related the whole lizard adventure to Bobby, who, like Missy and Mona, found the story to be quite amusing.

"Mrs. Williams, can I go talk to Mr. Fir?" Missy was tugging on Mona's arm while pulling on her blouse with the other hand. Mona looked down and nodded with a pursed-lip smile. "Sure, tell him I hope he feels better, Missy."

Missy happily skipped over to my broken branch, gently tightening the two pieces together and lightly closing her hand. Just as with the many times before, the energy of this child flowed throughout my body. My pain subsided, and the world seemed right again.

Mona and Bobby sat on the green bench and talked about Natalie and how they lived across from each other and how her new job at Publix was going. Bobby did most of the listening.

Meanwhile, Missy was beaming from ear to ear as she softly whispered, "Mr. Fir, guess what tomorrow is?"

Before I could answer, she blurted out, "Tomorrow is Wednesday! Wednesday, Mr. Fir. And do you know what that means, Mr. Fir?"

I decided to play dumb, even though I knew it was Wednesday, and I knew that Missy would be coming to Publix with Natalie. "No, what does that mean, Missy?" I asked.

"It means we'll get to see each other again, and it means that I am going to tell you a story, silly. Don't you remember? Mommy is bringing me with her, just like she does every Wednesday. She is only working half a day on Wednesday, and she needs to buy all the food for Christmas. I told her that I do not want a plastic tree, and I asked her over and over, again and again, if we could get you tomorrow and take you home."

My eyes brightened, and I asked, "What did she say?"

"Well, that's the really good part, Mr. Fir. She didn't say no. She said that she'd think about it. Isn't that wonderful, Mr. Fir?"

"Yes, it is, Missy, but usually when a parent says that they'll think about it, that's just another way of saying no. I don't want you and me to get our hopes up, but boy, if she says yes, I'll be the happiest tree in the world."

"Me too. I'll be the happiest kid in the world. Let's cross our fingers, OK, Mr. Fir?"

"I don't have fingers, but see the soft ends of my branches? I'll cross *them*, OK, Missy?"

"Missy, come now. We have to go." Mona was motioning for Missy to join her at the bench, where she and Bobby were winding up their conversation.

Missy released my broken limb and waved goodbye. When she got to the bench, she turned her head toward me and blew me a kiss. I could read her lips as she whispered, "I love you, Mr. Fir."

Hand in hand, Missy and Mona headed toward Mona's car with a shopping cart loaded with Christmas goodies.

CHAPTER 76

Tuesday, December 22
Bubble-Blowing Bobby

Bobby blew his first bubble, a doozy, as big as a softball. People walking in and out of Publix stopped to watch as the bubble grew in size. Their children oohed and aahed and gasped as this magnificent pink bubble grew to the size of Bobby's head.

POP.

Laughter and applause filled the breezeway, especially from the children, who were jumping up and down and shrieking with glee. Bobby stood and bowed to the crowd, his face covered with a film of pink bubble gum. He peeled the gum off his face and carefully separated his hair from the sticky gum. As the din of noise subsided, the crowd dispersed, and Bobby and I were again alone.

"Wow, can you put on a show. Did you ever think about going professional? I can see it now: "Radio City Music Hall. World Champion Bubble Blower Bobby Thornton, Live and in Person, December twenty-sixth to January first."

Bobby popped a few more bubbles while sitting in the middle of the bench with his arms spread out on the backrest. His chatter with me seemed to keep most people from sharing Bobby's bench. He asked how I felt. I told him that I felt great, except for the fact that I was still not adopted. He kept telling me to "Keep the faith...Keep the faith, Fir." Then Bobby looked at me and said that he had to run a few errands but would be back later in the afternoon, hopefully before dark. "But first, Fir, I have to go inside to the deli and grab a chicken tender sub for my ol' army buddy Nick. I'm running a bit late, so I'll say my goodbyes now, Fir. *Adios amigo y hasta luego.*"

"What does that mean, Bobby?"

"It's Spanish, Fir. It means, 'goodbye, friend...I'll see you later.'"

I knew it was Spanish, because trees are very smart. I looked over at Bobby and said, "*Que tenga un buen dia*, Bobby...Have a good day."

Bobby turned his head toward me with a puzzled look on his face and then hoofed it into Publix. He was mumbling to himself, "*Que tenga...?* Where'd he learn that?"

After paying for Nick's sub, Bobby jogged to the red truck and drove away. I was alone again. *That would be a good name for a song, "Alone Again,"* I thought, and I began to think of lyrics:

> *Alone again, alone.*
> *I need to find a home.*
> *I need someone who needs a tree,*
> *A Christmas tree,*
> *A tree like me,*
> *Alone.*

Alone except for Carl the cantankerous crow, who was perched in one of the oak trees, screeching and cawing at squirrels and blue jays and mockingbirds and robins and anything and everything that made this world beautiful. I thought to myself, *How can a creature be so angry and ill-tempered all of the time? Oh, well.*

CHAPTER 77

Tuesday, December 22, Afternoon
Ice-Cold Air in Natalie's Cool Car

Bobby returned to Nick's and saw Natalie's car sitting outside. Nick exited the building, waved Bobby over, and motioned for him to get in. *Vroooom.* The Chevy started right up, and ice-cold air filled the cabin of Natalie's Caprice.

"Wow, Nick! Great job! Brrrrr, how cold is it inside this car? Look, when I breathe you can see my breath."

Nick smiled at Bobby, grasped the back of his neck, and squeezed. "Remember how hot it was in Iraq and Afghanistan, Bobby? You and I used to be like each other's shadow, and you always told me that I was the coolest guy you had ever known? Well, I never thought that I was cool. In fact, I always thought I was kind of a nerd. As a kid, none of the other kids thought I was cool, and I was always picked on, but when I met you, that all changed. You were like...like my best friend. And you thought I was cool. That's what you told me."

"Nick, what's the point of all this psycho-babble that's coming out of your mouth?"

"Just listen, Bobby, and I'll explain. When we were over there, I made a pledge that since you thought that I was cool, I would dedicate my life to being cool, and not only that, but I would make other people cool too. That's why I'm in the air-conditioning business. So now that your Chevy's AC is fixed, you are cool, too, Sarge, just like me. We're two cool cats, and soon Natalie will be cool. So what do you think of that?"

"I think you've lost your mind, Nick, but I still love ya, man, and I still think you're cool, even if you are one wild and crazy guy this afternoon."

"You going to marry this girl? You seem like a different man since you met her."

"What do you mean, Cool Guy?"

"I don't know, exactly. I can't put my finger on it, but you just seem…well…happy. Very happy."

"Maybe it's because I'm so cool now." They both laughed, and Nick turned off the engine.

"How much do I owe you, Nick?"

"It's on the house, buddy. Think of it as a wedding gift, or a payback for the many times that you watched my back in the war."

"Thanks, Nick, but I always pay my way, *and* Natalie is my girl-friend, not my fiancée, *and* you were always there watching my back. So, that said, how much do I owe you?" The two friends walked inside, arms on each other's shoulders, and Nick wrote up a quick invoice for sixty-five dollars.

"This is for my labor charge, one hour. The parts were here in the shop. I harvested the parts from a Caprice I had in here last week. By the way, Bobby, this job comes with a lifetime guarantee, so if the air quits working for any reason, just bring it back, and Auto Air Repair will make repairs, with parts and labor covered one hundred percent." The two friends hugged, Nick took another bite from his chicken tender sub, and Bobby walked next door to the paint and body shop.

CHAPTER 78

Tuesday, December 22, Afternoon
Time to Paint the Chevy

Bobby had reservations about painting Natalie's car Viper Red, and as he walked into Dan's shop, he noticed a heavy book filled with paint swatches of every conceivable color to paint a car. This book must have weighed close to ten pounds and was almost eight inches thick. Dan's office had three armchairs, so Bobby picked up the book, took a seat, rested the book in his lap, and began turning pages. He saw purples of every shade, oranges, pinks, reds, blues, greens, blacks, and so on, but he kept returning to the tans, silvers, and whites.

Although he would love to paint the car Viper Red, he reasoned that she was an earth-tone girl. She wore a lot of light brown and white clothing, or light blues, greens, and yellows, and she seemed to like the softer pastels, so he settled on a silver, which would be a neutral color that he felt certain she would love.

Dan's other customers departed. He welcomed Bobby to his shop, and they shook hands. Dan reached for something in the cabinet behind him and clunked a can of Viper Red paint noisily onto the counter. "Let's do it, Bobby. The paint booth is available for the next twenty-four hours. Let me see the car. I need to see how much prep work we will have to do."

"No dents, Dan. No rust. Just burned up by the Florida sun. I think it's the original paint. Uh, Dan, would it be OK if we don't use the Viper Red? While I was waiting my turn, I went through your book and found a silver color that I really like."

Dan scratched his head and looked at Bobby. "But I thought she was your *fox*, so you wanted to paint the car red, you know, like a fox?"

Bobby looked down at his shoes, placed his hands on the back of his head, and then looked back at Dan. "Dan, I'm just not sure Viper Red is appropriate for Natalie. What do you think?"

"Bobby, I'll paint the car any color that you want, but I think that Viper Red is a win-win situation for you. Come with me."

Dan walked with Bobby to the area where his personal truck was parked, a space on the north side of his building that was shaded from the sun. As they turned the corner, Bobby saw an absolutely gorgeous red Ford F-150 pickup truck.

"Viper Red, Bobby. Also known as 'resale red,' for obvious reasons. Everybody wants to buy a red car. It just *pops* when you see it. What do *you* think?"

"*Wow*, is that your truck?"

"Yes, and a day doesn't go by that someone doesn't ask me to sell it to them. And I have enough of the paint left over from other jobs that I will not have to charge you for the paint. No, think about what I just said—*free paint!*"

"Free? You did say free, right?"

"Yes, Sarge. *Free*. Like, no charge. Like, on the house."

"OK, let's do it. When will the car be ready?"

"Well, if we start right now and I get her prepped, taped, and sanded today, I can paint it first thing tomorrow morning. It will take about two hours to paint and eight hours to dry."

"If I pay you extra, could you maybe paint it tonight? Then it could dry overnight."

"For you, Bobby, consider it done. Let me have the key." Bobby took the car keys off of Natalie's ring and handed them to Dan. Dan jumped into the car and started the engine. He rolled down the window and looked up at Bobby. "Where did you get such a good air-conditioning system? Feels like Alaska in here." They both laughed, and Dan asked, "How are you getting home?"

Bobby looked down at Dan and answered, "I was going to rent a car from that company that will come pick you up…uh… Enterprise, I think it's called."

Dan jumped out of the car and said, "No, that isn't going to happen." He went inside his office and came out with the keys to his pickup truck. He handed the keys to Bobby and pointed to where his truck was parked. "That's it, over there, the Viper Red pickup."

Again they both laughed, and Dan climbed into the Caprice while Bobby headed toward the pickup.

CHAPTER 79

Tuesday, December 22
Fir Is Adopted

Not five minutes had passed after Bobby left when a nice young couple came outside with Kenny to look at Christmas trees. There were only ten of us left, and I was the only Fraser fir. These people had certain requirements, and one of them was that they wanted a Fraser fir and *only* a Fraser fir. Stacy and Ron also insisted that the tree be seven feet tall. Well, I was a Fraser fir, and I was seven feet tall, so it was a match made in heaven. Kenny had me leaning against the wall so that my broken branch was not visible. He had watered me twice that day, and I was standing tall, and my needles were as supple as the skin of a baby.

Stacy touched one of my branches and remarked, "Ron, feel how soft he is. This is a healthy tree."

Ron came over and touched my needles. "Sold," he said. "Put him on my car, the Honda Civic right over there." Ron pointed to the car parked in the first handicapped parking space, nearest the store. Kenny wrapped me in mesh, lifted me up onto his shoulder, and carried me over to the Honda. These young people did not seem to be handicapped. They followed behind Kenny, and as we neared the car, Ron clicked his remote, and the trunk popped open. He quickstepped around Kenny, grabbed a blanket out of the trunk, and ran around to the passenger side to cover his roof so that it would not be scratched. Stacy danced around me to the driver's side, and the newlyweds worked as a team to smooth out the blanket, I'm sure so that I could have a comfortable ride to my new home. Kenny used a brown hemp cord to tie me securely to their roof. Ron and Stacy gave Kenny a five-dollar tip, slammed the car doors, and drove away. Stacy was so happy. I could hear her singing a Christmas carol all the way home, *my* home. I was happy too, so I hummed along with her,

> *It's beginning to look a lot like Christmas, everywhere we go.*
> *There's a tree in the Grand Hotel, one in the park as well,*
> *It's the sturdy kind that doesn't mind the snow.*

But there was no snow in Lake Worth, only houses garlanded with colored lights, big Santas filled with air, nativity scenes with wise men and the baby Jesus, and reindeer with red noses everywhere. As I lay on the roof of Stacy and Ron's car, I could see the cloudless blue sky of the heavens, and I thanked God for finding me a home. I also thought of Bobby. He had told me to keep the faith. *I will miss Bobby very much…and Missy, oh, my dear Missy. She was going to come to Publix tomorrow to tell me a story. How can I be both happy and sad?*

CHAPTER 80

Tuesday, December 22, Afternoon
The Ride to Fir's New Home

I was truly enjoying the ride home. I enjoyed the brisk breezes, which, with the wind-chill factor, made it feel like a chilly winter afternoon on my mountain in North Carolina. Ron and Stacy attended to several errands before taking me home to be decorated and to become a part of their family. First they stopped at the bank, where Ron jumped out of the car and went inside to use the ATM. Stacy needed some wrapping paper, Scotch tape, and ribbon, all of which were on sale at the local Walmart, and Ron was running low on cash. So the second stop was Walmart, to buy the Christmas wrapping stuff. It was all kind of exciting, especially being finally away from the Publix breezeway, where I had stood for so long.

But while they walked inside to shop, I lay on the Honda roof, baking in the Florida sun. Now, I don't know if you know how hot it gets in Florida, even in the winter, but when that sun shines directly on you for an extended period of time, the ultraviolet rays can burn you to a crisp. That's called sunburn, and if you don't put a good sunblock on, you can get totally fried. Well, trees don't get sunburned, but without water, they become very dry and dehydrated, and that is what was happening to me. Kenny always kept me watered. I was also beginning to feel weak and dizzy. Those are signs of sunstroke or heatstroke.

I waited and waited for Ron and Stacy to return, but there were so many people inside doing their last-minute Christmas shopping that the lines must have been humongous. It seemed like an hour had elapsed since they went inside, and there were so many cars in this parking lot that I feared they would never find their Honda and I would be tied on top of the vehicle forever. Speaking of which, Ron had tied me so tight that the bindings were almost cutting through my branches, especially when we were moving, you know, with the bumps and turns that make you bounce and sway. To further add to my discomfort, Kenny had wrapped me in that mesh again, only this time, the plastic mesh was white. My broken branch ached, I was hot, and I was thirsty. I was a mess.

Then I saw Ron and Stacy, pushing a shopping cart filled to overflowing. Ron had his arm around Stacy, and they were discussing baby names. I had thought Stacy was just a little on the chunky side, but it turned out she was pregnant. She was going to be a mommy, just like Natalie. *Wow,* I thought. *How cool is that?*

The engine started, the car backed out, and we were headed home, or so I thought. Stacy had a "*craving* for a milkshake," and between 4:00 p.m. and 6:00 p.m., Steak 'n' Shake had a two-for-the-price-of-one special (also called a twofer), so it was off to, hopefully, our last stop, and then home.

And so it was the last stop. Stacy ordered a pumpkin pie milkshake with pickles, while Ron came out with a more traditional strawberry milkshake. On the ride home, I could hear them talking. They settled on the name Michelle if the baby was a girl or Mark if it was a boy.

The Honda made a turn into their driveway, and after the engine was turned off and the doors opened, Ron proceeded to take me off the roof. He sliced through the cordage that secured me to his Honda and lifted me, so very gently, off the blanket.

My new home was beautiful, a pastel yellow with white trim, and it had a white front porch that wrapped around one side of the house and a two-car carport, where Stacy's new minivan was parked. There was a garden of roses, all in bloom and all of different colors and sizes. A trellis in the shape of a large fan held tightly to some small red tea roses and was positioned at the western end of the porch to block the afternoon sun. I had struck it rich. I was in a happy home, with two young people who loved each other and who would soon become loving parents. Of this I was sure, and now I was an essential part of their life.

CHAPTER 81

Tuesday, December 22, around 5:30 p.m.
Two Dogs and a Cat

I could hear a small dog happily barking inside the house, a modest two-bedroom home with one bath. I knew the dog was small because little dogs yap and big dogs woof. Medium-sized dogs just bark. I thought I heard a cat meowing, but I wasn't sure. Ron was making a lot of noise taking me off the car, and Stacy was chattering nonstop about how elated she was. I mean like real happy... elated.

While I was admiring my new home, Ron was being ever so careful with me as he lifted and carried me to a grassy spot near their front porch. He eased me onto the ground and walked up three steps to join Stacy, who was still talking about her new Christmas tree, *me*. A wooden swing hung from the porch beams, which were shaded by a trellis of red roses and their bushy green leaves—Christmas colors. Stacy led Ron to the wooden swing, where they sat down and Stacy held Ron's hand. "He kicked today, Ron. He's kicking, now. You want to feel?" Stacy guided Ron's hand to her stomach, and the baby kicked Ron's hand as if on cue. Ron smiled from ear to ear and put both hands on the side of Stacy's head. "I love you, Stacy."

Stacy and Ron started smooching and kissing on the swing while the dogs (there turned out to be two) barked and yapped and the cat, a Siamese, cried like a baby and I lay by the porch, waiting to be decorated. It was clear to me that there was a lot of love in this home. *Wow*, I thought, *I have won the lottery.*

Ron had worked hard all day as a block mason, and he was beat. He also smelled of perspiration. "Stacy," he said, "I'm going inside to take a shower, and let's take care of the tree this evening, OK?"

Stacy said, "OK, Ron. I have a tuna casserole in the oven with pasta, peas, and melted cheese on top, just the way you love it. I'll heat it up, and we can have dinner after your shower. While you bathe, I'm going to walk the dogs. I don't want any accidents on our new wood floors." Stacy leashed up the dogs, turned on the oven, and walked out the front door. The dogs sniffed me, and the male started to lift his leg, but Stacy jerked hard on the leash, which sent the larger dog tumbling to the ground. "No, Freddie, bad dog. You can't pee on my new Christmas tree." Stacy pulled that leash in the nick of time, otherwise I would have been soaked wet with yellow water. They walked down the sidewalk, and I watched as the dogs sniffed everything, tugged hard at their leashes, and pulled Stacy in all directions. More than once they ran around her in opposite directions, tying her feet up so that she could not walk until she untangled herself.

CHAPTER 82

Tuesday, December 22, 5:15 p.m.
Bobby Picks Up Natalie from Work

At precisely 5:15 p.m., Bobby pulled into the parking lot of Homes Depot, the real estate office where Natalie worked. Natalie's day ended at 5:30, and she had instructed Bobby to please not be late in picking her up. Bobby had learned from his mother to *never* be late for any appointment, be it a job interview, a doctor appointment, or a football practice.

"Never be late to class," she had said many times, "and never be late for dinner, and when you start dating, *never* be late in picking her up. Always show up early at a girl's home so that you can meet her parents, and always be well dressed and well groomed." She had admonished Bobby when he was late for anything, which was almost *never*. So here Bobby sat, in Dan's Viper Red pickup truck, with the radio tuned to 101.5 FM, a mellow music station that played soft love music and was hosted in the evenings by Delilah. He had showered and shaved at the community center, and he smelled of Polo.

Bobby fidgeted with the knobs and buttons of Dan's truck, smoothed his hand over the leather seats, and reclined his driver-side seat with its power button. *This is a cool ride,* Bobby was thinking. *I might just sleep in this truck tonight.* As he fiddled with the power windows and after playing with all of Dan's toys, he looked down at his watch and then drove in the direction of the real estate office.

There were no cars in the parking lot, so he assumed that Natalie was locking up and would be out shortly. His watch had the long hand on six and the short hand half way between five and six. Bobby looked at the door and then back at his watch. "C'mon, Natalie, it's 5:30." He was becoming antsy because Natalie had said 5:30, and it was now 5:30. "I'll give you five more minutes, Natalie, and then, if you're not out that door, I'm coming to get you." That five minutes passed slowly. As he sat behind the wheel, Bobby became more and more agitated and concerned. Had he not heard Natalie correctly? Had she said 5:00 p.m., or 4:30? Had something happened to her?

He thought about his phone. *Didn't I give her my number? Why doesn't she call?* Bobby began to panic and jumped out of the car, running full steam toward the front door. He grabbed the handle and pulled hard, but the door was locked. Bobby pounded on the door and put his face against the glass to see inside, but the lights were off, and it was obvious that this place was closed. Still, Bobby stood there, his breath fogging the glass as he scanned the inside of her real estate office, looking for any sign of life.

Bobby had failed to ask Natalie for her phone number, and he did not know where she lived.

"MONA! She lives across the street from Natalie. I'll just go back to Publix and ask Mr. Kemp or Kenny for Mona's address." Bobby ran to his truck, turned the key, and revved the engine. He was perspiring profusely, and the armpits of his shirt were wet with sweat. Even though it was cool outside, Bobby had beads of sweat on his forehead and dripping from his nose. The radio was playing a Taylor Swift song that he absolutely loved, but now, as his frustration turned to fear and anxiety, he slapped the on/off knob to silence his favorite female vocalist. *Where is my Natalie? Is she all right?* He put the truck in drive and backed out of his parking spot in the empty lot. His rear wheels were spinning so fast that they squealed and left a rubber mark on the pavement as he sped toward the exit, but Bobby had to slam on his brakes to avoid hitting a green Honda making a left turn into the real estate parking lot. It was Mona, with Natalie and Missy.

Poor Bobby was a mess. His heart was pounding, his head throbbed, and his eyes were filled with tears. He slumped forward, his head leaning against the steering wheel, and once he regained his composure, he placed his truck in park and jumped out of the pickup.

Natalie calmly opened the passenger door of Mona's car and was barely standing upright when Bobby wrapped his arms around her and lifted Natalie off the ground. He hugged her tightly and spun her around with her feet dangling off the ground. "Oh, Natalie, I was so worried that something had happened to you. I am so happy that you are all right."

"Bobby, you're crying, and you're soaked with perspiration."

Bobby lowered Natalie to the ground and said, "Yes, when no one answered the door, I thought the worst. My mind went wild with thoughts of why you weren't there and…and…well, I don't ever want anything bad to happen to you. I love you, Natalie."

Mona was behind the wheel, watching this spectacle in disbelief, and Missy, well, Missy was grinning from ear to ear. She liked Mr. Thornton. Her "Mr. Fir" had told her that he was a good man.

"What happened, Natalie? Why was the place all locked up?" Bobby asked as he wiped the sweat off his brow. "I darn near had a heart attack. Here, let me give you my phone number." Bobby reached into his pocket and asked for Natalie's number. Herman had told him that if he called someone, he could then save that call to his address book.

So, there in the parking lot, with the moon rising in the east, an almost full moon, and stars twinkling in a cloudless sky, Bobby called his girl, who was so close that their skin touched. The sun had long since set, and the temperature was rapidly dropping. Streetlights were casting ominous shadows throughout the parking lot when Natalie asked, "Where's my car?"

"Yeah, I knew you'd ask me that. I couldn't get it running right, so I dropped it off at my friend's. He will make it right first thing in the morning. He loaned me his truck. Why don't we go over to Grandma's Restaurant, and I'll treat everyone to one of the best home-cooked meals that you can find away from home? Tell Mona to follow me over there. It's near Publix."

"Oh, Bobby, I'd love to, but we've all eaten. It's a long story, and I'll tell you all about it tomorrow when you pick me up. I only work half a day tomorrow, so meet me at 12:30, and please, don't be late."

They both laughed and hugged tightly, and Bobby opened the door of Mona's car so she could get in. Bobby's mom had always taught him to treat girls with kindness, gentleness, and respect. She taught him to always open the car door for them so that they could more easily get into and out of an automobile. "That," she said, "is what a gentleman does." She taught Bobby many other things about being a gentleman, like assisting a lady at a dinner table by standing behind her chair to help her move the chair closer to the table as she is sitting down. Another lesson was about flowers. His mom said, "Bobby, girls love flowers. Always have a bouquet of flowers when you pick up your girl."

As Bobby was thinking about the lessons he learned from his mom, he suddenly slapped the side of Mona's car and said, "Can you wait just a sec? I almost forgot. I have something for you." Bobby ran to his truck and retrieved a massive bouquet of multicolored flowers. He skipped toward the Honda as if he were a teenage boy in love with his first girl. Behind his back were three bouquets of flowers wrapped in crinkly, clear cellophane. Flowers of red, purple, yellow, white, and pink. Beautiful green leaves and baby's breath completed the bouquet. "For you, Natalie. Happy Tuesday night." He handed her the flowers and shaped his lips into a kiss.

Natalie had a tear in her eye and a smile on her face as she watched Bobby get into his truck. She yelled to him, "Don't forget, 12:30." Then she silently whispered, "I love you too, Bobby Thornton."

CHAPTER 83

Tuesday, December 22, around 6:30 p.m.
Bobby at Grandma's Diner

B obby made his turn onto Jog Road and headed north toward Publix to sit with his friend Fir and talk for a bit, but his stomach had other plans. As he signaled to make a right onto Lantana Road, he saw the flashing neon sign that said "Grandma's Home Cooking," so instead of Publix, he turned right and backed his truck into a spot where no other cars were parked. Another of the many lessons learned from his father. "Son," Dad said to Bobby as the youngster was learning to drive, "always back into a parking spot. Most parking lot accidents are caused by drivers backing out of their spot; they don't look behind them, or they don't see anyone as they put the car in reverse and start backing out, and suddenly a car comes speeding through the lot or a pedestrian is behind their backing-up car. Bam, pow, crash, and guess what? It's your fault. If you back in, you simply get in your car, start 'er up, put it in drive, and off you go, no accidents, because you are looking through the windshield."

Bobby thought about his dad as he backed in, but those memories quickly evaporated as he smelled the aroma of fried chicken coming from Grandma's. The place was packed, but there was a counter stool available, so the hostess seated him immediately. The waitress handed him a menu, and Bobby started studying all the dinner specials. "Hmmm, it's between fried chicken, fried pork chops, and meat loaf." As Bobby was pondering his choices, the man seated on Bobby's left turned and in a deep voice cheerfully wished Bobby a merry Christmas. Bobby recognized this voice and smiled as he turned his head and greeted his dear friend Paul.

"Paul, merry Christmas to you, buddy. I was going to look you up tomorrow."

"Why, Bobby? You need me to help you with something?" Paul was noisily stirring his cup of coffee, his second cup.

"I've got something for you, Paul. A Christmas gift." Bobby reached into his pocket and pulled out a crisp fifty-dollar bill and handed it to Paul.

"Oh, God bless you, Bobby. I'm flat broke, and I don't get my disability check until next week." Paul jumped off his stool and almost knocked Bobby off his seat as he pulled him up and embraced him with a tight hug. "Thank you so much, Bobby. Thank you, thank you, thank you."

Bobby returned the hug and said, "Paul, you're always there for me. You always do so much for me. Merry Christmas." Bobby pushed him away and said, "Let me buy you a burger or some fried chicken, Paul."

"You're on, Bobby. I'll have the half pounder with fries, OK?"

"It's done," and Bobby called the waitress. "I'll have the fried chicken, steamy taters, and turnip greens, and my friend will have that monster burger with cheese and fries."

Bobby and Paul talked politics and religion and about almost anything that was controversial. They loved to debate, discuss, and argue about everything, and that is what controversy means, two totally different points of view discussed or debated by two or more people.

Paul looked to his left, where a hefty middle-aged man was eating gooey sunny-side up eggs. Paul leaned toward Bobby's stool, bumping his arm with his right shoulder. Paul cupped his mouth and motioned with his head for Bobby to look at the plate of eggs.

"What?" asked Bobby.

"Look at those delicious eggs, Bobby. They are cooked perfectly, with runny yolk and wet whites. This guy knows how to eat eggs. He can daub his toast in the egg or mix it with his grits or dip a bite of potatoes into the egg or eat it like I do. I mix everything together, grits, potatoes, and eggs. I cut my eggs into small pieces so that I will have egg in every bite. My favorite thing to do is, when I get everything mixed together, I like to spoon the mixture all over my toast, as if I were spreading peanut butter on bread. Mmmmmmmm, good."

Bobby was now staring at the man's plate of food while he envisioned Paul slicing and dicing and mixing everything together. "Yuck, Paul. Are you some kind of demented nut? Don't you know that you should make sure that your eggs are fully cooked? Don't you know that eggs come from chickens and that no one should ever eat raw chicken? You could get really sick. They call it salmonella, Paul. And raw egg is raw chicken, so you better make sure that your eggs are fully cooked. I like my eggs scrambled, with absolutely no goo floating around on my eggs. Salmonella, Paul. Raw chicken and raw eggs."

"You're nuttier than a fruit cake, Bobby. If they were worried about you getting sick by eating eggs that were sunny-side up, they wouldn't offer them on the menu. An egg is an egg. A chicken is a chicken. End of discussion."

But Bobby was determined to win this debate, so he leaned over and whispered in Paul's ear, "See how heavy that guy is? You want to know why he is so heavy? He has the salmonella sickness. Early stages, but it's clear that he's got it."

Just as Paul was preparing his rebuttal, the waitress placed two platters of hot, steamy food in front of Bobby and Paul. She refilled Paul's coffee cup and asked Bobby what he would like to drink.

"Water with two slices of lemon, ma'am."

Paul lunged at the half-pound cheeseburger like a starving lion would attack a careless zebra. Grease, melted cheese, and mayonnaise were dripping down his chin as Paul chewed on his first mouthful. He reached for the ketchup, unscrewed the cap, aimed the open end at his fries, and pounded the bottom of the bottle. Nothing came out, so he slapped the jar a little harder. Then again. Still no ketchup.

"You need some help, Paul? Looks like that little ol' bottle is more than you can handle. Looks like a 'big boy' job to me. Let me help you."

Bobby went to take the jar away from Paul, but Paul glared at him and said, "Don't!" Paul pulled the bottle close to his chest so that Bobby couldn't get it, but that's when it happened. The pounding had dislodged the clog, and red ketchup squirted all over his shirt and into his lap, and some even dripped onto one of his white tennis shoes.

Bobby howled with laughter, and Paul fumed. The diner grew quiet as everyone turned and stared at Bobby, who was snorting like a pig and slapping himself on both thighs. He jumped off his stool and doubled over as he replayed the ketchup moment in his mind.

Paul stood, a towering man of six-foot-five, and glared angrily at Bobby. Bobby looked up at Deep Voice and, seeing the anger in Paul's eyes, immediately stopped laughing. They stared at each other for what seemed like an eternity. A hush washed over the diner as the patrons watched the trouble that was unfolding. Then Paul started to snicker, then to chuckle, and then he began to howl. Bobby reached for a French fry and lathered it with ketchup from Paul's shirt. This made the whole restaurant erupt in laughter. Sometimes the worst things that can happen to a person turn out to be the funniest and the most memorable.

Bobby and Paul returned to their stools and resumed eating their dinners. Paul carefully tapped on the bottle and watched as a small puddle of red ketchup settled next to his fries. Paul looked at Bobby, who was watching his every move, and they both grinned from ear to ear. Bobby couldn't help but remark, "Well, Paul, I've got some good news and some bad news; which one do you want to hear first?"

"The *bad* news. Lay it on me, Bobby."

"Well, Paul, you've got ketchup on your shirt."

Paul shook his head and smiled. "And, wise guy, what's the good news?"

"The good news, big guy, and it really is good news, is that if you get hungry tonight, you can suck on your shirt."

This remark brought tears of laughter to both their eyes. Meanwhile, the heavy man sitting next to Paul had decided to leave. He had been splattered with ketchup too, but when he saw the size of Paul, he just eased his heavy self off the stool and waddled out of the restaurant, content to say nothing and just leave. His plate was empty.

Grandma's returned to normal, with glasses clinking, spoons stirring, utensils tinkling against dishes, and talking...lots of loud conversation. People go to restaurants not just to eat but also to enjoy each other's company. To socialize. To talk. And...to laugh.

Bobby quickly devoured his crunchy fried chicken. Years ago, he was a dark meat chicken eater, legs and thighs only, but as of late, he'd discovered that the white meat was the better choice. He had come to realize that the breast meat was healthier due to the lower fat content, and he was no spring chicken anymore, so he had to be mindful of eating the healthier food choices. The irony, of course, was that while he was devouring the chicken breast, which was fried, he was lathering his biscuits with oodles of butter, real butter. Grandma's only served *real* butter. Most diners offered the cheaper margarine. Bobby felt that margarine was like an imitation of butter. Bobby's mother had told him years ago that they used to take lard and mix it with yellow food coloring and artificial flavoring to make it look and taste like butter.

She said, "Bobby, if you want to eat something that tastes like butter, eat butter! Don't eat that imitation stuff. That's like eating plastic." She wasn't even sure that it was digestible. As Bobby unwrapped two pats and mixed it into his steamy mashed potatoes, he thought of her telling him that if you are going to eat margarine, you may as well eat a plastic water bottle. More butter flavored his turnip greens, slowly melting and disappearing into the delightful southern vegetable, which was hard to find anywhere but at Grandma's.

Paul was hunkered over his plate, stuffing ketchup-coated French fries into his mouth in rapid succession, as if he were afraid someone was going to steal his food. His burger was gone, and the heaping pile of fries had almost disappeared. "What are you doing for Christmas, Bobby?"

After forking the last of his taters into his mouth, Bobby looked over at Paul and said, "Well, big guy, I've been invited over to Natalie's house for Christmas Eve. What about you? I could always ask Natalie if you could join us. I'm sure she'd say yes."

"No, Bobby, I'm gonna be OK. I've been spending a lot of time at the library on Lawrence Road, and I met a lady there. Her name is Ann, and she has been teaching me all about the internet. She helped me set up an email account, showed me how to surf the web, and best of all, helped me get on Facebook."

"You are on Facebook? You have an email address? You told me that you could never learn how to use a computer. I think your exact words were, 'I'm not very smart, Bobby.' Do you remember telling me that?"

"Yep! But I was wrong. Ann showed me how, and it's really quite easy. She is a terrific lady, and we've been seeing each other for a couple of months now. Ya know, Bobby, all my life I've been told that I'm not very smart. When I was in school, I was told that I had a low IQ. All these years I've believed that...well...that I'm kinda dumb. But Annie said that's hogwash. She said that I'm as smart as a whip, and you know what, Bobby? I think she's right. But you want to hear the best part?"

Bobby was transfixed on his pal Paul, sitting on the edge of his stool, listening to every word. He lifted his water glass, took a big swallow, and then wiped his mouth with the napkin in his lap. "What's the best part, Paul?"

"My son found me on Facebook. I haven't seen him for ten years, not since the divorce from his mother. You know that story, Bobby. Probably the worst time of my life. That's when my world seemed to implode. My business failed, my wife left and took my boy with her, and she just disappeared with my son, Paul Junior. He was sixteen when she disappeared. Anyway, he found me, Bobby, and he's married. I'm a grandfather. We've got us a Paul the third. He's one year old. And the best part is they've invited me and

Annie over for Christmas. Isn't that just great? They live right here in Lake Worth."

"That's wonderful, Paul. I know you've missed your son. I'm so happy for you. Tell you what: meet me tomorrow morning at nine, and we'll get you spiffed up. You can't go to your son's house in a ketchup shirt. Go to the community center and get yourself cleaned up, shave, and then we'll go get you some new duds at the thrift store, then a haircut, and we'll turn you into one very handsome dude. I've got Dan's truck, so I'll pick you up at nine a.m. And Paul, be showered and shaved, OK?"

They left the diner and hugged, and each went his separate way. Paul headed toward the alley behind the Boost shopping center, and Bobby ambled slowly toward Dan's Viper Red truck. A toothpick was hanging from Bobby's mouth as he reached for the keys. Chirp, chirp. The lights flashed and the doors unlocked themselves. Bobby slid onto the soft leather seats and rubbed them with the palm of his right hand. *Boy, this is nice,* he thought. *I have to get me one of these trucks.* He turned the key, and the engine roared to life. Bobby felt like he was behind a team of horses, rearing in the air and ready to run. He put the shifter into drive and pulled out of Grandma's parking lot. Next stop, Publix, to see me.

CHAPTER 84

Tuesday, December 22, 8:30 p.m.
Fir inside Ron's House

It was 8:30 p.m. when the dishes were washed and the leftovers put away in the fridge. Ron and Stacy did not have a dishwasher, but a new Sears Kenmore was on the wish list—Ron had not told Stacy that Santa was going to install the dishwasher on Christmas Eve when he delivered her other presents. Ron hugged Stacy and lifted her into the air. "I love you, honey," he whispered in her ear. Her body shuddered as his warm breath tickled her fancy and as he nibbled on her earlobe. "I'm going to bring in the tree and get her ready to be decorated."

"How do you know it's a her, Ron?"

"The baby?" teased Ron.

"No, silly, the Christmas tree. You called it a her."

"I don't know, honey; it's just that she's so beautiful, like you, that surely she must be a girl."

Of course, I heard what Ron had said, and although I found it flattering that he thought of me as beautiful, I was sure that soon, when he saw how big and strong I was, Ron would realize that I was, indeed, a male, not a female. I was even considering talking with him after we got to know each other a little better, maybe even give him some advice. People don't realize that trees age differently from humans. We have *tree life*, which is different from people life. Let me explain it like in dog years. A dog year is equal to seven people years, so a seven-year-old dog is the same as a forty-nine-year-old person.

That means that a fifteen-year-old dog would be, uh…hmmm, seven times fifteen…er, uh…well, you get the idea. That would be an old dog. But trees are like, ten *wisdom years* to every human wisdom year. We are not old when we are fifteen years old, we are just very, very wise, and getting wiser by the year. I'm seven years old, but I am as wise as a seventy-year-old human. Get the picture?

Anyway, Ron was wearing a pretty pricy pair of sneakers that he had purchased at the local thrift store for ten dollars. They retailed new for around $1,500.00, but Ron did not know that. He only knew that they were his size and that they were like new. Most of the time, when Ron came home from work, he would remove his work boots, take a shower, put on some clean, white socks, and walk around the house in his stockings. But when he had to go outside, he would put on his Fendi leather high-top sneakers. As he walked through the house in these fur-lined shoes, his footfalls could hardly be heard. I only noticed him when the screen door flew open. I was so startled that I jumped into the air and rolled onto my sore, broken branch. Ron did not notice my movement because of the darkness.

The sun sets in Lake Worth around 5:30 p.m. in December, so I had been lying in the front yard for about three hours. It was cool, so I did not mind, but I was sure thirsty. Kenny had watered me shortly before securing me to Ron and Stacy's car, but that was hours earlier, and I was parched. Ron had set the red-and-green tree stand by the picture window of his living room so that one side of me could be seen from the street and my other side would be enjoyed inside the house. He filled the reservoir with cool water and then walked outside to remove my mesh bindings. Ron carried me inside and lifted me into the stand. He crawled under me and tightened the five eyebolts. The water was so good. I drank until I could drink no more, and then I settled in. I was home. The two dogs were sniffing at my branches the entire time that Ron was under me. The cat was not sure she approved of my presence, maybe because I kept whispering hisses at her. Maybe that's why the dogs were circling me. Maybe they thought I was a cat.

Stacy was busy tending to the leftovers from dinner, wiping down the kitchen counters, and spiffing up her dining area. Stacy seemed to be a fastidious young lady (*fastidious* means someone who is a neatnik, with everything clean and in its proper place—*I told you that I was really smart*). I heard Stacy putting a load of laundry in the washer, mostly Ron's dirty, wet, smelly work clothes, and then I heard the pitter-patter of her stockinged feet walking into the living room. She was here to see *me*.

"Ron!" Stacy screamed. "You've broken one of her branches. There is a massive hole in her back side."

"Stacy," Ron answered, as he tightened the last of the eyebolts, "I did not break any branches. I have been very gentle with this tree. If you notice, there isn't even one needle that has fallen on your wood floors, and for your information, this is a male tree. It's not a her; it's a him!"

"Whatever, Ron. Take him back to Publix. He is defective. He is broken. He is not perfect. This is our first Christmas together, and I want everything to be perfect."

"Stacy, it can't be that bad. Let me crawl out from under these massive branches, and I'll see what I can do."

OH NO! I thought as Ron scooted out from underneath me. *This is not good. Murphy's Law: Anything that can go wrong will go wrong, at the worst possible time!* I knew that this was too good to be true. I was so happy to be part of this family. We were going to have the merriest of Christmases, but now it was curtains. Ron would load me on that car and drive me back to the supermarket.

Ron stood next to Stacy, who had creases on her forehead, her arms crossed, and an angry look on her face. The two dogs were sitting next to Stacy, side by side, scowling at me as they stared at my broken branch, and the cat was pacing back and forth behind the dogs with her back arched, her fur puffed, her tail twitching, and a low-pitched snarl coming from her mouth.

"Stacy, I can use the garland and the lights to hold up that broken branch. It's no big deal, honey."

"Are you sure, Ron?" Stacy was one tear away from crying. The two dogs looked up at Stacy and then at Ron. The cat left the room and hid under the bed.

"Yes, darling. Tomorrow evening we will decorate him, and he will be the most beautiful tree in Lake Worth."

They hugged tightly and kissed, and Ron gently cupped Stacy's face. "Not to worry, baby. OK?"

"OK, Ron." They locked the front door, turned off the lights, and left the living room.

Whew, I thought. *That was close. I thought I was a goner.* I heard the television being turned on. It was the Channel Seven ten o'clock news. They talked about the robbery of a local convenience store. It was reported that a young man came in to buy beer, then demanded that the clerk give him all the money in the register, and he got away with thirty-five dollars, but with only one problem. The hold-up man left his driver's license behind when asked to show ID. Duh!

The weatherman said it would be a mild Christmas, typical for South Florida...no snow this year. In sports, the Miami Dolphins lost and were out of the playoffs.

Then it was lights out. Everyone went to bed, so I closed my eyes, exhaled, and thought of the beautiful decorations sitting in boxes neatly stacked by my side and about how beautiful I would look decked out in my garland, delicate ornaments, and multicolored lights...but try as I might, I could not fall asleep. I was too hyped up. Too excited. I could not believe my good fortune to have been chosen by Ron and Stacy and to have been so lucky as to be in this lovely home. I thought to myself, *Fir, this ain't half bad. You could learn to like living here.*

CHAPTER 85

Tuesday, December 22
Where's Fir?

After leaving Grandma's, Bobby drove across the street to see me. He parked Dan's pickup truck in a parking space that was so far from the store that Bobby had to squint to see the green Publix sign, but he was being considerate of Dan's truck. Bobby did not want someone opening a car door and dinging Dan's perfect red paint job, so he parked where nobody else parked, far, far away. His belly was full, the evening was cool, not cold, and his pockets were full of bubble gum. *It just doesn't get much better than this*, he thought as he jogged toward his bench. *I can't wait to tell Fir about Paul's ketchup mishap.*

He thought of Turk and how he should stop by the veterinarian tomorrow, since he had Dan's truck, and see how Missy's puppy was doing. Bobby had to stop for several cars that were driving through the crosswalk. This somewhat angered him, because pedestrians have the right of way. That's the law, or at least he thought it was the law. Anyway, Bobby was always careful in parking lots, careful not to get run over by a car backing out of a space and careful not to get squashed by a car that did not yield the right of way to pedestrians. After the second car zoomed by, he looked up and saw that I was gone.

A feeling of dread and despair swept over Bobby as he searched the breezeway for his friend; there were only a handful of trees left near the bench, and Bobby closely studied each tree, as if maybe I had somehow changed my appearance to play a trick on him. But I was gone. I was not there. Bobby asked the other trees, "Where is Fir?" but there was no response. *Kenny!* Bobby thought. *He will know where Fir is. Kenny probably moved him to the cooler. That's it!*

Bobby's despair was turning into panic as he entered the store to seek out Kenny. He spotted Mr. Kemp in the back of the produce department, clipboard in hand, performing some kind of inventory on bananas and apples. Bobby grabbed his arm, interrupting his count and causing the produce manager to turn his head and ask, "May I help you, sir? Oh, it's you, Bobby. What can I do for you?"

"I'm looking for Kenny, Mr. Kemp. I really need to talk to him. Do you know where he is?"

"You just missed him, Bobby. He had some kind of family emergency, so I let him leave early. Is there something I can help you with?"

Panic was turning into heartache. "Do you know where Fir is, Mr. Kemp?"

The produce manager cocked his head and laid his clipboard down on the bags of Gala apples. "Who?" he asked.

"Fir, Mr. Kemp. The Fraser fir Christmas tree that you had for sale out in the breezeway."

"Sorry, Bobby, but I have been doing inventory all day, and besides, that's Kenny's department. He is in charge of selling the trees. He'll be here first thing tomorrow morning, at seven a.m., sharp. You stop by then, and you can ask Kenny where this *Fir* might be, OK? Now, if you'll excuse me, I have to finish this inventory. It's almost closing time." Mr. Kemp picked up his clipboard and walked over to the broccoli.

Bobby was devastated. He walked toward the double doors leading to the area where the shopping carts were stowed, his head down and his eyes welling up with tears. As he approached the exit doors, the sensors triggered the mechanism that automatically opens the doors, and Bobby exited the building. He took one more look around the breezeway, but I was nowhere to be seen. Bobby lifted his hands to his face and started to cry. *"Big Boys Don't Cry,"* he thought. That was a song from the 1960s era, but "big" boys do cry, especially when their hearts are broken. He sat on his bench and sobbed. Several late-night shoppers left Publix, passed by his bench, and looked down at Bobby but kept their distance. Most people do not want to get involved when they see someone in obvious pain, but a little old lady with just one small bag of bread stopped and offered assistance. She was walking slowly and using a cart for support. She stopped and asked, "Is there anything I can do for you, Mister?"

Bobby looked up, his eyes red and his face wet. "No, ma'am, but thanks for asking."

She reached into her purse and handed him a twenty-dollar bill. "Young man," she said, "merry Christmas. Nobody should be sad during the Christmas holidays. Here, take this, and cheer up. It's Christmas."

Bobby stood, leaned over, and hugged the lady. "Thanks, ma'am, but I don't need money. I'm fine. I just lost my best friend, and I'm trying to deal with it."

"God bless you, son. I have a boy about your age. He lives in Ohio, and he has had some difficult times of late. You kind of remind me of him. Keep the faith, Mister. Your friend has gone to a better place. Don't worry about him, he'll be fine. Now, I have to go." She laid the twenty dollars on the bench and shuffled to her car. Bobby looked down at the money, shook his head, and contemplated what had just happened. *"Keep the faith." That's what I am always telling Fir. He's gone to a better place. Yeah, Fir is probably sitting in someone's living room right now, beautifully decorated, lights ablaze, and an angel on his head.* Bobby wiped his eyes, reached into his pocket for some gum, and leaned back on the bench. He looked up into the dark sky and exhaled. *He's gone to a better place.* Bobby stuffed the twenty into his pocket. *I'll give this money to Paul for his new clothes and his haircut. I'll tell him it's from Mrs. Claus.*

Bobby stood and felt a chill in the air. He shivered. There was a loud click behind him as the doors were locked, bringing to an end another busy day at Publix. He trod slowly toward Dan's truck, which was sitting alone at the far side of the parking lot. He sauntered toward the pickup. *He's gone to a better place.*

CHAPTER 86

Tuesday, December 22, around 11:00 p.m.
Trouble Sleeping

Yep, Ron and Stacy had a really nice home, and not only could I learn to like this place, but I was, indeed, *really* liking this place. I stood there in my cozy corner, drinking profusely from the water-filled green-and-red stand and admiring the darkened living room, which I guess you could say was my bedroom. Two frumpy overstuffed easy chairs sat side by side, separated only by an end table, or maybe you could call it a middle table. Ha, ha, a middle table...get it? Anyway, on this highly polished wooden table was a lace doily, upon which rested an early-American stained-glass lamp, a book, and a pair of reading glasses.

The far wall, behind the chairs, displayed a framed print of a charming farmhouse painted white and trimmed in yellow, not unlike the one Ron and Stacy had brought me home to. In this picture, cows grazed in lush, green, fenced pastures; range-free chickens foraged for bugs near a rusty tractor and a red barn; and a vegetable garden next to the house depicted the pastoral beauty of country life. I was transfixed by this work of art. It had a calming effect on me, for I was reminded of the farms visible to me in the valleys of North Carolina. As you undoubtedly recall, I was born in the last row of Fraser firs on Wildcat Mountain with an unobstructed view into the valley of farms and the bustling town of Murphy. So here I was, standing alone in this darkened living room of a beautiful little home in Lake Worth, and I just loved it.

The streetlight outside cast dancing shadows of windblown trees on my walls as the light spilled through the large picture window at the front of Ron's house. As I listened to the harmony of sounds coming from this darkened, sleeping home, my eyes began to feel heavy. I was really tired, and I knew that I needed to just let myself go and be lulled to sleep, but I couldn't seem to turn my mind off.

I think that part of the anxiety that was keeping me awake was that I had never slept in a house before, so maybe that was why I couldn't seem to fall asleep. Kind of like someone who has slept on the floor their whole life trying to fall asleep in a bed.

Anyway, like I said, living in this house wasn't half bad...except for that wacko cat sleeping under the bed. But hey, I had a bowl of cool water that I could drink from all night, it was a perfect seventy-three degrees in this air-conditioned home, I didn't have a stinking bear to deal with or feral cats spraying me, and I had not seen one cockroach or spider or mosquito in this house since Ron brought me inside, and I felt I must admit, *It ain't half bad!*

Ron and Stacy were sleeping on a huge king-sized bed that looked like a sleigh, she on her side hugging a long pillow and he on his back with a pillow over his eyes. His mouth was wide open. Beneath the bed was that psycho cat of theirs, claws at the ready, tail still twitching, with a throaty growl for a purr, making me think of my feral cats. The dogs were curled up on the carpet at the base of Ron's bed. They were lying end to end, tail to tail, touching each other, sharing body heat.

As I relaxed and reflected on how quiet it was in this house, I began to notice that it really wasn't quiet at all. Each room was indeed alive with sound. I listened to Ron's snores, coming from the bedroom—loud, snorting noises like the sounds pigs make when they eat. The cuckoo clock on the wall of my living room went tick, tock, tick, tock, and every half hour a screaming bird jumped out of a wooden door and screeched, "CUCKOO!" There was a humming drone sound coming from Stacy's kitchen—her refrigerator, which sounded like the motor was old and tired and on its last legs, but just when it sounded like it could run no more, it would make ice, and ice cubes would loudly tumble into its bin, "clop-kerplunk."

Just when I was getting used to these sounds of the house at night, I heard a new one: the clickity-click, tap, tap, tap of toenails briskly walking on wood floors as the dogs patrolled their home like little soldiers on sentry duty. This happened every half hour at about the same time that the cuckoo bird would sing. From the spare bedroom, I heard an electric clock whirring in the silence of the night as it spun the hour and minute hands round and round in its never-ending circle of life. I thought how awful it would be to be a clock, hung on a wall with spinning hands going nowhere…forever…wow.

But these sounds were my new reality, and they gave me comfort. I felt all the stress and anxiety of the past months leaving my body, and my eyes began to flutter. As I listened to the music of my new abode, I began to drift off. I was being lulled to sleep by the soothing songs of the home of Ron and Stacy, my new home. Soon I, too, was snoring, just like the cat under the bed, the dogs on their rug, the icebox in the kitchen, and Ron and Stacy. My eyes closed tightly, my trunk relaxed, my limbs drooped, and I was out cold, dreaming of Murphy, North Carolina.

My dreams always seemed to be about my peaceful life growing up in Murphy. As my body relaxed and I dropped deeper and deeper into my dream state, I listened to the hymns of those magical woods, the melodies of my beautiful mountain, and the songs and sounds of night. I was the conductor of an orchestra, and the musicians were playing the symphonic music of nature: frogs croaking to frogs, crickets signaling to crickets, owls hooting to owls, the wind whistling through us trees and rustling dry leaves, an occasional clap of thunder, and critters making the noises that critters make.

I loved those sounds, and as I've said many times, I missed the peace and tranquility of my North Carolina mountain, but what is, is, and what was, was. We must accept what is and not waste our time wishing that things would be the way they used to be.

A wise old sage once said, "Wish in one hand and spit in the other, and see which one gets full first."

CHAPTER 87

Wednesday, December 23, Morning
Missy about 6:00 a.m.

Missy awakened early, almost an hour before Lake Worth's sun would rise in the eastern sky. But on this particular morning, no alarm clock was needed to awaken Missy, nor did her mother have to drag her out of bed by both feet. Not today. It was Wednesday of Christmas break—no school—and today, Mona would babysit her until her mom got off work. Missy hated that word…*babysit*. She was not a baby, and she knew it, but she also knew that she was not old enough to tend herself, so she planned to go over to Mona's house after breakfast. Missy knew that Mona was old and needed looking after, so she would go across the street this morning to take care of Mrs. Williams. Missy knew that she was the *real* babysitter. Mona was kind of feeble and slow on her feet, and she couldn't bend over, and she couldn't run, and she could never find her glasses, so Missy knew that she needed to watch over Mrs. Williams until Natalie came home from work. Mona seemed to be lonely, and she always seemed to be losing things, so Missy would talk with her, and they would play cards, and Missy would help her find her lost things.

As Missy sat alone in her kitchen, she rubbed the sleep out of her left eye and thought how pleasant Mona was and how neat and clean she kept her house. Mrs. Williams had told her that they would make cookies that day, and as Missy sat at her kitchen table, she could almost smell the sweet aromas coming from Mona's oven.

Missy arose from her chair and went to the cupboard for a bowl, which she would fill with cereal. She gently set the bowl down on the breakfast table, but it made a clunk. The pantry door needed oil, so Missy tried to slowly open it so that the squeak would not awaken her mom, but all that did was to make the noise last longer, *squeeeeeeaaaaak...eeeeaaaakkkkk.* Missy listened but heard nothing from Natalie's room. That was good. *Mom is still asleep,* she thought. With the pantry door now wide open, she reached for the string that hung from the pantry ceiling and turned on the light.

The reason that there were so many different choices was that Natalie was always buying the BOGOs (you know, Buy One Get One free) from the cereal aisle at Publix. I guess she figured that she and Missy would never starve as long as they had cereal. *Which one should I eat?* Missy thought. *Captain Crunch, Cheerios, Special K, Sugar Smacks, Life, Raisin Bran, or one of those adult diet cereals that taste like cardboard?* She finally reached in and grabbed a box of Honey Nut Cheerios and carried it over to the wooden kitchen table. Her chair made a squeaking sound as she slid close to her bowl, causing Missy to turn her head and look toward her mom's bedroom. She was trying to be very quiet, but every move she made seemed to echo off the walls.

Missy poured Cheerios into a large bowl, sliced a banana, and dug in. Still dressed in her PJs, all she could think of was the story that she would tell me while her mom sat on the bench with Bobby. Missy had never told anyone this story, not even her best friend, Sarah. The story was about Sammy, her bulldog puppy. It was a sad story, a story about love and a story about loss.

Natalie was still sleeping soundly in her bedroom, on a bed that she used to share with Missy's father, Glenn, but since Glenn abandoned his girls, the bed had become a warm, safe place for Missy to go when she was lonely or frightened. Missy took another bite of crunchy Cheerios and then walked over to the sliding glass doors. She looked out into the backyard, which was still shrouded in the shadows of night, but she noted that the darkness was giving way to the awakening of early morning. A sliver of pale, yellowish moon, which hung like a backward letter *C*, was still floating lazily in the sky, and Missy imagined herself sitting on this moon with her legs dangling over the edge. She would swing to and fro, as if she were seated in a wicker basket chair suspended from the ceiling of a patio. She would watch the rising sun light up the eastern sky as the darkness and chill of night gave way to the light and warmth of morning. And Sammy, the bulldog puppy of her memories, would be with her, licking her face and watching the sunrise. Missy turned and returned to her bowl of Cheerios.

Missy missed Sammy. Missy missed her daddy too, but she did not miss the fussing and arguing that always seemed to go on between Glenn and Natalie. Missy put her elbows on the table and cupped her hands under her chin. She was looking at the cereal box, but she was thinking about how quiet it had been since her daddy had walked out in a huff.

She was also thinking about how when Sammy was still alive, she always poured much too much cereal into her bowl each morning so that there would be some breakfast for her puppy. Sammy loved cereal, so when her mom and dad were not watching, she would put her bowl down on the floor, and Sammy would quickly gobble up her leftover Cheerios and milk. Missy was sure that her mommy knew what she was up to, but Natalie never said anything. Her daddy was another story. When Glenn caught her sharing her food with Sammy, he had a hissy fit. He would start yelling at Missy and chasing Sammy away from the breakfast table. Sammy would run and hide under the bed. Missy would start to cry, and Natalie and Glenn would get into a big fight. Then Glenn would storm out of the house, get into his car, and speed off.

Today, just as every other Wednesday in her recent past, Missy would go to Publix with her mom to do the weekly food shopping. Of late her mother looked forward to the Wednesday trip to Publix so that she could visit with Bobby, the handsome homeless guy on the green bench. Missy's excitement this day was not to buy more cereal but rather to see me, but little did she know that I had been adopted. Missy and I had become dear friends...maybe best friends. Imagine that! A little girl and a North Carolina Fraser fir, *best friends*? Even though we were not both trees, even though we were not both girls, even though we were different in almost every way, we loved each other. Immensely. Can you imagine that? She was not even green like me, but she was still my best friend.

Her mom had to work until 3:30 p.m., after which Natalie would come right home, pick Missy up from Mona's house, and they would drive together to the supermarket and shop for groceries.

But wait a minute, thought Missy. *The Caprice isn't parked outside. How is Momma gonna get to work? Hmmm, well maybe Mr. Thornton is going to pick her up. Anyway, I've got too many things to think about to worry about how Momma will get around.*

Every Wednesday for as long as Missy could remember, Missy and Natalie had shared this special day. Missy always looked forward to shopping with her mother because it was their "girls' day," the one day of the week when the two ladies became sisters, not mother and daughter. They would sit side by side in a nail salon, each choosing a color. Natalie would take Missy to Jupiter Donuts for the best donut in the universe—that's why they called it Jupiter Donuts—or they would stop at Steak 'n' Shake for a BOGO. Missy liked the banana milkshake the best, and that's what she always asked for.

When they were at Publix, there was always the free cookie from the bakery department that Missy would nibble as they walked the cereal aisle while looking for the Captain Crunch that was on sale.

But the best part of all was their stop at the pet shop on the way home. Puppy Kisses was the name of the store on the southwest corner of Jog Road and Lantana. Puppy Kisses sold lizards, fish, turtles, rabbits, mice, all kinds of birds, and of course, puppies.

Actually, Puppy Kisses sold almost everything that a pet owner might need, and if you did not own a pet, they would sell you a pet. Missy used to buy her dried dog food for Sammy at Puppy Kisses, along with doggie vitamins and chew toys. But that was before the accident, and that was before Missy and I had met on the breezeway at Publix.

But best of all was the play area of the store, where children could sit on the linoleum floor with puppies climbing all over them, biting and pulling at their clothing and of course licking the ice cream and cookies off their laughing faces. It's hard to say who enjoyed this frolicking the most, the children or the puppies.

Today, however, was not about cookies or milkshakes or nail salons or puppies. Today was the day Missy would come to see me, her best friend, and she would tell me her best story.

But I wouldn't be there...

CHAPTER 88

Wednesday, December 23, 5:00 a.m.
Ron's Alarm, Walk the Dogs

I had been soundly sleeping for several hours, probably the best sleep I had enjoyed since being forcefully evicted from North Carolina, when I heard noises in the bedroom. Ron's alarm clock was sounding that it was time for him to awaken and start getting ready for work. The dogs were eager to go outside and pee, so they were prancing like tap dancers on the hardwood floors to alert Ron that they gotta do what they gotta do, and they gotta do it soon.

Ron had quickly turned off the alarm clock so that it would not awaken Stacy, who was so deep in her sleep that a bomb would probably not rouse her. But being the loving, considerate husband that he was, Ron shushed the dogs and tiptoed into the bathroom to wash the sleep out of his eyes and to brush his teeth. Ron used the toilet and shushed the dancing dogs a second time. He flushed, then turned off the bathroom light; grabbed his work clothes, shoes, and socks; and headed into the kitchen. This was his daily routine, and although the dogs knew that they must wait a while longer to go for their walk, they wanted Ron to know that their need to go should not be taken lightly. They were acutely aware that Ron did not like accidents; he yelled at them when they had accidents, and he hit them with that noisy newspaper when they had accidents. Ron would grab the sports section, roll it up like a tube, and spank them on the butt, but it was like being hit with cotton candy…so they would pretend to be in pain, and they would yelp and put their tails between their legs and stand by the front door or lie down on their backs with their bellies up in the air.

Ron opened the pantry and grabbed a can of Chock-Full-of-Nuts coffee, carried it over to his Mr. Coffee, put three scoops into his filter basket, added three cups of water, and turned on the coffeemaker. He slipped into his trousers, buttoned up his shirt, and put on his shoes and socks. The dogs were going crazy with enthusiasm. They knew that Ron was about to grab their leashes. He repeated this same routine every Monday through Friday, his workdays, and this was *Wednesday*.

"Ho boy, ho boy," barked Freddie. "We're going fur a walk, we're going fur a walk. Ohh, I gotta go. Ohh, I gotta go real bad. C'mon, Ron! Put the leash on already…" Freddie jumped up and down and ran around Ron in circles.

Shep just stood by the door, patiently waiting for Ron to leash her up and take her outside. She had to go potty real bad too, but she had class, and unlike Freddie, Shep never jumped around like an idiot, making a fool of herself.

As the smells of fresh, hot coffee engulfed the kitchen, Ron grabbed the leashes from the doggie drawer. These were all signs the two wagging tails recognized as *time to go*, but poor Freddie had to go so bad that he went right there on the floor, just as Ron was attaching his leash.

"Aw, Freddie!" Ron yelled, "Why do you have to do this? BAD DOG! BAD, BAD DOG!"

Freddie put his tail between his legs, dropped to the floor, and submissively turned his belly to Ron.

"Aw, Freddie, you are lying down in your pee. Man, what's the matter with you? I don't need this irritation so early in the morning. BAD DOG!"

Meanwhile, Shep stood patiently by the door, holding her water like a good girl as she waited for the door to open so that she could go outside.

Ron quickly ran into the kitchen, grabbed the roll of paper towels, and hurriedly returned to the scene of the accident. He soaked up the yellow puddle, held Freddie's long snout in his hand, kissed him on his black nose, and said, "It's all right, Freddie. I should have taken you guys out before I made the coffee."

With that, Ron returned to the kitchen, pitched the used paper towels in the trash, washed his hands, and returned to the front door. He leashed up the dogs, looked quickly at his watch, opened the front door, departed the house, and disappeared into the darkness of early morning.

Meanwhile, Stacy was restlessly tossing and turning in her bed. She was not aware of the drama that was taking place in her living room. No, Ron had been most careful to tiptoe around the house in stockinged feet and to be considerate not to make any noise that might awaken Stacy. If anything, the magical aroma of the percolating coffee would have aroused her senses and awakened her, but no, that is not what was causing her restless agitation. The previous night, when Ron had turned off the light and climbed into bed, Stacy had had a difficult time falling asleep. She could not stop thinking about my broken branch and the huge, gaping hole in my back side. Thoughts were racing through her mind as to where to put me so that my damaged limb would not be so obvious, but nothing seemed to work.

And then there was that god-awful snoring coming from her husband's mouth. He had what is known as a deviated septum, which is similar to having two raisins in your nose and still trying to breathe. Because his nasal passages were blocked, Ron's mouth was wide open, and he would inhale deep breaths of air, which he would then exhale through his mouth. The inhale sounded like someone trying to clear their throat of a stubborn wet hocker, or like the noise a hog makes when he is wallowing in the mud or eating a bowl of slop. The sound coming out of Ron's throat was actually quite humorous. Once his lungs were filled with air, he would close his mouth and exhale, which would cause his lips to flap against one another, kind of making the sound that a whoopee cushion would make. You know what a whoopee cushion is…it's that balloon-type rubber gizmo that you put under someone's butt as they are sitting down. It makes a sound like they are passing gas. Well, that is how his lips sounded as the air passed through them.

Poor Stacy and poor me were desperately trying to fall asleep, but Ron's snoring was so loud that the house seemed to shake. I know one thing. My needles were shaking like crazy, and I had to hold them tight so that they would not fall off. Stacy put ear plugs in her ears to muffle the sound, and by about three in the morning, she was finally able to fall asleep. I had no ear plugs, so I just had to gut it out. That said, as I mentioned before, I started concentrating on the melodious sounds of the house, a rhythm and harmony of noises that together formed an orchestra: tap-taps, whirrs, kerplunks, and snores, which lullabied me to sleep. At about 3:00 a.m., I finally drifted off.

To recap, Ron's alarm went off at 5:00 a.m. I fell asleep at 3:00 a.m. Do the math…five minus three equals two. Yikes, two hours of sleep. I needed more than two hours of sleep to keep my needles soft and supple. I had a busy day ahead of me. Ron and Stacy were going to decorate me, so I must have strong and sturdy limbs to hold up those heavy ornaments.

I know what you readers are thinking…that ornaments aren't heavy, right? Well, here's what I have to say about that. Although you may be correct in thinking that most ornaments don't weigh a lot, some of them are quite weighty. Just you try holding your arms out, with your palms facing up, and inside of each hand, hold one of those "light" ornaments. Now, stand there like that for twenty-four hours…or thirty-six hours…or seven days…no coffee breaks, no sitting in a chair to watch TV, no eight hours of sleep in a king-sized bed. Nope. This is a full-time job, twenty-four/seven, and it's not for slackers. It's not for the faint of heart.

Secondly, I needed my sleep because I needed to spend some quality time getting to know those two family dogs, Freddie and Shep. I was part of this family now, and as such, we needed to bond, to share war stories like the ones I had told Missy, to develop trust in each other. That's what family does: they watch each other's backs and stand by each other through thick or thin.

Finally, I needed my sleep because there was a real "nut" in this house: the Siamese cat. I truly believed that this *nut* was not a member of the family. She was an outsider, a loner, a mean-spirited beast, ol' Ms. Psycho Cat. I had to guard against the unpredictable antics of this loose cannon of a cat with the devil eyes and the slinky way she prowled around the house and walked in the shadows. I knew from the first minute that I saw her that she was no good, bad to the bone, and out to get me.

CHAPTER 89

Wednesday, December 23, about 6:00 a.m.
Stacy's Nightmare, Uh-Oh

So as I was saying, earlier Ron had left the house with both dogs, and I was alone with a restlessly sleeping Stacy, the symphony of house noises, and a phantom cat that had mysteriously disappeared sometime late last night. I felt myself dozing off again, when two things happened. Stacy started to cry, quietly at first, but I could definitely tell that she was crying. In short order, her cries became sobs, and she started talking in her sleep. I could hear her arms waving and her tossing and turning in the bed. Then she began to scream. She screamed a second time just as Ron, Freddie, and Shep were coming through the front door. Stacy sounded like she was being attacked in her bed. The dogs barked wildly, pulled loose from Ron, and high-tailed it to the bedroom. Ron ran into the kitchen, grabbed a huge butcher's knife, and ran right behind the dogs, whose long toenails were slipping and sliding on the wood floor. I was now wide awake and had no clue what was happening, but I knew that it wasn't good, whatever it was.

The barking dogs jumped into her bed and jolted Stacy out of her nightmare. Ron turned on the ceiling light, which temporarily blinded Stacy, but not before she saw her husband standing in the doorway with a large, menacing knife in his right hand. She screamed again, not quite out of her dream state and still not fully awake. Stacy was sweating profusely, and she was visibly shaken by the events in her nightmare. Ron surveyed the room, looking for any intruder who may have done harm to his dear Stacy, but he found no one, so he put the weapon down and lay next to her, where he held her close and hugged her tight. Freddie and Shep were all over her too, busy licking the salty perspiration from her face and the wet tears from her eyes.

"It's all right, Stacy," Ron whispered. "You were just having a bad dream, honey."

Stacy pushed the dogs away and hugged Ron tightly. Her nose was wet with fluid. She wiped her eyes and nose on Ron's shoulder and whispered back to Ron, "It was so real, Ronnie. I dreamed that I was asleep in our bed with you next to me, and all of a sudden I sensed that someone was in our room. Then I felt a…a… like, like a hand, grabbing me around the neck. I opened my eyes, but it was dark in the bedroom. I thought maybe it was you, you know, playing with me like you do, trying to scare me, but you were sound asleep on your side of the bed. I could hear you snoring. Ronnie, this guy was huge, he must've been seven feet tall. I could only make out a big, dark body standing over me. And he was choking me, harder and harder. I fought back though, pulling his long, bony fingers off my neck and pushing him away. I think I knocked him down, Ronnie. I tried to wake you up to protect me, but you just rolled over on your side and put the pillow over your ears." Stacy started to punch Ron for not helping her—not hard punches, but she furrowed her eyes and banged him on the chest four or five times and said, "You rat. You should've helped me… but nooooo, you just rolled over and stayed asleep. A fine husband you turned out to be."

Ron started to laugh. "Stacy, it was a dream…your dream. If this had been my dream, I would have punched the guy out. I would've karate-chopped him and slammed him down on the floor like Steve Austin of the WWE."

"Like who?" murmured Stacy, who was once again holding her husband tightly in her arms.

"Steve Austin. The wrestling dude on TV, you know who I mean. Anyway, tell me the rest of your dream."

"Well, Ronnie, it's like I said: I pushed him away, but he quickly recovered and came at me again. I was *so* scared, and you wouldn't help me at all...you just kept on snoring. I punched you in the ribs to try and wake you up, but all you did was grunt and tell me to knock it off. Then he grabbed me again, but this time I had my legs bent and my knees under my chin so that I could force him off of me with the power in my legs. It was so dark in our room that I could barely see anything but shadows, but I sunk both feet into his rib cage and pushed hard, and he went crashing against the wall. He felt like a skeleton, Ron. No skin on his body, just bones. I jumped out of bed and turned on the lights, hoping you would awaken, and I ran from the bedroom. The dogs were cowering by the front door, and the cat had somehow crawled under the living room couch."

"Good grief, Stacy. This is one of the scariest dreams I have ever heard. What happened next?" Ron's eyes were as big as saucers as he concentrated on Stacy's every word.

"I heard him struggling to get to his feet while I was trying to unlock the front door, but there was no gizmo on the door. There wasn't even a doorknob. No way to get outta this house. I was trapped, Ronnie, and I just knew that...that I was going to die.

"The only light on was the one in our bedroom. The rest of the house was dark. I was clawing at the door with my fingernails, trying to somehow pull it open, but it was no use. Freddie and Shep were between me and the door, whining and scratching at the door, trying to get outside. Behind me, I heard the sound of heavy feet pounding against the floor as this massive hulk of a beast approached me from the hallway. I turned toward the monster in my house, balled up my fists just like you taught me, and prepared to defend myself..."

"Stacy...Stacy...? Are you going to tell me the rest?" Ron had been hanging on every word, but Stacy had just quit talking. Her eyes were welling up with tears, and then she became very angry toward Ron.

"Ronnie, I want you to take that Christmas tree right out of here this very minute. RIGHT NOW! Do you hear me? I do not want that tree in this house. *Is that clear?*" Stacy's voice was breaking up, and she started to cry.

Ron held her close and with one hand gently patted her back while the other hand stroked her long, brown hair. He said nothing as he tried to console her. He cupped her chin in his hands and kissed her on the forehead. Looking into her eyes, Ron whispered, "OK, darling, whatever you want, but could you just tell me what the tree has to do with your being so upset?"

Stacy and Ron walked into the living room, where I stood meekly in the corner. They sat down on the couch and both sat there staring at me, neither one saying a word. Freddie jumped up on the couch, Shep laid down on the laminate next to Ron's feet, and then the psycho cat came into the room and started hissing at me. Both the dogs were staring at me as if I had done something wrong, but I'd done nothing but stand in that corner, minding my own business.

Ron looked at Stacy, who was now clear-eyed and composed. "Stace, why do you want the Christmas tree taken back to Publix?"

Stacy looked at Ron and then at me before she spoke. "Ronnie, in my dream, that tree came into my room and tried to choke me to death. It had lost all of its needles. It was nothing but branches. Its branches had hands and fingers. It had evil, menacing eyes and clumsy legs and large, woody feet. It chased me all over the house. It upset the dogs, and the poor cat may have to see a cat psychologist. I may have to see a psychologist to get my head on straight, Ronnie, and it's all that tree's fault."

I watched intently as Ron shook his head back and forth, all the while looking down at Shep. Shep's chin was on the cool wood floor, but her eyes were on me. Ron scratched her behind the ear, looked up at Stacy, held his large, muscled hands around hers, and said, "Stace, it was just a dream, honey."

"I don't care, Ronnie. It's a premonition. I don't like that broken branch. In my dream he chased me, with that broken branch dragging behind like a dinosaur tail. It was scary, Ron. And all the needles fell off…what if that happens? I bet it will, Ron. It's a premonition."

Oh, boy, I thought. *Whew!* There is an adage, which is a kind of a saying, called Murphy's Law. I think I mentioned this to Missy when she was telling me about her father, but Murphy's law goes like this: Anything that can go wrong will go wrong. Just when I thought everything was great, that I had found the perfect, happy home, BAM! Something goes very wrong. Man, I liked this place. I did not want to go back to the breezeway. I liked it here. I liked Ron. I liked Stacy. I liked the two dogs, and I could even learn to like that wacko cat.

Ron got up and walked over to me. He held one of my supple, soft Fraser fir fingers in his hand, turned to face Stacy, and asked, "Are you sure, Stace? His needles are so soft, and he's incredibly beautiful, except for his broken branch."

Stacy responded with a stern admonition. "Either he goes, or I go, Ron. I'll go spend Christmas with my mother."

Ron looked at me and quietly whispered, "Sorry, buddy." Then he kneeled down and started to loosen the bolts that held my trunk steady and upright in the stand. Soon I was being carried outside and tied to the roof of the car for my ride back to Publix. I could see the cat watching me from the picture window. I could see her smiling. Ron started the car, and we drove off.

CHAPTER 90

Wednesday, December 23, about 7:00 a.m.
Mr. Fir's Wild Ride

The ride back to Publix was bittersweet. I was bitter about leaving Ron and Stacy's happy home, but it was sweet to know that I would never see that cat again. I guess you could say that I was bitter about not having the opportunity to show Stacy how beautiful I could have been when decorated, but it was sweet to know that I would soon be reunited with my dearest friends, Bobby and Missy.

The humiliation of being returned to the orphanage of unadopted trees at Publix was taking its toll on my feelings of self-worth. I was beginning to feel unloved, ugly, and unwanted. I knew that I was loved by Mary, but where was she now, when I needed her most? Anymore, Mary only existed in my dreams. But Missy loved me. And Bobby! Bobby definitely loved me. Turk too. I'd almost forgotten about the little puppy that I helped hide from the dogcatcher. Just as I was growing very depressed over being kicked out of Ron and Stacy's house, I snapped out of it. I wiped the redness from my eyes and decided that I would enjoy my ride back to the breezeway. As Ron's Honda reached speeds of forty-five miles per hour and the wind galed through my branches, I decided to turn something bad and sad into something good and happy. Today was Wednesday, and every Wednesday Missy and Natalie came to Publix. I was going to see Missy again. I smiled at the thought of her holding my broken branch and listening to my stories.

Ron was speeding. He seemed to be out of control. I could hear him yelling at the other drivers to get out of his way. Ron was ranting and raving like a madman. The angrier he became, the faster he drove. Speed limits posted in residential neighborhoods generally range from twenty-five to forty-five miles per hour, but never sixty-five, which was how fast Ron was now driving. I was tied to his roof with bungee cords, which are adequate tie-downs if you drive no more than thirty-five miles per hour, but sixty-five? I grew quite unsettled when my first bungee snapped and went flying through the air and caromed off the car behind me. I became concerned that we may have an accident if Ron did not slow down.

His car went faster and faster, seemed to hit every bump and every pothole, and turned corners going much too fast, but it was kind of like being on a roller coaster. I thought of this ride as one at Disney World or Coney Island, and I yelled, "WHOOPIE," as we bobbed and weaved around cars, through stop signs, and, as they say in the nursery rhyme, "over hills and dales," whatever that means. The tips of my branches are incredibly strong, like powerful fingers, so I reached down to each side of the car and held on for my dear life. Fortunately Ron's air conditioning was not working, and he had rolled all the windows down, so I was able to snake the end of each limb through and dig my tips into the Honda's headliner. Like tentacles from an octopus, my branches were holding on, four on each side of the car.

I spotted blue-and-red lights flashing behind me on Hypoluxo Boulevard, and the police car seemed to be pursuing Ron's Honda. We couldn't have been more than a quarter mile from Publix when Ron began to slow down so he could make the turn into their parking lot, but I saw what he didn't see. "UH-OH!" A beautiful, emerald-green Dodge 4X4 pickup truck with custom wheels and heavy-duty bumpers was traveling east as Ron made his turn into the Publix parking lot. The crash was unavoidable. Ron had simply ignored all oncoming traffic as he traveled westbound, and turning left without yielding the right of way, he collided his driver-side door with the massive steel bumper of the pickup, causing me to lose my grip and go flying through the air. As good fortune would have it, though, I landed in the bushes of a beautifully landscaped area adjacent to the Office Depot. I must've been airborne for five or more seconds, tumbling end over end through the air before landing softly in the flowered hibiscus hedges. The crash attracted onlookers who were entering and exiting Grandma's Diner, patrons of Home Depot and Office Depot, and food shoppers from Publix. Kenny, my caregiver from Publix, who was sweeping up pine needles on the breezeway, recognized me immediately and ran to the hibiscus bushes to render aid for me if I was injured.

"Fir, you OK?" Kenny asked as he leaned over me and started removing red flowers.

My trunk had landed like a lawn dart right in the middle of the largest bush, and my lower branches cushioned my landing. I might add that the hibiscus is an incredibly strong Florida shrub, and it saw me coming and literally caught me in midair.

The blue lights came to a stop right next to Ron's crinkled Honda, and I saw a thick ticket book in the hands of the police officer. Ron was OK, the other driver was OK, and I was OK, so I guess you could say that all's well that ends well. But for Ron, his day was in tatters. First, Freddie peed on his floor. Second, he had to console his hysterical wife, Stacy, who wouldn't stop crying. Thirdly, he had to bring me back to Publix, and fourthly, he totaled his car in a traffic accident. I do not know if thirdly and fourthly are words, but you know what I mean. Oh, and fifthly, the officer was writing poor ol' Ron a whole bunch of tickets...And lastly, he was going to be late to work.

"*C'est la guerre.*" (That means, "So goes the war.")

Kenny hoisted me up onto his shoulder and had started toward the breezeway when Ron called out, "Hey, you! Bag boy! I want my money back. That tree has a gaping hole in its hind side."

Kenny politely turned and responded, "Yes, sir. Just stop by and see me after you finish with your business, OK? My name is Kenny." Then we proceeded toward my place by the bench. As we walked, Kenny told me that Bobby was panicking, that he had been to the store looking for me and became quite upset when I was gone. I told Kenny that I had missed Bobby, too, and that I had missed Kenny as well.

By the green bench, Kenny set me down, leaned me against the wall, turned on the hose, and soaked me down real good. The water was great. I thought to myself, *Fir, this breezeway ain't half bad.*

Then Kenny leaned over, stuck his big, basketball-sized head into my branches, and whispered, "Good to have you back, Fir. I missed you."

CHAPTER 91

Wednesday, December 23, 8:00 a.m.
Fir Back at Publix

Remember when I said, "What is, is"? Well, here I was, back at Publix, and it was what it was, and I accepted that. Does that make any sense? My choices were to feel sorry for myself and have my own pity party or accept what was and make the best of it.

So I decided to be a happy tree and to keep my chin up. (I know what you all are thinking, "Fir, trees don't have chins. Right?" Cut me some slack here; it's my story, and I'm trying to be upbeat, OK?)

I looked around and noted that there were only two Scotch pines left unsold. I didn't recognize either of them, and I believed that they were from Canada, because they spoke with a French accent. They seemed like nice enough chaps, though, and they welcomed me and wished me a merry Christmas. I reciprocated in French, "*Joyeux Noël.*"

I thought they were going to fall over when I spoke to them in French. They got big smiles on their faces, and we chatted in French for the next fifteen minutes. It's funny how a little thing like talking to someone in their own language can create a bond that will quickly develop into a friendship. No doubt about it, these two Scotch pines and I had become bosom buddies.

Just as they were telling me about the harsh winters in Quebec, Canada, where temperatures dropped below zero and snow drifts could completely bury a tree, a man came running from the parking lot and into the store. He raced by me so fast that he looked like a blur.

Then I saw three more tiny missiles flying through the breeze-way at a very high rate of speed, and they were on a collision course with me. I held branches over my eyes, certain that I would be involved in my second crash in less than two hours, but instead of the three brown rockets blasting into me, my sparrows landed gently near my trunk and hugged me with their wings. I was kissed and hugged by these three adorable birds in the same way that parents would kiss and hug their missing child.

Then, behold! My friend, the cantankerous crow Carl, hopped close, looked up at me, and smiled. He had missed me too. *How cool is this?* I thought.

And then there was Ollie, sitting high overhead with sleepy eyes. Ollie had been awakened by the commotion on the breeze-way. "*Whooo* is back?" he hooted. "*Whooo* missed Fir?"

Iggy, munching on three red hibiscus flowers, which were hanging from his mouth, lumbered slowly toward my bench. Four squirrels who lived in the oaks of the parking lot—Scudo and Isabella, Salvatore and Carmella—surrounded me, their nervous tails twitching and their cheeks swollen with acorns. Ten mottled brown-and-white pigeons cooed as they pecked at crumbs found beneath my branches. In unison, all my feathered and fuzzy friends and Iggy said, "We love you, Fir. We missed you. We're glad you're back."

What a morning. I was blown away.

Then Kenny came out of the air-conditioned Publix, with Bobby close behind. "See, Mr. Thornton, he's right here."

Kenny, all six feet, five inches of him, stood motionless as Bobby ran toward where I stood, embraced me, and held me close.

Carl was startled and retreated to the trash receptacle. The squirrels scattered, returning to their lofty homes, where hungry mouths needed to be fed. Iggy simply looked up at Bobby and continued to chew on his flowers. And my sparrows? Well, they simply enjoyed the moment. As far as they were concerned, all was well in the world.

When Bobby released me, he walked over to Kenny, looked up into the tall bag boy's eyes, and then leaned into Kenny for another hug. It was clear to me that Bobby had missed me.

Kenny turned and walked back into the store. Bobby sat on the bench, lowered his head, placed both hands over his face, and mumbled something to himself. After lifting his head, he wiped his right eye with his fingers, stood, walked over to me, and said, "Fir, I'm glad you're back. We'll talk later, but this morning I am going to be really busy. I have to go help Paul buy some new clothes. I have to go see Nick and pick up Natalie's car, and I need to see the Boost guy about problems I'm having with my phone."

As he turned to leave, he stopped and said, "By the way, I'll see you at 3:45 this afternoon. That's when Natalie and Missy will be here to do their weekly grocery shopping. See ya, buddy." And with that, Bobby jogged across the parking lot to the Viper Red truck.

CHAPTER 92

Wednesday, December 23, 9:00 a.m.
Bobby Picks Up Paul at the Community Center

Bobby pulled into the community center at precisely nine o'clock in the morning. He looked up into a cloudless, sapphire-blue sky, took a deep breath of cool Florida winter air, and opened the door to the dining room, where a hot breakfast was being served to the needy.

He immediately spotted big ol' Paul eating a steamy stack of pancakes, scrambled eggs, and home-fried potatoes.

Paul was a big eater, and his stack of hotcakes had to be at least six inches high, and seeing the sweet syrup dripping down the sides, Bobby began to salivate. Paul's eyes met Bobby's, and Paul motioned for his pal to go through the serving line and join him with a platter of food.

Paul looked great. He had already been to the barber and was as spiffy as Bobby had ever seen him. Paul was clean shaven and had one of those old-man haircuts, where the sides are cut real short and what little hair remains on the top is combed neatly and precisely to hide the developing bald spot.

Bobby filled his plate with taters and eggs and four links of sausage. He never really was a pancake man. He opted instead for a toasted bagel with butter and, noticing that Paul had no drink on his table, grabbed two small cartons of 2 percent milk. He carried his tray to Paul's table, pulled up a chair with a blue plastic seat, and sat down.

"How's Natalie, Bobby?" asked Paul as he forked a massive bite of hotcakes into his mouth.

"She's terrific, Paul. In fact, I'll be seeing her this afternoon at 3:45."

"You mean like a date?"

"Yeah! Like a date. Natalie and I have a date at three forty-five p.m., so you and I have to hustle outta here and do our business, Paul."

The Lake Worth Community Center was a nonprofit organization that fed hot meals to the hungry. Like most food banks, they relied on charitable contributions to make ends meet. Those unselfish people who did the cooking and cleaning were all volunteers, and many of the folks who offered their time as cooks and staffers were homeless men and women like Bobby. Natalie was also one of the compassionate souls who helped out at the center. The local churches also did fundraising, donated food, and provided volunteers to work at the food kitchen.

There was a wooden box near the door, which was for donations, although none are required from the distressed folks who come to the center to eat during their times of personal hardship. Written on the box in large black print was a sign that said, "Donations greatly appreciated, but not required."

Bobby dropped a twenty into the collection box as he entered the dining room this morning, the same twenty that had been given to him yesterday by the elderly lady at Publix.

Bobby drank the last of the milk from his plastic carton, leaned back in his chair, and stared at his empty plate. "Boy, that was good. I didn't realize I was so hungry. You almost finished, Paul?"

"Two more bites, and we can go. You do know that Sonia will give you seconds if you're still hungry, don't you, Bobby?"

"I know she will, but I'm fine. I feel just right. You gotta know when enough is enough, Paul."

As Paul shoveled in the last of his eggs and potatoes and wiped all traces of food from his plate with his final piece of pancake, he looked at Bobby, then looked over at Sonia, then back at Bobby. He smiled and said, "Yep, I suppose you are right. Enough is enough."

CHAPTER 93

Wednesday, December 23, 10:00 a.m.
Do Not Pick the Flowers

Bobby and Paul exited the building with full bellies and smiles on their faces. Paul was excited to be celebrating Christmas with the son he had not seen for many years. He was thankful that he would not have to spend another Christmas alone.

Millions of people in this country have no one to enjoy their holidays with, to share laughter, food, drink, friendship, and love. Unless I was adopted in the next two days, I would be one of those sad, lonely, depressed souls who would be alone on Christmas Day.

Looking down at his wristwatch, Bobby noted that it was about ten in the morning, which gave him almost six hours to complete the remaining tasks on his to-do list. Barring no complications or unforeseen roadblocks, that should be ample time to get everything done and be on time to meet Natalie.

Each winter, when the weather cools in South Florida, the City of Lake Worth plants multicolored flowers in the landscape beds of the Public Works Department, the administration buildings, and the community center. Pink and white impatiens, yellow marigolds, pink and red geraniums, and purple pansies bordered the walkways leading to the parking lot where Nick's Viper Red pickup truck was waiting.

Bobby was a step or two faster than his older friend Paul, so it did not surprise Bobby that he arrived first at the red Ford truck. But what did surprise Bobby when he turned around was that Paul was nowhere near the parked truck. Bobby looked back toward the community center from whence they came and spotted Paul kneeling down and picking a bouquet of flowers.

Bobby ran toward his friend, waving his hands in a manner that would tell Paul to *stop picking the flowers*, but Paul did not see Bobby. Paul was too busy selecting the healthiest and most colorful of the flowers for his bouquet.

Slightly winded after his forty-yard dash, Bobby placed his hands on the sides of his head, looked down at his buddy, and exclaimed, "Paul, what in the world do you think you are doing?"

Paul held up his beautiful cluster of flowers for Bobby to see. He then brought the bouquet back toward his nose, took a deep breath, and then stuck the colorful bunch up against Bobby's nose so his friend could take a whiff. "Ain't they beautiful, Bobby? I was going to ask you to drive me by Ann's house, and then I saw these flowers, and I thought how much she would love a bouquet of fresh-picked flowers."

Bobby was exasperated. "Paul, you can't be picking these flowers. They are planted here each November to beautify the common areas. If everyone picked the flowers, there would be no flowers to enjoy when you sit on the benches or stroll along the walkways. There is also a sign over there"—Bobby pointed—"that says, 'Do not pick the flowers.' They could give you a fine if they catch you picking the city's flowers."

Bobby extended his hand and helped Paul get to his feet. He then grasped the big man's arm and escorted him toward the red truck. Two chirps accompanied the unlocking of the doors, and after both men climbed inside, they pulled out of their parking spot.

"Will you drive me by to see Ann? She only lives about two blocks from here. OK, Bobby?" Paul kept smelling the flowers, but most annuals have no noticeable scent, or if they do have an aroma, it is very slight.

"Sure, Paul. Show me the way."

CHAPTER 94

Wednesday, December 23, 10:30 a.m.
Bobby Meets Paul's Girl

Paul had told a little white lie, probably unintentionally. Ann lived three blocks from the community center, not two, as the big man had told Bobby. Actually, it was probably not even a lie at all, if you think about it. Paul did not own a car, so when he visited his girlfriend, Ann, he walked. And when he walked, he took the shortcut behind the municipal buildings, along one of the drainage canals, through a park, and finally to Ann's back door. Ann's house backed up to the park. So if you walked, it was two blocks, but if you drove, it was three.

The red truck pulled into a circular drive that fronted Ann's three-bedroom, one-story home. An older, faded-red Toyota pickup truck was parked in the carport.

"She's home!" blurted Paul as he grabbed the door handle and excitedly jumped from the Ford.

He skipped toward the front door like a lovestruck teenager, and Bobby watched as he hid the bouquet of flowers behind his back. Paul rang the doorbell, then turned around and waved to Bobby with a huge smile on his face. The upscale wooden door opened, and a tall, lovely woman about Paul's age put her arms around the big man, stood on her tippy toes, kissed him, and invited him inside.

Paul handed her the handpicked flowers, which brought a smile to her face and tears to her eyes. She hugged Paul tightly, and they held each other close for what seemed like forever. Ann's eyes met Bobby's, and she released Paul from their loving embrace.

"Who's in the truck?" asked Ann as she squeezed Paul's hand and asked to be introduced.

Bobby looked down at his watch and saw the short hand approaching 11:00. His day was ticking away, and so little seemed to be getting accomplished. Breakfast was not on the to-do list, nor was driving Paul over to his girlfriend's house. Bobby saw the two lovers approach his truck, so he pushed the button to roll down his window.

Paul introduced Ann, and then he introduced Bobby as his "*best friend ever.*" That blew Bobby away. Ann invited the boys in for a cup of coffee, and although the clock was ticking, Bobby remembered his mother's many lessons about politeness, etiquette, and the social graces, so he graciously accepted.

Ann's home was modestly furnished with a threadbare sofa and chair, thrift store knick-knacks, and scratch-and-dent appliances. Her plastic dishes and chipped coffee cups were vintage garage sale. Ann, however, had a roof over her head; a truck; one of those old-fashioned, one-hundred-pound, nineteen-inch TV sets with rabbit ears; and air conditioning, compliments of the breezes blowing through jalousie windows. Ann Jones had worked two jobs every week for the past ten years. She had saved her money and paid cash for her home and cash for her used truck, and she had borrowed no money from anyone to buy anything.

Ms. Jones, the ex-Mrs. Jones, had been married to a most difficult husband, who was what I would call a freeloader. He chose not to work for a living but rather stay home, drink beer, and watch TV all day while Ann washed his clothes, cleaned his house, bought his groceries, cooked his meals, mowed his grass, and worked at a full-time job and one part-time job just to make ends meet.

The marriage had lasted five years. They were divorced ten years ago, and Ann's story was still being written, but it looked like she would live happily ever after.

Bobby listened to her story for thirty minutes, ate three homemade blueberry scones, drank three cups of Keurig coffee, and had a delightful time with Paul and his wonderful girlfriend. As Bobby swallowed his last bite, he realized that the three cups of coffee required a pit stop at the bathroom, so he looked at his watch and said, "Ann, we really do have to be on our way. I have three pressing appointments, and time is not on my side, so we are going to have to go. I've thoroughly enjoyed your hospitality, and your scones taste better than those sold in the Publix bakery."

Bobby and Paul stood, and Bobby asked if he could borrow her restroom before they left.

Of course, Ann said yes, and she pointed and said, "At the end of the hallway, Bobby." She heard the bathroom door close, and she looked up at Paul with her sparkling blue eyes and said, "Paul, you've got a really good friend there."

Ann waved goodbye to the boys in the red Ford and watched them pull out of her circular driveway. She walked to the mailbox as the truck drove away. There was only junk mail, which was not unusual, since Ann had only insurance and utility bills to worry about. Her lawn needed cutting, so she walked to the utility shed, pulled out her like-new green-and-yellow John Deere, added gas, and tugged once on the cord. It started immediately—another great deal she had made when her neighbors sold their house and moved to Georgia.

As she mowed her lawn, Ann thought about Paul.

CHAPTER 95

Wednesday, December 23, 11:00 a.m.
Paul at the Thrift Store

"No more stops, Paul. OK?"

"No problem, Bobby. I just wanted to give those flowers to Ann. What do you think of her, Bobby? Ain't she a fox?"

"You've got yourself a keeper, there. And she seems to really like you a lot, Paul. I couldn't help but watch you two sitting next to each other on the couch. Ann kept her hand on your knee, and she was scrunched so close that I doubt I could pry you guys apart without a crowbar."

Bobby made a left turn onto Kirk Street and reached over to hike up the AC. He turned his head to peek at Paul, who was leaning back with a smile on his face.

"Those scones were the best I ever ate. And, Paul, you know what else?

Paul looked over at Bobby and said, "What?"

"She is one mighty fine-looking woman, Paul."

"Thanks, buddy. That means a lot to me. I knew you'd like her. She likes you too, Bobby. I could tell that right away."

Bobby pulled into the Salvation Army Thrift Store on Lantana Road, found an empty parking space, and parked his truck. He then turned off the engine and looked over at Paul. "You ready to do this?"

Paul nodded, both opened their doors, and they headed toward the entrance, where the traditional red Christmas kettle sat next to an old, white-bearded guy who looked like Santa Claus. Bobby dropped a five-dollar bill into the kettle and was graciously thanked by the bell-ringing man dressed in red. They shook hands and wished each other a merry Christmas. Paul shook Santa's hand, too, and apologized for not being able to make a donation. The jolly man, who outweighed Paul by at least fifty pounds and who was even a bit taller, responded in kind, "Hey, man, you don't gotta make no donation. Just have a merry Christmas, and don't ever forget that the Salvation Army is here for you if you need us."

Paul and Bobby lingered next to the bearded man and talked a bit before going inside. "That was right nice of you, Bobby, to give that man five dollars." Paul patted Bobby on the back, and then Bobby patted Paul on the back and explained how the Salvation Army works.

"That donation was not for the man with the beard, Paul. It's for the poor, the needy, the hungry, disaster relief, and much more. The donations, nationwide, will probably exceed one hundred and fifty million dollars this Christmas season. But what I think is particularly cool is that the money raised here in Palm Beach County stays here in Palm Beach County, to help the needy and homeless here…at least, that's my understanding. According to what I've read, a typical red kettle can generate four hundred and fifty dollars a day, and that man with the beard could be a volunteer, or he might be an employee of the Salvation Army. People who are having trouble finding a job can apply to be a bell ringer, Paul."

"Hey, Bobby, maybe I can get an application."

"We'll ask inside, but the job only lasts until Christmas Eve, and that's tomorrow, Paul. Besides, you are going to your son's house for Christmas. When are you supposed to go over there? I'm sure that Natalie would give you a ride. I could ask her, if you like."

Just as Bobby and Paul were turning to go inside the thrift store, a tall, thin thug wearing a blue hoodie came running out of the store. The glass entry door flew open with such force that it shattered when it hit Bobby's head. Bobby was knocked temporarily senseless, and the momentum sent him crashing into Paul and Santa.

Hoodie Thug grabbed the red kettle, which was overflowing with Christmas donations, and raced toward a waiting van. Paul lifted the stunned Santa and bleeding Bobby up from the ground, and the chase began.

The thief's white panel van was parked on the grass between the sidewalk and the road. The rear doors of the van looked damaged, as if a car had rear-ended it in the recent past.

A three-foot-high, trimmed ixora hedge surrounded the parking lot and served the dual purpose of a landscape fence around the parking area and a buffer zone to minimize noise from the busy roadways.

The man in the hoodie ran south toward the driveway, which leads cars into and out of the thrift store parking lot. He then had to turn left and run toward the sidewalk and then left again along the sidewalk toward his van.

Bobby and Paul were athletes. They jumped the hedge, arriving at the van just as the bad guy was trying to pull open his rear door, but it would not open. It was damaged. It was broken. Like football players, Bobby and Paul tackled the hoodie thug. He went down with a grunt and fumbled the red kettle. Bobby recovered... TOUCHDOWN!

Santa had a cell phone, so he had dialed 911, told the dispatcher about his stolen kettle, and given them the address.

Sirens sounded and blue lights appeared as four police cars arrived at the scene.

After all the commotion had subsided and he and Paul had given their statements to the police, Bobby looked at his watch. It was 12:15 in the afternoon.

CHAPTER 96

Wednesday, December 23, 12:30 p.m.
Heroes at the Thrift Store

Santa hugged Paul, and then he hugged Bobby. His eyes were sparkling and moist, his cheeks were rosy, and he was acting very jolly. "You young men are real heroes," he said, holding up the dented red bucket for them to see. "There was one thousand, three hundred and ninety-two dollars and nineteen cents in this kettle. That's enough money to provide a week's worth of groceries to a family of four for twenty-three weeks, or to put it another way, enough to feed twenty-three families of four for one week. The Salvation Army thanks you. Go inside and buy what you need, but your money is no good here. Whatever you buy, it's on us! Merry Christmas, and thank you."

The hero Paul climbed back into the passenger side of the Viper Red Ford with three pairs of slacks, five shirts, a pair of size-thirteen dress shoes, size-thirteen white tennis shoes, two belts, a tie, and a like-new Samsonite Fiero suitcase with spinners. He was all set for his holiday with his son, except socks. There were no socks at the thrift store.

"Bobby, I need socks. Can we stop at Walmart or Marshalls for some socks? Maybe we'll get lucky and catch another bad guy."

Bobby looked at his watch. It was 1:35.

"Sure. But this is the last stop, OK, Paul?"

"OK. Last stop."

"Paul, we were a pretty good team back there. You jumped that hedge like a young man, and you can run almost as fast as me. Not bad for an old guy."

389

"Bobby, I was the first one over the hedge, and I made the tackle. All you get is an assist. Shoot, if a referee had been there, you might have been flagged for piling on." They both laughed as the truck pulled into Marshalls on Lantana.

CHAPTER 97

Wednesday, December 23, 1:15 p.m.
One More Stop

B obby stayed with the truck as Paul hoofed his way through the crowd, shopping at Marshalls. All Paul needed were socks. He wandered through the store, looking in every direction for the socks department.

Every woman in Lake Worth must be here, he thought as he tried to make his way around the herd of ladies blocking every aisle. Paul towered over most everyone in the store, so he stopped behind a very heavy, short woman and scanned the store, trying to locate the socks.

Socks are white, and he spotted a section of the store where a lot of white things were hanging on racks, but it was on the other side of this large store, in the opposite direction from where he had been walking. Paul did a quick about-face and bumped into a lady carrying a shoe box, two blouses, a skirt, and an oversized purse. She lost her balance and fell sideways into a circular rack of women's slacks. Her Christmas gifts went airborne, seemingly traveling in slow motion; the rack fell onto two small children, and the woman who collided with Paul fell hard on the wooden floor.

As Paul bent over to help the embarrassed lady up from her sitting position, she socked him in the nose. Paul was unfazed by her powder-puff punch and again offered to help her to her feet, but she rebuffed his offer. The furious woman hollered and screamed at Paul as if he had knocked her down on purpose. Paul apologized a second time, but she was not interested in anything Paul had to say. Paul held up his hands and backed slowly away as the manager came over to check on all the commotion. A crowd of women gathered around to watch the show, staring first at the middle-aged female on the floor and then at the big man who had knocked her down. As she searched for her right high-heeled shoe, she continued to rail at poor old Paul as he walked ever so slowly toward the front door.

The manager helped her up, picked up her purchases, and led her over to his own personal register to ring up her merchandise. He also gave her an extra 20 percent discount for her misadventure with Paul. But Paul still had no socks.

Meanwhile, in the parking lot, Bobby had found a pull-through parking space, which gave him an unobstructed view of the department store's front door. He turned on some soft music, leaned back, and looked at his watch. It was two o'clock.

Bobby felt tired. He closed his eyes and hummed with the music.

He thought about Paul and hoped he would hurry up and find his socks; the clock was ticking.

Bobby could see that he would really have to hurry if he were going to make it to Publix by 3:45. So far, his day had not quite worked out the way it was planned, but as a wise man (Bobby's father) once said, "Go with the flow!"

He once asked his dad just exactly what that meant, to "go with the flow."

"Well, Bobby. It means that things don't always go as you would like for them to go…"

Bobby's thoughts became dreams as he closed his eyes and dozed off.

"Go with the flow…Go with the flow…" Bobby was talking in his sleep.

He was back with his dad, a child again, driving to the golf course on a beautiful Monday morning, with not a worry in the world.

Bobby was eight years old when they had this discussion. Bobby was in the front seat, sitting next to his father. Back then, children did not have to sit in the back seat, there were no airbags in cars, and although seat belts had been invented, not all cars were so equipped, and there were no seat belt laws.

It was an early-morning drive to the Cypress Golf Course, where Bobby had an eight o'clock tee time. Bobby grew up in Broward County and had been playing on the Broward Junior Golf Association Tour from the age of six. He had won three trophies already, and that day was an important tournament. If he won, Bobby would win another trophy and would represent Broward County in the state competition held in Orlando. However, traffic was heavy that morning with people on their way to work, and his dad seemed to be catching every light. But the worst part was that if Bobby was late for his tee time, he would be disqualified.

Normally, they drove south on State Road Seven to Prospect, where they made a left turn and followed the winding road to the golf course. However, because they were running late, he watched his dad pull into the left turn lane at Atlantic. The arrow turned green for drivers turning left, and Dad's car was moving again.

"Why'd you turn here, Dad?" Bobby asked his father, who was now traveling fifty in a forty-five m.p.h. zone. Bobby's dad looked over and said, "I decided to go with the flow."

"What exactly does that mean, Dad? Go with the flow?"

"Well, the cars going straight ahead on State Road Seven were stopped at the red light. They couldn't go until the light turned green again. And, Bobby, the cars traveling south on State Road Seven were catching every red light, so when I saw the cars in the turn lane were moving, or flowing, I made the turn along with them. I went with the flow. Like logs floating down a river, Bobby. They go where the current takes them. They go with the flow."

Dad did the same thing several more times, and they arrived on time. A lesson learned. Always be willing to modify your plans...Go with the flow.

As Bobby was reminiscing, he heard a tapping on the window. It was Paul, who was waving his hands and motioning for Bobby to unlock the doors. Bobby reached down and hit the button that unlocked the doors. Paul climbed in and said, "Let's go, Bobby Baby."

But Bobby was still reliving that day so long ago at the Cypress Golf Course. He leaned his head back against the headrest, closed his eyes, and remembered the awards presentation. Bobby had won his fourth trophy that day, and he did end up going to the state tournament. Bobby was almost asleep again…

"Bobby."

"BOBBY?"

"BOBBY!" Paul reached over and tugged on Bobby's ear.

"Ouch, what's your problem, Paul?"

"No problem, buddy. I just wanted to ask if you could stop at Burger King, across the street. I have some coupons. It's two o'clock, and I'm hungry. You hungry?"

"I could eat, Paul. What coupons do you have?"

"Let's see…hmmm, what are you in the mood for?"

"I like their Whoppers. You got a Whopper coupon?"

"Yep, 'Buy One, Get One Free.' Let's go, Bobby. My treat."

Bobby adjusted the rearview mirror, fastened his seat belt, started the engine, and drove forward. He had parked in a pull-through space.

The heroes stood in line behind a young couple with two kids. They studied the overhead Burger King menu, even though they knew what they would order. High-definition pictures of chicken sandwiches, gigantic burgers, and steamy fries made Bobby's mouth water. The Whoppers were larger than life, and each was piled high with mounds of lettuce, tomatoes, and pickles and topped off with mayonnaise on a huge sesame-seed bun.

The children were both talking at once and pointing to all the things that they wanted to eat. The father—Johnny Lopez—was his name, pulled out an old, worn leather wallet, which was empty except for his driver's license and a twenty-dollar bill. His wife ordered two Whoppers, two large fries, two Junior Whoppers, two small fries, and four small Cokes. The bill came to twenty-six dollars and some change. Johnny, the husband, looked embarrassed and asked the man at the cash register if he would take off one of the Whoppers, one large fry, and one Coke.

The Burger King man did as instructed, and the register recalculated the price. "That will be eighteen-seventy-six, sir. Is that for here or to go?"

Johnny started to give the clerk his only twenty-dollar bill, when Paul tapped him on the shoulder and offered Johnny four of his coupons. "Show these coupons to the Burger King man and ask him to ring it up with these discounts," said Paul, as he proudly extended his hand with the four "Buy One, Get One Free" coupons. The third order was the same as the first order, which meant that everyone had a burger, everyone had a fry, and everyone had a Coke, and best of all, the new price was only $14.76. Paul wished the family a merry Christmas, shook Mr. Lopez's hand, grabbed Bobby by the arm, and led him toward the door.

Bobby's mouth hung open, and he broke into a smile. He put his arm around the big man's shoulder, and they walked arm in arm out of Burger King and climbed into the chirping Viper Red truck.

CHAPTER 98

Wednesday, December 23, 2:15 p.m.
Last Stop?

Bobby looked over at Paul as he turned right on Lantana. Paul still had no new socks, and he hadn't eaten lunch, but he sure looked happy. In fact, he was grinning as if he were listening to a funny joke but had not yet heard the punch line. Then, his smile broke into a full-blown belly laugh…He'd heard the punch line.

Bobby smiled, then grinned, and then laughed out loud with Paul, each hero laughing at his own private humor.

It's funny how laughter is contagious. One person laughs, then another starts to chuckle, and next thing you know, the whole room erupts in laughter…and not a single person knows why they are laughing except for the person who laughed first.

The cabin was suddenly quiet as Bobby turned right onto Jog Road and headed north to Southern Boulevard. Both men were deep in thought. Bobby looked over at Paul and caught him chewing on one of his fingernails. "You know, Paul, that's a bad habit you've got there."

"What? What are you talking about, Bobby?"

"Biting your nails, you goofball. Look at the ends of your fingers, Paul. You have nothing but nubs. Your fingers look like hot dogs. Let me ask you a couple of questions. How would you pick a penny up off the ground? A person needs nails to pick up a penny. And how do you scratch? A person needs nails to scratch an itch. I'm not even going to tell you about how important fingernails are for tending to noses and ears, but I am going to ask you a very serious question, OK?"

"Ask away, Bobby."

"OK, Paul, why do gorillas have such large noses?"

Paul tilted his head slightly sideways, looked at Bobby puzzled, and said, "I don't know, man. Why *do* gorillas have such big noses, smart guy?"

"Because they have big fingers, Paul."

The two heroes looked at each other, and laughter again filled the cabin. When the merriment finally settled down, Bobby had been driving for about twenty-five minutes, and he was almost at Dan's Like-New Paint and Body Shop. Dan had two locations, and because Bobby wanted to expedite his Caprice paint job, Dan had had to use the drying oven at his second location. This had been just fine for Bobby, who had seemingly had so much time on Wednesday, but now, with Paul making so many stops, time was not on his side. If Paul wanted to make one more stop, Bobby would have to lay down the law and say, "No," or he would be late picking up Natalie. This would be totally unacceptable.

CHAPTER 99

Wednesday, December 23, 2:50 p.m.
Dan's Paint and Body

Bobby looked at his watch. It was almost three o'clock. He pulled into Dan's, and the first thing he saw was Natalie's Viper Red Chevy Caprice. It was gorgeous. After parking the truck, Bobby went inside to settle up with Dan. Paul followed along behind his dear friend, pulling along with him the Samsonite filled with clothes but no socks.

Dan was standing behind the counter, talking on the phone to someone who wanted to repaint an old Jeep. He gave him a price for the basic paint job and asked the fellow to come in and choose a color. With the appointment made, Dan hung up and flashed a smile as he shook Bobby's hand and then hugged him like the brother that he was. Bobby introduced Paul. They exchanged pleasantries, and Dan said, "I've got some good news for you. Let's go outside and look at Natalie's car."

As they approached the Viper Red Chevy, Dan pointed out the quality of his work. He explained that all rust was removed when they prepped the car using a rust inhibiter. He pointed out that there were no serious issues to deal with. Dan also said that his son had block sanded most of the car before spraying on the primer coat, then block sanded it again before the base coat and the clear coat were applied.

Neither Bobby nor Paul had any clue what Dan was talking about. Bobby thought a block was something you walked around in a residential neighborhood, and Paul thought that sand was something you found at the beach.

Dan wanted Bobby to know that this was a quality job, that he used quality paint, and that Natalie would be driving around in a car with a showroom-quality paint job.

Bobby needed to leave. He was running out of time. When Dan turned his head and opened the car door, Bobby looked down at his watch…3:07…thirty-eight minutes to get back to Publix.

"Bobby, the surprise I told you about," Dan said, and he grabbed Bobby's arm, ushered him to the front passenger seat, and invited him to look inside and inspect the new interior. Dan had installed new carpeting, new floor mats, a new headliner, and custom camel-colored leather seats.

Bobby nearly fainted. "Holy cow, Dan, how much did this cost? I can't afford this."

"I called in a few favors, Bobby, for old time's sake. None of this work will cost you a dime. Consider it a wedding gift to you and Natalie."

Paul's mouth dropped open, and his eyes became dinner plates. "You and Natalie are getting married?" he asked, both of his huge hands cradling his head.

"I wish," answered Bobby. "Nothing would make me happier, but so far, we are just good friends."

"Really good friends, Paul, from what I hear," added Dan.

Paul whistled. Bobby hugged Dan, thanked him profusely, and handed back the keys to Dan's Viper Red truck. Dan gave Bobby the Chevy keys. Bobby opened the trunk, which was also newly carpeted, carefully lifted Paul's suitcase into the massive trunk, and walked around to the driver-side door. After one last hug between Dan and Bobby, Bobby got in and pulled the car out and onto Southern Boulevard.

It was 3:15.

CHAPTER 100

Wednesday, December 23, 3:15 p.m.
Speeding to Publix

Fifty-four miles per hour in a forty-five m.p.h. zone is *speeding*, but under the circumstances, Bobby felt that going just a little bit over the speed limit would be OK. Besides, he had always been told that unless you exceed the posted speed limit by fourteen miles per hour, you do not have to worry about being stopped by a cop. And so it was that Natalie's glossy, Viper Red, eight-cylinder wannabe muscle car was flying west on Southern Boulevard at fifty-four miles per hour.

Everyone knows that red cars receive more speeding tickets than cars of any other color—more than white cars, more than black cars, more than pink cars. Pink cars? Anyway, about two miles ahead, hiding behind a large, shady oak tree, sat a motorcycle cop with a radar gun aimed at the cars traveling west on Southern Boulevard. His name was Bob Thompson, and he wrote more speeding tickets in Palm Beach County every year than any other cop. Thompson had been written up in the *Palm Beach Post*, was honored as Officer of the Year three of the last five years, and had brought over three hundred thousand dollars in revenue to the county in speeding tickets.

"Aren't you traveling a bit too fast, Bobby?" asked Paul as he double-checked his seat belt while looking at the Chevy speedometer.

"Yes, Paul, but I have to pick up Natalie from work, and I am running behind schedule."

"Where does she work, Bobby?"

"Homes Depot, Paul."

"Oh, that's right there by Publix. Which department? Paint? Tools? Garden?"

"No, no, no, Paul. *Homes* Depot. The real estate office a little farther from Publix. She does secretarial work, bookkeeping, and even sells houses and condominiums. She gets off at three thirty."

"Oh…Well, I think you can slow down. It's only three o'clock right now."

"No, Paul, it's three-twenty-one right now."

"Not! My watch says three o'clock. I think your watch is fast, Bobby."

"Geeez, Paul, you're right. I purposely set my wristwatch ahead so that I would not be late, but I forgot. I'm twenty minutes fast." Bobby slowed down to forty-five just as Thompson's radar beam hit his windshield. As Bobby cruised by the motorcycle cop, however, the police officer turned on his blue lights—the driver behind Bobby was zipping along at sixty miles per hour.

The Caprice turned left on Jog Road, returning to Lake Worth along the same route Bobby had traveled earlier when driving to Dan's Paint and Body Shop.

For some people, it is almost impossible to fall asleep in a moving car, but for others, a car is like a cradle, swaying back and forth and rocking the baby to sleep. Within a few more minutes, Paul was sound asleep. Bobby glanced over at his dead-tired friend and smiled as he thought about how much closer together this adventure-filled day had brought them. No doubt about it. They were on the same team: heroes who had bonded for life.

Paul was sitting in an upright, statuesque position, swaying to the right and then to the left as the Caprice weaved in, out, and around traffic. His head bobbed forward as Bobby slowed and then stopped at traffic lights, and when the light turned green, Paul's head would bob backward again. Paul's mouth hung open, and a deep, hoarse growl bubbled from his mouth. He sounded like a large dog warning you to stay away from his food.

Bobby chuckled as he watched his bobble-headed friend and listened to his strange-sounding snores, but Bobby was not paying attention to the road as he should have been. The traffic signal on Jog and Forest Hills had turned amber, and the car in front of Bobby chose to slam on its brakes and stop rather than possibly run a red light. Bobby slammed on his brakes, too, and managed to stop just short of a rear-end collision. Paul went flying forward and would have crashed into the dashboard had his seat belt not cut into his chest, causing him to yelp in pain, "Youch!"

Paul was jolted awake by the sudden stop; his head whiplashed backward, and the dream of frolicking with Ann was popped like one of Bobby's bubbles.

Paul looked over at Bobby and said, "What happened? Are we OK? I must've fallen asleep."

"We're fine, Mr. Bobblehead. I just needed to wake you up and ask where you would like to be dropped off."

"Wait a minute, wise guy. Are you telling me that you slammed on your brakes and skidded down Jog Road just to wake me up? Is that what I'm hearing?"

"No, no, no, Paul. I was just trying to avoid hitting that White Subaru in front of me. He should have gone through the intersection; he had the yellow light, but he suddenly stopped, so I had to stop. But Paul, now that you are awake, where would you like to be dropped off?"

"Oh, I get it. You woke me up by accident, by not having an accident, right?"

"Right! So where do I drop you, Paul?"

"Well, let's see. Let me get my bearings. We're on Jog and Forest Hills…hmmm, that's around the corner from Ann's house. Hmmm, it's also near McDonald's. I have some McDonald's BOGO coupons. We're also not far from Target, and I still need socks, Bobby."

"You need new underwear, too. I was thinking about that while you were sleeping."

"Yeah, especially after that skidding stop you just made."

Bobby and Paul both turned to look at each other, broke into a smile, and then laughed out loud. The light turned green, and Bobby snuck into the left turn lane and turned east onto Forest Hills. Two blocks later, he pulled into Target and dropped Paul off at the door. "Be quick, Paul. Give me your McDonald's coupons, and I'll go grab us some fast food. Please hurry. Seriously, Paul, I have to pick up Natalie at three thirty, and I can't be late."

Bobby looked at his watch. It was 3:30 according to Bobby's watch, or 3:10 on Paul's watch. "Hustle, Big Guy. Get your underwear and socks and be out here in ten minutes, OK?" Bobby knew that he could grab two Big Macs and be back at Target by 3:40/3:20, five more minutes to drop Paul off at Ann's, and five minutes after that to get to Natalie's real estate office.

"This is doable," he said out loud.

Bobby pulled the red Caprice out onto Forest Hills Boulevard and one block later turned into McDonalds. Not a single car was in the Drive-Thru lane, so Bobby pulled up to the huge menu board where orders are placed.

A pleasant, almost musical voice from a static-filled speaker said, "Welcome to McDonalds. I'll take your order when you're ready."

Bobby hollered at the sign, "I'm ready!"

"Yes?" asked the scratchy voice.

"I have a coupon," hollered Bobby.

"You don't have to yell, sir, I hear you quite well. You say you have a coupon?"

"Yes, 'Buy one Big Mac and get one Big Mac free.' That's a BOGO."

"Would you like a drink and some fries, sir?"

"No, just the two Big Macs, and don't forget that I have a coupon."

"I know, sir, you have a coupon. Would you like an apple pie, sir?"

"No, just the two Big Macs. Nothing else, and I have a coupon."

"I understand, sir. That will be four-twenty-four. Please drive around to the first window."

Bobby drove to the first window and presented his coupon for the free Big Mac, together with a five-dollar bill, but that is when the happy voice he had heard before changed to one that was more hardened and matter of fact.

The voice now had a face, a body, two arms, a name tag, and two very big, blue eyes that were actively searching for an expiration date on Paul's coupon. She turned to Bobby and, with a half smile on her face, said, "I'm sorry, sir, but this coupon is expired."

Bobby had not checked his coupon, but for the first time all day, he was speechless. Bobby lowered his head, looked down into his lap, closed his eyes, placed his hands on his knees, and shook his head back and forth.

"What exactly are you saying, Miss?" asked Bobby, his head still down and his eyes still closed.

The young lady, whose name tag said "Julie," responded in the same cheerful tone as when she had taken his order just two minutes before, "Sir, that will be eight-fifty for two Big Macs. You'll need another three-fifty, sir."

Bobby was becoming agitated, but he realized that this young woman was just doing her job and that she did not deserve to be yelled at by a grumpy customer, and Bobby was beginning to feel very grumpy. He asked, "Ma'am, can you cut me some slack, here? Why don't you just honor the coupon? It can't be expired more than a day or two."

Julie leaned out of the Drive-Thru window and was so close to Bobby's face that he could feel the warmth of her breath, or was it the fire from her mouth, and she whispered to Bobby in a menacing voice, "It expired three months ago, sir. You should've thrown these coupons away back in September, sir." Her eyes had darkened, her brow was furrowed, and her face had taken on the look of the fire-breathing dragon that she had become.

"Uh…can I speak to the manager?" requested Bobby.

The smile returned, the happy face reappeared, and the musical voice was suddenly back.

"Certainly, sir," said Julie.

Seven cars had pulled behind Bobby, and he was now holding up the line. The very pleasant young lady asked Bobby to pull over to one of the parking places to the right of the Drive-Thru lane and said that the manager would come out to talk with him. Bobby looked down at his watch. He had been here for six minutes and did not have time to wrestle with the manager over a free Big Mac. He looked at Julie, asked if he could have his expired coupon back, thanked her for her time, and started to pull out of the lane, which now had ten cars behind him, all honking horns. But before he could drive off, Julie offered a compromise. "We do have twenty chicken McNuggets for five dollars, plus tax. Would you like to change your order, sir?"

Bobby couldn't control himself any longer. He looked into the young lady's eyes, furrowed his brow, and said, "Miss Julie, if I wanted twenty chicken nuggets, I would have ordered twenty chicken nuggets. I wanted two Big Macs, ma'am." And then Bobby drove away.

Paul was standing at the entrance of Target when Bobby drove up. Paul was holding two plastic sacks, one in each hand, and he proudly held them up for Bobby to see. As the door slammed and Paul sat down, he did not notice the scowl on Bobby's face. Paul was too busy reaching into one of his Target bags so that he could show his buddy the new socks that he had purchased. The big man retrieved a bundle of black socks, which he held in one hand, and a sleeve of white socks, held in the other. "Half price, Bobby. Everything in the store seemed to be half price, this being almost the last shopping day before Christmas."

Bobby was seething, and the seat belt alarm was beeping because Paul had still not clicked it. Bobby's face was red with anger, and his head was throbbing. "WILL YOU PLEASE fasten your seat belt, Paul!" Bobby angrily yelled. "I can't stand that bloody beeping! It's driving me crazy."

Paul still did not notice that Bobby was out of sorts, because he was busy clicking his seat belt. "Yeah, 'Click It, or Ticket.'" said Paul as he reached into his underwear bag.

"What?" said Bobby.

"You know, the seat belt law, Bobby? If you don't have your seat belt clicked, the cops can give you a ticket, 'Click It, or Ticket.'"

Paul grabbed a package from his bag, which contained six pair of men's briefs underwear, all six of different colors. "Aren't they beautiful, Bobby? I got the last package in my size, and like the socks, they were half price. By the way, where are the burgers? I'm famished."

The Viper Red Caprice passed the Salvation Army Thrift Store, and the heroes saw Santa still ringing his bell. Bobby made the turn onto Kirk while telling Paul about the expired coupon episode at McDonald's and about how the young lady got him so ticked off.

Paul apologized. "Bobby, I should have told you to not use the Drive-Thru but to go inside instead. Julie usually works that window, and well, that girl Julie never cuts anybody any slack. If you had walked inside to the counter, they would have honored the expired BOGO. So we don't have a Big Mac; what's the big deal? Ann will have something for us to eat. She probably has a big pot of beef stew on the stove, or chicken-n-dumplin's. Why don't you come in and eat a bowl of something or maybe a couple of her world-famous scones?"

"I'd love nothing more, Paul, but I only have about five minutes to get to Homes Depot, where Natalie works. I'll take a rain check, though."

Bobby pulled into Ann's circular drive. The lawn had been freshly cut and edged and looked great. Paul grabbed his Target bags while Bobby unlocked the trunk and retrieved Paul's new suitcase filled with shirts, trousers, and shoes.

After giving Paul a man-sized hug, Bobby got back into the Viper Red Chevy and started its eight-cylinder engine. The ruckus brought Ann outside to see just what was going on. "Hi, Paul! Hi, Bobby. You guys hungry? I've got fried chicken on the stove. Just took it out of the Crisco; potatoes are boiling and should be ready for mashing in five minutes." Ann was waving them both toward her front door.

Bobby looked up at Ann and said, "Fried chicken? That's my favorite food. If I were on death row and asked what I wanted for my last meal, I would say fried chicken, or maybe a Big Mac, if I had a coupon."

Paul looked at Bobby, and Bobby looked at Paul, and they both burst out in laughter.

Ann asked, "What's so funny, boys?"

Paul turned to Ann and said, "I'll tell you later while we eat Bobby's portion of the fried chicken. He can't join us, Ann. He has to pick up his Natalie from work in five minutes."

Ann looked disappointed, but she said, "Hold on, Bobby. I've got something for you." She returned with a paper plate wrapped in aluminum foil and handed it through the window to Bobby.

Paul asked Ann if there were two scones under that foil, and she said, "Yes."

Paul looked at Bobby and said, "Sir, your coupon has expired. Give me those scones back."

The two men burst into laughter yet again. Ann scratched her head and asked for a second time, "What's so funny? I don't get it."

"I'll tell you later, Ann," repeated Paul.

Ann circled the shiny Caprice, admiring its glossy red paint and the soft, camel-colored leather seats. She stopped at Bobby's open window, kneeled down, and placed her hand on Bobby's arm.

"Merry Christmas, Bobby," she said. "You're a good friend to Paul. Please know that you are always welcome here, and any time your sweet tooth is acting up or you would like to join us for a hot, home-cooked meal, just give me a call. You do have my number, don't you?"

"Uh, no, I just got this phone on Monday, and I only have two phone numbers in my address book."

Ann asked for his number, dialed it, and when Bobby answered his red phone, she said, "Hi, Bobby. This is Ann. Would you like a piece of fried chicken for the road?"

Bobby's mouth began to water.

"Sure," he said, and Ann quickly ran inside to wrap a fat, juicy chicken breast in tin foil. She was back in a flash and handed the warm package to Bobby, leaned her head into the car, and gave Bobby a small kiss on the cheek.

Paul reached over and gave Bobby a strong handshake and said, "Thanks for a wonderful day, Bobby. I told you that Ann had taken a liking to you. Merry Christmas, buddy. Say hello to Natalie for me and wish her a merry Christmas, OK?"

As he drove away, Bobby looked in his rearview mirror and saw them waving goodbye. He waved back, rolled up his window, and headed to Natalie's office.

Bobby looked at his watch. He had three minutes to get to Homes Depot. Three minutes later, he was pulling into the realtor's parking lot. Bobby backed into a space that was highly visible from the front door. He wanted Natalie to be *blown away* when she saw her car. Her Christmas present. Bobby opened the windows, turned off the engine, and eagerly stared at the front door of Homes Depot, watching for Natalie to exit her office.

Only two other cars were parked in the small lot, but they were on the other side of the building, probably vehicles that belonged to employees.

Bobby looked down at his wrist. The time was 3:50. Bobby decided to reset his watch with the correct time, which was 3:30. He pulled at the little stem on the side of his crystal until he heard a faint click, and then he rotated the big hand until it pointed to the number six. He then pushed the stem down to click it back in place and held his watch to his ear to confirm that it was indeed ticking.

Time to leave, Natalie, he thought. *Come on, pretty lady, punch out and come see your new car.* Bobby was so excited that he could hardly wait to see her face when she walked out of that building.

While Bobby sat waiting, his mind was going wild with thoughts. *What if she doesn't like the color? Did I ask her if she likes red? I should have bought a big bow to put on top of the car, with ribbons.*

Bobby's stomach started to growl. That chicken sure smelled good. He would save the chicken breast and scones until tonight.

He could eat it by his campfire before going to sleep. That's when he realized that he had not eaten since breakfast with Paul. *Maybe,* he thought, *Natalie and I can share a sub. Or I could eat some chicken tenders.* That made Bobby laugh—the McDonald's girl had tried to sell him chicken tenders.

Then the door of the Homes Depot opened, and it was Natalie.

CHAPTER 101

Wednesday, December 23, 3:30 p.m.
Bobby Picks Up Natalie in Her New Caprice

Natalie's hands came up to her cheeks as she stared at Bobby sitting in the Viper Red Chevy Caprice. Bobby watched as she descended the three steps and walked toward her car. He opened the door, removed the keys, and walked toward her. Her eyes darted from the gorgeous red car to the man with the gorgeous smile, the man whom she had come to love. She wrapped her arms around him, and he hugged back.

Bobby released Natalie, lifted her right hand, and placed the keys in her open palm. He held her left hand, and they walked toward the Caprice.

"Merry Christmas, Natalie. I fixed your broken window mechanism, and I changed your oil."

"You changed my oil? You did more than change my oil, Bobby. I don't know what to say. How? Where did you get the money to do this? It's beautiful, Bobby. Red is my favorite color. How did you know?"

Natalie's eyes were moist, and teardrops of happiness were trickling down her face. She held him tightly and said, "Thank you, Bobby. It's the best Christmas gift ever. I love you, Bobby."

Bobby Thornton had wet eyes too, and he put his hand on the back of her head as she rested her face on his shoulder.

The heavy glass door of the real estate office opened, and out walked Penny, one of the associates who worked at Homes Depot.

Penny stood on the stoop and watched her dear friend turn and then wave her hand toward the red Chevy.

"Is that your old bucket of bolts, the Caprice?" Penny asked.

"Yep," answered Natalie, "but she ain't no bucket of bolts no more. Pardon my English, Penny, but isn't she beautiful?"

"Yes, she is, Natalie. Introduce me to your friend."

Penny walked down the three steps as Natalie and Bobby wiped their eyes. Natalie hooked Bobby's arm and met Penny halfway to the middle of the parking lot.

"This is Mr. Robert Thornton, Penny. He's a dear friend of mine."

Bobby held out his hand, and Penny did likewise. They shook hands, and Penny said, "He's very handsome, Natalie."

Bobby blushed, and Natalie smiled.

"Yes, he is," Natalie agreed.

Penny shook hands with Mr. Thornton again, hugged Natalie, whispered something in her ear, and waved goodbye. "Gotta go. Merry Christmas!"

"See ya Monday, Penny."

Bobby walked Natalie back to the car and opened the door for his dearest friend. She looked up at him and exclaimed, "Bobby, what did you do with my old seats? I loved those seats, Bobby. Can we get them back?"

Bobby had a puzzled look on his face, and he frowned and wet his lips as he tried to figure out what to say. That's when Natalie smiled and said, "Got ya!"

"Whew, Natalie, don't do that to me. I was hoping that Dan's friend hadn't thrown them out."

"Who's Dan?"

"I'll tell you all about Dan and Nick and Paul and the day I've had when we sit on the bench at Publix. Deal?"

"Deal!" said Natalie. "Let's go get Missy."

Natalie started the engine. It purred like a kitten. The AC was blowing icy cold air. She fiddled with the electric windows and raised and lowered them while she drove. Natalie smiled all the way home. She had Bobby slide over on the wide bench seat and sit in the middle so that she could rest her right hand on his knee.

"I just love this car, Bobby. Thank you."

The Caprice pulled into Mrs. Williams's driveway. Natalie got out of the car, walked up to Mona's front door, and rang the bell. Missy answered and said, "Yes, may I help you?"

"I'm looking for my daughter. Missy is her name. Would you know if she's here? I understand that Mrs. Williams is watching her for the day." Natalie enjoyed playing this game with Missy, but Missy was very good at it, maybe better than Natalie.

"Your name, Miss? Or is it Ms.?"

"Natalie. I live across the street."

"Please wait here, and I'll ask Mrs. Williams if she knows of a… uh, what did you say her name was?"

"Missy is her name."

"Yes, Missy. Please wait here. We don't allow strangers in the house."

Missy turned to walk away, and then she did an about-face and ran to her mother and threw her arms around Natalie's waist.

Bobby was somewhat puzzled as he watched the mother and daughter behave as if they were total strangers, as if they were playing parts in a Broadway play.

"Hi, Mr. Thornton. Won't you please come in? Mrs. Williams and I made cookies today. Would you like a cookie?"

"Absolutely, Missy," said Bobby, who was starving. "I might even have two if you don't mind."

"No problem, Mr. Thornton. Two it is, maybe even three if you're a good boy."

Natalie and Bobby looked at each other and smiled.

CHAPTER 102

Wednesday, December 23, 3:45 p.m.
Cookies at Mona's House

Missy grabbed Bobby by the hand and led him to the rear of the home, where Mona sat in her easy chair, watching a game show. Natalie held Bobby's other hand. Mrs. Williams rose from her La-Z-Boy and greeted her guests.

"Mrs. Williams?" Missy was tugging on Mona's hand as she looked up and asked, "Can Mr. Thornton have a cookie? I told him that he could! He's really hungry and said that maybe he can eat two cookies, or maybe even three."

"Sure," said Mona, and she placed the heaping platter of cookies on the breakfast table. Mona brought three glasses, three dessert plates, a carton of milk, and three coffee mugs to the table. She invited her three guests to be seated and offered everyone a choice of fresh coffee or cold milk.

"So, Missy, did you wear Mrs. Williams out today?" asked her mother.

"Oh, no, Mom, we just played cards and made cookies. Oh, and we played hide-and-go-seek too. I didn't wear Mrs. Williams out at all. Just look at her. She's not worn out, are you Mrs. Williams?" Missy looked over at Mona, who was seated next to her at the small wooden table.

Mona shook her head and said, "Heavens, no. I'm not the least bit worn out, Natalie. We just did girly things all day, and we read some interesting books, stories, and articles too."

"Yes, Mother, Mrs. Williams read me a story about a Christmas tree just like Mr. Fir. It was so exciting. There were foxes and possums and mice and a little girl just like me. And, Mom, Mrs. Williams is a really good reader, just like you. Mom, are you ready to go to Publix? I need to talk with Mr. Fir."

Natalie shook her head and looked over at Bobby, who was gobbling down his fourth oatmeal raisin cookie and already half-finished with his second glass of milk.

"Yes, dear, we're almost ready to go, just as soon as Bobby is finished with his cookies."

"These cookies are delicious, Missy. You said that you made them?" Bobby swallowed his fifth cookie and chased it with the last drops of his second glass of milk. He leaned back and patted his tummy. "Mmm, good. Best darned cookies I ever ate. Good job, Missy."

"Mrs. Williams helped me, Mr. Thornton. I'm glad that you liked them. Are you full? Mommy said that we can go see Mr. Fir when you are finished with your cookies."

Mona, Bobby, and Natalie laughed, and then Mona asked if Natalie would pick her up a loaf of bread, the soft Publix brand that costs less than two dollars. She handed Natalie a five-dollar bill, which Natalie refused. "I'll use my BOGO coupon, Mona. I also need a loaf of bread, but we can't use two loaves, so I'll use the coupon and bring you the other."

Mona walked them to the door, waved goodbye, shut the door behind them, and walked back to her La-Z-Boy. She plopped down, said, "Whew," and fell fast asleep.

CHAPTER 103

Wednesday, December 23, 4:00 p.m.
From Mona's House to Publix

Missy was the first one out of Mona's house, and she shrieked with glee when she saw the red Caprice.

"Mama," she squealed, "our car is beautiful. When did you have it painted?" Missy ran over and pulled open the back door. The new-car smell of fresh leather filled her lungs. She laid her head on the seat and inhaled the sweet smells of newness. Missy rubbed her hands on the soft surface, and then she looked up at the headliner. "Mommy, the old, saggy ceiling is gone!" she exclaimed. Missy fastened her seat belt and called out to Bobby and Natalie, "Come on, guys, get in! Let's go show our new car to Mr. Fir."

The doors slammed shut, and Natalie pulled out of the driveway. Less than five minutes later, they were parking at Publix in a spot far from the store, where few people ever parked. Natalie had learned Bobby's lesson. Park far away, and your car won't get dinged. During the short trip to Publix, Missy chattered nonstop about the cold air conditioning, the new carpet, the soft seats, the gorgeous red color, and how the motor was so quiet that you could barely hear it running. She also played with the window mechanisms that Bobby had fixed, rolling them up and down, until Natalie fussed and told her to stop.

Missy could hardly wait to tell Mr. Fir about their new Chevy Caprice.

CHAPTER 104

Wednesday, December 23, 4:08 p.m.
Missy Tells Her Sammy Story to Fir

I knew that Natalie and Missy would be here to see me at exactly 3:45 p.m., unless something unforeseen happened to cause them to be late, but I doubted that. Missy had never been late. Not yet. Missy told me that she would spend all day every day with me if her mom would let her. She told me that she had been on Christmas break since school let out on Friday and that she didn't have to go back until January 4. We had talked a lot about a lot of things when she and Natalie had come to see me this past Sunday. We would've talked longer, but Bobby had other plans. That was the day they went on their picnic.

Missy had worked all week on her story, the best story of her short life, and she could not wait to come to Publix to tell it to me. I couldn't wait to see her and to feel the energy flow from her small hand as she held my broken branch.

But Natalie had told Missy that there was no way in the world that she would let a Fraser fir babysit her daughter, and although I get it, I still wished she were there with me. I was so doggoned depressed after that morning. Thank God I had my sparrows. They were so happy to see me again. No sooner had Kenny leaned me against the wall and sprayed me down with water than Eddie and his two fuzzy brown brothers perched on the branch by my face and started kissing me with their cute little yellow beaks. I loved these guys. I don't know if you have ever watched two birds kiss each other, but they are quite affectionate. They open their mouths and kind of gently nibble at each other's beaks, and if they have food stored in their craws, they share with their loved ones. That's what my sparrows were doing to me. Actually, it tickled, and I started to laugh, and then they laughed along with me, and soon all us trees and critters on the breezeway were engaged in roaring laughter. Even Cantankerous Carl, the crow, was laughing.

My sparrows were a delight, and guess what happened? My sadness and depression went away. It's kind of hard to be sad when you are happy. Other than Ron and Stacy, nobody had wanted me. Nobody except Missy, but her mother had said that they could not afford a real tree this year, so I had become very sad and disheartened during this, the last day before Christmas Eve.

Oh, I was looked at, lifted, and turned, but once people saw the extent of my damage, they would toss me aside and buy another tree. Often I was roughly handled and thrown to the ground like trash that was no longer wanted or needed. Kenny would always pick me up when he noticed that I was not standing proud with my Scotch pine cousins, but Kenny was not always on the breezeway. He was also a bag boy and had other duties to attend to in addition to watching over us trees. So sometimes I would just lie there for hours, watching people walk by, but nobody seemed to care, except Bobby. Boy, if he saw me on my side, he would get really angry and walk into the store and start ranting and raving. Then he would come out and gently pick me up, talk softly to me, and set me up close to his bench.

And then there was the catastrophe with Ron and Stacy. Adopted at 2:00 p.m. on Tuesday and returned at 7:00 a.m. on Wednesday…seventeen hours in a happy family. I thought I should not even share that story with Missy.

So here it was, Wednesday, the day before Christmas Eve, and I was still homeless, but as I stared off into the distance, I saw Missy. She was closing the rear door of a glossy red Chevrolet Caprice. As Missy came closer, I could see that she was walking between Bobby and her mother, holding hands with both of them and swinging their arms as she walked.

My heart fluttered with happiness at seeing my dear Missy, and then Missy did something really neat. She brought Bobby and Natalie over to me and introduced us. "Mr. Fir, this is Mr. Thornton, and Mr. Fir, this is my mother, Miss McCord." Then, she looked up at Bobby and Natalie and introduced me to them. "Mr. Thornton and Miss McCord, this is Mr. Fir."

Natalie and Bobby each reached over, grabbed the end of a branch, shook my limb, and said, "Pleased to meet you, Mr. Fir."

Bobby said, "We don't mean to be rude, but we are going to sit on the bench for a bit while you talk with Missy. I hope you won't be offended, Mr. Fir."

"Offended? I have been thinking about this day for a whole week. Go sit down, Bobby. Missy and I have some catching up to do."

Bobby and Natalie sat down on the green bench, close together and holding hands.

Missy walked around me, located my broken branch, and with that high-pitched little girl voice said, "Hi, Mr. Fir. I've missed you. Today I get to tell *you* a story. It's not a *best* story; it's actually a *worst* story, but I want to tell it to you anyway."

"What is your story about, Missy?" I asked.

"It's about my bulldog, Sammy, Mr. Fir."

Uh-oh, I thought, *this is going to be a real tear-jerker of a story.* Bobby had already told me about Missy's father and Sammy, the bulldog puppy, and about what happened on that fateful night. It is a sad story, and it made me cry, but I knew that I couldn't tell Missy that I knew all about what had happened to her puppy.

"OK, Missy, tell me about Sammy."

"One day this past spring, Daddy brought me home a puppy. I was so happy, Mr. Fir. The little fellow seemed to take an instant liking to me, and I to him. We played tug-of-war, and we chased each other, and we went for walks together. When I walked Sammy, Mommy made me hold on tight to his leash so that he would not get loose, but as he grew bigger, he became much stronger, and it took all my strength to hold him when I took him outside to do his business. Mommy and Daddy made me walk him twice a day, once in the morning before school and once in the evening before bedtime. Daddy would get really mad at Sammy when he messed in the house, and he would hit my puppy with a newspaper. I just hated to see poor Sammy getting a spanking. I knew it was my fault for not walking him. Daddy always yelled at me after spanking Sammy, and he would make me clean up the mess.

"Daddy would yell at me and stand over me, shaking his finger. 'Missy, you wanted a puppy, so I went out and bought you a puppy, but *you* are responsible to walk him and to feed him and to water him. Look at his bowls, Missy. They are both empty! You are a bad girl, and I'm sorry I bought you that puppy. Now go feed and water him, and you are restricted for a week, except to walk the dog."

Little Missy had a pained look on her face as she told me her puppy story, and her voice began to tremble as she continued.

"Well, right after Sammy's whipping, and after I cleaned up the mess on Daddy's new wood floor, I hooked up the leash to Sammy's new red collar. Mommy had bought the collar a lot larger than Sammy's neck because he was growing so fast that she said he would quickly outgrow the collar if she didn't buy the larger one.

"Sammy had his little curly tail between his legs, and I was crying because Daddy was being so mean toward Sammy and me. Sammy was happy to be leaving the house for his walk, and I was happy to be getting away from my daddy. As I said before, Sammy was growing into what my mom called a teenager, and he was very strong. Bulldogs are all muscle. They have short legs, big necks, and muscular chests, and they are very stubborn. They do not like to listen and don't always come when you call them. I was being pulled down the block toward the stop sign by a very strong dog. He was smelling everything from trees to fire hydrants, and he would stop for no apparent reason and sniff at grass where he sensed another dog had been. I think he smelled their scent. Then he would leave his scent and again start pulling me down the sidewalk. I yanked hard on the leash, and I yelled at Sammy, but he paid no attention to me. He just kept going.

"Suddenly a Siamese cat sprang out from behind a bush, hissing and snarling when he saw Sammy. My bulldog went wild, barking, yelping, running around in circles, and pulling hard on his leash. He was shaking his head and jumping in the air like a rodeo bronco trying to buck free so that he could chase the cat. The cat, though, knowing that Sammy was on a leash, stood his ground. He arched his back and hissed and growled at Sammy. This behavior by the neighbor's cat made Sammy furious, and he ran around me, causing the leash to become entangled around my legs. I fell down, and suddenly Sammy slipped out of his new red collar and took off after the cat. The cat high-tailed it across the street with Sammy in hot pursuit. That's when it happened. A car came speeding down the road just as my brown-and-white puppy was crossing the street, and my Sammy was left lying in the road, bleeding from the mouth. Tears were cascading from my eyes as I lifted my lifeless puppy and carried him home.

"My father blamed me for Sammy's death, Mr. Fir. He yelled at me and screamed about how much a purebred bulldog costs.

"Daddy was so angry with me that I knew I was about to get a spanking. He and my mother got into a big fight, and then Daddy stormed out of the house.

"The next day, Daddy came home, packed a suitcase, moved out, and left me and my mother alone…and it's all my fault."

Missy was weeping as she whispered this story to me. Her small hand never once, however, released my broken branch. Her love, her affection, her energy was flowing into me in torrents.

I didn't know what to say. *God,* I prayed, *I love this little girl. I need for her to take me home. Please, God, make it happen!*

I looked over at Bobby and Natalie, sitting close together on the bench. There was love and affection and energy flowing on the bench too. Natalie rose from her seat and asked Bobby if he could stick around a while longer. She said that she needed to pick up a few things for Christmas Eve and would only be inside Publix for no more than thirty minutes.

Natalie looked over in my direction and noticed that her daughter was almost completely hidden by my lower branches, but she could hear Missy quietly talking to me, in a voice that was just barely audible.

"Missy, let's go. Tell your friend that we will be back in a few minutes, OK?"

"OK, Mama!" Missy looked up at me and wiped her eyes. She was so upset, and her tears had left wet spots on the pavement.

"Missy," I said, "I will be here when you come back out of Publix, and we'll talk some more, and we'll hold hands again, OK?"

"OK, Mr. Fir."

Missy released my branch, walked over to Natalie, and grabbed her hand, and the two McCord girls walked into the store. Natalie did not notice Missy's red eyes or tears, because she was still looking at Bobby as they walked away from the bench.

Bobby stood and walked around to the back of the bench. He looked at me and said, "Life is good, Fir. I feel as if I am being reborn. It's as if I became stuck in a river of mud. I feel like my legs are suddenly incredibly strong and I'm able to walk out of the quicksand that had been holding me down. I can walk, Fir. I can dance. I can laugh. I'm alive again, Fir."

Bobby slapped himself on his backside as the doors closed behind Natalie. He jumped into the air and looked up into the perfectly blue Florida sky. He raised his arms up toward the heavens and whispered, "Thank you."

As the afternoon sun began peeking at his bench, Bobby sat down and leaned back his head. He allowed the sun to warm his face just as Natalie had warmed his heart. Bobby did not recall ever feeling this happy, and he anxiously awaited Natalie's return from her shopping. Bobby was tingling and vibrating and seeing life as he had never seen it before.

Missy and her mother would be inside Publix, doing their last-minute shopping, for about thirty minutes, but to Bobby, it would seem like hours. Bobby was in his own celestial world of extreme happiness, a time warp where time without Natalie seemed to pass in slow motion.

CHAPTER 105

Wednesday, December 23, about 5:00 p.m.
Missy and Natalie Finish Shopping

Upon seeing Natalie in the checkout line, Bobby put two sticks of peppermint-flavored gum into his mouth and started to chew. This was not bubble-blowing time; this was sweet-smelling breath time. The smiling faces of Natalie and Missy graced our presence and returned to share our company. Bobby stood up as Natalie approached. I was already standing when Missy walked near.

Missy returned to my side and again reached gently for my broken branch. I had cried while Missy was inside the store shopping with her mother. I knew not what to say to her when she returned, but when her warm little hand grasped my damaged bough, I knew exactly what I was going to say.

"Missy, your father did not leave because of *you* or anything that *you* had done. Life is very complicated, and no matter how old we become, we cannot understand why things happen as they do."

Missy wiped her nose on her left sleeve, and with her right hand, she wiped the tears from her eyes. "But Mr. Fir, my daddy was very mad, and he glared at me and just walked out of the house and got into his car. Momma went after him, but he drove away very fast."

This little girl was breaking my heart.

"Missy, bad things happen to all of us, and when they happen, we ask ourselves, Why? What did I do to deserve this? Was it my fault? What could I have done differently? But Missy, life just happens."

I paused and then continued, "Good things happen, and bad things happen, but we just have to go on living and not blame ourselves for the bad things. I was living the most wonderful life you can imagine on my lush, green mountain in Murphy, North Carolina. All the animals loved me, and the flowers and the bushes loved me, and the insects loved me, and the sun loved me, and the moon, too, especially the moon. It kept me company every night when everyone else was asleep. And I loved everything, even the grouchy crow who frequently pooped on my head. But one day a group of big, mean-looking men with chainsaws walked through my grove and cut every single tree, all my friends, to the ground. My Mary screamed and cried, but there was nothing I could do. I'm just a tree, Missy, and you are just a little girl. There is only so much that we can do. I blamed myself for not being able to help Mary, but Missy, I'm just a tree. Your daddy left because it was time for him to move on, just as it was time for me to move on. And there was nothing either one of us could do, Missy, because I am just a tree, and you are just a little girl."

Again I paused, thinking about what I would say next, and then I said, "My destiny is to find a family, brighten their home at Christmas, and become part of their love and joy during the holiday season. You have a destiny too, and so does your mother. Don't blame your father for moving on, and don't blame yourself for your father leaving. Stuff just happens in this world. There is a greater power in the heavens that will watch over you and your mother, and me too. We will all be fine! We'll be all right. You are a very special, beautiful little girl, Missy, and I love you very much."

My sparrows were quietly sitting on one of my branches, at eye level to Missy. They were listening to every word and staring into Missy's eyes. They, too, had little bird tears in their eyes as they felt the pain and sadness in this loving little girl.

The crow, Carl, was perched on one of the benches nearby and had not moved since Missy returned to my side. Carl did not caw, the sparrows did not sing, and the unsold trees just stood there, listening to Missy and to me.

"Missy, you just remember one thing, a most important thing that will guide you throughout your life."

"What's that, Mr. Fir?"

"Everything always works out for the best, Missy. We don't always understand why things happen as they do or why they happen when they do, but everything works out for the best. Life has a way of sorting things out and making things better than they were before."

"But, Mr. Fir, I caused my daddy to leave, and now Mommy and I are alone. How can that be better?"

"Just have faith, Missy. Have faith. I would not have met you if I had not been cut down by those mean men. I have been blessed to be your friend, Missy. And I have my sparrows and Bobby and even that grumpy old blackbird over there on that bench. Yes, Missy, I'm blessed, and it's almost Christmas. Soon I will be adopted, and I will celebrate Christmas in a happy home with happy children and maybe even a doggie."

"I wish I could take you home, Mr. Fir. I love you, Mr. Fir." And with no advance warning, Missy wrapped her little arms around me and hugged me tightly.

There wasn't a dry eye in the breezeway, except for Natalie and Bobby, who were so engrossed in their own conversation and laughter that they heard nothing of ours. Even the old black crow had shed tears, which were dripping profusely from his eyes.

"Missy, we have to go," summoned her mother.

Bobby stood, and Natalie moved close to him and gave Bobby a loving hug. Bobby never saw it coming, and he stiffened up. But the softness of her skin and the gentleness of her embrace melted his tension, and Bobby returned the hug.

Hand in hand, Missy and Natalie headed for their new car. Natalie turned and smiled at Bobby.

"Pick you up at seven o'clock Christmas Eve, OK?"

"You bet, Natalie. I'll be right here. See ya then! Bye, bye, Missy."

"Bye, Mr. Thornton. See you Christmas Eve."

Kenny came out and gave us trees a good soaking. There were only a handful of us left. Carl flew down to share the water with my sparrows. Everyone was in the Christmas spirit, and I was hoping so much that a miracle would happen and that I would be Missy's Christmas tree, decorated with lights and shiny bulbs and lots of garland. And, of course, a star or an angel on my apical meristem. (Remember what I said before? That's the top of my head.)

CHAPTER 106

December 24, Christmas Eve
A Very Long Day

Christmas Eve at the supermarket began like any other day, with vendors pouring through the front doors starting at 5:00 a.m., when the service entrance was first unlocked. The bread men had already been to the bakery and were first to arrive, drinking coffee in the parking lot while they waited for the lights to come on. The deli employees were told to punch in at 5:30 a.m. and begin making platters for the myriad Christmas Eve parties that would usher in the arrival of Santa.

The din of activity awakened my sparrows, but they remained in hiding within the safety of my branches. The noisy blackbird bullied his way through the western corridor, seeking sustenance from McMuffins, donuts, and other fast food hastily discarded into the trash. This monster-crow ruled the Publix breezeway and parking lot.

"Caw, caw," he warned. I understood his screeching to mean, "This is my domain."

There were only five of us trees left. Mr. Kemp had not scheduled any more Fraser firs to be delivered on the twenty-fourth. Most shoppers had long since purchased and decorated their trees, but I was optimistic about the prospect of finding my new home, since there were only five of us left to choose from.

My thoughts wandered to the home that my humans would live in. Maybe it would have a fireplace and a puppy like Turk and a little girl like Missy. The family would turn on Christmas music, open boxes of decorations, drink eggnog, and decorate me.

I would spread my strong limbs to hold shiny strands of garland and sparkling lights, some blinking, others bubbling. Some would twinkle, like starlight. Then there would be the delicate decorations, colorful and precious. And with my center branch, my scion, held high, I would proudly display a magnificent star or a majestic angel.

My excitement was building as the clock approached 7:00 a.m.—that's when the doors would open and the parking lot would begin to fill with cars. Patrons would stampede the store and fill their buggies with last-minute needs. Everything in the store seemed to be on sale. Pumpkin and apple pies were three dollars apiece, and the pecan pies had been reduced to four dollars.

Kenny came out front and shooed off the blackbird that was scavenging in the trash can. He was an angry bird and let Kenny know in no uncertain terms that this was his realm and he was the king. "Caw, caw, caw."

Kenny swept the fallen needles with a straw broom, connected the hose, and watered us well. We had to look our very best. This was *our* day. He then walked over, turned me around so that my best side faced the shoppers, and in the spirit of Christmas, discounted me to 50 percent off. Kenny repeated the process on the remaining four trees and afterward went into the store to report to Mr. Kemp.

It was a beautiful day in Lake Worth. A cold front had moved through, dropping the ambient temperature to sixty-five degrees. Mothers clothed their children in warm jackets, and old people wore sweaters. The cool weather made me nostalgic for the cool climate of North Carolina, where I was born. But just as I was reminiscing, I was lifted into the air by a giant of a man and carried into the sunlight.

"Look at this one, Madge! Only eighteen-ninety-five." I was twirled around and around so that his wife could see me from all sides.

"Naw," she said, "there's a big broken branch on the back."

The big man tossed me aside as easily as if I were a toothpick and he had finished cleaning his teeth. He picked up one of the Scotch pines, spun him around for Madge, and called Kenny to help him load the tree in his truck. My friend was so happy to be adopted that his needles were puffed up like the soft feathers of a happy sparrow. His name was Nick. We all had names, and we all talked to each other.

Trees communicate with each other by way of a nonverbal language understood by most all living things. An energy conveys feelings of joy or pain, tranquility or imminent danger, new life or even death. Nick was elated with his new family and was thrilled to be going to his new home to be decorated. I had not noticed the twin daughters standing next to Madge. I sent my blessings and congratulations to my friend Nick, and then he was gone.

I knew that I would probably be next. I was so excited, but the day did not bode well for me. There were only four of us left after Nick departed, and by three o'clock in the afternoon, I was the only tree left. Kenny swept the fallen needles that had been left behind by my good friends, gave me one last drink, stood me up good and straight, and again turned me so that my broken branch was facing the wall.

At 4:00 p.m., patrons began arriving to pick up their party platters. No one paid me any mind as they hurried to the rear of the store with yellow receipts in hand. A long line began forming at the deli, where orders for huge, eighteen-inch rounds of steamed shrimp, deviled eggs, and assorted cheeses were matched to their respective yellow tickets. Fruit and veggie platters, chicken wings, and assorted bakery platters were carried to waiting cars by shoppers who did not even know I was there.

The setting sun slowly drifted toward the horizon as the afternoon waned, and Publix's parking lot slowly emptied as last-minute shoppers headed home to celebrate the arrival of Santa.

By 5:00 p.m., the supermarket was largely deserted, and the department managers began preparing for the holiday's six o'clock store closure. Kenny was directed to check the parking lot for buggies, sweep the storefront, and empty all garbage cans. The crow was busily feeding on the remains of a turkey sub sandwich when Kenny approached the trash receptacle. Startled by this sudden intrusion by the bag boy, the massive blackbird violently flapped his wings in a noisy retreat to the unoccupied bench.

"CAW, CAW!"

My sparrows snickered at seeing this selfish bully of a bird lose his Christmas turkey dinner to the big, black mouth of a trash bag. They had found the sub first, but it had been stolen from them by the aggressive crow.

CHAPTER 107

December 24, Christmas Eve
Bobby Finally Arrives at Publix

And suddenly Bobby was there, standing right in front of me, staring at me with the eyes of a dear friend. He could sense my sadness. He could tell that I had been crying. Bobby reached out to me, and with the soft touch of a sparrow, he gently closed his fingers around my broken branch. He mumbled something in a whispered voice, but I was unable to make out his muffled words. His eyes were closed as he spoke, and his head was bowed. The melancholy of my self-pity was gone. I was not alone and forgotten. I was with Booby. I felt his love.

Bobby turned toward the bench where the curmudgeonly blackbird was perched. They stared at each other, the crow turning his head and focusing on Bobby with one shiny, black eye.

"CAW, CAW!" Bobby flapped his arms as if they were wings and lunged at the defiant creature standing on Bobby's bench. The blackbird flew away, noisily retreating to higher ground.

Bobby pointed to the bench, where he had placed a small kennel with a barking dog inside. It was Turk. My spirits were raised almost immediately. I asked Bobby to bring Turk over so that I could see him better and so that I could say hi. Bobby obliged. He turned and walked to the bench, opened the gate, and lifted the small, furry puppy into his arms. Turk had a red collar, to which Bobby fastened a red leash. He set Turk on the breezeway floor, and the small dog ran to me as if I were a long-lost brother. He squeezed under my lower branches and lay next to me, where he felt safe. We talked about the dogcatcher, the veterinarian, and the new collar and leash that he had and about how he was going to be Missy's Christmas present.

While we talked, he snuggled close to me and shared his warmth. Bobby watched and listened to me talking to my dear friend Turk. He was such a loving little puppy, and I was so excited for him and for Missy, but at the same time, I was saddened that I would not be a part of their Christmas Eve and their Christmas Day.

Bobby was scanning the parking lot for Natalie, but since she had not yet arrived, he decided to take advantage of the opportunity to wrap the stuffed animal that he had bought earlier.

Bobby had agreed to meet Natalie at Publix at 6:30 p.m. because he just had so much to do to get ready for Christmas Eve with his girl. He was donned in the new clothing Natalie had given him at the community center on Friday night, and he looked good. Bobby had stopped by the center earlier to shower and put on his sweet-smelling, foo-foo aftershave lotion. His teeth were sparkling white, his hair was combed, and the man looked like a handsome prince. Bobby also had to visit Chase Bank to withdraw money to pay Walker, the vet, and he needed to see several homeless friends whom he had become very fond of. Then there were the presents he bought for Nick and Dan, which he'd had to deliver. Bobby hadn't worked so hard since he last worked a full-time job.

Bobby was wrapping a white, fluffy, soft-as-satin teddy bear, which Publix had marked down to 50 percent off and Bobby had thought would be a perfect gift for Missy. They also had Christmas wrapping paper discounted to 75 percent off, so he purchased a roll with Santa Clauses in sleighs pulled by reindeer. He opened the roll of paper, laid the bear on top, and carefully folded the sides together to be taped. The Scotch tape was also on sale. As he completed taping the ends of his package, the crow flew overhead with angry wings that almost hit Bobby as he flew by.

"What the...? I guess that's his way of saying merry Christmas to me, Fir."

"Yep, that's the way he is, Bobby," I answered.

Bobby leaned back, extending his arms onto the backrest, when he heard the automatic doors of Publix open and the locks click. The lights inside the supermarket were turned off, and one by one the employees, dressed in their dark green vests, filed out of Publix, walking briskly toward their cars. Mr. Kemp and the store manager, Judy Wright, were the last to leave. Judy activated the alarm system and secured the last of the doors.

Mr. Kemp saw Thornton sitting on the bench, looked down at Bobby's Christmas present, and nodded to the homeless man. "How ya doin', Bobby? Merry Christmas. I see that Santa has already brought you a gift."

Bobby stood and extended his hand. "Merry Christmas to you, Mr. Kemp. No, these presents on the bench are for a friend. I bought that one"—Bobby pointed toward the wrapped stuffed bear—"here, at your store. Could I ask you a quick question, Mr. Kemp?"

"Sure, Bobby." Bobby turned and pointed at me. "See that tree over there? What are you going to do with it?"

"Well, Bobby, on Saturday we'll have to carry it around back to the dumpster. It has a broken branch, and nobody wanted to buy it."

"I do, Mr. Kemp. I want to buy *this* tree. How much? I have money, Mr. Kemp."

"Bobby, the store is closed. It's too late. You should've bought it when we were open."

The store manager was standing next to me, watching and paying close attention to the drama playing out in her breezeway. She watched Bobby's eyes look down and noted his sudden change in demeanor. She reached into her pocket, retrieved a marker, and scribbled something on my tag.

"Do you have a dollar?" she asked.

"Yes, ma'am. I have twenty dollars."

"Well, Bobby—do you mind if I call you Bobby?"

"Oh, yes, ma'am, Bobby's fine."

"Well, Bobby, the tag says one dollar, but as Mr. Kemp said, we're closed. Why don't you take the tree and come by the store on Saturday to pay for it? OK?"

"One dollar? Are you sure?"

Judy bent down and pulled firmly at the tag, breaking the green string that held it to my trunk.

I was holding my breath as Bobby blurted out, "OK!" Then he ran up to Ms. Wright and gave her a big hug. "Merry Christmas, merry Christmas, thank you so much, ma'am."

Mr. Kemp and Ms. Wright retreated into the early-evening darkness of a largely deserted parking lot.

Bobby walked over to where I stood and again put his hand around my damaged branch. Bobby had kept his word and adopted me!

CHAPTER 108

December 24, Christmas Eve
Where's Natalie?

A peaceful calm settled over the shopping center as darkness shrouded the city of Lake Worth. Every night, parking lot lights provided illumination so that shoppers would be reasonably safe walking to and from their cars, and the common area walkways were also well lighted for pedestrian traffic.

We were indeed alone, Bobby and me, and Turk made three, and Teddy made four. Earlier in the day, Bobby had walked over to Walker's Veterinary Clinic and picked up the fluffy brown puppy. He was fat and happy and perfectly at home in his kennel, but he had fallen sound asleep lying next to me under my branches. I looked at the kennel and saw a big red bow on the kennel, and I knew Missy would be thrilled with having her own puppy again.

My sparrows had moved on, choosing to roost in the large oaks that landscaped this parking lot. From their lofty perches, they could be the first to spot potential food and danger. We had bonded over the weeks preceding Christmas, but we had different destinies, and tonight I would grace a little girl's home, or go to the field to live with my homeless friend. Either way, I was happy.

Bobby was getting anxious and somewhat agitated. Natalie was supposed to pick him up at 6:30, but it was already 7:30 p.m.

Has she forgotten? he wondered. *Or is she just running late?*

CHAPTER 109

Happy Ending

Then he saw Natalie's car turning into the parking lot. She pulled up right in front of the Publix and rolled down her passenger window. "Sorry I'm late, Bobby. It couldn't be helped. I'll tell you all about it later. Anyway, get in. We're going to have a nice evening."

Missy was sitting in the back seat and looked as if she had been crying.

"Hi, Missy," said Bobby. "I've got a surprise for you. Actually, two surprises for you."

And with that, Bobby turned and came over to where I was standing, picked me up by the trunk, and carried me over to the car. He gently set me down and smiled at Natalie's little girl.

"He's all yours, Missy. I bought him for you and your mom. I know you love him, Missy, and you know what? He loves you too. He is so excited to be going to your home for Christmas."

Bobby had rescued some orange mesh that Kenny had deposited in the trash. He carefully wrapped me up so that none of my other limbs would become broken on our ride home. Bobby is so thoughtful and considerate, a genuinely tenderhearted man. He even brought a blanket for me to lie on so that I would be comfortable riding on the top of Natalie's car.

Missy's eyes cleared up almost immediately. She was still sniffling as she jumped out of the car and wrapped her small arms around me.

God, I loved this little girl. My eyes were glassing up, and my nose was beginning to get the sniffles too, just like Missy's.

"Mr. Thornton, what's in that big cage over there? The one with the red bow on top."

"That's your second surprise, Missy. Why don't we open that little metal door on the end and see what's inside?"

Missy ran to the kennel, and as soon as she opened the gate, little Turk jumped into her arms and repeatedly licked her face. Missy fell to a sitting position, where Turk washed all her tears away.

"He's mine, Mr. Thornton?" Missy asked. She was looking at Bobby in disbelief. "For real, Mr. Thornton?"

"For real, Missy. His name is Turk. I'll tell you how he got his name after we get Mr. Fir decorated, OK?"

Missy jumped up with the doggie in her arms and ran over to me. I was a mess. My eyes had so much water flowing from them that you would think that Kenny had just hosed me down.

"See our new puppy, Mr. Fir? His name is Turk. Isn't he beautiful?" And then Missy looked at Turk. "Turk, this is Mr. Fir. Isn't he beautiful?"

Natalie stood next to Bobby, her arm around his waist, watching a happy daughter, who hadn't been happy for a long time. She looked up at the proud man standing by her side and said, "Thank you, Bobby. Thank you so much. You've put the smile back on my little girl's face. This is the best Christmas ever."

Well folks, all I could say was, "This is going to be my best Christmas ever too."

I was so looking forward to that night—the laughter, the merriment, the Christmas cheer, and the love that I would give to little Missy, and she to me. And, of course, Turk, Bobby, and Natalie.

The world is a beautiful place, and one need only look for the goodness, and somehow the goodness always seems to find you.

Bobby put the kennel in the trunk. Missy and Turk climbed into the back seat, and Bobby spread the blanket on the top of Natalie's very hot red Chevy.

So there I was, comfortably and securely tied to the roof of our car and slowly exiting the Publix parking lot. I looked back at the breezeway and thought of the blackbird and wondered what happiness he would find this Christmas Eve. Then I thought of my sparrows, and I saw them watching me. I called to them and asked them to follow us to Missy's house. They immediately took flight, dancing in the air and singing sparrow carols all the way home.

Our car pulled into the driveway of a beautiful home only a few blocks from the shopping center. Natalie turned off the engine, three doors all opened at once, and my new family exited the vehicle. Bobby untied the cords that secured me to the roof while Natalie unlocked her front door. Missy was holding Turk in her arms but staring at me with her mouth agape and her big, blue eyes fixated on Bobby's every move.

"Be careful, Mr. Thornton. You know he has a broken branch. Isn't he beautiful, Mr. Thornton?"

"Yes, Missy, I daresay that he's the prettiest Christmas tree in Lake Worth, maybe even in the whole state of Florida. And I'll fix his broken limb when we get him inside, and he will be like brand new."

"Oh, Mr. Thornton, that would be wonderful. Mommy's right."

"About what, Missy?"

"About you, Mr. Thornton. You are a very nice man." Bobby turned a light shade of red as he contemplated what Missy had just said, but the little girl didn't notice. She was too busy looking at me and playing with her new puppy.

"Now Santa Claus has a place to put my presents, Mr. Thornton. This really *is* going to be the best Christmas ever."

It was approaching eight o'clock at the McCord residence, normally Missy's bedtime, but this was Christmas Eve, and there was a tree to decorate, songs to sing, and food to eat. Natalie had prepared a platter of shrimp and cocktail sauce, a plate stacked high with egg salad and tuna sandwiches, and a massive bowl of buffalo chicken wings. She also had her huge holiday dish piled high with fruit for Missy. Missy loved honeydew, watermelon, red seedless grapes, and strawberries.

Natalie had her stereo turned on to 101.5, and Delilah, Palm Beach County's most popular radio personality, was taking requests and dedications. Natalie walked into her bedroom and called the station.

"Merry Christmas, this is Delilah. Would you like to tell me your story?" Delilah is a DJ who plays love songs for people who are "smitten"; hopeful songs for those listeners who are sad; and soft, mellow, oldie-goodies for people who want to remember friends and loved ones from the past.

"Yes, Delilah, my name is Natalie."

"Merry Christmas, Natalie. Tell me about your Christmas Eve."

"My husband abandoned me and my daughter about seven months ago. Tonight he came by the house to pick up the last of his things. He rang the bell, and my daughter and I went to the door to see who was there. Glenn asked if he could come in. Missy was ecstatic and readily invited her daddy to come in and have something to eat. She was so happy to see her father. Her eyes were glowing, she was giggling the way little girls laugh, and she hugged him tightly around his waist. Glenn did not hug his daughter back. He pushed her away and walked through the house to our garage. Glenn opened the garage door and loaded his golf clubs into the trunk. Then he climbed into his car and drove away.

"Glenn was not alone. In his car were his new girlfriend and a little girl sitting in the back seat about the age of my daughter. She watched us through the rear window until they had disappeared from sight. My daughter was devastated. It took me an hour to calm her down and get her to stop crying. And he didn't even bring her a present or wish her a merry Christmas."

"Natalie, your daughter's little heart must have been broken!"

"Yes, Delilah, but God works in mysterious ways. After Glenn disappeared into the darkness, I put my daughter into our car and we picked up a friend who was all alone on Christmas Eve. No one should be alone on Christmas Eve. He and Missy are in the living room right now, decorating a tree that he bought for her. He also bought her a precious puppy. He is a kind, gentle, and companionate man, and he could ill afford to spend his last cent on a Christmas tree for Missy and me. There are some really good people in this world, and if you don't despair, the good people will seek you out. I would like to wish Bobby a very merry Christmas. Can you play something for him?"

"Your story, Natalie, is very touching. Rarely do I find myself without words, but right now I am speechless. We wish you, Missy, Bobby, your Christmas tree, and your new puppy a very special holiday season. I'll play something special for you, Natalie."

Natalie hung up the phone and went into the living room, where Missy, Bobby, and I were listening to Delilah and Natalie on the radio.

"That's what Christmas is all about," Delilah said, "love, kindness, and friendship. If you are listening to our program right now, open your arms wide, reach out, pull someone close, and hug them tightly."

"And for you, Bobby and Missy and Natalie, we are going to play, 'Have Yourself a Merry Little Christmas.'"

When Natalie walked into the living room, we all stared up at her. Missy yelled, "Mommy, we just heard you on the radio! We have all been listening to you and Delilah. Even Mr. Fir was listening."

The music began to play as Natalie stood there watching the three of us sitting on the floor by the radio. Bobby and Missy jumped up, and we all hugged each other, just as Delilah had told us to do. I got the biggest hug ever from Missy, and I even got a hug from Natalie. She said, "We all love you, Mr. Fir." And then the song began to play:

"Have yourself a merry little Christmas,
Let your heart be light.
From now on our troubles will be out of sight.

Have yourself a merry little Christmas,
Make the Yuletide gay.
From now on

443

Our troubles will be miles away.
Here we are as in olden days,
Happy golden days of yore.
Faithful friends who are dear to us
gather near to us once more.

Through the years we all will be together,
If the Fates allow.
Hang a shining star upon the highest bough,
And have yourself a merry little Christmas now."

Turk walked over to the front door and yapped, the sound little dogs make. Then he turned his head, looked up at Missy, and yapped a second time.

Bobby said to Missy, "Your puppy wants to go outside to do his business. They potty-trained him for you at Walker's Veterinary Clinic. Here is his leash, Missy. Why don't you take him out into the front yard?"

Natalie opened her arms and gave Bobby a warm hug. "Merry Christmas, Bobby. I'm glad you're here."

"I'm glad too, Natalie."

The next three hours were total happiness for my new family. We listened to Delilah's Christmas carols and the sad stories that people told her, and we sang along with the Christmas songs as they played on the radio. Natalie, Bobby, and Missy decorated me with blinking colored lights, garland, and ornaments and topped me off with a beautiful winged angel in a white robe.

Bobby and Natalie feasted on shrimp, chicken wings, and all the other goodies that she had prepared for this wonderful Christmas Eve party, and Missy ate fruit until I thought she would pop.

When my last ornament was placed on the only empty branch I had left, Natalie spread a satin skirt under me and around my green-and-red stand. Bobby had filled my stand with purified water from plastic Zephyr Hills bottles, and it tasted *so* good. Then Natalie went over to the wall that controlled the lights. She flicked it on, and I lit up like a…like a…uh, like a Christmas tree. I was magnificent!

When Missy finally fell asleep, it was well after midnight. Natalie offered the guest room to Bobby and promised him a wonderful breakfast of bacon, eggs, pancakes, and grits on Christmas morning.

The house lights were all turned off except for my colored lights, which were draped over all my branches. I was so beautiful, and I was truly happy.

Santa came that night, but everyone was asleep except me. Santa left presents for Natalie and Bobby and a beautiful red Schwinn bicycle for Missy.

CHAPTER 110

Friday, December 25
Christmas Morning

The home erupted with the high-pitched screams of a happy little girl as she discovered all the presents under my decorated boughs.

Turk was barking his little puppy barks, wagging his tail, tapping his toenails on the wooden floor, and following Missy everywhere she went.

Bobby and Natalie came running into the living room just in time to see Missy rubbing her hand on the shiny red fenders of her new bike. She raced toward her mom and threw her arms around her mother's waist. Next she hugged Bobby. And then she came over to me and walked behind me, by the wall, to hold my broken branch in her small, warm hand. But my branch was no longer broken, because Bobby had fixed it.

"Merry Christmas, Missy," I whispered

"Merry Christmas, Bobby," I whispered just a bit louder.

"Merry Christmas, Natalie," I said.

Natalie looked up at Bobby and down at Missy. "Did you hear that?" she asked. Bobby and Missy just looked at each other and smiled.

And we all lived happily ever after.

THE END

EPILOGUE

Remember when Missy told me that her best story was really her worst story? Well, here I thought my story would turn out to be my worst story, but it turned out to be my best story. Go figure.

ACKNOWLEDGMENTS

Special thanks to Robert Karl, with whom this story had its origins. He became the Bobby in this manuscript, as I texted to him the woe that I experienced as I walked into Publix Supermarket one cool day in November. Two things happened that day; both made me feel hollow inside, and I had to talk to somebody. Robert, or Bob, as I call him, was in Murphy, North Carolina, at the time, and I knew that he would understand. The first thing that bothered me was that a fifty-three-year-old female elephant at the Miami Zoo had died of constipation. I heard this on the radio of my car as I pulled into Publix and found a spot to park. I was devastated. I knew that Bob would understand, so I sent him a text. As I got out of my car and started my walk toward the Publix entry, I saw the Fraser fir trees, and I stopped dead in my tracks and just stared at them. Already crestfallen from the death of the elephant, I sent a text to Bob about the trees. I wrote about their happy life before coming to Florida. Bob told me that this would make a great story, so I sent him more texts. When I arrived back home with my groceries, I decided that Bob was right. This story just had to be written. As the years went by, Bob kept encouraging me to finish the book. I truly believe that I would never have written or finished this book without his support and undying encouragement. Thank you, Bob.

My sweet granddaughter, Jordan, needs to be thanked. She is a straight-A student at All Saints Catholic School. She reads above her grade level, and I remember one summer when she visited me in Summerfield. I had a rough draft completed, and I gave her a copy of the first twenty pages for her perusal. Sarah Allen was visiting, so I had them alternate reading the story. I was really testing to see if eleven-year-old children could read what I wrote and if they could enjoy the content. Jordan bugged me to finish the story and have it published. Sarah asked me if I would mind if she interviewed me. I was blown away, but I said yes, of course. She went into her bedroom, grabbed a yellow legal pad and pencil, sat down, and began asking me questions. She finished the interview with, "'I wish I had thought of that!"

My cousin Ladonne Patterson spent hours editing my manuscript for punctuation and spelling errors. I thank you, Ladonne.

And finally, thank you to my wife, Ann Thomas, my soulmate for forty-seven years. Every word, every sentence, and every paragraph was read to her many, many times. She was my content editor and would not let me stray from the true goodness of this book. Thank you, Ann.

Made in the USA
Coppell, TX
08 July 2020